Ed Lehner, a retired professor of graphic design from Iowa State University, has written poetry for over forty years and recently began writing short stories. *The Awakening of Russell Henderson* is his second novel. He lives with his wife, Julie, and Emma the cat, in Durango Colorado. He can be reached at www.elehner~~~~~~~~.com

Enjoy the Journey

Ed H

THE AWAKENING
of Russell Henderson

Ed Lehner

AIA PUBLISHING

A Note on Places and People

Almost all the places that Russell and Hanna encountered are ones that I've experienced myself over the many summers my wife and I spent camping throughout the West, not in a Westfalia van, but in a tent, in our Chevy van or, in later years, a pop up camper. I've driven most of the roads, hiked many of the trails, and enjoyed many of the experiences Russell had. Some of the characters are composites of folks I encountered over the years, but everyone in this book is as completely fictional as is the story itself.

Acknowledgements

I wish to thank my wife, Julianne Ward for her support, patience, encouragement, as well as for her editing and astute constructive comments while writing The Awakening of Russell Henderson. I also wish to thank my beta readers, Linda Hinde and Rini Twait for their comments and encouragement.

"All new beginnings lay shrouded in mist." *Nina George.*

"What a long strange trip it's been," the great philosopher, poet, and musician Jerry Garcia once said. Isn't life really all just a strange trip from birth until death, sometimes being stranger than others? Strangeness began in earnest for me on a camping trip to the west when I picked up a woman hitchhiker on the second day out.

Chapter 1: Dana Departs

I like numbers. Numbers don't lie; they don't criticize; they do not discriminate, and, if you use the right numbers, you get a right answer. Numbers are black or white, never allowing for any grey areas. Numbers, work, and responsible behavior is the way this planet operates, and that's the way I operate. I like my life orderly and functional with little or no room for surprise.

My name's Russell Henderson. I'm thirty years old, six feet tall, in fairly good shape, brown-haired and brown-eyed. My parents raised me to be orderly, disciplined, and frugal, to look at the world as a place of hard work, and to have realistic expectations of what that work produces.

After a double degree in economics and accounting, graduating with honors in three years, I was accepted into the University of Iowa Business School and earned my MBA—all by the age of twenty-three. I wanted to be a millionaire by the time I turned thirty, and I'd already exceeded my goals sevenfold by the time I turned twenty-nine.

Recruiters knocked on my door a year before I even got my MBA, and the longer I remained non-committal, the higher the monetary rewards went up. Finally, feeling like an NBA superstar, I signed on—with a substantial signing bonus—with a Chicago investment bank, Americo Financial.

Dana and I met during my MBA time while she was in law school at the U of I. She was from Des Moines and had short dark hair and deep brown eyes. I found her quite handsome and charming. We dated for about a year and married right after we both received our advanced degrees. We were young and in love, so marriage seemed the right thing to do.

We found an apartment in a downtown Chicago high-rise, close to our respective offices. Ultra-modern, it had bare concrete floors, lots of glass looking out over the city, two bedrooms, a big kitchen, and a large living area for entertaining. We furnished it with modern practical furniture. For me, frills were unnecessary. Any other decorations and such, I considered a waste of money. However, despite that, Dana did manage to add a few homey touches.

Work started for each of us right after returning from our honeymoon in Mexico: Dana at the Chicago D.A.'s office and me at Americo. Immediately, we both put in long hours, and, after our day, usually met for a late dinner, went home, crawled into bed, made love once every week or so, and got our five to seven hours of sleep. Weekends, we kept free from work and study to sleep in and enjoy the city: museums, galleries, or just walking along the shore of Lake Michigan.

We led an idyllic life, trying to be in love and nesting. I found my work challenging, fun, and rewarding, and Dana loved her work as an assistant D.A. As time went on I put in even more hours and started to make good money, better than either I or my employer thought I would for at least a few years. The money kept coming in, and I worked harder and harder.

Extensive research, numbers, and risk assessments were my forte, and every client I worked with went under intense scrutiny. Risk assessment became my mantra in work as well as in play. Run the numbers, be cautious, do the research—always risk assessment.

Research—a singular activity—was more fun and far better than client meetings and the parties to which I was expected to go. The idle chatter that went on at parties and dinners, I found boring and meaningless. I usually found myself in a one-to-one conversation, which felt comfortable for me. When more than one or two individuals participated in a discussion, I never managed to keep up with the rapidly changing ideas. By the time I'd absorbed what was being said, the topic had already moved on, and so I moved on, usually ending up pretending to look at artwork or book collections, sitting by myself out of the way, and, usually, drinking too much. Dana also found these parties boring and hated them as much as I did.

Our life for the next three years became a blur, and I couldn't recall much that happened. We still managed to keep Sunday for ourselves, but they became less and less fun. I was usually exhausted. Our sex life diminished, along with sharing time together.

We had no time to make, or have, any mutual friends. Our colleagues at her and my work were the only people we really had any contact with, and only when at work or sometimes for a few drinks late on a Friday night.

Our life together completely diminished; we became like two strangers living in the same apartment. We took a two-week vacation in Puerto Rico and tried to fall back into love. The plan didn't succeed. We came back after the first week.

On December 19, my thirtieth birthday, I left work early and stopped on the way home for a bottle of champagne. I planned on ordering out for dinner to be delivered when Dana got home, but when I walked into our apartment, something wasn't right. It took me several moments to realize what was wrong; Dana's family photos and knickknacks had gone

My comfort level dropped like the temperature right before a midwestern thunderstorm. I looked around for anything indicating her presence, but her closet, her drawers, her medicine chest were all empty. Her luggage, the pieces of silver given to us by her family at our wedding, her books; every last trace of her existence had disappeared. I fell into a chair, dazed, stunned, not believing what I realistically knew to be true. She'd gone.

An hour passed before I could get up. I went to pour myself a scotch and saw a plain envelope on the counter.

Dear Russell,

As you may have gathered by now, I have moved out. I have moved out for good. I have left you. I'm sorry to have done it this way, but I wanted to avoid any drama. It seemed this would be easier for both of us, quick and easy.

To keep it short, I haven't been in love with you for years now, if ever. I've been miserable, and you, in your narrow world of finance, didn't have a clue. I've been lonely and was dying inside, until I met Susan. I worked as assistant prosecutor on a case involving her. She's a well-known and successful gallery owner. We started meeting for dinner to discuss her case. Then one thing led to another and we became lovers. She cares for me like you never did. She listens to me. She makes me feel wanted. She makes me laugh. She makes me happy. I never really knew how miserable I was until I met her.

Do not try to contact me. I do not want to talk to you with your stupid arguments about the reality of your work, the reality of your feelings, about all the reality of your bullshit world you live in. I've changed my cell number, and our receptionists at work have been

told to screen all my calls. Please do not try to contact me. I'll get a restraining order if you do.

My attorney will be serving you with divorce papers in the next few days. I'm not asking for much. I just don't want to be married to you anymore. Truthfully, while this may hurt, you are the most boring self-centered person I have ever known.

Dana

The next few minutes seemed like hours. I couldn't believe she thought I was boring. Hell, I thought she liked hearing me talk about my work and about my successes. She never really had anything to say that mattered: her work, her feelings, books she read, things she wanted us to do together that neither of us realistically had time for. Work was my reality.

I had another scotch, put a frozen pizza into the oven, tried to eat, but couldn't, so threw it all away. I drank some more until I was on the verge of being completely drunk, tried to watch some basketball, and went to bed.

The next morning, I went to work as usual—only with a hangover—and tried to pretend nothing had happened. At 1:30 p.m. my secretary buzzed me, saying that Roland Pierce was here to see me. He didn't have an appointment, but I thought he might be a potential client. When Roland Pierce—a sallow little man with reddish eyes and a bad comb-over on a bald head—came into my office, his rumpled, ill-fitting suit made it readily apparent that he wasn't a potential client.

"Are you Russell Henderson?" he asked.

"Yes, I'm Russell. How can I help you?"

"By considering yourself served." He handed me a thick envelope. "Thank you and have a nice day." He turned and walked out the door.

I stared at the envelope like it might explode into flames. When I eventually opened it and looked at the papers, I discovered that she wanted a quarter of my holdings, which would be over $1,500,000.

And she said she didn't want much!

I called my attorney friend, Marcus, who asked me to bring the papers tomorrow and he'd be happy to look at them.

"Do you have time right now?" I asked.

"Ah, yeah … yeah, sure. I have a few minutes between appointments if you can get here now."

I told my secretary to cancel my appointments as I'd be gone for the rest of the afternoon, then I walked to Marcus's office in the next building.

Marcus was about my age. We'd met when I consulted on a case he'd had, and he became the only guy I ever hung out with outside of work, meeting for lunch once in a while. As a junior partner in a large firm, he had a private office that looked like a typical movie set: dark wood paneling, a huge desk, and plush leather chairs. Tall, blue-eyed, blond-haired with a boyish grin, and in good shape from running and the gym, Marcus was single and always in love with some beautiful woman.

He greeted me with his usual strong handshake: "Hey, buddy, not good news, eh? That just sucks. I'm really sorry, man. Hope I never have to go through this sort of shit with a woman."

"Hell, you're never going to get married, so what are you worried about?" I said with a hollow laugh.

"Yeah, maybe not, but one never knows. Let me see those papers."

We sat in the comfortable chairs while he looked through the several documents, sometimes pausing and rereading certain passages. Finally, he looked up with a serious look, not saying anything. I could tell he was thinking what to say, what to tell me, how to break the bad news.

"Well, I'm not a divorce attorney, but my initial response is to tell you to take Dana's offer. A quarter of your assets is not going to hurt you. And then this can all be over and done with without a major amount of attorneys' fees and an unknown outcome. It could end up costing you a lot more. You make a boatload of money, a lot more than she does as an assistant D.A. She could ask for, and most likely get, alimony. You don't want that!"

"But if I could talk to her," I said, "we could straighten this all out. Maybe I'll call her at her office and lie about who it is … if we could just talk—"

"I would strongly advise against doing that," Marcus said sternly. "She was quite clear about you not contacting her. I can only guess, but I'd wager that there's a restraining order already completed and ready to be filed if you try to see or call her. Do not add fuel to the fire. Her terms seem fair and she, from what I've read, seems to have made her decision."

My stomach turned. This wasn't what I wanted to hear. I told Marcus I'd consider it and thanked him. We talked a bit more and confirmed lunch plans for Thursday, then, with his next appointment waiting, I left. I walked down the street to my building, pondering what Marcus had told me. I realized how bewildered and in shock I truly was. I couldn't believe Dana had left. Why? What did I do wrong? I thought we had a reasonably good life together. I thought she enjoyed our time together.

Then I realized that we didn't actually spend that much time together. I worked seventy, plus, hours a week. She'd been at home by herself quite a bit of the time, or so I'd thought, but apparently she'd been out with her lover. How long had she been seeing that woman?

I was making a lot of money. My plan was to retire early and then spend our time together. She should've been happy that I cared that much for our well-being. It was confusing.

Going home was hard; the apartment now seemed cold and foreboding. I opened a beer and sat in the dark living room, feeling like a hollow shell, as empty and cold as the apartment in which I sat—alone.

The next few weeks passed slowly. Christmas and New Year, with all the parties to which I didn't go in order to avoid the Dana questions, just added to my growing depression.

Dana and I usually went to my parent's for Christmas, but I couldn't face them, so I called and lied, saying Dana and I were going to Mexico and wouldn't be able to come this year. I drank a lot and didn't eat or sleep much, so I drank more, trying to self-medicate, which only made matters worse.

Days became a fog from lack of sleep and hangovers. I couldn't concentrate on work, and when I almost lost a major client, Gordon, my boss, summoned me to his office. He closed the door and explained how he wasn't at all happy with my performance. I tried to explain everything, and I assured him that things would change for the better, that this client debacle wouldn't happen again.

The deadline approached for me to sign or contest the divorce, so I consulted with a divorce attorney. He told me exactly what Marcus had said and charged me $1000.00 for two hours' work.

My appearance suffered: I lost weight; bags appeared under my eyes, and I badly needed a haircut, but I kept going to the office every day because there wasn't anything else to do. My productivity plummeted to zero. One day Gordon called me into his office and told me to go home. He didn't want to lose me. I made the firm a lot of money, but, on the other hand, he told me in no uncertain terms, to get myself together or I was history.

On my way out, one of my co-workers, who knew about Dana leaving, stopped to talk to me. After commenting that I looked like shit, he recommended that I see a doctor he knew to get something for sleep. I did. The doctor prescribed antidepressant medication and sleeping pills. I tried both, and could finally sleep, but felt hung over the next day from the meds. I still felt listless, barely able to move. Finally, I gave up; I just didn't care anymore. I signed the papers. I was divorced. I had failed. It was done.

The doctor recommended a psychiatrist. He listened a lot and asked a lot of questions about family, my marriage, work, feelings, anger, so on and so on. I wasn't the best patient, being petrified of giving him much other than superficial information. I could tell how frustrating this was for him. He recommended journaling, writing down answers to his questions, just for myself; his thinking being that the journaling exercise might help me to open up. I didn't bother; pills and whiskey were easier.

Chapter 2: Late Winter Blues

It was February, winter's last attempt to depress everyone with dark, dreary, cold days. The remaining snow lay dirty and frozen in piles of ugly slag. I managed to get myself out of the apartment to walk down by the lake—when the weather permitted—or hang out at my favorite coffee shop, reading books I'd always wanted to. I even got out my old guitar from high school and early college days and tried playing again, but I had no social interaction other than with my doctors. Boredom and loneliness were my new friends.

Putting dread aside, I finally drummed up enough courage to call my parents with the news of my divorce. My mother answered:

"Russell, how are you? We haven't heard from you in ages. We missed you at Christmas. How was Mexico? How are things in Chicago?"

"Ah, yeah, been busy, Mom, as always. Ah … news is; well, ah … Dana left me, Mom; she divorced me," I blurted out.

"What? How could you get divorced, Russell? Were you having an affair, fooling around? It must've been something you did to cause this, because we liked Dana. It was probably because you didn't have children like your sister and brother. No family! No wonder you failed! I am so disappointed in you. Wait until I tell your father. This is a disaster. What will we tell people? Hope you're satisfied! This is just an example of your irresponsibility! We didn't raise you to be a failure."

I tried to get a word in. "But Mom, it was Dana who—"

She yelled back into the phone, almost screaming, "No buts, Russell! You work this out! Nobody in our family ever gets a divorce! You work this out and don't call again until you do! Do you understand?"

With that last tirade, the phone fell silent. I sat there with the phone to my ear, waiting for something more, maybe for some understanding, some consolation, some support. After a long, dead silence, I put the phone down, poured a drink and sat, staring into space. I drank until I was drunk, and eventually staggered into bed, fully clothed, and slept a dreamless night in a drunken stupor.

The next morning, feeling more like crap than usual, I called my older sister, Karen, and told her the story, which she already knew since Mom had called her and talked for over an hour about what a failure I was. I told her how I was depressed, and on medication, and how my work had suffered, that I was on leave. Karen was a bit more understanding, offering some consolation and support. She ended the conversation by saying that she'd do anything she could to help, that maybe I should come and spend some time back in my hometown with her family. I told her I'd think about it, then thanked her, and we ended the conversation.

The rest of the morning I spent staring out a window, not seeing anything, drinking coffee to clear my head and considering all that had happened and was happening. Chicago held nothing for me anymore but bitter memories. I called Karen back and took her up on her offer to stay with her and John for a few weeks.

I called Gordon and told him that I wanted at least a year's sabbatical. If that wouldn't work, I'd resign. He told me to take my time, get the help I needed. He didn't want to lose me and would welcome me back anytime. With that resolved and not knowing what I'd do in Chicago for a year, I spent the next two weeks selling, giving away, or throwing away the few things I had, except for some clothes, books, and a few other items I didn't want to part with. I let go of the apartment, rented a Ryder truck, and moved everything to my home town. There, I rented a storage unit for things I'd kept that I didn't want to take to Karen's.

Before I left Chicago, I contacted a guy I knew who was an investment counselor. He helped me create an investment portfolio that would offer me a monthly income off the interest after setting up a substantial accessible cash reserve.

I moved back to my hometown.

Chapter 3: Iowa

Karen used her college degree in computer science to work as office manager in the John Deere dealership on the edge of town. Her husband, John, was a lawyer in a firm in Iowa City, a fifteen-mile commute. John had two boys from his first marriage.

Karen and John welcomed me into their newer four-bedroom house on a small acreage west of town. It felt funny moving in with them. I emphasized that this would be short-term until I found my own place, that I needed to figure out where I wanted to be or what I wanted to do with my life first. In the meantime, I'd do what I could to help out and stay out of their way as much as possible.

The next day, I went to see my parents on their farm seven miles southeast of town. They lived in the updated farmhouse built by my dad's grandfather. My brother, Donny, lived three miles away in a double manufactured home. After driving through the Iowa landscape of bare fields awaiting spring tilling and planting, I found Dad and Donny in the machine shed getting machinery ready for spring field work. The large building housed three large tractors, a combine, tillage, and planting equipment, and smelled of diesel fuel, oil, and fertilizer.

"Russell, good to see you, boy," Dad said. "How're doing? Heard you moved back. Big city life finally got to ya?" He chuckled.

Donny stuck his head out from behind one of the tractors. "Yeah, he's back with his tail between his legs 'cause he couldn't handle his woman. Always was a loser." He laughed. "Heard she run off with another woman. Wait'll the boys around town hear this."

Brother Donny, a bully who thought he was better than anyone else, wasn't the brightest bulb in the chandelier. We never got along as kids. He'd get in trouble and then blame me, and Mom always took his side. I couldn't stand him.

He still considered himself some sort of super jock, having been a big deal when he played football in high school. I remember him being the biggest one on the team—also the slowest in both mind and body. He'd achieved small-town hero status, but I always thought he only did so well because he was bigger than everyone else.

However, no college showed any interest in having him play for them, so he enrolled at Iowa State with big plans of walking onto the football team. He washed out of that after the first week and washed out of college first semester sophomore year. He came home, saying they weren't teaching him anything and that college was a waste of his time. He then went to work for Dad. A year later, he married Alice, a local girl, after getting her pregnant with their only child, Zoe.

He drank pretty heavily off and on, mostly on, had several DUIs, and his license revoked twice. He'd been arrested twice for bar fights. But, as always, Donny could do no wrong and our mother always went to his rescue and got him out of trouble.

I ignored him and tried to continue talking to Dad, but he wouldn't shut up. "Big city boy comin' home with his tail between his legs. Ha, ha, always knew you're a loser." He laughed. "What ya gonna do now, loser? Did the big city bank fire the loser?"

"Shut the fuck up, Donny. I've been here two minutes, and I'm already sick of your mindless bullshit. Any new DUIs lately?"

He came towards me with his fists clenched. "Fuck you, you little shit. I'll fucking tear you a new ass—"

"That's enough! Both of you!" Dad said in a sharp voice. "Donny, get back there and finish putting that oil in, and shut the hell up! Russell, I don't need this from you either!"

"Sorry, Dad. I think it'll be better if I just leave. It was good to see you."

"Aw, you don't need to run off just because of ..." He nodded towards where Donny stood behind the tractor.

"Is Mom up at the house? I'd like to say hi."

"Naw, she went into Iowa City for some groceries and a few things she needed to do. Should be home soon, though. You could wait?"

"Thanks, but it might be best if I left. Tell her I said hello. I'll see her another time."

As I turned to leave, Donny said, "You don't need to come around no more. Nobody really gives a shit about you ... loser."

I flipped him the finger and left.

* * *

With Karen and John working all day, I volunteered to become a housekeeper to earn my way. I bought the groceries, cleaned their house and country acreage, and transported the boys to and from school and their activities.

During any downtime, which was a lot, I hung out at the town coffee shop/restaurant/news stand/gossip bar. I found it interesting being back in old, familiar territory, but as the first week went by, it became apparent how little I had in common with anyone anymore. Some people had never left after high school. Some had taken over or worked at family businesses like implement dealers, small manufacturing plants of farm-related products, the hardware store, the grain elevator, seed and fertilizer outlets. Others were now farmers, worked as tradespeople, laborers, or drove trucks. Most had gotten a girl pregnant or married their high-school sweetheart and had their own families. Some took up the task of being the town drunks.

Almost everyone who'd gone to college didn't return, electing to live in bigger cities where there were better-paying jobs. The few who did come back came back as school teachers or worked at, or started, online businesses; a few sold insurance, and one, I knew, was now a doctor. Everyone wondered why I'd come back after life in the big city. All expressed guarded regret when they found out about my divorce, like it was a contagious disease.

We shared the usual small-talk, reminiscing about high school days, families, sports, work, then the conversation would be lost. We clumsily departed with false promises of "See you soon," and "We'll have to go out or have you over for dinner sometime." Truth was, there was nothing left for me here. I had nothing in common with anybody anymore; everyone knew it, and no one was interested in hanging out.

Nothing had changed; boredom and loneliness were still my main companions, no real friends, nothing to do. I felt listless, gained weight, and started frequenting the bars, joining the town drunks some afternoons, playing Euchre for dimes and drinking—too much sometimes. One afternoon I got drunk and missed picking up the boys from school. Karen and John were really pissed. I couldn't blame them. I'd been to the local clinic and was able to continue my sleep and antidepressant meds, which were helping with sleep, but I needed a life, something to do, and I didn't want to go back to Chicago.

One day when I left the coffee bar, I saw a pristine 1987 four-wheel-drive Volkswagen Westfalia campervan parked right behind my car with a "For Sale" sign in the passenger's side window.

I remembered back to when I was in summer school and a few of the guys I knew had summer jobs, many out west in to Colorado, Montana, Idaho, and other exotic sounding places. They worked at resorts, national parks, as river guides, as ranch hands, while I stayed at home and studied. In my world, money had been my adventure.

Now I was thirty years old, in good health, and had no responsibilities. What the hell? I got out my cell and called the number.

"I'm interested in your van. When can I take a look and get more information?"

"Where are you?"

"Standing here looking at it."

"Yeah, I see you."

A man in his mid-forties walked up and introduced himself as Doug. He needed to sell the Westfalia since his two kids were growing, and they needed something bigger to accommodate them. He said the engine had been recently overhauled, everything else was mechanically sound, and he had all the service records. Fully outfitted with pots, pans, eating utensils, bedding, and towels, it was ready to go. As completely irrational as it was for me to do something so outrageous without first analyzing and carefully thinking it through, I bought it on the spot, writing Doug a check for half. I'd pay the rest when I picked up the van and got the title, which I planned to do that night.

I got into my sister's minivan and went to pick up the kids at school. While driving there, I realized that this was the most crazy, non-thought-out, spur-of-the-moment transaction I'd ever made in my entire life. I always pondered any decision, did an extended risk assessment, sometimes even when getting a cup of designer coffee. And now I'd just bought a Volkswagen Westfalia campervan on a whim to go camping out west. This was not my normal, careful, well-thought-out modus operandi. It was a little unnerving. I hadn't even driven it. I took a few deep breaths and arrived at the school.

Karen got home around five thirty. I already had dinner on for us to eat at six when John got home. I told her what I'd done and what I planned to do. Karen's mouth fell open, and she just stared at me, unable to speak.

Finally she said, "You did what? You've never camped in your entire life! You'd hardly drive across town, much less across the country! Have you lost your mind?"

Wondering the same thing, I said, "Karen, I'm always so uptight. I control my life to a fault, always play it safe. This whole idea scares the hell out of me, but I'm happy I bought that Westfalia, and I've made a decision to try to do this. I can't stay mooching off you any longer. There's nothing for me to do here. I don't want to go back to Chicago or to work right now. We'll all just have to see how it turns out."

"Are you going to tell Mom and Dad?"

"Hell, no. They'll find out soon enough, and I hope to be well gone when they do. Mom hasn't spoken to me since I moved back. I called her several times and she didn't answer, left her voice messages, but she never called back. Anyway, they'd probably have a complete breakdown if they knew what I was going to do."

The more we talked about it during dinner, the more excited and confident I became about this road trip to explore the west. After dinner, Karen took me to get the van. The boys rode along, excited about Uncle Russell's new car. At Doug's house on the other side of town, I quickly went through the service records he had in a folder. Everything looked in order and all up to date. I checked out everything that had been done to the engine. It all looked good. We finalized the deal and did the title transfer. I paid the remainder and then owned a little mini-house on wheels.

The boys wanted to ride home with me, so we transferred the jump seats to the Westy, and off we went. It was a fun little car to drive, sitting with your butt over the front wheel. Not having even done a test drive, I wanted to see what I'd bought and how it would drive on the open road, so we went out on the highway for about five miles or so and turned around. Though not very speedy, it got up to seventy miles per hour okay and felt solid. I grew more excited with every mile.

The next day I went to the library and asked the woman at the desk what she might recommend for road books. She suggested *Zen and the Art of Motorcycle Maintenance* by Robert M. Pirsig, *Blue Highways* by William Least Heat-Moon, and the aptly named *Out West* by Dayton Duncan. I got a library card and checked out all three. I dove into *Out West* first and devoured it, then went on Amazon and ordered a used copy. I read the other two, also buying *Zen and the Art of Motorcycle Maintenance,* which they had at the local bookstore. *Blue Highways* was good, but there was too much about the east to suit my needs.

In the meantime, I went through everything in the Westy and discovered that it had everything I could imagine needing for my trip: a few pans to use on the little two-burner propane stove, a nice ice chest, a rear seat that folded out into a small two-person bed, and various little storage cubbies for clothing, food, and such. The top hinged at the front and popped up so I could stand inside. I had to pare down what I was able to take, but it wasn't like this was an African safari in the remote bush country; there would be Targets and Walmarts along the way. After several test runs, camping out in nearby state parks, figuring out how to operate all the little nuances and making sure everything functioned properly, I was ready.

Not wanting to leave anything to error, I spent countless hours with maps, online resources, campground directories, Google Maps, and anything else I could find to help plot my route. Once I'd accounted for every mile of the trip, I considered myself and the Westy ready to go.

After doing some online research in preparation for any weather I might encounter in the mountains of the west, I shopped for appropriate layers of fleece, rain gear, zip-off pants, shorts, quick-dry underwear, t-shirts and socks. The van was ready to go with a new tool box with basic spare parts that I discovered through further research might be needed, as well as tools needed to perform any basic repairs, plus a manual, of course.

May arrived with longer and warmer days, and I wanted to get going. Karen and family, while appreciating all I was doing, were ready for me to not be living with them anymore. I sensed a little stress.

I had all the essentials and my old Martin guitar, having illusions of sitting around a campfire, strumming and singing the few old Neal Young and Bob Dylan songs I used to know.

As much as I didn't want to, I felt an obligation to call my parents to let them know my plans. "Hi, Mom. How're you and Dad?"

"I hope you're calling to say that you and Dana have gotten back together. I know you're living with your sister. You came out to the farm only once when I wasn't home. Donny reported on how nasty you were to him. Are you going back to Chicago? And what about your job? It's about time. I'm sure Karen is tired of you freeloading like that."

"Mom, please just listen for a minute; I called you several times but you never answered or called back. I'm surprised you answered now." I continued on to tell her my plans. All she could say was, "Oh, Russell, I am so disappointed in you."

The phone went dead. I stood there for a while with my cell at my ear, waiting, wanting the least bit of understanding. But it was not to be.

Chapter 4: The Beginning

I left eastern Iowa on Saturday morning the week before Memorial Day and headed the twenty miles north to I-80 at Iowa City. From there I drove west across Iowa through mainly rolling hills of farmland and little towns to I-25, then north at Council Bluffs. All of it breezed by from the isolation of an interstate highway that only required stopping for gas or the call of nature. I stayed my first night in the little town of Missouri Valley, Iowa. The first day had run smoothly and precisely— just as I'd planned.

I had dinner at a local diner in town; it felt strange being alone, not knowing anyone—everyone strangers. I felt a pang of loneliness and fear. After a good sleep, I rose early, filled up with gas, and headed to the Interstate. It was then that I veered from my plan.

She stood by the on-ramp with her large backpack and a guitar, thumb up in the hitchhiker position. She wore loose, khaki cargo shorts, a shapeless light-blue t-shirt, hiking boots, and a grey baseball cap on backwards.

Whatever possessed me to stop, I don't know. Loneliness? I pulled over and swung open the passenger door. In the rear view mirror, I saw her grabbing her backpack and guitar, then walking slowly towards the van, giving it the once over. She looked in, scrutinized me with her emerald-green eyes, smiled a cold, crooked smile, and asked, "Where are you headed?"

"West," I replied. "How about you?"

"Eventually San Francisco, but right now, I'm heading to the Rosebud Reservation to see an old friend. You headed up that way?"

"I'll be going through there. My itinerary's all mapped out, but San Francisco isn't included. I'm planning on heading west on Highway 20 when we get to Sioux City, then up through the Lakota Reservations on to Mount Rushmore. How far do you want to go?'"

"I meant the Rosebud. Didn't expect you to take me to the Bay. But I'll be happy to have a ride up to the Res," she replied.

"Jump in, then, and let's go."

She got in and threw her stuff into the back. I accelerated the Westy up the ramp and headed north to Sioux City.

Rolling loess hills, created by strong westerly winds eons ago and now covered in farmland, vineyards, and pasture land, border the Missouri Valley on the east side. The Missouri River, originating in Montana, borders the other side, but all I could see were trees, the river itself rarely being visible.

I felt her silent presence, and smelt her scent of fresh air and earth, both satisfying and also indicative of a need to bathe. With a discreet, sideways glance, I determined that she was attractive. Her short, tangled, dirty auburn hair stuck out from under her cap. Her face, arms and legs were darkly tanned. I noticed a tattooed bracelet around her left bicep and another of a flowery vine on her forearm. I guessed her age to be mid to late twenties.

"So, ah, I'm Russell. What's your name?"

"Good to meet you Russ, I'm Hanna. Where're you from?"

I responded all too tersely, "Ah, I prefer to be called Russell, and I'm from a small town down in eastern Iowa and more recently, Chicago."

"All righty, then … *Russell*."

I didn't respond to her dig, and we rode in silence after that, eventually reaching Sioux City. I got off I-25 onto Highway 20 and crossed into Nebraska. For the first miles, everything looked like Iowa. Then, ever so slightly, the landscape changed to fewer trees and corn fields, and more open grassland. The flatness eventually changed into grass-covered hills—the Sand Hills, a fragile landscape of thin vegetation that held the sandy soil at bay from the powerful winds that blew across this area.

Finally she broke the silence: "Sorry if I offended you, Russell. I can sometimes be flippant and should just keep my mouth shut. My mother always told me to think before I speak, and I still don't sometimes."

That mellowed me, and then I felt a little stupid myself. "That's okay, I didn't mean to be so sharp; it's just that I like everything in my life to be orderly, predictable, safe. Change upsets me. That's why I have this trip all planned out … everything, places I want to see, campgrounds, mileage. I like to stick to my schedule."

"But isn't that sort of boring sometimes?" she asked.

"It's not boring to me. It's the way I like to live my life. I don't like surprises," I replied.

She seemed to consider that for a moment before saying, "I guess I like to experience the unexpected, live without an agenda, see what might come my way … like hitching and meeting you."

We dropped further discussion.

Chapter 5: Niobrara Camp

I planned to spend the night at a campground by the Niobrara River. When we came to the turn-off, I told her I was stopping for the night.

"Do you want to get out and hitch into Valentine, about fifteen miles down the road?" I asked.

She shook her head. "I can camp there. I have what I need."

We found places to set up our camps, paid our fees in the drop box, and settled in. It was early in the season; we were the only ones there. New spring leaves on the trees shaded our campsites, and the river flowed only a hundred or so feet away.

She got out, grabbed her pack and guitar from the back, walked over to a site she'd chosen, and set up her camp. I raised the camper, then walked over to the river. The weather was warm and the water looked inviting, so I changed into my swim trunks, went back to the river and waded in. Cool water washed over me, cleansing two days of driving from my body and mind. I glanced down the river and saw her naked body slide into the water about fifty feet away. I looked away, not wanting to let her know I'd seen her. I didn't want her to think I was spying on her. I didn't know if she'd seen me or not. All I'd seen of her was a slender female body.

I was enjoying the cool water when I heard her behind me:

"Hi, water's great, feels wonderful."

I turned; she stood a few feet away in waist-deep water. All I saw were her naked breasts, but I immediately averted my gaze up to her eyes.

She smiled. "Russell, you're blushing. I embarrassed you. I'm really sorry. I can also be a bit of an exhibitionist, along with other faults." She chuckled and dipped down into the water so that only her head showed. "My parents always took me to 'clothing-optional' beaches around home when I was a kid, so I guess that I can be naked if I want. Since there were only the two of us, guess I thought it would be okay. Shouldn't have— sorry."

"I just wasn't expecting you to be naked." For the first time I could clearly see her emerald-green eyes, high cheek bones, and warm, full-lipped smile. "Never seen a naked woman before except my wife, ah, my ex-wife, I mean." I realized that I'd never actually seen her naked.

"Oh, I'm really sorry. Recent?"

"Yeah, almost six months now."

"Wow, none of my business, so I won't ask any more questions."

"It's okay, and thanks. Hey, I'm getting cold. I bet you're really cold with no clothes on."

She laughed. "Good one, Russell."

"Yeah, I'm just a barrel of laughs," I said somewhat too sarcastically. "You can get out first. I won't look."

"It's okay, really; let's just get out."

We walked out together, my eyes looking away. She wandered over to her towel and wrapped it around herself. I went to the van, dried off, and got dressed, then I opened a bottle of wine and, wanting some companionship, called over, asking if she wanted some.

'I'd love some wine," she replied. "I'll be over in a minute."

She appeared shortly, and, dammit, she looked beautiful with her big smile and the almost electric energy she gave off. I invited her to sit on one of my two folding camp chairs and offered her a plastic cup of wine.

She took a sip and looked at me, now sitting opposite her. I thought the way she cocked her head and twirled a loose strand of hair in her fingers the sexiest thing I'd ever seen a woman do, but I immediately cleared my mind of that thought.

She smiled and said, "Russell, would you mind taking me up to Mission tomorrow? I don't think it's much out of your way, and I can see my friend John. I really don't want to hitch on the Res. It can be dangerous. Then I could maybe go with you to Rushmore.

"I've been hitching now for over a month, and the only rides I get have been with smelly truck drivers who smoke a lot and guys in big pickups, all of 'em wanting to get in my pants. You don't seem that sort. I think I can trust you. Can I trust you?"

At first I didn't say anything, wondering if I wanted a passenger. "Thanks, I guess," I replied eventually. "I think that was a compliment. I hadn't planned on a passenger. And yeah, you can trust me. Promise. And I don't smoke, and I like to shower every day. I suppose I could take you up there as long as we don't stay too long so I can get to Rushmore on schedule."

She looked at me with the I-can't-believe-you-said-that sort of look I'd sometimes gotten from Dana, then continued, "That'd be great. It's not easy being a woman hitchhiking around this country. After reading Kerouac's *On the Road* last year, I had this illusion of freedom on the road, but I think I'm about fifty years too late. I'm so tired of old men in pickups and truck drivers all thinking that I should fuck them just because they give me a ride."

I stayed quiet for a while. I'd never heard a woman use the "f-bomb" before. Then it was my schedule: I had my plans; I had my itinerary; now there was this Hanna woman wanting to go along with me. I wasn't too sure about this. But she was really pretty and seemed nice in a peculiar sort of way. It might be nice to have her along, at least for a while, maybe. I felt another pang of loneliness.

"Well, Hanna, I'm willing to try it for a while, but as soon as it's not good for me ... or you, we'll need to part ways. Agreed?"

She smiled. "Thanks, Russell. Thanks. It's agreed, then. I'll help with gas. I can afford to pay my way, don't want to be a freeloader. I won't be a problem. I promise."

"Okay, then." I didn't need her help with gas, but decided to let her contribute, figuring there was no sense in arguing about it. I poured us some more wine. "So, how long have you been traveling?"

"I left the end of March and headed south through California, then Arizona, New Mexico, and up into Iowa. Just wanted to see the country, but I'd gone far enough east when I hit Iowa and was ready to head back home. You picked me up and here I am. I admit there were many times I was tempted to get on a bus for home, but ... yeah, here I am. I have a secret stash of money if I ever need a ticket."

"Wow," was all I could say, then, "Hey, I'm getting hungry. Why don't you join me for dinner? I have some cold chicken in the cooler that my sister sent with me. Also there's stuff for salad. It all needs to be eaten before it spoils. I'll get started."

"I can help." We both got up.

I got everything out, including bowls, forks, and olive oil. Hanna got the greens ready while I cut up the chicken, some onion, and a tomato. I also had some bread that I toasted on my stove. In a few minutes we were eating.

I asked her about herself.

"I'm twenty-six. My mother, Meg, is a fairly successful artist. I've never met my real father. Mom's work is represented by several Bay Area galleries as well as galleries in Los Angeles, Chicago, and New York. Her work sells great.

"Her partner, Frank, is a woodworker. He also writes poetry and hangs out at City Lights Bookstore, going to readings, and talking with his writer friends. He's had three books of his poetry published.

"What about you? What do you do, and where do you live? You said you were divorced. Want to talk about it?"

"I don't want to talk about my divorce," I replied, realizing immediately that I'd been short with her. I continued on more gently, "Sorry, that didn't come out very well. I just don't want to talk about it."

"Understood, but sometimes it helps to talk. I can't imagine how painful something like that might be. Sometimes talking about stuff helps; if you ever want to, I'm a good listener, no judgement. Promise."

"Thanks; I'll keep that in mind. As for the rest of your question, I worked in a bank in Chicago until last winter, then moved back to my home town in eastern Iowa, where I've been living with my sister and her family until I left on this trip yesterday. Interesting, it already seems like forever that I've been out, but it's only been two days."

That feeling of fear and loneliness came over me again. I missed Karen, John, and the boys, my stability, even my parents—my safety net. I started to think this whole trip was a big mistake. I felt myself having a panic attack like I read about in the waiting room of my psychiatrist's office: my breathing quickened, my heart beat faster, and I started to sweat. I fell painfully silent.

"Russell, are you okay? What's going on?" Hanna asked gently.

"Nothing! I'm fine! I have to pee!" I answered all too harshly.

I jumped up and walked away, embarrassed, not wanting to show any of what I was experiencing. I went into some trees. My life was a mess. I felt dreadfully alone and scared. I sat down by a tree until I got myself together.

Hanna shouted, "You okay, Russell?"

I walked back and sat down. "I'm sorry. I'm feeling … I'm feeling alone and out of my element. Maybe I'm not suited for this and should just head back home tomorrow."

"But, Russell, a few minutes ago we planned to travel together. You seem like an okay guy. I thought we would hang and travel for a while."

"Thanks, Hanna, but I think this trip was a big mistake. I probably won't be a very good travel companion. To be honest, I'm scared."

"Scared of what, Russell? Of what you might discover about the world? It's great to be out. I love traveling and seeing new things and places."

"I don't know, Hanna. I like knowing familiar places. It feels safer, more predictable."

"Ah, sure, okay," she responded. "Not sure I understand, but yeah, if you feel that way."

"I don't want to talk anymore. Let's clean up." I stood and gathered the dishes.

She gave me a sad look but said no more. We cleaned up, and Hanna went to her tent. I sat in the Westy, feeling dumb and stupid. She started to play her guitar, then sang some song I hadn't heard before. She had an amazing voice, clear and sweet. I listened, absorbed in her music and the lyrics. I started wondering why I'd gotten so emotional. Truth is, I'd never really been free from family all my life, until right now. The University of Iowa was less than twenty miles away from home; I visited my family almost every weekend. Then in Chicago, only a few hundred miles away, I was with Dana. I'd never really been on my own.

Only after the divorce had I really been alone, and then I moved in with my sister. My parents thought I was a complete failure, and I felt like one. Was I scared of myself, afraid of what I might find out, afraid of this trip? Was that why my doctor wanted to me to write a journal?

Then there was this Hanna—frightening with all her openness and free spirit. She didn't seem afraid of anything. I didn't understand her ability to act so free of responsibility. I was always so strictly guided by my parents and my church. How could she be so undisciplined? I couldn't grasp that idea. One had to be self-disciplined, work hard, be responsible, not be frivolous but assess risks, every risk. I wasn't sure I had adequately assessed this risk.

I turned off my reading light, closed my eyes, but couldn't sleep. My mind raced with worries. Finally I took a sleeping pill. At last, sleep found me.

Chapter 6: Rosebud

The next day, my first thoughts were of last night and our conversation. I remembered that I'd decided to head back. I'd take Hanna to Valentine and head back to Iowa.

I looked over to her campsite and saw her sitting by a tree, looking out towards the river, still as a rock. I watched her for a few minutes. She didn't move. I got dressed.

"Good morning, sunshine," she said cheerily as I opened the sliding door into the new bright day. "Sleep okay?"

"Yeah, I did, thanks. How about you?"

"Great. Hope my singing didn't bother you."

"No, not at all; it was wonderful. You have a beautiful voice and know your way around a guitar."

"Thanks, that's nice of you to say. I was a music major in college, specializing in voice. I took some classes in guitar, learned a lot from some friends, then had some lessons after I graduated. I like writing my own songs, but do some covers as well. Sometimes when I hit a town for a night, I look for an open mike at a bar or coffee shop. It's fun and I usually make a few bucks in tips."

"Wow, really? That sounds really nice."

She nodded. "I see you have a guitar in your van. Let's play together sometime. Oh, right, I forgot, you're heading back today—really hate to have you leave before you even get started."

She gave me that look again, the hair twirling thing, and said, "Hey, come on, why not give it a few more days and see what happens. You said you were planning on going up to the Lakota Reservations. Let's do that and head to Mount Rushmore at least. Come on, give it a go. I know a guy that moved back to the reservation. I have his number. That's why I want to go there."

I thought for a moment. *Dammit, that look just melts me. Maybe another few days, then head back.* "Okay, Rosebud it is, and sure, call your friend. Then … then maybe to Mount Rushmore? I don't know what got into me last night. I just missed everybody and … and … well, you know."

"It's okay to be lonesome and miss your family. I understand. I've really missed my mom and Frank since I've been out."

Not wanting to go into this conversation any further, I said, "Let's make some coffee, have something to eat, and hit the road."

"Yahoo! Let's do it!" The way she looked at me, with excitement in her eyes, made me think for a moment that she was going to hug me, but she hesitated, and the moment was lost. I realized how much I would've liked a hug from her right then.

We ate a quick breakfast of some power bars and fruit, made some coffee for my two travel mugs, packed up, and hit the road. Valentine, a real cowboy town, had a main street lined with feed stores, a saddle shop, two western clothing stores, a huge farm and ranch store, and a stock yard. Lean, raw men—and some women—wearing cowboy boots, denim jeans and shirts, and big hats walked down the main street. I drove slow, gawking as

33

we moved up the street. It was like the Old West, but real with real people, not a TV show or a movie.

Driving farther north, on the road to Mission, the biggest town on the Rosebud Reservation, the land changed again, now to empty, rolling grasslands that opened up to an enormous clear blue sky, expansive land with endless herds of imaginary buffalo coming over the horizon, hooves thundering, clouds of dust so vividly described in the Zane Grey books of my youth. I was in the West and overwhelmed by it all. I wiped a tear.

Hanna apparently noticed. "Are you okay?"

I didn't say anything, only nodded. I couldn't ever remember my emotions being so on edge and didn't understand why this was happening. I was always so controlled, but now …? We continued on in silence, lost in our thoughts.

Driving into Mission, there was an old store with faded boards and dirty windows looking almost ready to fall down with two pickups and three cars parked in the lot.

"Can we stop here?" she asked.

I reluctantly pulled into the dusty parking lot, and we walked inside into a very clean and organized array of Native American beaded jewelry, silver jewelry, books, hats, some beaded denim jackets, assorted cooking products, and craft supplies. We spent an hour looking around an assortment of things that neither of us had ever experienced before. I ended up with the book *Black Elk Speaks*. Hanna bought a bundle of sage, a long print skirt, and a beaded bracelet.

She grabbed a straw cowboy hat and put it on my head. "Russell, you should get this straw hat. You look really cool."

It fit nicely. I found a mirror and checked it out. "Yeah. I like it, but don't think it's really me. Thanks."

She looked at me and gave me her beautiful smile. "Then I'll buy it for you and make you wear it."

34

"No, I don't want it!" I hissed.

"Okay, then!" She scowled. "Sorry! I'll put it back!"

When we were paying for our purchases, the Anglo woman cashier asked, "So, you two married?"

Hanna and I looked at each other and almost in unison, said, "Oh, no, just friends."

"Oh, sorry; it's just that ya both look so cute together."

I knew I was blushing. I looked at Hanna. She was smiling happily at the woman.

"Thanks, but really," she said, "I'm just hitching a ride with Russell for a while." She looked over at me with big eyes.

"So, where ya headin' next?" the woman asked.

Hanna replied, "Thought we'd look around Mission for a while, check it out."

"There's really not a lot to 'check out' here. Folks here are pretty poor and struggle just to survive. But you might want to go to the Sinte Gleska college. It's something the Lakota people are really proud of. Pretty nice what they've done out there. Tryin' real hard to get the young people an education of their culture and other stuff. Should go check it out."

"Thanks," Hannah said. "Really love your store. It was fun to look around. Hey, I know a man lives up here; actually he's at the college. Maybe you know him, John Running Deer?"

"Sure, I know John. He works out there. He might be there."

"Thanks. I'll try to look him up."

"Come back when you're by again. We'll be here," she said with a sweet motherly smile.

We left the store and followed the directions the woman had given us to the college.

"God, Russell, you don't have to be such a shit," Hanna said. "I was just trying to have fun. I liked that hat on you."

35

"Well, sorry I'm not your idea of fun. I didn't want that dammed cowboy hat!"

She folded her arms across her chest and went silent.

I drove with purpose through the nondescript, run-down town, finally finding the college. It was different from what we'd just driven through, looking modern and up-to-date with a large building that resembled a teepee, another that might house classrooms and a gymnasium, and another resembling a two-story log home that looked like it might be a residence hall. I located what looked like the administration building, parked, and we went in.

An attractive young Lakota woman sat at the receptionist desk. "May I help you?"

"I'm looking for a friend I knew in San Francisco," Hanna said. "He moved back a few years ago. John Running Deer? Is he around?"

"Yes, John's here. You can find him down this hall, Office one hundred twelve." She pointed to her right. "You can go on down."

I followed Hanna to John's office. She peeked in. "Hey, John, remember me? Hanna?"

A tall, lean Lakota man with long, shiny black hair got up from his desk. From a man's point of view, he was a good-looking man, about my age, maybe a little older. "Hanna, what a surprise! What are you doing here? So good to see you. Come in and sit down."

"Hi, John. Likewise," Hanna said. "This is my friend, Russell."

He came over and shook my hand. "Welcome. Russell. It's nice to meet a friend of Hanna's. Please. Sit. Do you need water?"

We both declined.

"Hanna, tell me everything that's happened since I left," he continued.

Hanna talked about the friends they had, what they were doing, where they were, who was married, and who had children.

I got antsy to get going towards Mount Rushmore and, strangely, felt a tinge of jealously, but I tried to be patient and let them reminisce.

"How's Donna?" Hanna asked.

"Donna's great. We just had a new baby girl, Ann Marie."

"A new baby! Oh, can we come by to see them?"

"We'd love to have you. Donna will be thrilled to see you. Come by early. We're having a sweat tonight, around five thirty. Can you and Russell come?"

"Of course we can come—"

I interrupted. "But, Hanna, we were going to—"

"Rushmore will still be there tomorrow, Russell!" Hanna said, somewhat sharply, then, looking back at John, she said, "Of course we'll come."

"Okay, I have to catch up on a little work. Come by whenever. I'll be there around five or so. You're welcome to camp there for tonight."

He scribbled something on a piece of paper and handed it to her. "Here are the directions."

"See you tonight, John. Thanks." Hanna got up to leave, and I followed.

We walked out, got in the Westy, and drove away.

"Hanna, what's a sweat?" I asked. "I thought we were going to Rushmore. I really want to get going. I have it scheduled."

"Russell, do you have any idea what an honor it is to be invited to share in a Lakota sweat lodge? You can leave if you think you have to keep a schedule, but I'm staying. We can leave in the morning."

"But what's a sweat? Have you ever done this before?"

"Yeah, maybe six, eight times. John used to have sweats out on this guy's land out north of Sausalito. It's like a sauna, only this has much more meaning than a sauna. It's a sacred ceremony, held in an enclosed dome-shaped structure covered with canvas or whatever to create a dark, tight space.

"There's a pit in the middle, and it's filled with hot rocks. The entrance is closed, and the leader calls on the spirits to come. He pours water on the stones, the heat engulfs you, and you sweat—sweat hard.

"There're usually four prayer rounds when the participants pray for whatever they want to pray for. It usually lasts around an hour or so. There are breaks between the prayer rounds when the entrance is opened and you can leave if you want to or need to. Nobody ever does. More hot rocks come in and the next round begins. It's really very spiritual. What do you think? Are you game?"

The description overwhelmed me a little. "I don't think so, Hanna. It's not something I think I should do. While I don't go to church anymore, it sounds pretty pagan to me."

"Oh. Come. On. Russell. Lighten up. It's not going to turn you into a pagan. My God. You really are uptight."

"I don't think it's appropriate. You go ahead if you want."

"I want, and I also want you to participate. Come on. Try it, and if it's too much you can leave. Seriously. No one will think anything of it. Please?"

"Thanks, but no thanks. I think I'll head out. I'll take you out to John's and then get going. Really, thanks, but no."

She sighed. "I'm sorry, Russell, if that's what you want. But can we stop by that store for a minute? I need to get an appropriate dress."

"Sure." I made a left and drove back to the store.

Hanna jumped out. "Just be a minute."

About five minutes later she came out and we followed the directions to John's house, a nondescript ranch with a dusty drive and parking area—stark, no lawn or shrubs. A few other houses were scattered about. They all looked the same—sad and desolate. I pulled in.

Hanna got out and looked at me with a pleading face. "I really wish you would reconsider."

"Thanks, but no. I need to get going. I think I'll just head back down to last night's camp and then home. It's getting late. It's been nice to know you, and best of luck … with everything."

She gave me one final look of puzzlement, shrugged, shook her head sadly, then retrieved her things from the back, turned, and walked away. I watched her for a moment, drove back to the highway, and headed south a few miles and pulled over onto the shoulder.

My emotions were completely in conflict with my rational mind. I wanted to get out of there and go back to Iowa to my secure reality. But I wanted to see Rushmore. And, for some stupid reason, I sort of wanted to do this sweat thing. This strange woman intrigued me, and I wanted to know more about her. What would happen if I was adventurous for once? If I went back there to see what would happen? After arguing with myself for about five minutes, I was breathing hard and my heart was racing. I took several deep breaths, got calmed down, turned around and headed back. I found Hanna putting up her tent.

She looked up and smiled her radiant smile when she saw me getting out. "You came back!" She ran over, and this time she hugged me—hugged me really tight.

I hugged her back, felt her body, smelled her scent, and something went through me like a gentle bolt of lightning.

"I'm so happy you came back. Are you gonna do the sweat?"

"What do I have to wear?"

"A swimming suit and t-shirt will be fine. This will be a wonderful experience for you. I know. I just know." She squeezed my hand and put her other hand on my face, looking at me with the most tender, sweet look I'd ever experienced. I thought she might kiss me, but she let go and turned away, saying, "And bring a towel."

At four thirty, John arrived home. Another man—older, but how old I couldn't say—followed him in an old rickety pickup, rattling and sputtering to a stop in a black cloud of exhaust. John brought him over and introduced him to us as Raymond. He shook our hands, nodding his acknowledgement. He had long raven-black hair, dark eyes, a deeply lined face, and wore blue jeans, work boots, a denim shirt, and a baseball cap.

Raymond looked at me. "You, Russell, come help me with the fire." He motioned me to follow him.

I looked at Hanna. She smiled and nodded, so I followed.

He led me to what looked like the sweat lodge Hanna had described and pointed to a wood pile. "Bring over some wood and put it here." He pointed to a place next to a pile of rocks.

I did his bidding, loading up a few pieces of the split wood and placing it where he said. "Ow! I got a sliver."

"Let me see." Raymond looked at it and carefully pulled it out. "Wait here." He went to his pickup and brought me a new pair of leather gloves. "Here. Use these. No more slivers. Now, bring more than that. We'll need a lot more. Need a big fire."

While I brought the wood, he stacked it neatly into a precise order including the rocks, which, I guessed, the fire would heat for the sweat. His attention to his work and his precision impressed me.

I kept on bringing wood until Raymond said, "Enough. There's a bucket by the door. Get it and fill it with water over at that hydrant and put it inside to the right of the door."

I got the five-gallon bucket—it had a ladle in it—and did as ordered. When I went over to Raymond and gave him his gloves back, he refused.

"No. Those are yours now. Wear them so you don't get no more slivers. You earned them."

His kindness overwhelmed me. Me, who could afford these gloves by the dozen, and he gave me his pair of new ones. "Thank you," I choked out. I couldn't remember ever experiencing such a simple act of kindness.

Raymond started the fire, and it grew blazing hot. I noticed that a few other people had, somehow, magically appeared. They used an old shed close by as a changing room, then hung their towels and clothes on a long wooden pole that sat on top of two posts. Hanna came over dressed in the long shapeless gray dress she'd bought from the store.

"So, we're about ready. Like my new dress?" She smiled and twirled around.

"Very becoming, Hanna. But what do I do?"

"Just pay attention and follow what everybody else does. It's not a big deal. When the time comes around for you to speak or pray—"

"Oh, no. No; I'm not praying."

"Then just pass. It's okay. There's no pressure. Just enjoy. I'll sit next to you. John is leading, so he'll go in first. We can join in right after since we're sort of special guests."

I started to get really nervous.

Hanna noticed, smiled at me, and took my hand, reached up and gave me a peck on the cheek. "You'll be fine. I'll be right next to you."

Her kiss was unexpected, warm, and reassuring. It also made me feel what I'd felt before, that gentle lightning bolt in my chest.

John came over. "Hanna said this is your first time. Just watch what everyone else does. You'll be fine."

"Yeah, she's prepped me. Guess I'm ready."

"Then let's go. Follow me."

He walked to the entrance, got down on all fours, and crawled in while saying something I didn't understand. Hanna followed, and I followed her into the dim light, crawling clockwise around the pit in the center. John and Hanna got situated, and I located next to her, sitting cross-legged. We sat on bare dirt. The odor of earth, sweat, and some other smell I couldn't define filled the air. Others followed: six other men and five women packed in, each saying something in Lakota. I felt uncomfortable in confined places to begin with, and to be crowded in with strangers made it even more uncomfortable. I took some deep breaths, trying to relax. My heart was pounding in my ears.

John welcomed the two of us as guests. Everyone acknowledged us with something that sounded like "Ho."

Once we'd settled, Raymond placed red-hot rocks into the pit with a pitch fork. Then he lowered the flap, making it pitch black. A blast of intense heat hit my body, making me feel as if I'd walked into a blast furnace. John began a chant with words in his native Lakota language. Though I didn't understand, I guessed he was calling in the spirits as Hanna had told me. I found the chanting entrancing, and a calm settled over me.

Some sort of primal emotion built in my chest. I looked around in the pitch black and saw shapes moving about; I felt a jolt of fear and immediately closed my eyes. John finished his chant, and I heard the sizzle as he poured a ladle of water on the rocks. The steam hit me like a body slam. It was unbelievably hot. Sweat started to pour out of my body.

One of the participants spoke in Lakota. After some time, the first person stopped speaking, and everyone said that word that sounded like "Ho," and something in Lakota sounding like "Mit—sake," or something like that. Then another person spoke. It was hard to breathe. I became more and more uncomfortable, calm replaced by nervousness and fear. The round proceeded until it came to my turn. All I could mumble was, "Pass."

Then Hanna began: "Thank you, Great Spirit, for the honor of me being here and sharing in this sacred time. Thank you for my safe journey. Thank you for my meeting Russell." She stopped.

I felt a lump form in my throat.

John shouted something in Lakota and opened the flap. I felt a rush of cool air and, thankfully, could breathe. Hanna said I could leave after a round. I fought the urge. After what I guessed to be about five minutes of silence, Raymond shoveled in more red-hot rocks and closed the flap. It began again. A blast of steam and then a pungent scent, similar, but more pronounced than what I'd smelled when I'd entered. I later found out that John had spread sage onto the rocks.

The next round began and came to me. I again passed. Hanna went on about her mother and Frank. John finished the round and opened the flap again. More rocks, flap closed, steam, sage, prayers. I felt dehydrated and woozy. The round came to me again.

"I'm honored to be here, and thank you, everyone. I'm on a journey to find my life. Please pray for me."

Everybody said, "Ho."

I couldn't believe I'd said anything. I wanted to cry. I wanted to leave. But I stayed. I thought I would surely die. Strangely, I surrendered to that idea. Right then, I wasn't afraid of dying. My family would wonder, maybe look for me. I didn't really care. They wouldn't even know where I was or what had happened to me. I'd simply disappear off the face of the Earth. I felt an incredible calm.

The sweat lodge continued into the fourth round. This time, during my turn, I went on about my divorce and my poor relationship with my parents, and then everyone said, "Ho."

Hanna talked about something I didn't hear. John finished with a closing prayer. The flap opened.

I followed Hanna and John out and inhaled the most amazing fresh, sweet, cool air I could ever remember. I was alive. I felt as if I'd been reborn. I felt giddy and wanted to cry. I wanted to run and scream, "I'm alive."

Everyone came over and shook my hand, making me feel as if I'd joined a fraternity. I couldn't believe I'd done it. Feeling thirsty, I followed others over to the hydrant, stuck my mouth under, and drank until I was about to burst.

After a lot of talking, laughing, and drinking water, the group said their goodbyes and began to leave.

"Donna has food ready," John said. "Let's go eat." He motioned us to follow.

Raymond banked the fire and followed.

"Russell and I'll go change and be there in a minute," Hanna said. She grabbed my hand and led me towards our camp.

"Dinner?" I said. "I don't know these people and feel uncomfortable going to his house for dinner."

"Don't be silly. John is very nice, and so is Donna. I've known them for a long time. I'll be there. Don't worry so much."

Despite the sunny sky, I heard a crack of thunder while we walked to our camp. I looked around and saw a small thunderstorm scudding along to the south. Rain and lightning headed more cracks of thunder. In Iowa, huge fronts brought a wall of storm, covering the sky from horizon to horizon. I found this funny little storm under a clear sky another weird and wonderful experience I was having only two days from home.

We changed, returned to the house and knocked. A slender, dark-eyed woman with waist-long, raven-black hair answered the door. "Hanna. Oh, Hanna. It's so good of you to come." The two women hugged, then the woman looked at me and said, "Welcome. My name's Donna. How long have you and Hanna been together?"

"About two days," I replied.

"Please, come in." She smiled and turned.

The house was plainly furnished with older, worn furniture. The walls held several abstract paintings and drawings, and a large, shallow drum. Delicious smells of food cooking permeated the house. I realized I was starved.

Hanna walked with Donna to the kitchen, explaining our meeting on the way. They went to a baby carriage and Hanna's eyes lit up.

"Come here, Russell; come see this baby."

I wandered over and looked at a little person sleeping soundly. "She's beautiful. Wow. I don't remember ever seeing a little baby this small. She's amazing. Can I hold her?" Why I asked that, I don't know. I'd never held a baby, even my niece, Zoe, since I didn't get along with my brother and only saw the little girl once when she was about two.

"Thanks. You can hold her when she wakes up," Donna said. "Her name is Ann Marie. She's four weeks old. Go in and sit, Russell." She motioned me towards an adjacent room. "John will be out shortly, and we'll eat. I'm happy you're here to join us."

I left Hanna staring at Ann Marie and went into the dining area. Raymond already sat at the table. He motioned me to a chair next to him. "Come, sit here."

I joined him. "Thank you again for those gloves today. That was very kind of you."

He looked at me, nodded, and took a drink of water. I did the same and we sat in silence.

John appeared and sat as Donna brought in a big, steaming bowl of stew. Hanna brought in another bowl piled high with some sort of pastry I discovered was Fry Bread. John blessed the food; we passed everything around, then ate. The stew was great, thick with beef, carrots, onions, and some other vegetable I didn't know. The fry bread was warm. I coated a piece with butter and tasted it—delicious. Everything was delicious, and I tried to take my time and not inhale my food.

Raymond passed me a dish of jam with large chunks of berry in it. "Try this on your bread."

I did and found it wonderfully good. After we'd finished, Donna served coffee, which I respectfully declined—I'd be awake all night. After some conversation, Donna and Hanna cleared the table while the three of us men sat without talking until Raymond stood, shook my and John's hand, thanked everyone, said goodbye, and left.

Only the two of us now. John asked me about myself, the usual stuff: where I was from, what I did, and did I have plans with Hanna? I replied that we'd just met and were only traveling together for a while.

46

"I can tell she really likes you," John said. "We were good friends back when I lived in the Bay Area. I lost track of her since I moved back here three years ago. She's had some hard times, so be careful and don't hurt her."

"Hard times? Like what?"

"She'll tell you when she wants to."

I asked about Raymond.

"Raymond is my uncle," John replied. "He always tends the fire for our sweats. He was married and had five children. All but one of his children died, all violent deaths: drugs and alcohol. His wife died last year."

I said nothing for a while. I didn't know what I could say to that. "Is there anything I can do to help? I got a sliver, and he pulled it out and gave me a pair of brand-new leather gloves. I'd like to repay him somehow."

"He doesn't expect anything. He's a good man. He likes you."

"Really? He likes me?"

"You're the first person he ever asked to help him with the fire. It's an honor, and he selected you."

A lump formed in my throat and I said nothing. I remembered his old pickup and had an idea. "What's Raymond's last name?"

"Same as mine, Running Deer."

"So, Raymond Running Deer. Live around here?"

"About two miles down from here. He has his old house that his family lived in. It's been hard."

"I can't imagine. I like him, too."

Donna and Hanna returned from the kitchen. Donna carried Little Ann Marie. "Here, Russell, you wanted to hold her." She handed her to me.

I immediately regretted my request to hold her. "I don't know how."

"Just make a cradle with your arms like I am. Here."

I did as instructed and received the little package. I must have looked scared because Donna said, "She won't break."

I stared at her little face and felt a delightful warmth. Her eyes opened, and she looked up at me with beautiful coal-black eyes and wiggled her tiny fingers. She was the most amazing little person.

"Russell, I need to go," Hanna said. "I'm really tired. John, I'd like your contact information."

They exchanged phone numbers and email addresses, then she looked at me questioningly.

"Yeah, I'm ready," I said. "Thank you, John, for everything—allowing me to participate in your sweat. Thank you, Donna, for dinner. It was delicious."

Donna took little Ann Marie from me.

"Come back, Russell, and bring Hanna," John said.

"I'd like that. Thank you again."

I thanked Donna again; we said our goodbyes and left for our camp.

"So, Russell, what did you think?" Hanna asked as we walked.

"I don't know. I don't want to talk about it right now. But I do have a question; what was everybody saying after someone said their prayer? Like, mit—something?"

"I know what you mean. I can't remember the words exactly, but the translation is something like 'all my relatives', which sort of means 'we are all connected'. The Lakota believe that all life is connected: moon, stars, sun, earth, plants, animals, humans, everything, all part of the same. It's very profound when you consider what it truly means, that all the universe is sacred and is one. It's also a basis for Buddhist philosophy. It gives us reason to respect all life, no matter what."

I considered this while we walked to our camp area. I found it hard to accept. "So, what you're saying is that I'm connected to animals and plants? Like I'm the same?"

"Exactly."

"I'm sorry, but I can't accept that. It just doesn't compute."

"I can understand. It's a hard concept, I know, but once you understand and accept it, it changes your whole realization of yourself and how you fit in this life. Just think about it."

"Yeah, maybe Black Elk's book will help. Hey, do you remember seeing a car dealer here in Mission?"

"We went by a small Ford dealership on the way in. Why?"

"Just wondering …. Thanks, Hanna. Thanks for talking me into this. It was a special experience."

"You talked yourself into it."

Even in the dark, I could see her smile as she turned to me and gave me another peck on the cheek. "Good night." She squeezed my hand, then crawled into her tent.

I lay awake for a long time, thinking of the day and all that had happened. I thought of Hanna's pecks on my cheek, her hugs, her easy affection. I couldn't ever remember anything like that from my mother or Dana. Finally without the help of any drugs, I fell easily into a sleep with vivid dreams, but by morning they'd disappeared into that place where dreams go.

Chapter 7: On to Mount Rushmore

The next morning I woke early and was getting out of the van when Hanna came up behind me.

"Good morning. Sleep okay?" she asked.

"Like a rock. And I feel great today. It's a beautiful day, isn't it?"

Hanna smiled and said nothing.

"Hey, I want to stop by that Ford dealership for a few minutes. I have something I need to do."

"But you wanted to be off to Mount Rushmore. I already delayed you a day."

"It'll only take a little while. We have all day," I said happily.

After a quick breakfast, we found the dealership.

"Coming in?" I asked her.

"No. I want to call Mom. It's been a while."

I went in, and an hour later, my business finished, we left for Mount Rushmore.

"What were you doing in there?" Hannah asked.

"Just checking on something."

"Just checking on something? For an hour? Like what?"

"Pricing new pickups."

"You wanting to buy a pickup? Here? I don't understand."

"Just checking on one was all."

We drove through the town, and I noticed how austere it all seemed, dreary and sad—the opposite of Valentine. The people looked weary and tired, but those I'd met were so kind and beautiful. It made me sad.

After Mission, we headed west under the big, clear blue sky—forever west in silence, lost in thoughts of last night. We followed Highway 18 past Parmelee, Martin, and Kyle—all sleepy, desolate towns displaying the poverty and sadness of the Lakota people.

My thoughts went to Hanna. After almost eight years of being married to Dana, I'd gotten used to her: her habits, her scent, her clothes, her different attitudes and idiosyncrasies. It felt strange being with a different woman. I found myself sometimes responding to her as I would've with Dana, which made me feel uncomfortable. Had being with someone so long shaped me into a mold of that person? I certainly didn't want to get involved with Hanna. She was too strange and different from me, not what I thought a woman should be. For now I appreciated her company, but after Mount Rushmore, we'd go our separate ways.

We entered the Badlands National Park, and I drove slowly and deliberately through the ghostly moonscape of multi-hued spires and bluffs tortured by weathering. I saw an overlook and pulled in. An unbelievable scene spread out before us. I stood there in awe; my chest almost ached with the wonder of this landscape. My awe brought a lump to my throat, and my eyes welled up with tears.

Hanna broke her silence: "This is so amazing. I had no idea that any place like this could exist on the face of this planet. What do you think?"

Seeing this along with everything that happened yesterday had filled me with unknown feelings, and I couldn't answer her.

I was too choked up. I simply looked at her, smiled a weak smile, and nodded.

"You okay? What's wrong?"

I turned and walked away. I couldn't let her see me like this. I was a man and was supposed to be strong. I had no idea of the emotions working on me. I pulled out my handkerchief, blew my nose, and wiped my eyes as discreetly as I could.

Hanna joined me, right by my side. "It is pretty overwhelming, I know. I felt a lot of emotion as well. It's okay, Russell; it's okay." She took my hand in hers, and that did it, I started to sob.

I hadn't cried since I was five years old. Everything seemed to be bursting out of me: my parents, expectations, rigidness, Dana, the divorce, failure. Then, doing what I did yesterday, something so crazy, yet an incredible experience. Thank goodness it was just Hanna there. That was bad enough. But instead of being judgmental, she put her arm around my shoulder until I was finally able to stop the flood.

"I'm sorry, Hanna. I'm really sorry. Please don't think of me as a crybaby."

"Russell, it's okay ... and *crybaby*? That sounds like parent talk made to make you a 'big strong man.' Russell, it's okay to feel. It really is. I like a man who can let go with his emotions. It's healthy for you, rather than holding it all inside. This was truly pretty overwhelming."

"Yeah, the view's amazing, and I guess after last night ... I don't know, these past few days have really affected me. Sorry."

"Nothing to be sorry about." She squeezed my hand, and we walked back to the van.

Back on the road, Hanna's cell chirped. She checked the text and sat staring out the windshield. "Russell! What did you do?"

"What?"

"That was John. Somehow a new Ford pickup was delivered to Raymond a while ago. Russell. Do you have any idea about how that might have happened? Raymond said it was from you!"

"Me? No. Of course not."

"That's why we stopped by the Ford place! You fucking bought Raymond a new fucking pickup! What the hell! Who are you?"

I didn't say anything.

"Dammit, Russell! I want to know!"

"Okay. So, yeah, I did it. I bought him that truck. I wanted to. It was supposed to be anonymous."

"You. Wanted. To. You spent like, what, thirty, forty, fifty thousand dollars for a man you met for a few hours yesterday? What the hell! Who are you? Are you fucking rich?"

"I wanted to do this for him. He showed me more kindness yesterday than I can ever remember anyone ever doing before. I'm not rich, but I have a little money saved, and I'm so damn happy I did what I did. I want this man to have something, and his old pickup was a piece of shit."

"God, Russell. You are the strangest man I have ever met ... that I've ever known. I don't know what to say."

"Say nothing."

She didn't say anything for a moment. "What you did for Raymond ... I don't know what to say; it's the sweetest thing ever. John said to tell you that Raymond will adopt you as his nephew when you come back. He told John to tell you that you're a good man."

I didn't say anything. I felt warm inside, very happy, and that now familiar lump in my throat.

I managed to break the silence. "Hey, there's a Woodalls Camp Guide in the glove box. See if you can find something, preferably with electric hookups so I can charge my laptop and cell phone."

She found an RV Park about ten miles from the monument, reserving a spot that would accommodate the van and her tent. We arrived about an hour later and checked into a tree-shaded place with a swimming pool and a small store for basic essentials.

Chapter 8: Mount Rushmore Camp

Our camp set up, I asked her if she wanted to go to the pool.

"Sure, it'll be great to cool down."

"You'll probably have to wear a suit here," I said.

"Really, and why would that be? So you aren't embarrassed?"

I laughed. "I think little kids, and maybe their parents, might be a little disturbed."

She laughed and we changed into our suits. I poured us some wine in the travel mugs, and we found two poolside lounge chairs, deposited our drinks and towels and plunged into the cool, refreshing water to soak away the day. I needed to clear my head of all this emotional stuff and get myself back into my normal, controlled self.

Hanna wore an attractive two-piece, but modest, suit. She was beautiful. I tried not to have any thoughts of her other than that I simply enjoyed her company.

Once cooled and refreshed, we got out, dried off, and reclined on the chairs, basking in the last of the afternoon sun and enjoying our wine and the quiet. With the sun setting and the temperature dropping, we headed to the shower building. I took a long hot shower and shaved off my three-day growth.

Back at camp, I suggested we go to the mom-and-pop restaurant next door to the campground for dinner. We entered into a 1950s vintage establishment that wasn't retro at all, but original. Cracked red Naugahyde chairs sat around pale-green Formica tables with chrome edging. Chrome and red Naugahyde stools lined a long lunch counter with drink fountains, a pie safe, a malted-milk machine, an array of candies, and the coffee urn sat on the back counter. Smells of fried onions, French fries, and grilled burgers floated out from the kitchen, adding to the ambiance.

A not-so-retro, young waitress dressed in tight jeans, sneakers, and a pastel-blue t-shirt brought us water and asked for our drinks order. Hanna ordered an ice tea, and I, a chocolate malt. We both studied the overhead menu, decided what we wanted and ordered. Sensible Hanna ordered a salad with grilled chicken; me, a cheese burger, fries, and a small side salad. The waitress left, and we sat, looking around the restaurant.

"This is like a restaurant in my home town when I was growing up," I said. "It had the same smell, ambiance, even almost identical fixtures. But it was torn down ten years ago. This is a true relic of the past."

"It's so cool," Hanna responded. "Never had anything like this in San Francisco where I grew up. It feels weird, but homey in a way."

Our food came. We ate without conversation, enjoying our food. My burger was great, and the rich, thick, and tasty malted milk brought back childhood memories.

We finished eating, and I grabbed the check. Hanna wanted to pay her share, but I refused, saying I suggested this so I would pay, but she insisted on leaving the tip.

On the way back, we stopped by the store and asked about getting to the monument, crowds, and such. The woman working there gave us directions, adding that the big crowds would begin the coming Memorial Day weekend. The season would start in earnest then. She suggested we get there early, none-the-less, and added that this campground was ninety-five percent booked starting Thursday.

We walked back to our campsite, planning tomorrow on the way. It seemed like a good idea to get an early start before the big throngs of tourists showed up.

I crawled into bed, and my mind went to Hanna. I enjoyed her company, finding her nice to be with. I realized that if I hadn't met her, I would've turned around and headed back to Iowa yesterday. But after tomorrow she'd be on her own, and I'd be heading home—home to what?

Up early, I went over to the store and paid to stay for another night. I got us coffee in the travel mugs, then we grabbed some power bars and headed off to see Mount Rushmore.

The parking lot was already filling when we arrived. While I was concentrating on finding a parking spot, Hanna said, "Oh, stop and look … there they are."

I stopped the van and looked to where she pointed: four huge ghostly faces carved by many men, and what would now be considered ancient machinery, into the side of a mountain.

We headed toward the entrance, climbed a few steps to purchase our passes, then walked down a promenade past the visitor center toward those gigantic edifices of George Washington, Thomas Jefferson, Theodore Roosevelt, and Abraham Lincoln.

A kiosk gave us some background on the sculptures: Doane Robinson first conceived the project, with the idea of promoting tourism in the area by creating carvings of western heroes like Lewis and Clark, Red Cloud, and Buffalo Bill Cody. However, a sculptor by the name of Gutzon Borglum, who got involved with the project, thought that the sculptures should have more of a national focus. He wanted the four presidents, and his idea eventually won out. U.S. Senator Peter Norbeck secured federal funding for the project, and construction began in 1927. The four faces were completed between 1934 and 1939. The initial concept had the sculptures from top of head to waist, but funding dried up in 1941, and the heads are as we see them today.

Both of us stood for a few moments savoring the moment, like after opening a wonderful present on Christmas morning, then we ambled down the promenade to a viewing platform for a closer view. After studying the faces for some time, I felt a huge sense of the history of our country, which I'd never paid much attention to before. I really didn't know much about any western history other than my Zane Grey novels. I also had never been to a national park before yesterday.

We headed toward the museum, where we saw a display of pictures, models, samples of the hand tools used by the four hundred or so workers, survey equipment, and other assorted artifacts.

At the gift shop we checked out books and t-shirts. I saw a nice women's tee and told Hanna she should have it.

"Nice, but too expensive," she said.

I quietly bought it for her, but Hanna didn't find anything. We walked out, taking one last look before exiting the park. Now, three hours later, tourist buses were disgorging throngs of tourists who flooded the park. Thankfully we'd gotten there as early as we did.

Since it was only eleven thirty, we decided to drive the twenty or so miles down to Custer State Park. We paid our entry fee and stopped to look at the map. A short two-point-four-mile hike to a place called the Cathedral Spires sounded good, so we parked the van and set off. At the trail head, Hanna got her water bottle out of her day pack—two things I didn't have. She admonished me, saying I should always carry water and that, because the air was drier, your sweat evaporated quickly, and you could be dehydrated before you knew it. Depending on where you were, you could be in serious danger if you didn't have adequate water and stayed hydrated. I took her advice and promised that a water bottle would be my next purchase.

The air was truly different here, sharper and clearer. I attributed that to less humidity.

After a strenuous hike up a difficult trail, we came to the viewing place and looked across a deep, pine-tree covered canyon to the Cathedral Spires rock formations. We sat for a while, enjoying the solitude and beauty of the area, then headed back towards the van. On our way out of the park, Hanna told me to stop. She pointed to seven buffalo about a quarter mile away. Neither of us had ever seen buffalo before, and we took several pictures from our smartphones until a car came up behind us and we moved on.

Hanna had seen something about a hike up to Black Elk Peak. She wondered if we shouldn't stay another day and do that hike tomorrow. My schedule had lost all meaning by now; and what was another day? I could head home then. We stopped at the park store to ask about it. The manager showed us a map on how to get there. He told us the trail started at an elevation of about 6,200 feet and had an 1,100-foot elevation gain in three and a half miles and to allow four to five hours for the seven-mile round trip.

I asked if we could stay the next night in our spot. He said that we could, but he did have it reserved the following night. Hanna showed me a day backpack with a water bladder and suggested I needed it for the hike. I tried fitting it on my back, and it felt comfortable enough, so I bought it along with a water bottle to have in the van.

I pulled my laptop out to check news and weather, and also took a look at my portfolio, which was doing nicely. I was spending hardly any money, except for the truck I'd just bought from my cash reserve, so I was making money every day. *I could spend all summer out here if I want.* Everything I'd seen the last few days had whetted my appetite for more. I decided to keep on going until after Memorial Day and go back then. Having Hanna with me felt comfortable. I honestly didn't think I could do this by myself. I didn't think I could exist alone. I needed companionship, but I wanted to keep on going.

In the late afternoon Hanna knocked on the side of the van. "Hey, want to hit the pool?"

"Sure," I said. "I'll change and be out in a minute."

I poured some wine for each of us into the travel cups and met her outside, where I gave her the t-shirt I'd bought. She wasn't as excited as I thought she'd be. We walked over to the pool, located ourselves, and went in. The water felt good after the day of touristing and hiking. We swam for a while, then got out and sat down.

"Russell, I don't want you buying things for me," she said. "I have my own money. I told you I'd pay my way. I know you have money, but don't, please, just don't."

"I'm sorry. I enjoy having you with me, and I wanted to treat you. It's really no problem for me, seriously not a problem."

"You're missing the point. I want to pay my own way. I don't want to be indebted to you."

"You're not going to be indebted to me, but okay … I still get to treat you once in a while, though—promise I won't make it a habit. It's just that having you with me is keeping me sane."

She giggled. "Okay, as long I'm keeping you sane, but not all the time. Promise?"

"Promise."

"Do you want to talk about the sweat?" she asked.

"No, I really don't know what to say other than it was an interesting and amazing experience. I'm happy I did it, but it's not something I feel I need to do again." The subject was dropped.

We lay there, enjoying the last of the sun. When it began to set, we hit the shower building and met back at camp.

"Let's go over to the mom and pop for dinner again," I said. "I'm too tired to want to get anything together tonight. I promise I won't buy your dinner tonight."

"Sure, let's, and I want to buy."

I didn't object.

We walked over, found a booth, and our waitress from last night came over to take our order. Being more sensible than last night, I ordered a salad with grilled chicken and iced tea. Hanna had the same.

I kept noticing her tattoos and had to ask, "Did they hurt much?" I pointed at her arm.

She smiled. "Not really, sort of like a mild bee sting that lasted a long time."

"Why did you get tattoos?" I asked, immediately regretting the question.

She turned and looked out the window, not saying anything for a while. Then she said, "I really don't know. Some of the people I was hanging out with a while back, you know, it was when …" Her voice faltered. "Never mind." Her chin started to quiver.

"I'm sorry; didn't mean to pry. It's none of my business. I didn't want to upset you."

She said nothing. I let it drop, and we said nothing more until our food came. We ate, talking about the day and our hike tomorrow. I told her I planned to continue on for a while longer and asked if she wanted to keep on with me.

"That's great. Yeah, I'll be happy to keep you company," she laughed, "and sane."

Up early again, we got coffees at the store, had a power bar and some trail mix, filled our day packs with water and some snacks, and headed to the trail. With the uphill grade I found it harder and longer than the day before. I was soon sweating and short of breath.

"Wow, I am so out of shape," I said, panting.

"You're at higher altitude than in Iowa, and there's less oxygen," Hanna said. "You'll be fine, just need to acclimate to altitude is all. It'll take a few days."

After stopping to get my breath several more times, we arrived at the summit, where one could look east far out onto the green plain that met a blue sky dotted with fluffy white clouds. To the west, endless mountains faded into blue haze. An old fire lookout tower stood right next to us. We checked it and found it locked.

We sat to have some snacks and water and enjoy the distant views, then we headed back down. Around a tall rock we spied a mountain goat grazing on some tufts of grass. He saw us, considered us for a moment, then nonchalantly continued his grazing. The downhill hike back to the van was much easier than going up.

Back at camp we went for another swim and relaxed by the pool until the sun began to disappear. I suggested we eat out of my fridge to finish my supplies. We could get groceries tomorrow.

The next morning, we headed down to Rapid City and found a large supermarket at the edge of town where we bought what we'd need for a few days. Then we drove to Interstate 90, heading towards Gillette and Sheridan, Wyoming, taking a short detour to see Devil's Tower.

Chapter 9: To Wyoming

We got to the Devil's Tower Park around eleven thirty. The tower, a lone sentinel of vertical ridges and striations, rose almost 1,300 feet above the Belle Fourche River. Several people were climbing this monster like spiders, constantly grasping for purchase. Just watching them made me queasy.

An information kiosk gave us several geologic explanations for the tower, one being that it was a volcanic plug, any debris created by it, such as volcanic ash, lava flows, and other debris, having eroded away many millennia ago. We watched the climbers for a while, checked out the visitors' center, then left to get on the road west to Gillette, Buffalo. From there we drove on up to the little town of Story where Hanna had reserved a campsite.

After seeing a sign reading *No Services for the Next 70 Miles*, we stopped in Gillette for gas and found ourselves in the middle of an oil patch. Well pumps dotted the otherwise barren landscape and slowly rose and fell in a hypnotic rhythm, like robotic creatures from the Star Wars movies. We found a noticeable increase of truck traffic on the interstate, seemingly part of the oil and gas extraction industry. The air smelled and tasted of oil.

We got to Buffalo where Interstate 25 intersected with 90, then continued north on I-90 to the exit to Story and onto a winding road up into the foothills of the Bighorn Mountains.

Chapter 10: Story Camp

We arrived the Friday of Memorial Day weekend and found the campground chock full of all sizes and shapes of tents, camping trailers, vans, and recreational vehicles. We'd been lucky to reserve a spot. A tall pine forest interspersed by cottonwoods lined a little creek.

On the way in, we saw a restaurant that served Mexican and American food. Since I hadn't eaten Mexican cuisine before, I suggested we give it a try.

"We have tons of food, Russell," Hanna said. "Why eat out again?"

"Because I've never had Mexican before. I'd like to try it out is all."

"Really? You've never had Mexican? Where've you been?"

"Pretty sheltered and conservative in my eating, I guess—mainly a meat and potatoes sort of guy." I finished with a chuckle.

She smiled. "Oh, for pity's sake, all right. You are such a little boy sometimes."

"Is that a compliment?" I asked.

She shot an exasperated look at me and said nothing. We set up our camp and walked through the campground to the restaurant, where we faced a thirty-minute wait. The hostess said we could sit at the bar and she'd find us when a table became available.

"Pretty full?" I asked.

"We're really busy throughout the summer up here, weekends especially. And this weekend ... well, you can see for yourself," she replied as she turned away.

Hanna and I sat on stools at the bar. A large bartender of an undetermined age with a huge handlebar mustache, a shaved head, in a white shirt and black suspenders, stood in front of us, both hands on the bar. "What can I get you?"

"What do you recommend?" I asked.

"We have great margaritas."

"That's tequila, right?"

He looked at me quizzically. "Ah, yeah, tequila."

"Okay, I'll have one."

"Make it two," Hanna added.

"Frozen or on the rocks?" he asked.

"On the rocks," Hanna replied.

"Me too," I said.

"Salt?"

"Please," Hanna replied.

"Me too," I said.

The bartender went to make our drinks.

Hanna turned to me with a sarcastic grin. "Never had a margarita before either, have you?"

"Ah, no, never have," I replied sheepishly.

We sat and observed the bustling activity in the large restaurant, which looked to have been built from the native pine trees in the area. Wait people ran everywhere, taking orders, serving food and drinks. Young bus boys and girls refilled water glasses and cleaned off and set up tables as fast as they could.

The place was full of happy people, eating, drinking, talking, and laughing. Cowboy hats were everywhere.

Our drinks came in huge thick glasses, like a wine glasses on steroids. We each took a sip. I was taken with the combination of the sour from lime and the sweetness, which I found out came from Cointreau, with a slight bite from the tequila. It was really good, going down all too fast. I ordered another.

"Pace yourself, Russell; these are a little more potent than the wine you're used to drinking."

The next one arrived, and I made myself slow down; it wasn't easy. The hostess arrived to take us to our table. We picked up our drinks and followed her through the crowded dining room, weaving between tables and dodging wait people. She sat us at a table for two in a dark corner—nice and cozy feeling and a little quieter. She handed us menus, then disappeared.

The menu boasted a wide range of steaks, chicken, and Mexican dishes. I hadn't a clue about burritos, fajitas, tacos, quesadillas, or the chili sauces—red, green, hot, mild—not a clue.

"Hanna, I need help here."

She laughed and directed me to some dishes that she felt would be okay for a novice. Hanna ordered chips and salsa to share, and fish tacos. Then she and the waitress looked at me. I stammered and frantically tried to make a decision. Hanna saved me by ordering for me—a house burrito smothered in mild-green chili sauce with rice and refried beans. The waitress shot me a look, turned on her heel and left.

"Thanks for saving me. I had no idea what to do."

"I'm pretty sure you'll like the burrito." She smiled at me, looking directly into my eyes, head cocked, twisting a lock of her hair, and those green eyes. *Does she know how sexy she is?* I looked away, pretending to look around the restaurant.

"Do I make you uneasy, Russell? I'm sorry if I do. You're just sort of nice to be with is all," she said with a serious look.

I didn't know how to respond, so all I could do was say weakly, "Thanks, I like being with you too, Hanna."

I liked her name. Hanna seemed to fit her; I had no idea why I even thought that.

"So, Hanna, what about you?" I asked. "You told me you studied music in college, a little about your parents, but that's all I know about you."

"Okay, I really like you so you should know this about me. I'm sorry, but I have to be honest. I'm really a wanted murderer for something I did in San Francisco. I'm on the run." She said it with a dead pan expression.

I looked at her with wide eyes—and probably a dumb expression—not knowing whether I should believe her or not.

She cracked up. "God, Russell, I'm kidding. Do you always take things so seriously?"

"Well, nobody ever really kidded me much before."

"Russell, you have to lighten up. I'm making it my objective to get you to have fun."

"I have fun!" I responded somewhat defensively.

"So what's the last totally outrageous fun thing you did?"

"Going into a Lakota sweat lodge!" I said with a little haughtiness. "Then, maybe, I don't know, maybe hiking and swimming back at Mount Rushmore? I lived a quiet life, Hanna. Very quiet. Thank you for helping me to experience some new things. I'm happy I stopped for you back there in Iowa."

"Well, we're going to have fun. I'm going to get you to enjoy life and have fun."

"Knock yourself out." I smiled, not too worried since I was heading back after Monday.

We sat without speaking for some time. Hanna broke the silence: "You asked about me. As I told you, I've never met my real father. My mom lived in a commune north of San Francisco back in the nineties and apparently met him there. Mom has never told me much more about him, other than that he had two children of his own—twins. They'd be about three years older than me. From what she told me, it was a pretty wild place, so when she found out she was pregnant, she moved back to my grandparents' home down by Santa Cruz to have me.

"She lived there with her parents until I was about three while she went to school to finish her degree in fine art. Then she took me to inner city San Francisco to an artist commune loft of sorts. I really don't remember much about it other than some people about Mom's age and a few kids I played with— nice people. Everyone took care of me and the other kids, like a big family."

She stopped talking and gazed unfocused eyes somewhere else, then said wistfully, "I often think that somewhere I might have a father and a brother and sister. I pressure Mom to tell me more, even just his name, but she always brushes me off, saying that it's not important, that I don't need to know. I guess it's something she wants to forget. But then there's Frank; he's been a great father to me."

The chips and salsa arrived. "Enough of that, let's eat!" Hanna said as she dipped a chip into the salsa. "Wow, pleasantly hot," she remarked. "Try some."

I did, and not knowing about salsa, took a big dip on a chip. It was hot! hot! hot! It burned my mouth so I could hardly breathe. I took a big drink of my margarita that sort of salved the burn. Tears trickled down my face and my nose ran.

"Holy shit!" I said, almost too loudly. "Why didn't you warn me?"

"I started to but you already had it in your mouth," she said, laughing. "It's pretty hot stuff. But good, if you take only a little at a time."

I had my first lesson in Mexican cuisine: be careful of the salsa.

The hot salsa crisis settled, she continued with her story, "Mom met Frank about the time I was six, and we moved out to his place in Berkeley. I went to a Montessori school, took music lessons, which I was really good at, especially singing, and ended up getting a full ride at the Department of Music at U.C. Berkeley, and, ah, where I graduated Magna Cum Laude, I might add," she said with a big grin. "What do you think of that?"

"Brilliant. That's wonderful. I'm traveling with a real scholar," I said with a big smile.

"Then, for the last five years, I haven't done much with it. Recorded some samples for recording companies, which never panned out. I write my own music and tried some producers, but no go. So I made some home recordings and put them on some social media sites, but nothing took off. I still sing around in some open mikes at coffee houses and some of the college bars and work mainly as a barista in a coffee shop near our house.

"Mom's art took off right before I started high school, and we moved to a house in Sausalito. I still live with Mom and Frank. It's a big house, so I have my own space; Mom has her studio and Frank his workshop. Never been on my own until this hitchhiking trip. So that's about it."

Food arrived and our focus changed to our plates, each ordering another margarita. The burrito was really tasty. I'd seriously been missing out on a whole genre of food. The green-chili sauce had a distinct, mildly hot spiciness, complemented by the meat, cheese, and bean filling in the burrito. The rice and refried beans were a new treat. All in all, it was delicious.

After eating for a few minutes, I said, "I hope you haven't given up on your music. I loved hearing you the first night we camped in Nebraska. Couldn't quite hear all the lyrics, but it sounded beautiful. I wish I played guitar as well as you do. Maybe you're trying the wrong producers and record studios."

"Maybe. I sort of lost interest after my rejections and then I … it's a really tough business. I'm seriously planning on trying to find real work somewhere when I get home, try to find something to earn a decent living for once, doing what, I don't really know. Maybe inspiration will hit me on this trip. Heaven knows I need something …" She ended on a note of despair.

"You'll find something, I'm sure. Just find something to make money and work hard at it. You'll see."

"Yeah, right, easier said than done." She ended the discussion by taking a bite of her food, followed by a drink of her margarita.

We continued eating in silence, concentrating on our food. When finished, Hanna looked up from wiping her hands on her napkin. "Hey, let's get a sopapilla for desert."

"What's a sopapilla?" I asked.

"It's like a puff pastry served warm with honey. They're really good, and the honey settles down any burn from the hot food."

The waitress came by to pick up our empty plates, and we made the order, which appeared moments later—a very large pastry with a small pitcher, like a coffee creamer, only filled with honey. We split the still-warm, hollow pastry and poured in the honey. I found it delicious, and it quieted the lingering heat from the hot salsa.

The night grew chilly due to the higher elevation, so I went to the camp store and bought a bundle of wood and a newspaper to start a fire in the fire ring at our campsite. I got out my camp axe and split off some kindling, crumpled the newspaper, stacked the kindling and lit the fire. The wood was dry and it caught quickly. We both put on long pants and fleece tops for warmth, then sat in my camp chairs and listened to the crackling fire and sounds from around the campground: quiet conversations interspersed with laughter; children's voices and chatter; somebody playing a guitar and singing old cowboy songs. We both got warm, and I asked Hanna if she wanted a glass of wine. She nodded, so I got an open bottle from the fridge along with two glasses.

Hanna spoke first: "So, Russell, tell me more about yourself. You haven't shared much."

"Well, I was born and raised in east-central Iowa, on a farm. I was brought up to be a hard worker, respectful, and disciplined. I learned that pretty much everything is either black or white. So, I worked hard at school, got into college, got my MBA, all by the time I was twenty-three. I went to work for a large investment bank in Chicago and made a lot of money. But then … then Dana left me for a lesbian woman—can you believe it, a lesbian woman, she left me for a lesbian!" I was a little drunk and my voice rose with my anger.

"Okay, Russell, I know this must piss you off, but try to keep it down. Okay?"

"Yeah, sorry. I haven't really talked about this and, well, yeah, it makes me mad, just makes me mad. You know, Hanna, I was working sometimes seventy hours a week to earn enough money so Dana and I could live well, retire early, and live somewhere nice, have leisure." I took a large gulp of wine and refilled my glass.

"Then I tell my mother, and she lambasts me, like it was all my fault. I feel like I've been disowned by my parents. They think I'm a failure. Nobody in this family ever gets divorced is what she told me. She scolded me like I was a child.

"I'm happy I'm out here and they don't know where I am. My sister, Karen, she's the only one in my family who even gives a damn about me right now." I ended almost shouting again and took another large swallow of wine.

"Shhhhh. Not so loud. Wow!" was all she said for a minute, then she asked, "How many siblings do you have?"

"Sorry." I was beginning to slur my words. I didn't care. "There's my older brother, Donny. He works with my dad on the farm and will probably take it over when Dad retires. He's married to Alice and has a daughter, Zoe. I don't have much communication with him. We never got along. He's a bullheaded bully and a drunk. Then there's Karen, older, too. She's married to a nice guy; they have two boys, really cool little guys. Her husband John's a lawyer. Karen's an office manager at the John Deere dealership. She and I've always been pretty close. Don't really know any aunts, uncles, or cousins; our families were never very close."

"So, if I may ask, why do you think Dana left?" Hannah asked. "Just the 'other woman' or something else, like, maybe, because you were never around much if you were working so many hours?"

"Makes no difference. She should've been happy. I was doing it all for us. She just didn't appreciate what I was doing."

"But, Russell, she might have wanted something else, like to have you around more and spend time with her so she could talk and share her thoughts with you. And listen to you, to just be with you."

"Nah, she's a lawyer; she was around people all day. She didn't need me to talk to."

"If that was your attitude, I can understand why she left you," Hannah retorted. "She married you, Russell, not the people she worked with. She needed someone to be intimate with, she needed you."

"Naaah, she's just a loser, running off with a lesbian. She wasn't a lesbian when I married her, I know! Hey, they should take all those lesbians along with the lazy blacks and Mexicans and send 'em out of the country. Then it would be a much better place."

Hannah didn't say anything for a few moments, then with anger in her voice she said, "Russell, I can't believe what I just heard. You've made me really sad with what you just said, very sad. I didn't think you were like that, such a bigot. I don't understand. I thought I liked you, but what you just said is so … so repulsive, I can't find words. Fuck it! I can't be with you. Tomorrow, I'm gone. I can't be around your bigoted bullshit! So, fuck you! Good fucking night!"

She got up, knocking over her chair, threw the rest of her wine in the fire, chucked the cup on the ground, and went to her tent.

I sat there for a while, thinking I'd be leaving anyway, and then I heard her crying. I sat a while longer, starting to sober, realizing what an ass I'd just been, spouting off stuff from when I was in grade school and high school, things I hadn't thought of for a long time, things I'd hidden away. I remembered how my colleagues at work had started to shun me after one of my rants one night while having drinks after work. I remember going on about how certain people like blacks are substandard and lazy. The only good ones were the athletes. They were naturally good and didn't have to work as hard as white guys. I was tired of supporting all the rest of those lazy good-for-nothing druggies. They never asked me to go out for drinks again after that.

I got up and went to her tent. "Hanna, I'm sorry for those things I said. I'm really sorry."

"Get the fuck away from me, you god-dammed bigot!"

"Hanna, I'm really sorry. I really am. Please don't be angry with me. I don't want to make you mad. I'm sorry. Please talk to me."

"You're just a big god-damned bigot. I have friends who are lesbian. I have African-American friends. I have Hispanic friends. You think they don't deserve to be here? Maybe you should fucking leave! Go away! Please just go away and leave me alone."

"Hanna, please, can we talk? I had too much to drink. That all just came out. This was the way I was brought up. It's what my parents, my church, my community all led me to believe. Please, I'm so sorry. I don't want you being mad at me. You're my only friend in the whole world right now. I have no one else."

"Tough shit!"

"Please. I am so sorry. It was stupid of me. I feel really bad about all that. I do. I really do."

"Oh, god dammit, Russell, you are just so fucking infuriating. Drinking is no excuse! It just lets you say what you really feel. Dammit, Russell!"

She came out of her tent and stood staring at me, her cheeks wet with tears. "I can't be around people who think like you. I just can't. So please just leave me alone!" She started to go back into her tent, but I grabbed her arm and turned her to face me.

"Hanna! I'm sorry for what I said. It was what I was taught as a kid. My mom taught me that stuff. I never knew any different. I know that's no excuse, but I can do better. Really. I can. Just, please, don't leave! Not like this!"

"Don't you touch me, asshole!" She jerked away from me and stepped back, looking at me with a ferocious, sad anger. "So, I'm supposed to help you fix your pathetic life? I thought you were a nice guy, then what you said, how you acted; it was so vile to say what you said. Just go to hell! I don't need a fucking ride! Leave me alone! Touch me again and I'll scream. I'm out of here." She turned away.

"Hanna, please, let's just talk. Then you can do what you want. But I want to talk about this."

"What the hell? You think you own me? I don't want to talk to you! I don't need this! Please. Just get away from me, you bigot asshole!"

I felt really horrible and choked out, "Hanna, please, please, can we just talk for a minute. I feel bad about what I said. I do."

She stopped and slowly turned. "Russell, you are such a son-of-a-bitch … but, for a minute, then go."

"Thanks, let's go and sit, please?" We walked back to the fire, and I added more wood. She sat down.

"One summer when I was maybe seven or eight my mother took me and two of my friends into Iowa City to the swimming pool. It was July and hot. Mom sat outside in the shade to keep an eye on us. My two friends and I were playing. They saw another kid they knew and left me to play with him. I then ran into two other boys and we started to play—splashing, jumping off the diving boards, chasing each other, just having fun.

"I saw my mother motioning for me, and I went over. She told me I shouldn't play with those dark boys. They were dirty. She didn't understand why they were even allowed into the public pool.

"I looked over to where they were waiting for me and realized that they had darker skin than me. I hadn't noticed. I disobeyed my mother and went back and played with them the rest of the time we were there.

"She didn't speak on the way home, even after dropping off the other boys. When we got home, she grabbed me and beat me, screaming at what a disobedient little brat I was, that I was dirty from playing with those dark-skinned boys. She made me take a bath, and she scrubbed me with a hard brush. My skin was raw afterwards.

"My mother beat my sister and me a lot. Dad never did, not like that. He was always pretty mellow. It was always my mother. As I remember, Dad was never around, always in the fields, working on machinery, in town doing business ... and whatever. My brother would do something stupid, and I'd get blamed for it. Donny would sit there and laugh—"

I stopped and took some deep breaths before continuing. "I learned not to trust her. I learned to stay away from her and Donny as much as I could. I'd hide away a lot, in the machine shed or the old barn ... I was never good enough ... never. That's no excuse, I know, but I— "

I choked and tears welled in my eyes. I sat staring into the fire, knowing I was pretty drunk and shouldn't be telling her all this. She'd think I was some sort of loser wimp. This was stuff I'd put away a long time ago. I hadn't even told my therapist about this. It was all about Dana back then. The doctor had asked me about my childhood, but I'd lied and avoided his questions.

She broke the silence. "God, Russell. I'm sorry. That was abuse, Russell. God, I'm so sorry. I'm ..." She fell silent for a moment. "I want you to know, I had and still have very good friends who are Hispanic, African-American, gay, lesbian, writers, musicians, actors, alternative-culture people. That's my scene. And for you to suddenly say those things. It really hurt me, Russell. It really hurt. You need to understand what you did, how that hurt. Do you?"

All sympathy had disappeared. I felt daggers penetrating me. "I do, Hanna, I do. And I'm sorry to have hurt you. That was the last thing I ever wanted to do. It just came out. It was stupid of me. I don't really think I feel that way. I met John and his family, the others at the sweat, and Raymond. They were so nice to me. I liked them. They're the only people of color I've ever been around except for the swimming pool incident. There were a few people at work, but I always avoided them."

We fell quiet again for a while until she said, "I guess I grew up sheltered as well, but in a different world. If anything, I was almost over-nurtured. I knew there was bigotry and hatred out there, but never experienced it firsthand. My mother and Frank were always so open to everyone, everything. I was always around all these amazing people of all races, colors, beliefs."

"We've sure been brought up different," I said. "Hearing you, I feel a little envious, like I was deprived, programmed, or something. I'd like to meet your parents sometime."

Things had quieted. I felt her anger had diminished, but I detected a wariness from her. She'd distanced herself from me. I realized it would be hard to regain her trust.

"Again, I'm sorry. I'll definitely think before I open my big yap from now on."

"I hope so." Hannah looked at me, her smile shimmering in the firelight. "You know, I'd like to hang around here for a few days and see Sheridan and more of the area. Would you be up for that?"

"Sure, have nothing better to do. My plans have evaporated … and, you know, I'm starting to not really care. Tomorrow morning, I'll go to see if we can keep our spot for the next two nights." Then I added, "I was thinking I might head back on Tuesday, but I'll see how it goes."

"If you want, I understand. I've kept you going longer than you wanted, and I appreciate it," she said with resignation. "It'll be nice to hang around the next few days."

The next morning, we went into the camp store. The woman at the desk said she was sorry, but our spot had been reserved for the weekend and the campground was full through Monday. She told us to check over at the restaurant/lodge, where we ate last night, and see if they might have anything.

Luckily, they'd had a last-minute cancellation for one of their cabins. The rate was a little high, but it was Memorial Day, the start of the season. Hanna looked at me and shook her head, but I smiled at her and booked it through Sunday night.

"I can't afford to pay my share of the cabin cost," she said as we walked out.

"I'll pay; I owe it to you after last night. And we deserve a nice place for a few nights," I replied.

She shrugged her agreement.

The cabin was rustic, but fully equipped with stove, refrigerator, dishes, and a spotless full bath. It had only one bed, and I told her I'd sleep on the couch. We both showered and headed off to explore Sheridan, taking a quieter, more scenic back road.

Chapter 11: Sheridan

As we drove, I apologized again about last night, adding that she saw the world so differently from me.

"Well, Russell, I've studied and been a practitioner of Buddhism since I was a little kid. One of the main practices I've learned and worked on for a long time is loving kindness and compassion for all sentient beings, and that means for *all* sentient beings, not just whoever or whatever you select to be compassionate for. It means every human being, every living creature, as well as our planet. No exceptions! Kind of like what I told you back after the sweat."

"I'm still having trouble understanding that," I said. "There are nasty, evil people out there and animals that would kill and eat you. How can you be compassionate towards a drug dealer or a murderer?"

"No exceptions means no exceptions, Russell," she replied. "By the way, have I told you I do like your name? I like to say it. Sorry about the 'Russ' early on. But, I digress.

"First off, you have no idea about the drug dealer or murderer, what led him or her to their life, their circumstance. We can't judge other people's actions. Didn't your Christ say something similar like 'do not judge, don't cast stones,' something like that? And critters that would like to eat you, that's their nature, and you need to respect that. It's just who they are.

"And I want to add that most anger and fear is the result of a lack of love. If you can love yourself, love all sentient beings, fear will fall away."

I pondered all this for a few miles, trying to understand what she'd just said. I think I liked the concept, but still wasn't sure I could accept all of this; it was contrary to everything I'd been taught and believed.

A few more miles on, I said, "You've given me some things to think about. I'm not sure I can accept it all, but I'll consider it for sure. I might need help. What is this 'Buddhist' thing?"

"Buddhism is a philosophy. His Holiness the Dalai Lama maintains this and I truly believe it. There are no gods to worship or anything like that. There is a lot of meditation practice involved, though. The writings and teachings can be endless."

We were approaching Sheridan and dropped the conversation. The town was busy with a lot of folks on the Main Street sidewalks, strolling and shopping. American flags flew from every lamppost and storefront. We found a place on a side street, parked, then joined the Main Street strollers.

First, we visited a locally owned and busy bookstore.

"I like independent bookstores," Hannah said, looking around the stuffed shelves. "I do all I can to support them, but living out of a backpack kind of limits how much I can read."

We browsed through the store. I wasn't looking for anything in particular, but Hanna picked up any number of books, reading cover blurbs and looking at the opening pages.

When we came to the religious section, divided into sections for various faiths, Hanna went directly to the Buddhist section. She pulled out several and handed them to me. "These might be helpful in explaining what I talked about on our way here. They'll give you a deeper understanding of compassion and Buddhist philosophy, if you're interested, of course."

I took them from her and leafed through them. I trusted her and felt they might help me better connect with her. She was diametrically opposite of Dana, not so rigid about everything, so much more open—and opposite of myself as well. She kept piquing my interest to know her better, know more about how she thought, how she moved through this world.

"Thanks, Hanna. I'll be happy to look at them, if they'll help me know you better."

She gave me a serious look. "Not to know me better, but to know yourself better."

I thought about that for a moment, and we continued on towards the cash register. A display of journals, pens, pencils, and markers sat on the counter.

"Have you ever journaled?" she asked.

"Journaled?" I looked at her, remembering what the doctor back in Chicago had advised me to do.

"Journaling is writing about your thoughts, feelings, experiences, or whatever strikes you. It's a way of self-growth, spiritual growth, healing, or just keeping track of where you've been or plans about where you're going, whatever might strike your fancy at the time. Some people sketch as well as write. Something else you might want to consider. I keep a journal, have for the last ten years."

I remembered I used to doodle in my notebooks a lot when I was in school but hadn't since I started working at the bank. It might be interesting. I could write about my adventure, which was ending next week. I wasn't sure at that moment that I wanted it to end.

"In truth, my psychiatrist recommended that I should do that, but I didn't pay much attention to his advice, sort of blew it off. Maybe it'd be a good idea. It seems I've a lot I could write about these days. Any recommendations?"

"Psychiatrist?"

"I'll explain that later; so, recommendations?"

"Hemingway always used a Moleskine." She pointed at a section of all sorts of blank books waiting to be filled.

I pulled out the smallest-sized one. An elastic cord held it closed, and a small ribbon marked your place. I looked at a larger version, and eventually selected it. I had nothing to write with, so I looked at pencils and found a nice automatic one with a retractable tip, then I added an eraser and a Moleskine ballpoint pen as well. We paid for our purchases and returned to the busy sunlit street.

We came across a saddlery shop. I walked on by, but Hanna stopped and shouted, "Hey, Russell, let's go in here, they have a museum. Should be fun."

Museums didn't really appeal to me, but I followed her in, and my mind changed at what I saw.

Dozens of saddles, bridals, lariats, hats, boots, western wear, racks of spurs, and any other cowboy accessory anyone could imagine made up the shop display.

An older, rangy-looking fellow with silver hair and a big mustache came over and asked, "Can I help you folks with anything?"

I said, "This is just amazing, all these saddles, and the ropes … or lariats?"

"Well," he said, "we supply equipment for working ranches as well as people who ride for pleasure. There's a lot of ranches and horses in our neighborhood. We also have an online catalog and get orders from all over: Montana, Utah, Idaho, Colorado, Nebraska … Europe, even.

"We have saddles ranging from actual working ranch saddles to pleasure as well as rigging for outfitters. They're all slightly different. Some of the more expensive ones have more tooling and glitter, of course. We have one show saddle over there worth over $10,000."

I gasped. "$10,000?"

"Sure, come on over and have a look." He led the way.

It wasn't a saddle; it was a work of art with extensive, intricate tooling, embellished with silver trim in various places.

"You should check out the museum," the man said. "It's quite a collection. The owner and owner's father have gathered it over the last sixty or so years. It's out back." He pointed us to the door, and we moved on, thanking the man.

The museum—a collection of western ranching paraphernalia from forever, so it seemed—proved to be even more intriguing. As well as saddles and tack, it also displayed artwork, Indian artifacts, guns, wagons, and coaches. We spent the better part of two hours in the place.

I wanted a saddle, but that was absurd. I didn't have a horse, hadn't ever been on a horse. Back in the main store, the array of boots tempted me, but I demurred and ended up getting a pair of Wrangler jeans. Hanna passed up buying anything, and we left to continue exploring. Lunchtime had passed, and we were both starved, having had no breakfast, so we found a brewpub and each ordered a burger. I got a beer and Hanna an iced tea. Well fed, we continued on, passing by a yoga studio.

"Just a minute." She stopped to look in the window. "They have a meditation and yoga class tomorrow morning at nine. Would you want to come? I haven't done any yoga in so long and my meditation has been spotty at best."

"Geez, Hanna, I don't know. I've never meditated ever, don't even know what it means. And yoga? What's yoga?"

"Oh, come on, really? Yoga is simply some serious stretching and can be a good workout. It's for all levels, so expectations won't be high. It'll be fun. Really. I bet you'd get a kick out of it."

"Ah, let me think on it, okay?" *Risk assessment!*

"Sure, let's keep on going."

We finished our tour on Main Street, and I suggested that we head back. With our cabin we had access to a sauna and a spa. Hanna liked the sauna idea, so we left for Story.

We saw a supermarket on the way out of town, and I pulled in. "Let's get some real food for tonight, maybe some salad stuff, steaks or chicken?"

"That sounds fun. We have a table and chairs, a stove and refrigerator. Let's get wood again and build a fire. Salad greens, a tomato, an onion, an avocado, olive oil for dressing, and let's get some chicken, some rolls. We have butter."

So we did a quick shopping tour and hit the road again.

"You can be fun, Russell. You were actually pretty spontaneous back there for someone, ah," she chuckled, "someone like you? No offense intended."

I laughed. "None taken, know what you mean."

Back in our cabin, we put the cold food into the fridge and set off to find the sauna. It looked nice, with showers, towels, and changing rooms outfitted with lockers. I changed into my swimsuit and went into the sauna; Hanna followed shortly after, wrapped in her towel.

"Tell me you're wearing your swimsuit," I said.

"No, we're in a sauna, silly boy." She undid her towel.

I couldn't look. I was becoming attracted to her fully clothed; naked, I would lose my mind.

"You don't have to look away, Russell. I was just teasing, I have my suit on." She chuckled again.

"Hanna, you're a beautiful and attractive woman, and … and, naked next to me— "

"It's really okay. You could just act normal. Just because I might be naked doesn't mean I want to have sex with you. But I'm flattered about what you just said about being beautiful and being attracted to me. I don't mean to lead you on, but, really, I just want to be friends … no more than friends. Truth is, I just got out of a nasty relationship a while back. That's the primary thing that spurred this trip. I guess, like you, I just wanted to get away."

"I'm sorry, Hanna. I can understand from a first-hand point of view. Want to talk about it?"

"Not now, maybe sometime." Then she said flirtatiously, "We could both take our suits off and both be equally naked."

"Naaah, I don't think that would be a good idea, but thanks for the invite." I knew how embarrassed I'd be if she saw what was happening inside my swimming suit at that moment.

We sweated out until both of us were bordering on dehydration, both having stupidly forgotten to bring water. Having enough, we left the sauna and went outside to cool down. The air was warm and humidity-free, smelling of pine and mountains. I found the cool, dry Wyoming air scented with pines, along with the nearby gurgling stream, satisfying to the mind, body, and spirit. We sat and enjoyed.

"This must be as close to Nirvana as one can get on this planet," Hanna said. "It's perfect. I love this place. Maybe you could buy a house for us here and move in together. That'd be great."

"What? Move in together?"

"No, not really, just dreaming … just dreaming. But a dream I might like someday." She turned to me with a look I didn't grasp.

Around five thirty, cooled down, we returned to the cabin. I went over to the headquarters and got two bundles of firewood, made some kindling, and got it all ready for a fire, then I prepared the chicken ready for frying while Hanna worked on a salad. Everything ready, I opened a bottle of white wine, and we sat and smiled at each other, toasted ourselves, and enjoyed our repast.

Finished and full, we cleaned up, and I started the fire. We sat on the couch, finishing our wine and enjoying the peace.

Hanna slid over next to me. "You know, Russell, what I said this afternoon … about buying a house here and moving in together? I was actually half serious." She put her hands on my face, turned me to her, and kissed me. She then settled back next to me and put her head on my shoulder.

I was a little unnerved by the kiss and didn't say anything for a minute, thinking about it, what it meant. "Geez, Hanna, that was … unexpected … but nice. Thanks. But you know I don't want to get involved right now, and neither do you."

"Yeah, sorry. You're right. But you can be a sweet guy. You need some work, but I think I can shape you up." She chuckled. "I like that you seem receptive to things I've given you a hard time about." She chuckled again. "I'm really not that sure about anything, myself, but it's been fun exploring together, and for a few more days until you head back home."

I sucked in my breath and didn't comment. I just laid my head over against hers, savoring her scent and the silkiness of her hair against my face. After Monday, I'd probably never see her again.

Though only nine thirty, we both felt tired and decided to head to our respective beds.

"So, are you up for yoga tomorrow?" Hanna asked. "I think you'd like it."

"I never did anything like that. It's not like a religion or something weird, is it?"

"No, not the practice of yoga and meditation. Yoga is stretching out your body in a systematic way, and meditation? Meditation is simply quieting the mind. The practices come from the Hindu religion, I guess, but, no, you won't be made into a Hindu by going to a yoga and meditation class."

"I don't know, Hanna, What do I wear? It's not a naked thing, is it?"

"God, get over the naked thing already," she answered, laughing. "Do you have gym shorts? Your swimsuit and a t-shirt will be fine."

"I'm not sure I want to do something like this. Let me sleep on it, then see how I feel in the morning. And thanks for today, and for being my friend. I'm really happy I met you."

"Me too. Good night." She went into the bedroom and closed the door. I crawled into my sleeping bag on the couch and lay awake a long time, thinking about that kiss.

Chapter 12: The Yoga Class and Bighorn Battlefield

We woke to another beautiful, sunny Wyoming day. While having coffee and a light breakfast, I asked, "So, will there be other guys there?"

"How would I know? Let's go and find out, okay? You can always back out after we get there. You could go for a cup of coffee or something."

Both needing to do laundry, we gathered our dirty clothes and piled them into the grocery bags from yesterday, then left for Sheridan, arriving in front of the yoga studio about ten minutes ahead of time. I grabbed my swimsuit and reluctantly followed Hanna inside. An incredible-looking thirty or maybe forty-something slender woman with long blonde hair sat at a desk in the foyer.

"Hi, welcome. I'm Summer. I'll be your teacher today. It's fifteen dollars for drop-ins. Are you local? Haven't seen you before."

Hanna introduced us. "We're passing through and saw your sign yesterday. This is Russell's first-ever yoga class, so be gentle." She finished with a chuckle.

I was about ready to leave, but Hanna, sensing it, grabbed my arm. "You are not bailing out now."

Summer told us where the changing rooms were and that she locked the front door during the class so everything would be safe.

Reluctant to explore another new 'Hanna' adventure, I felt as if I were about to have a panic attack, but I calmed myself by taking a deep breath and exhaling slowly. I managed to change my clothes and head back to the foyer. Hanna emerged from the women's change room in some tights and a tank top. *God, she's beautiful.*

The studio, a large room with abundant natural light, wood flooring, and walls barren of decoration, felt quiet and serene. Others already sat on the floor ready for the class—all women, ages somewhere from early twenties to maybe fifty or older. They all looked slender and in great shape. That, I liked, of course, but I also felt a little embarrassed being the only man. Hanna led me to a closet and handed me a rolled-up rubber mat, a blanket, and a long cotton belt.

"We'll need the mat and maybe the rest," she said.

Hanna moved right up next to a woman in the second row. I wanted to hide in the back but unrolled my mat next to hers, following what she did. She struck up a conversation with the woman next to her like they were old friends. I wanted to get up and run away.

Summer walked to the front of the room. "Namaste and good morning; so happy to see all the familiar faces. We have two visitors with us today, Hanna and Russell. Welcome them to our little studio."

The students all looked over at us and smiled. I knew they were really looking at me, all thinking, *"What's this man doing here. He should know better. This is for us women."* I was slowly dying inside.

Then, somehow, in unison, they all said, "Welcome, Hanna and Russell," as if they'd rehearsed it. I wanted to crawl under the mat I sat on and melt into the floor.

"Hanna tells me this will be your first yoga class, Russell? Don't worry, it's a small group of regulars today, so I'll be able to spend time with you and help you out. We like new people, especially men."

They all stared at me, smiling.

Please God, let somebody just shoot me … now!

Summer then announced there'd be forty-five minutes of yoga followed by a thirty-minute meditation.

Dammit! I wanted to ask Hanna about meditation. I whispered over to her, "What is meditation?"

She frowned, shook her head and whispered, "Shhhh!"

Summer demonstrated the first pose—simply raising your hands over your head and stretching upward. *Pretty easy; no problem.* Then Summer came over to me and helped me correct everything I was doing wrong, which was pretty much everything—pull in your belly button, tighten your core muscles, arms touching your ears. Tighten your buttocks. All of a sudden, simply stretching turned into something way more complicated. I never knew I was so stiff. The same thing happened with every pose we did: I watched Summer demonstrate; she made it look easy, but when I tried to do it, it was impossible. She helped me make corrections, but I still found it hard. Then we did a relaxation pose, lying flat on our backs, but as with every other pose, there was a right way and a wrong way. I found this to be the one I liked the best: simply relaxing.

Summer announced that the forty-five minutes was up, and everyone sat up and arranged blankets to sit on. I rose slowly, exhausted, sweating, and hurting everywhere. Muscles I didn't even know I had were hurting. Everyone else looked like they'd just come from the beauty salon.

Summer said that we could either sit on our blankets or grab a chair from the back if we wished. Everyone folded their blankets just so and assumed a cross-legged position, upper bodies ramrod straight. I tried the same and immediately got up and went for the chair. I couldn't sit like that; I was too stiff.

Summer sat in the front and directed us: "Today, I'd like us to meditate on our breath. Get your body anchored and focused. Close your eyes now." Then more softly, "Take three deep breaths. In … out … in … out … in … out. Now, just follow your breath … I'm breathing in; I'm breathing out. I'm breathing in; I'm breathing out. I'm breathing in; I'm breathing out. When thoughts come, observe them and let them go; feel your body relax; let your mind be quiet."

I did as she directed, but thoughts raced all around my head: *Am I doing it right? What am I doing here? I could be doing laundry. We could be driving somewhere to see something. What will we do this afternoon?*

I kept trying to focus on my breathing and worked on letting thoughts go. More and more, I managed to focus on my breathing. Then, something very strange happened. I felt as if everything drained away: all my anxiety, fear, worry, Dana, parents, failure, everything that always seemed to be occupying my thoughts … all slipping, slipping, slipping away. I felt light, like I might float away.

A soft, quiet voice came from someplace far away: "Okay, let's slowly, gently come back. When you're ready, slowly open your eyes, and take some deep breaths. Slowly get up when you're ready. And thank you so much for being here. See you all soon. Namaste."

Everyone said, "Namaste," then people talked and laughed.

"Russell, Russell, hey, you okay?" Hanna said. "Time to wake up."

I didn't want this blissful feeling to end—I'd never felt so relaxed—but I slowly opened my eyes, turned, and saw Hanna standing by me.

"Hey, you okay?"

"I … I think so. Wow! That was interesting. That was really nice," I mumbled with a tongue that felt numb.

Summer came over. "You okay, Russell?"

"Ah, yeah … thanks," I mumbled dumbly. "That meditation thing was something else."

"Your first time?" Summer asked.

"Yeah, it is. Amazing. I want to do it again. I like it."

"I've seen first-timers have a really deep meditation," Summer said. "Have you had a lot of stress in your life recently?"

I nodded. "You could say that. This was nice. I can't believe how much lighter I feel. Thanks, Summer. I appreciate it."

"No problem. Will you be joining us again?"

"Doubt it; we're planning on leaving tomorrow."

"Well, I really enjoyed having you both. Please come again if you're ever in the neighborhood."

I got up, and she gave me a big long hug. "Be safe out there on your journey."

Hanna asked one of the women about a laundromat, and, being Sunday morning, it was deserted. The washers were huge, so Hanna suggested we wash both of our clothes in the same machine. I thought there was something rather intimate about that, but we got everything going and sat down.

"So, what does 'Namaste' mean?" I asked.

She thought for a moment. "It's a Hindi greeting or salutation, roughly translated, it means, I honor the god in you, or the god in me salutes the god in you."

"Nice. Just wondering. Hey, I really need to call my sister and let her know I'm okay and where I am."

"I should call Mom, too. We haven't talked in a week, and she'll be concerned."

We turned on our phones and went to opposite ends of the waiting area for some privacy. I had seven calls from Karen. I punched in her number, and she picked after three rings.

"Dammit! Russell, where are you? Have you talked to Mother? She's driving me crazy! She calls about every hour to see if I've heard from you. She's blaming me for not stopping you from doing this 'hare-brained thing' as she calls it. Please call her and take the heat off of me! She even blames me for encouraging you. I'm so tired of her I want to scream!"

"Okay, okay ... I'm sorry, really sorry. I'll call her and try to get her off your back."

I told her where I was but gave no other details or my plans about heading home. Right then I wasn't sure I really wanted to.

"I'll call Mom right now. I love you, Sis," I said.

"Ah, yeah— Russell, please be careful. We're worried."

"I will, and don't worry. Talk to you soon."

I hung up and, with hesitation, punched my parents' number. Mom picked up in a few rings. "Hello?"

"Hi, Mom, it's me, Russell; how are you?"

"Russell, where on God's green Earth are you? What do you think you're doing, running off like this? You just make me so—"

I cut her off: "Mom, I'm in Sheridan, Wyoming. I just talked to Karen. Please leave her alone. She had nothing to do with this. It's not her fault. Please, I'm not a child and can make my own decisions about where, when, and why I want to do something!"

Upset, I disconnected the call. Her controlling attitude always made me nuts. Anger, fear, and heaviness replaced all the peace and lightness I'd felt a short time ago. My phone chirped, and I stupidly answered. It was Dad.

"Russell, please, you shouldn't hang up on your mother like that. She's really upset. She's just very worried about you and wants you to come home. She's afraid of you being so far away. She feels you're wasting time traveling around."

"Dad, it's just … it's just that she's the reason I feel so messed up … all her discipline and pressure, I'm tired of it. I'm out here trying to live my own life finally. Please tell her that. I'm sorry, Dad. I'm really doing fine. I do miss you all, but this is something I have to do. I hope all is well there. I'll talk to you soon. Tell Mom to please not worry. I'm seeing a lot of the west and having a great time. I'll be fine."

"I'll tell her. Don't know if it'll help. She just worries about you is all. Be careful out there, and please call more often and let us know you're okay."

"I will. Nice to talk with you."

We ended the call, and I turned off my cell. I was happy to talk to my dad, but I wasn't sure he understood what I was trying to say. I felt bad for him. He shouldn't have to justify Mom. I sat for maybe five minutes and tried to get focused. But, of course, I felt the usual pang of guilt. What if she died and I never saw her again? But I didn't want her rigidness anymore now that I'd had a taste of freedom, now that I'd had this meditation experience that made me realize how loaded with hurt and stress I was. I'd discovered so many things about the world already in this last week. Going back to Iowa would be for what purpose? This trip was scary, but I wanted more, wanted to go all the way to where or what I had no idea. I wanted to keep discovering, go for the ride. But the guilt wouldn't go away. I was sitting there looking at my feet when Hanna finally came over and joined me.

"Hey, what's going on?"

I told her about the conversation. When I'd finished, neither of us said anything for a time.

She broke the silence. "Russell, one thing I learned is, when you start waking up, you can't go back to sleep. Another thing, guilt comes from fear and attachment. What we fear losing, we've already lost. Make sense?"

"Yeah, maybe, sort of, but not really. I was feeling so happy. Now I feel like shit. And I'm scared."

"Scared of what? Of what you've started to uncover in yourself?"

"Maybe. Right now, I wish I could just go back to being my old self before I started all this."

"Russell, do you really want that? I'm seeing somebody changing, like a butterfly breaking out of its cocoon. Growth is hard. Very hard. I've hit many bumps in the road like you're now experiencing. Believe me, I have. But the good news is, it gets better."

She reached down, took my hand and held it in both of hers. "You're a special guy, Russell. I'm sorry you're going back on Tuesday."

"I've just made a decision not to, at least not right now. I've no idea what I'd do back there right now."

"That's wonderful, Russell; good for you. Can I keep going with you, then?" she asked with a flirtatious giggle.

"Of course you can. I hope you will."

She leaned over, giving me a peck on the cheek. "Hey, our wash is finished. Let's get our stuff into the dryer so we can get out and do something."

While the clothes dried, we walked over to a nearby coffee shop and asked the barista what there was to see. She mentioned the Little Bighorn Battlefield, about an hour's drive north, said she thought we might find it interesting, but without going into any detail. We thanked her and headed back. Hanna checked it out on her phone. I kept mine off so I didn't see how many calls I had back from my mother. While we folded our clothes, we talked about it and made the decision to head north into Montana to see the place where Custer was defeated and his troops annihilated on June 25 and 26, 1876, on the eastern side of the Little Bighorn River.

* * *

We crossed the state line into Montana and a short time later came to the battlefield site. We exited the Interstate and drove onto the road leading up a hill to the entrance gate, where we paid our fee and got a map, then we carried on up to the visitors' center and took a look at the museum, which contained artifacts along with exhibits showing a full-size Custer and soldiers in the uniform dress of the time. Paintings, old letters, and maps showed how the battle commenced.

After leaving the building, we walked towards a monument farther up the hill. On our way up, we passed a fenced-in area of scattered white headstones that marked the spots where soldiers had died. At the monument, we looked to the west, where the view spread out for what seemed like hundreds of miles over rolling grasslands, still green from winter and spring moisture, and to far distant mountains. Down below, along the Little Bighorn River, the combined tribes of Lakota, Northern Cheyenne, and Arapaho had gathered to camp.

An eerie sensation come over me, as if I could feel the ghosts of all those who died here. Then sadness washed over me. I could almost feel the fear, the anguish, and the hopelessness of these soldiers, knowing they couldn't escape their fate. So many poor, uneducated refugees from the Civil War with nowhere else to earn their keep other than the army. Most were just young farm boys, derelicts of the times. Then I wondered how the Native Americans felt as they were hunted down and were systematically driven from their historic lands.

I noticed Hanna wiping her eyes and reached out and took her hand. She leaned against me and rested her head on my shoulder. We stood like that for a long time, each of us lost in our own thoughts, until we eventually headed back down towards the center. Right next to the center sat another graveyard of hundreds of gravestones, all in perfect order, like the pictures I'd seen of Arlington National Cemetery.

Continuing on, we came to a circular stone monument that told of the battle called the Battle of the Greasy Grass by the Native Americans. Several steps led up to the monuments to the fallen Native Americans. I thought about how they must have felt, peacefully camped, knowing the United States Government wanted their land and to destroy their way of life, if not their very existence. I wondered if John or Donna or Raymond had ancestors that fought here—or any of the others in the sweat lodge.

I felt happy we'd come, but almost wished we hadn't. The place unnerved me, and, coupled with talking to my parents earlier, I needed to leave. We drove back to Sheridan in silence, both of us digesting what we'd just seen.

"Hanna, I need some food," I said after a while. "How about you? Let's stop at the brewpub and get dinner. I'm drained and don't want to fuss with dinner."

"Exactly what I was thinking, but I'm paying tonight."

At the pub we found a booth, sat down, and ordered a beer and food.

"Hanna, there's something you need to know about me, something I need to tell you."

She looked at me with some concern. "What ... is it something bad?"

"I told you I made a lot of money, well, it's really a lot of money. Truth is, I'm sort of wealthy. I can easily afford to buy you dinner, and it would be an honor to do it, if nothing else but to repay you for all your kindness, all that you've taught me, for being my friend, for forgiving me, for just simply hanging out with me." A lump formed in my throat. *Damn, my emotions are out of control.*

She looked at me for a long moment. "You seem so normal, driving an old Westfalia Van—camping. Then, when you just up and bought that truck for Raymond, I thought you were ... I don't know what I thought, but it still doesn't change the fact that I want to buy dinner tonight. Okay?" She smiled at me. "And thank you for what you said about being my friend. You're becoming a very close and special friend, Russell; you truly are."

I smiled. "Thanks; that means a lot. Even with my weird history?"

"Yeah, even with that. The Universe never gives us more than we can handle, and it sometimes gives hard lessons. Apparently, you're having to work through some dandies right now. I had to after ... after, oh, never mind, not now with—" She let it hang, looking somewhere beyond me with unfocused eyes.

"Thanks. I think I heard someone say somewhere, sometime, 'What doesn't kill you will make you stronger,' or something like that."

Our food came, and we both wolfed it down all too quickly. Hanna paid and, satiated by our burgers, fries, salads, and beers, we left for Story, stopping on the way out of town to replenish the wine supply.

At our cabin, we unloaded, and I walked over to the lodge and got more firewood for the night. A fire going, I opened a bottle of wine.

"Hey, get that guitar out, and let's play some tunes," Hanna said.

"Aww, I'm not in your league at all," I replied. "Don't want to look stupid."

"Come on, I won't do anything special, just basic chords with some transition chords. I'll keep it simple, and you can follow along. Come on. Please."

"Oh … all right," I whined, "but don't make fun of me." I got out my Martin D-18 while she got out her old beat-up Gibson small body.

We tuned our guitars, then I strummed through some chords to warm up and try to re-familiarize my fingers with what they were supposed to do. "I'm really rusty, haven't played this thing for a while."

"You'll do fine. Just have fun. This one's in G with an A minor thrown in. Listen and watch, you'll pick it up." She laid out the chord progression and rhythm for me, then moved into an intro and began to sing in her sweet voice.

If I couldn't ever love this woman for anything else, I could love her simply for her voice. I started in, following her chording and rhythm clumsily at first, but I got better as the song went on. With her finger-picking and me strumming, I thought it started to sound pretty good. The chord progression was easy enough. I watched her left hand working the frets. Her finger-picking style pulled out a basic melody interspersed with arpeggios, all tastefully done.

She finished, looked at me and smiled. "See, you did great. I want a glass of wine; how about you?"

"Me too. I'll get some."

We played until my un-calloused fingers became sore. It was a fun evening, playing music with her by a crackling fire, sipping wine, someplace in Wyoming, far away from all my cares. I realized how comfortable I felt with her.

We got ready for bed. I was about to crawl into my sleeping bag on the couch when Hanna came over and hugged me and said softly into my ear, "That was really nice. You play much better than you think." She looked up into my eyes and gave me a sweet, cool kiss. "G'night, Russell, see ya in the morning."

"Thanks. Yeah, it was fun. Good night to you as well."

I lay in my sleeping bag on the couch, thinking about that kiss and the warm flood that filled my chest, a feeling that was not desire as much as how I felt from being with her. I thought about tonight and the day, about what Hanna had said about loving kindness and compassion to every sentient being, no exceptions. I thought about my parents and how the conversation with my mother hadn't gone well. I thought about what Hanna said about how we can't judge because we can't really know where anyone is coming from or what they might be thinking. Maybe what I thought was her controlling attitude was simply that she was worried about me and didn't know how to be any different.

I wondered about their childhood, how they were treated. My father's parents weren't around much, were really old, and they died before I was old enough to really get to know them. I knew Dad was raised on the farm; he was the youngest of three siblings, and both his brothers had died at a young age. I had absolutely no idea about Mom's family or her history. I needed to call and apologize to my mother and at least try to help her understand. I felt better after my introspection and fell into a sound sleep.

Chapter 13: Memorial Day, Ten Sleep and Beyond

After a light breakfast, we headed south and then over the Big Horn Mountains and through the little town of Ten Sleep, simply because we liked the name, which came from the fact that the town's location was "ten sleeps" or ten days travel southeast to Fort Laramie, west, or northwest, to Yellowstone National Park, or northeast to Stillwater River in Montana and the Indian Agency there.

On the drive over the Bighorns, we saw the beautiful Alpine Lake and deer grazing in the tall grasses along the winding but gentle road that climbed high enough that all the trees disappeared but for a few in the deep gullies. We checked the elevation: 8,200 feet, the highest I'd ever been. Then we descended into the canyon of Ten Sleep, a small village with two saloons, a mercantile store, a convenience store and a motel. We didn't stop, but continued on our way to Yellowstone.

Right after Ten Sleep, I felt the Westy wobble and pull to the left. I drove off the road and discovered what I'd feared; the left front was going flat. As I got out the jack, a pickup pulled in behind me and two men in work clothes got out and started towards me. When I saw they were Mexicans, I began to panic.

"Hey, man. Flat tire?" one guy said. "Want some help?"

"It's okay; I think I can get it."

"Naw, let me and Manuel help. Give me the jack and go get the spare."

I didn't argue and did as he said. When I brought the tire to the two guys, they already had the car up and were removing the wheel. Hanna talked to them like old friends. I just acted dumb, not knowing what to say to Mexicans.

"Hey, man, here, take this." The one called Manuel gave me the flat and then took the spare from me. I put it in the van, and when I returned they were already lowering the jack.

"Make sure you get that fixed," the first man said. "There's a tire place in Worland. Don't want to be out here with no spare, man. Come on, Manuel, let's get back up to the ranch. Boss-man'll be wondering where we are."

I didn't know what to say. "Thanks ... can I give you anything?"

"Awe, no, just happy we could help out. Where're ya headed?"

"Yellowstone."

"Pretty up there, I hear," Manuel said. "Travel safe. Oh, when you go through Lovell, stop at Angelina's, right on the main street, for some great Mexican food. It's my sister's place." A moment later they were in their truck and gone.

Back on our way, I said, "That was really nice of those guys."

"Yeah. Two really nice guys. They work for a rancher up towards Lovell. They said they were fixing some fence down on another parcel the rancher owns. Both are second-generation immigrants, working with green cards, always worried about having to go back south."

"I didn't know what to say to them, how to talk to them. I felt stupid."

"Talk to Mexicans the same way you talk to me. They're just like us, only with darker skins and beautiful accents."

"It was really nice of them. Really nice. People out here seem nice, helpful, considerate, more so than Chicago, that's for sure."

"There's a lot of empty space out here. I think folks are more inclined to help out people they see in trouble. They're more willing to take the time."

I gave her a confused smile and we continued on to the little town of Worland, where we got the tire fixed and changed back, then on north to Greybull. While driving through that town, we spotted the Museum of Flight and Aerial Firefighting. Neither of us were interested to go in, but we drove by slowly and saw several old planes parked off the town's airport.

Hanna had called to make camping reservations at Yellowstone, but they were full until tomorrow night. She then checked Lovell, our next town, and got a reservation there for the night. We arrived at Lovell shortly after noon, found our campground, and asked the camp manager if there was anything to go see. He recommended we drive up to see the Medicine Wheel, about thirty-five miles east.

We made some sandwiches and followed his directions out of town on a nice road, straight and easy, crossed Big Horn Lake, and, a few miles later, we began to climb—and I mean climb up the windiest, steepest, narrowest road with major drop-offs that I could imagine only in my nightmares. The Westy ground along in low gear. I was petrified, hanging onto the steering wheel in a white-knuckled death grip.

After what seemed forever, thankfully, the road started to level, straighten, and widen out. We arrived at the Medicine Wheel turnoff and drove a few miles up a gravel road to a parking area. After about one and a half miles of walking up a graveled path, we came to the designated national monument.

Large wooden posts connected by three strands of rope decorated with bandanas, scarves, feathers, bundles of sage, jewelry, and many other things lined the outside of a big circle. A sign directed us to walk to the left, in a clockwise direction, on the path that followed the fence. Seven other people, all Native Americans, walked slowly and reverently. Realizing that this was a sacred place, we followed suit, silently and respectfully. At the far end, we walked on a path out towards the edge of a cliff, and the distant view took my breath away.

"My god, this is so amazing," Hanna said. "I can hardly breathe. I almost want to cry with the utter magnificence of where we are."

It took me a moment to clear the lump from my throat to speak. "Yeah, me too," was all I could say. Again, like at the sweat, something deep and primal welled up inside me. This was so special. I felt strange, like electricity or energy of some sort. I couldn't understand was running through my body.

Yellowstone National Park sat out to the west, and beyond that was seemingly forever. Hanna turned and started back. I could have stayed there forever, but turned and followed, and we continued on our journey around the wheel.

We stopped at the information kiosk and read that the wheel was probably built anywhere from around 500 to 1,500 years ago. It's close to eighty feet in diameter and has twenty-eight spokes radiating from the center. Studies have shown that they have astrological alignments with various stars and the summer solstice sunrise. We discovered we were at 9,600 feet in elevation.

"Are you ready to head back down?" I asked.

Hanna paused for a moment, wiped a tear, took my hand, and said, "Not really, but let's go."

We had one last look and headed back down to the van. "Are you okay?" I asked.

After a moment, Hanna replied, "No, not really." She paused to wipe another tear. "But let's go before I change my mind and stay."

We turned around and left, heading back down the road—the road I dreaded. I shifted the Westy into second as we started down, thinking that maybe first gear might have been a better choice, but the Westy held firm, and we wound our way down. It seemed less scary than the trip up.

Silence filled the van. I looked over at Hanna. She was looking out the side window. I couldn't help but hear her sniffles. If I didn't have to focus so intently on driving, I probably would have been sniffling too.

Back at the campground a little after four, we decided to walk around the campground to wear off our afternoon. Hanna reached for my hand as we strolled, both surprising and pleasing me.

We passed by some big RVs and fifth-wheel travel trailers; Hanna pointed to a large, sleek van camper. "Russell, now that I know you have money, maybe we should get one like that." She giggled. "Then we could travel in the style a lady like me deserves." She turned and looked at me with big, pleading eyes.

"Ah, I don't think so. Can you imagine trying to herd one of those things up the road we were just on?"

"Aw, please? If you truly love me, you'll obey my desires."

Was she just teasing me? I couldn't tell, but figured she was trying to bait me, so I decided to play along with her game. "My dear woman," I looked at her with the softest, saddest eyes I could muster, "although my love for you knows no bounds, the answer is still no."

"Aw, you say you love me, but you don't really. You're just after my body. I know your type." She pouted. Then she looked up at me, laughed and squeezed my hand, asking seriously, "How do you think of me, Russell?"

I hesitated at the question and then said, "Well, I'd be lying if I said I wasn't attracted to you. We've known each other like a week? I'm happy we met. And, I guess, I hope we can continue for a while as friends."

A little farther on, she stopped, turned to me and said, "I'm really sorry I was teasing you before about the motorhome. But my last question was serious. I needed to know where I might be headed. I'm happy we can be friends. I'd like to hang out for a while."

"Thanks. It's just … it's just you're easy to talk to, easy to be with. And very interesting, I might add." She moved in so close, it was almost hard to not lose my balance. "In the little while I've known you," I continued, "you've opened my eyes to a lot."

For the rest of the way back to our camp we walked in silence. There, she turned to me, placed her hand around the back of my neck and pulled me down to a quick kiss on the cheek, followed by a long hug. "Let's get out the chairs and sit for a while before dinner. I'd like some wine, please, kind sir."

"Anything for m'lady … except a motor home."

She giggled and sat into my offered chair. I opened some wine, poured two glasses, and sat down beside her.

"Would you consider going down to find that place that Manuel told us about?" she asked. "His sister's place, Angelina's, for some Mexican? I bet it's authentic and would be really good."

"Sure, I'd be game." Finished with our drinks, I got directions to the restaurant, which was within easy walking distance.

The place was what one might call a "hole in the wall", barely noticeable and nondescript, with a small hand-lettered sign in the window.

"Are you sure about this?" I asked.

"Of course, let's go in."

Inside was bright with good smells of spicy food. A female voice with a Mexican accent said, "Seat yourselves anywhere you want."

Posters and art from Mexico decorated the soft-white painted walls. Several families and couples were already eating.

A woman of nondescript age with a long, thick braid of black hair hanging across her left breast, and wearing tight jeans and a white ruffled top, brought menus and water to our table. "Hello and welcome. I'm Angelina, would you like something more to drink than water? We have iced tea and our margaritas are really good, made with all fresh ingredients. Plus we have a good selection of beers."

We each chose a margarita and perused the menu. Angelina came with our margaritas and we ordered our food. A few minutes later, another couple with two children came in.

"Hey, man, you came to my sister's place. Good choice."

It was Manuel—and his family? Angelina greeted them with hugs.

Hanna got up. "Manuel. Hi. Yeah, we took your advice. Great to see you again."

"Meet my family: this is my beautiful wife and mother of my two beautiful babies, Rosa and Eduardo; this is Alejandra."

Hanna greeted them graciously and invited them to join us.

"We would love to."

I cringed, but wanted to be gracious, so I got up and helped gather more chairs. Manuel had cleaned up from his work clothes and wore a broad smile, his black eyes twinkling.

Alejandra, a truly beautiful woman with soft, dark eyes, had her long, black hair in a ponytail, and she wore skinny jeans and a white t-shirt with glitter around the neck and shoulders that seemed to accentuate her warm smile. The two little ones carried their parents' looks, Mom and Dad seemingly blended into each one.

Manuel explained to Alejandra how he and Juan had helped us out with the tire. I got up and told Angelina to hold our food so we could all eat together. They each ordered margaritas and milk for the little ones. My nervousness quickly evaporated, and I joined the animated conversation. Hanna related how we'd met and where we'd been, and Manuel and Alejandra told their story. They ordered their food, and Angelina served us all together. I was surprised at how much I enjoyed their company. I found them so nice and full of life. I felt his hard, calloused hands when I shook it in greeting—callouses of a laborer, a ranch hand who worked hard to support his family. I knew men like that back in Iowa, but most were sullen with the life they'd been dealt.

Alejandra worked as a receptionist in a law office. Being with them made me feel warm and happy, like we could maybe be friends, like I was missing something, like maybe I needed to work on a ranch or something to see what it was like, to live in a community like this where people were independent, yet would stop and help a stranger in need, a place where I could fit in.

Hanna and I were the only two Caucasians in the restaurant, and Manuel introduced us to several of their friends during dinner. As soon as we finished, they had to leave, needing to be up early the next day for Manuel to begin his ten-hour day and for Alejandra to get the kids to her mother, who babysat them while they both worked. The night had gone all too quickly.

111

I insisted that I buy their dinner to repay Manuel for his kindness. After a little argument, I won out. After our goodbyes, Hanna and I started down the street.

An older man dressed in boots, jeans, denim shirt, and a black cowboy hat came up to us and said, "You people shouldn't go into that place. Gotta watch them wetbacks—steal ya' blind or stick a knife in ya if ya ain't careful—can't be trusted, that bunch. Word of advice, stay outa that place and away from their kind. Gubment oughta ship 'em all back to Mexico where they belong. Buncha dirty drug dealers and crooks, stealin' all our jobs." He turned and walked away.

My heart fell. I almost told him to fuck off, that I didn't appreciate his advice, but I held my tongue. I didn't want that asshole to ruin this night. Then it occurred to me that he spoke as my mother had some twenty years ago, and that I was that man less than a week ago, a man with the same prejudices and bigotry. Hanna and I looked at each other, shook our heads, and walked on in silence.

My brain tried to compute all this, and what could best be described as a sort of confused dizziness came over me. I later found out that lessons come unexpectedly when we're ready, when we need them, and to pay attention.

That night I had strange dreams about sitting beside a path on the side of a mountain. Seven men with bald heads, wearing long saffron robes, came by. The one in the middle turned and talked to me, but I couldn't understand or remember what he said.

Chapter 14: Yellowstone

On the way to Cody, Wyoming, and to the east entrance to Yellowstone National Park, we listened to a nineties alt-country band CD with acoustic guitar, bass, fiddle, and pedal steel drums that did the kind of sad songs to which you might drown your sorrows in whiskey. One particular song about being on the road, lost with no direction or destination, seemed to precisely describe where I was with my life. We drove and listened. After listening for a bit, Hanna sang harmonies to the chorus.

I thought about what I'd seen and experienced out here so far, the vast far-reaching landscape, the towns we'd visited, Manuel and his family, the locals I'd talked to, and I got a sense of a different mentality out here, a mentality of "we can do it by ourselves," a sort of independence different from the east, of strong communities where people did what they did because they liked doing it, and they contributed to something bigger than just their own lives. I saw a lack of big box stores and restaurant chains and more little mom and pop stores and eateries, hardly any McDonalds. Every house had a satellite antenna pointing to the heavens for their television, and most likely any internet service.

It hit me that the remoteness of these little towns, the isolation of the farmers and ranchers, long distances between towns, and the sometimes staggering distances to any major city, meant that people out here had to count on themselves to survive, and they created communities around that ideal.

Then I mused on the early settlers and how it was for them. They had to be completely self-sufficient. They had no grocery stores or "amazon.coms" around back then and, more than likely, the majority of residents in remote places like Ten Sleep, Worland, Lovell, and so many others were descendants of these pioneers.

* * *

Traffic increased when we came into Cody, the town being full of tourists with large lumbering motorhomes and travel trailers. T-shirt and souvenir shops sat on every street corner. Weaving slowly through the traffic along with the rest, we eventually made it to the west end of town, where traffic became less congested.

Hanna spotted a large sporting-goods store, and we decided to pull in to take a break and look around to see if either of us needed anything. A young rugged-looking guy in shorts, flip-flops and an un-ironed faded print shirt greeted us, asking if he could help us. I explained that we were going to be camping at Bridge Bay in the park and would he recommend anything we should have. He asked what we were camping in, and I told him about the Westy and that Hanna was in a tent.

"Does it have an LP tank and a heater?" he asked.

"No, just the camp stove with a small butane tank."

"You'll be at 7,800 feet elevation up there. It can still get down to almost freezing this time of year, especially at that elevation. Do you have warm sleeping bags?"

I looked at Hanna with questioning eyes. "I haven't a clue. We're traveling from the mid-west. This is our first time out here. Can you look at what we have and give your opinion?"

"Sure, be happy to."

I got our bags and saw skepticism creep into his face. "Ah, maybe okay. Do you have any blankets?"

"No."

"I can honestly say that you probably won't be comfortable in these bags up here. Where're you going after here?"

"We were thinking Glacier."

"Get some warmer bags. Don't want to pressure you, but Glacier will be even colder. I was backpacking up there last July and know first-hand that it can freeze at night up there."

I glanced at Hanna and said, "Show us what you'd recommend." He led us to the sleeping bag section.

"Are you going backpacking?"

"No, just day hikes," Hanna replied.

"I have these on sale. They're really good bags and can zip together if you want. With both of you generating body heat, you'll be toasty all night long. These'll do you good, even below freezing."

Hanna replied quickly, "I like the concept. I get chilled easily and like to be warm when I sleep. Let's get them."

"Only if I can buy," I whispered to her.

"I'll let you get these. My funds can't afford even one. Thanks, I owe you."

"You owe me nothing." We walked to the cash register. "Anything else we might need?" I asked.

"There're no showers at the campsite you're going to, so I might recommend a solar shower: a large black bag you fill with water in the morning, then leave it in the sun and you'll have a nice warm shower when you get back to your camp in the evening. I'd add a small, light tarp for privacy," he said, looking at Hanna. "How's your butane supply? And food? You can get stuff in the park, but it's pricey."

"We need to find a grocery store, but maybe four butane tanks."

"There's a grocery store right next door." He got the butane cylinders and rang up our bill. We put our purchases in the van, then walked to the grocery store, restocked our food supply, and headed out.

"So, you're willing to sleep in the same sleeping bag as me?" I asked.

"Only if I might be freezing to death," she replied, laughing.

At the park entrance, all the lanes had several cars and campers ahead of us. I pulled into the shortest queue and waited quietly for our turn.

Ten minutes later we got to the gate, paid our fee, and received directions to the Bridge Bay Campsite. We were following a slow line of traffic when, suddenly, everyone stopped, and people got out of their vehicles. We joined them to see what was going on: six deer grazed alongside the road and everyone gawked and took pictures. We both chuckled to ourselves, remembering the deer we'd seen in the Bighorns.

"Probably a first for these folks," I said.

"Hmm, suppose so," Hanna said. We returned to the van and waited. She put her hand on my arm and looked at me. "You okay?"

"Yeah, just been thinking I need to call my parents, and I still haven't called Karen. Really need to talk to her—see what's going on at home."

"Maybe call her when we get set up? See what's up. Then call your folks," she suggested.

Over an hour later, we made the thirty miles to the campsite. We must have stopped a dozen times to look at everything from buffalo to chipmunks. The slow progress frustrated me, but Hanna kept telling me to take deep breaths and be in the moment. I really didn't understand what "be in the moment" meant and made a mental note to ask.

Tall pine forests with intermittent areas of tall grasses and sage cover Yellowstone. In one such open area, we spotted maybe a dozen buffalo grazing. Other than that, the trip felt like going through a tree tunnel, which made me feel claustrophobic after spending so much of the last few days in open, treeless, rolling hills and plains.

We paid for four nights, found our site that had a breathtaking view of Yellowstone Lake, and got situated.

Since it was still early enough in the afternoon, we walked to where we'd paid our fee and asked the ranger if there was anything we could do or see today. He suggested we just sit and relax and, later, take a walk down by the lake, that there's always wildlife feeding that time of day. He also repeated the warning we'd been given on entering the park, "Do not ever approach wildlife. These are wild animals, and they can and will attack humans." He went on to tell us of all the incidents, injuries, even deaths that had occurred in the park, simply by tourists being stupid. When we assured him that we were not stupid, he chuckled and told us to enjoy the rest of our day.

Back at camp, I dug around and found the journal I'd bought last week in Sheridan, grabbed a chair and sat down, wanting to start this journaling thing and to chronicle all that I'd seen and done since I left Iowa. I tried writing down my thoughts and searching for my feelings, but I found it hard to find my feelings. However, something occurred to me as I wrote, thinking where my life now was—I was thirty years old, a workaholic, a recovering bigot, and alone. I realized that my life overall was unrewarding, empty, and now in limbo. Here I was, divorced, not working, and wandering about in a tiny campervan with a strange woman I didn't know. Here I was, out on my own, far away in a national park with wild animals and not a clue about what I was doing. But when I stopped to think about it, I'd never felt more alive than I did right then.

Hanna interrupted my thoughts: "Hey, I'd like to walk over to the camp store and see what's going on; it's about a mile. Wanna come?"

I considered it for a moment. "Sure, it'd be good to move." I stood and put my stuff away.

"What were you writing, if I might ask?" she said. "Don't tell me if you don't want to."

"I started writing in my journal. It started me thinking about more than just this trip, about a lot of things." I told her what I'd been thinking.

She acknowledged me with a nod, but didn't say anything until we'd almost arrived at the store. "I'm a great believer that things happen for a reason. For instance, Dana divorced you. You took a sabbatical. You decided to do this trip. You met me. We sort of connected. You're starting to view your life from a different perspective, far away from all the influences of your parents, your job, your marriage, your community. It can be very frightening … and I want to add, I think you're being very open to change."

I thought for a moment. "I don't know, Hanna. I've always wanted things to be orderly and not messy. This all seems so disorderly and messy. But you've opened my eyes to a lot of things in the short time I've known you. I'm still trying to process all the experiences I've had in this last week. One week?

118

Seems like years, and I think I'm starting to enjoy it, but, deep down, I'm scared."

She looked straight ahead and then, after a few long moments, answered with a flatness in her voice, "Life can sometimes be messy. Messy can be interesting and fun, but I found out it can also be just plain crappy."

I wondered what she meant by that last remark, but let it go.

At the store, we looked around at the array of t-shirts, souvenirs, food, books, and some camping essentials—nothing I needed.

Hanna came up and grabbed my arm. "Guess what? There's an open mike tomorrow night at the Old Faithful Inn. Free pizza and beer for anyone who plays and tips are okay. Let's do it!"

"Sure, we can go up for it. You'd be great."

"No, silly," she said, smiling excitedly at me, "I mean both of us! You and me. It'd be so much fun."

"Naah, I'm not good enough to play with you. I've never played in front of anyone before. You'd do great by yourself and don't need me messing up your songs."

"Russell," she said sternly, "don't be a spoilsport. The other night you were spot on with your rhythm, your chords, everything. I want you to do this with me. Please. It's important to me." She looked at me with those pleading eyes that caused me to melt. "We can go through four or five songs tonight and get them tight. You'll be great. Promise. Hmmmm?"

She did her sexy, coy routine on me: head cocked, twirling a loose strand of hair.

I love it when she does that. Does she know what that does to me? "Okay, let's see what happens tonight and how it works out. Then … maybe. What if they hate me and throw things?" I said with a chuckle.

"The audience won't be expecting super-pros. For God's sake, have you ever been to a fucking karaoke night? Now that stuff is usually really awful. They'll love us. Promise."

"Let's see what happens. No promises, but maybe."

"Yay!" She squealed and gave me a quick hug. "Let's go practice."

She almost dragged me back to camp with her excitement and eagerness. I liked seeing her being so happy.

Since we had a fire ring, I got two bundles of firewood and lit a fire. We opened a bottle of wine, and after a quick dinner, got out our guitars and proceeded to play for the next three hours. Two hours in it'd gotten downright cold, so I doused the fire, and we cramped ourselves into the van on the bed, now folded into a bench seat, and continued until my fingers became sore.

"Gotta get some good callouses going there, Russell," she said smiling. "That was a great session. You're doing great. You'll be fine. Seriously. I really mean it. I do have my professional pride, ya know, wouldn't let just any hack back me up," she said, laughing.

We put our stuff away and got reorganized. We could feel the cold creeping in, and we were tired.

Hanna gave me a peck on the cheek, and we said our good nights. She got her new sleeping bag and left for her tent.

The next morning I saw her sitting facing the lake—meditating, I guessed. I dressed quickly and warmly, and quietly joined her. I tried doing what I'd done in Sheridan, but my thoughts wouldn't let my mind rest. I tried following my breath like Summer had instructed, but my mind was full of parents, recent events, Hanna, and everything else a busy mind wanted to conjure up. I found it frustrating.

Hanna touched me gently. "Let's go and get some food."

As we walked to our camp, Hanna said, "I'm going to wear that new skirt I bought back in Mission. Why don't you wear your new jeans? We'll be really cool."

The reality of tonight and the open mike hit me. Panic and fear shot through me. "Hell, I don't think I've ever been cool in my whole life, but I'll try. Sure. Let's be cool."

I tried to make sense of what I felt about Dana and my failed marriage—how devastated I still felt. I didn't want that to happen again. I liked Hanna, but should I keep traveling with her or call it quits and be safe? My heart said to stay with her as long as it worked. My head said, "Run!"

* * *

After driving over to Canyon Village, about forty-five minutes away, to see "The Grand Canyon of Yellowstone" and the deep, thundering waterfall, we went to Norris, about thirty minutes away, and walked the boardwalk. The colorful thermal pools seethed and boiled, periodically burping up stinky smells from deep in the bowels of the earth. The temperatures hovered around 200 degrees, beautiful and terrifying at the same time. After a number of stops and short hikes in the area, it was time to get to the Old Faithful Inn early enough to see the famous geyser and get ready to play at around five.

In spite of the gawky, slow-going tourists, we managed to get to the inn about three thirty and signed up for the open mike. A smiling, eager young woman we guessed to be a college student and seasonal worker took down our names and said that we were the first ones to sign up for tonight and she was thrilled to have us. We could start right at five and play as long as we wanted if no one else signed up. Beer and pizza would be provided. We thanked her and walked outside.

An information kiosk gave some park history by the main door, which we stopped to read:

Yellowstone National Park contains the headwaters of the Yellowstone River, from which it takes its historical name. Towards the end of the 18th century, French trappers named the river Roche Jaune, which may have been a translation of the Hidatsa Tribe's name 'Mi tsi a-da-zi' (Yellow Rock River), but most believe that the river was simply named for the yellow rocks seen in the Grand Canyon of the Yellowstone.

The park covers an area of 3,468.4 square miles that include lakes, canyons, rivers and mountain ranges, mainly located in Wyoming, but spilling over into neighboring Montana and Idaho. The U.S. Congress established it, and President Ulysses S. Grant signed it into law on March 1, 1872. The first national park in the U.S., it's also widely held to be the first national park in the world. The park has vast forests and grasslands that are home to abundant wildlife, including grizzly bears, wolves, and free-ranging herds of bison and elk. The Yellowstone Park bison herd is the oldest and largest public bison herd in the United States. Also, hundreds of other species of mammals, birds, fish, and reptiles have been documented, including several that are either endangered or threatened.

Another of the park's great attractions are its many geothermal features, especially Old Faithful geyser, one of its most popular features, fueled by the Yellowstone Caldera, the largest super-volcano on the continent still considered to be active. It has erupted with tremendous force several times in the last two million years. Half of the world's geothermal features can be found in the park, fueled by ongoing volcanic activity. Lava flows and rocks from volcanic eruptions cover most of the land mass of Yellowstone.

Native Americans have lived in the Yellowstone region for at least 11,000 years, and aside from visits by mountain men during the early-to-mid-19th century, serious exploration didn't begin until the late 1860s. Since then researchers have examined more than a thousand archaeological sites.

Hundreds of structures have been built since the park's creation and are protected for their architectural and historical significance.

The Greater Yellowstone Ecosystem is the largest-surviving, mostly intact, ecosystem in the Earth's northern temperate zone. In 1978, Yellowstone was named a UNESCO World Heritage Site.

Finished, I turned on my cell and found I had service. I also had eight calls from my sister and two from my parents. I thought I might as well get it over with and called Karen first.

"Russell, Mom is so worried about you," she said. "She's driving me nuts thinking I should know where you are or what you're doing. You never answer our calls. Our calls always go to voice mail."

"Karen, I'm really sorry that Mom's been bugging you. I have my phone off most of the time because cell service is spotty out here at best. I'm sorry. I don't want them to worry. I'll call them.

"I'm really enjoying being out here. It's given me time to think. I met a woman, actually picked her up hitchhiking back in Iowa, and we're having fun. We're in Yellowstone, and we're going to play an open mike tonight at the lodge here."

Karen answered more quietly, "Russell, I'm really happy you're enjoying yourself, but please call Mom and Dad more often. They worry about you. They truly want you to be happy, but they worry. Just please talk to them."

"I'll call them. Promise. You know, even when I was living in Chicago, they called me constantly, not to see how I was doing or how I was, but always telling me how to run my life, what I should be doing, complaining that I wasn't coming home every weekend, how I didn't appreciate them, stuff like that. I realize they worry, but they've smothered me, especially Mom.

"It's good to be away. I'm doing fine, seeing the most amazing wonderful places. You can't believe how big all this is. You need to bring the boys out here sometime. It'd blow them away."

"I have to go, Russell. I'm finishing up here at work and have to get a few more things done before I leave. Thanks for calling. Please call Mom and Dad." Then she gave a sarcastic laugh. "It must be nice, being irresponsible."

"Yeah, right. Good to talk to you. Love you, Sis."

"Me too." She disconnected.

Hanna was standing right next to me. She turned. "You okay? I sort of overheard. Your sister?"

"Yeah, Karen. I guess Mom and Dad are having a worry fit and I need to call them. I really don't want to. Think I'll wait 'til tomorrow."

"I need to call my mom too; haven't talked with her for a few days, and she'll be worried. Stick around. You can listen if you want."

She speed dialed. "Hi, Mom, how's everything?" Pause. "That's great. We're in Yellowstone. Got here yesterday. It's so amazing; so beautiful." Pause. "Yes. I'm still with Russell, and he's just great fun to be with." Pause. "I know, Mom." Pause. "Yes, he's really nice." Pause. "No. We haven't … yet." Pause. "Yes, M-o-t-h-e-r, I know, and yes, I will." Pause. "We're at Old Faithful, and it's going to erupt in a few minutes. We're playing an open mike together tonight here at the inn and I gotta go. Love you, Mom. Love you so much, and I'm so happy, really happy." Pause. "Yeah, I'll tell him sometime, depending on … you know. Bye, love you … and Frank, too. Say hi."

She looked at me and smiled. "God, Russell, I'm so happy right now." She hugged me. "Mom hopes she can get to meet you sometime. She just wants to give you the once over and give her approval, especially after the craziness of my last boyfriend."

"Boyfriend? So I'm a boyfriend? And what craziness?" I asked.

She looked at me with what looked like panic in her eyes, shook her head, and looked away, ignoring my questions. "Not now. Maybe some other time. Com' on, Old Faithful is ready to go."

Old Faithful was scheduled to erupt in about ten minutes, and a crowd of eager tourists were gathering. We found a niche and waited. A few moments later, there was a slight rumbling sound, and then a little bit of water and steam shot out of the center of the area. Then, whoosh, steaming hot water shot thirty or forty feet into the air. Oohs and ahs came from the crowd; pictures were snapped, and then the waterspout faded back into the earth, like a garden hose being turned off. A cheer went up from the group, after which everyone stood gazing at the last few sputters, seemingly reluctant to disperse, as though expecting a repeat performance.

It was a quarter to five, so we got our guitars and went into the inn. I felt like I was going to the gallows. Hanna sensed my panic.

"Take some really deep breaths. It'll help you relax. You'll be fine. After all, you're with me and I won't ever let you down," she said, turning, giving me a reassuring look.

We tuned up off to the side of the low stage, then ran quickly through the beginning of three tunes to get our fingers moving. Hanna took my hand and led me onto the small stage. The lounge was about three quarters full—various couples and families having drinks, some having food, talking quietly. Some clapped mildly.

I felt like throwing up, so took in deep breaths, almost hyperventilating, while Hannah, completely calm and in control, whispered that the sound system looked to be really good and someone would run a control board to balance out the different microphones. She showed me how to work my guitar microphone, what distance I should be from it, and advised me that I needed to listen to the monitors, that we would both be facing front, and that would be the only way to really hear what she was playing and singing.

She smiled at me. "Just do what you can do and follow me. If you get lost, just back off a bit until you find your place. I'll announce the songs, same order as we planned last night. You'll do fine." She reached up and gave me a quick peck on the cheek. "Let's break a leg."

She then played a few chords and sang a few phrases into her mike. The monitors were really loud, and she motioned for the sound guy to lower them a bit.

She tapped her mike, which was already active, and said, "Hello, everyone, my friend, Russell Henderson is here with me tonight. My name is Hanna Martin. We're from San Francisco and are happy to do some tunes for you. Here we go, and one and two and three—" She launched into her intro and began to sing.

I waited a few measures, then gently came in with her, playing with her just as I had last night. What I heard sounded good. Her voice was so pure, it almost made me want to cry. All my jitters started to fade away. I was enjoying this. It felt good.

We finished the first song, and Hanna said, "Thank you." She backed away from her mike and turned towards me. "You okay?"

Applause started with whistles and whoops. It was amazing, totally amazing, and it felt good, really good. I flashed a huge grin back at her. "Yeah, I'm great."

We played what we'd practiced, and with Hanna's chatter between songs, took up almost an hour. Hanna announced that we were done, and the crowd shouted, "More! More! More!"

I looked over at her and told her to keep on if she wanted, and I'd bow out. I'd done everything I'd practiced with her and didn't want to try to fake my way through stuff I didn't know. Hanna said she'd play a few more songs solo, and I gave a nod and a wave to the audience and slipped off to the side. She continued with some of the sweet, soulful ballads she'd written.

She finished about six forty-five and thanked the applauding crowd. People came up and dropped one, five, even ten-dollar bills into the tip jar. Many wanted to talk with her about her music. Some asked if she had any CDs, was she on tour, was she ever coming to whatever town or city they were from? They kept her occupied for the next half hour before things settled down. I even had a few people coming up to tell me how much they appreciated my playing. I felt like a rock star.

After we put our gear away, the manager came over and gushed about how we were the best group they'd ever had in the open mike. How long are you staying? Could we play again tomorrow night? Would we want a steady gig?

We said we weren't sure of our plans tomorrow night, thanked her, said our goodbyes, and went for food and drink. The tip jar held $137.00. Hanna wanted to split it, but I refused.

We sat at a table and had pizza and beers. "So, you okay?" she said before chomping onto a huge slice of "the works" pizza.

"Yeah, that was great. Man, you were awesome. You're a total pro. I'm impressed with my girl."

She looked at me with a cocked eyebrow. "Ah, your g-u-r-l ...?"

"Just a figure of speech ... a bad figure of speech?"

She laughed. "If you can be my b-o-y."

"Anytime."

Starved, we wolfed down our pizza and quaffed our beers until we were stuffed full, then we packed up and headed back to camp—about an hour's drive.

After riding for about fifteen minutes, Hanna said, "You were really good tonight. You can play really well. I liked you backing me up like you did. You had a nice way of adding to what I was doing. I'd like to work some more tunes up and go back on Thursday if you'd be up for it."

"Ya know, as scared as I was, once we started and I settled in, I had a blast. It was really fun. Yeah, I'd be up for it."

"Then let's."

It was past nine when we got back and got the Westy set up. Hannah said good night.

"Were you warm enough last night out there?" I asked as she headed out to her tent.

"I was a little cold but okay."

"The bed is big enough in here, and you'd be up off the ground. You might be more comfortable."

"Are you asking me to sleep with you?"

"No! Well ... yeah, but just so you'd be warmer. Nothing more. Promise."

"Oh, darn," she said flirtatiously, "but, yeah, I'd like that. Thanks."

She came back in. "Zipped together or separate?"

"Separate would probably be a good idea."

As discreetly as we could in close confines, we got undressed and into our respective bags.

She snuggled slightly over next to me, gave me another peck on the cheek and said, "You're becoming more than just a travel companion, Russell, and I'm not sure I know how to deal with it … good night."

"Ah … yeah, good night." She didn't move away, but stayed next to me. Her breathing slowed into sleep.

Sleep didn't come so easy for me as I lay there, thinking how nice it felt having her sleeping so close and considering what she'd just said: you're becoming more than just a travel companion, and I'm not sure I know how to deal with it. I thought of the conversation with my sister. Could it ever be the same when I went back to Iowa? Probably not. I closed my eyes and eventually fell into welcome sleep.

In the morning, Hanna still lay tucked in next to me. I yawned and stretched a little, awakening her.

She did a cute little moan and tried to get a little closer, which was really impossible. She looked up and smiled. "Good morning."

I caught her scent and could hardly contain my feelings. I quickly unzipped and rolled out and into my clothes so she couldn't see what was going on. "Hanna, I'd like to take a chair over by the trees and try to meditate like yesterday, like we did last Sunday … maybe twenty or thirty minutes? I had a real hard time yesterday. Maybe it'll be better today."

"Sure, I'll join you."

"Great. It's still chilly; let's bundle up."

Dressed as warmly as we could with most of the clothes we had with us, including stocking caps, we took our chairs over by the grove of trees so we had a clear view of the lake.

"Remember last Sunday?" Hanna asked me. "Summer won't be here to lead us, but just remember what she said and go with it. So you're on your own. Take three deep breaths. You okay?"

"Sure ... think so."

I sat and closed my eyes. The first thoughts that came to mind were of my discussion with Karen yesterday, then my parents, then Dana, Chicago, my job, all the old stuff. Then Hanna appeared in a fantasy life. I tried again focusing on my breath as Summer had instructed. Slowly, all thought grew quiet, and all I knew was that my mind was empty, empty of thought, other than me knowing my mind was empty of thought. I sat in this state for what seemed like ten minutes. I felt the sun on my face growing hot and slowly opened my eyes. I blinked and looked at my watch. I'd been there for almost forty-five minutes. I looked around. Hanna was gone. I felt great. Good. Happy. Back at camp, I found Hanna eating a bowl of cereal.

"Hey, meditation man, you okay?"

I nodded. "I didn't think life could ever be like this; it's a beautiful day in a beautiful place with a beautiful woman. It couldn't be any better." I walked over and took the liberty of giving her a peck on her cheek. "I think I'm letting myself go, Hanna. I'm doing things I could never have imagined doing only a few weeks ago. I don't think I can ever go back to any of my past life. It's all fading: Dana, job, Chicago, family, the midwest in general. I feel free! I want to go and scream from a mountain top, I'm free!"

She placed her hand on her cheek where I'd kissed it and smiled. "Slow down, happy boy. You apparently had a wonderful meditation session. That's great. I've been there. It's exhilarating. I know. But you're still here … on this planet. Your shit is still all here, hanging around and can come back and bite you on the ass, and it most likely will, given time. Trust me on this; I've been there. There are still responsibilities. As they say, I'm sort of paraphrasing here, but, 'What do you do after you attain enlightenment? Chop wood, carry water.' You still have to chop your wood and carry your water, Russell. Make sense?"

That brought me back to reality. I stopped and thought about that for a moment. "Yeah, you're right. But I enjoyed the moment, darn it. Can't take that from me." I let go a chuckle, realizing that everything hadn't just disappeared, it was all still there.

"Well, truth is, all we have is the moment," Hanna said. "The past is gone, never coming back. The future, we aren't there yet. We always just have the moment. But everything we've done is still there: all the good things and all the bad things. Your issues with your parents are still there and will need to be resolved sometime because the law of karma's always in play … and that's another story we'll talk about sometime."

"How come you know all this stuff?"

"'Cause I began studying this stuff when I was like fourteen. I think I told you that before. My mom had studied Buddhism all her life. Her parents were serious Buddhists, studied in Kathmandu and Dharmsala and places like that. So I guess I'm sort of third generation."

"Gives me a lot to consider, oh wise woman."

She laughed. "Not that wise, really not, but thanks anyway. Hey, what d'ya want to do today? I'm personally toured out. Wouldn't mind just going up to Canyon Village again and sitting by the waterfall and reading and relaxing, then coming back and working on some more tunes?"

"Sounds good," I said. "I'm tired of all the driving and would be happy to sit and read and write in my journal. Yeah, let's go up there. I liked that spot. We can take lunch and come back here and I'll buy you dinner at the hotel restaurant. Like a date."

"A real date? With a guy? I'm not t-o-o sure a-b-o-u-t that," she answered.

"Aw, just please give me a break, already, let's get outa here."

We spent the day just hanging out by the falls. I wrote in my journal about my parents, my sister, trying to put into words on a page exactly how I felt. It was hard, but I filled about ten pages with thoughts of self-pity, remorse, anger, frustration, Hanna, this trip, everything, until I was finally drained and had to quit. I sat for a while, watching the falls, considering it all. I had journeyed through fear, anger, sadness, this trip, the exhilaration, and, lastly, how I was feeling about Hanna, all in around two hours.

I cleared my head and opened one of the books I'd bought in Sheridan called *The Dalai Lama's Little Book of Buddhism*. It was filled with excerpts from his teachings, which were straightforward and easy to read, but while seeming easy, it also caused some pause and refection to seriously understand the depth of each little teaching. Reading it made me feel good and helped me better understand a little of how I was feeling about my parents, the church I grew up in, my siblings, and how I felt about Hanna. Those few pages contained much wisdom.

By then it was early afternoon. "Hanna, we should probably get going. I'm getting hungry, and I bet you are too."

"Yeah, now that you mention it." She stood and stretched.

Just watching her, looking at her move, turned my mind to jelly. I realized how sexually frustrated I felt and decided to talk with her on the drive back. Her sleeping next to me might not have been the best idea.

On leaving Canyon Village, I said, "Hanna, I need to talk. The truth is, sleeping with you so close to me last night, well, it's just driving me crazy. Please understand, but I'm willing to go and sleep in your tent. I'll be warm enough."

"Truth is, I am too," she said, then she paused a long moment before continuing with a shaking voice, "I'm sorry. I sort of feel the same way. But … not right now. Please bear with me. I'm sorry. But not right now. Okay? There's some things I … things I just can't talk about right now, just not right now. I'm sorry … but not now. If it's all the same to you, I'd like to leave here. I know we have one more night, but I'd like to head north, maybe. You said you wanted to go to Glacier?"

"Yeah, I do, eventually, but you wanted to do the open mike tomorrow night. We could work on some songs? I'd be up for it. There's no rush to be anywhere. Let's just hang out and play music and head out Friday. Sound okay?"

"Really? You want to do the open mike again?" she asked with a laugh. "You were so scared the first night."

"Yeah, I'm over my stage fright and would like to do it."

"Let's do it, then."

We got back to camp and went up to the hotel for dinner. It was late when we got back, so we crawled into our sleeping bags; neither of us mentioned sleeping in the tent.

On Thursday morning, we reviewed what we'd played the first night and then worked on more of Hanna's material. Some of the new songs were more complex than what we'd already done. She sketched out chord charts for me. My fingers became sore, and I needed to stop in order to be able to play later.

In the early afternoon, we went to the lodge and signed up for the open mike, then fooled around there the rest of the afternoon, sitting on the expansive porch, reading. Around three thirty, I took a few deep breaths and called my parents.

"Hi, Mom, it's Russell. How're you doing?"

"Russell, where are you? We thought you were coming home like we told you to. Are you on your way?" she asked expectantly.

"I'm in Yellowstone National Park, Mom. It's amazing out here, and please stop worrying about me. I'm doing fine. There's no need for you to worry."

"Well, we do. What on Earth are you doing out there anyway? I told you to stop running around wasting time. You need to get home and get back to work and patch things up with Dana. We didn't raise you to be like this."

"Mom, with all due respect, I'm not coming home anytime soon. I'm planning on heading up to Glacier Park tomorrow and eventually maybe to San Francisco to meet my friend Hanna's mother. So it will be, I don't really know ... it'll be a while; I'll let you know where I am."

"Glacier Park? Never heard of it ... and San Francisco? That's in California. That's so far away. What about your job? And who is Hanna?"

I tried to explain where Glacier was and tell her about Hanna and how we were traveling together and had become friends, but it was like talking to a wall. She ignored everything I'd said and launched into her usual rant about irresponsibility, Dana, work, family; why couldn't I be like my brother and sister? What had she done wrong? And so on.

I'd heard enough and managed to interrupt when she took a breath from her tirade: "I'm fine, Mom. Good to talk to you. Hi to Dad. Love you both. Talk to you soon." I disconnected, took several cleansing breaths—as Hanna called them—turned off my phone, and went to find her to get ready for our set.

Once again, we were the only act and, with our new music plus what we had done the last time, we played until seven-thirty before we thanked everyone and stopped. My fingers were almost bloody, and we were both starved.

Chapter 15: Corwin Springs, Bozeman, and Glacier

After a brief stop at Mammoth Hot Springs, we drove north towards Bozeman on Highway 89. Close to noon we stopped at a little restaurant in the village called Corwin Springs. The restaurant proved to be a conundrum with white-linen table cloths, classical music playing softly over the sound system, and a full menu of all locally grown organic food.

On asking our server about this seemingly incongruent classy restaurant in cowboy country, he explained that it was part of the New Light Church that had bought a 10,000 acre ranch some years before. Many believers had relocated here: doctors, lawyers, stock brokers, and such, many now working either in the community or long distance via the internet. There was the usual ranch work as well as a farm that grew produce for the restaurant and for the rest of the community. The restaurant had a world-class chef to fulfill the culinary needs of those who'd come from larger cities.

After our delicious lunch, we drove along the Yellowstone River. The land changed from the high pine forests and mountains of Yellowstone back into the grassy, rolling Montana landscape as we'd seen at the Little Bighorn site. Small irrigated farms sat on the side of the river. We traveled on, lost in our thoughts.

Again, I marveled at the expanses of land. Having only known the mid-west where all land was farmed—now all mainly in mono-culture crops of corn and beans—I was unaccustomed to seeing so much unfarmed land. I knew this was due to the aridness of the west, but the expanses made me feel open, like light years away from life as I'd known it. I'd never felt such freedom, like I could do anything I wanted out here, like anything was possible.

At Livingston, we headed west on I-90 towards Bozeman. Hanna found us a campground adjacent to a hot springs on the edge of town. As we checked in, Hanna asked the woman behind the desk if there might be any open mikes in town that evening. She mentioned the weekly Friday night one at a place called Mike's Pizza starting at six. We set up the camper and headed to the springs to soak away the road.

"So, are you up for playing tonight? Pizza and beer?" Hanna asked while we walked to the springs.

I considered her request, and replied, "Yeah, my fingers are sore, but why not? I'll suffer through it."

She grabbed my hand and gave it a squeeze. "Great; pizza places are always good. Most folks there tend to be more appreciative than some of the rowdy bars I've played in. It should be fun."

The springs had a number of pools, from the almost-scalding 'lobster pot' to the ice-cold pool immediately next to it and everything in between, plus a larger pool for swimming. We found that if you went into the ice-cold pool, then into the lobster pot, the super-hot water was actually bearable; each, however, only for short times. After about an hour of soaking in the various pools, we ambled back to our camp and relaxed, drinking copious amounts of water to hydrate our drained bodies as we soaked up the Montana sun. In the quiet, I slipped into a meditative state without trying. I was just there, at total peace with the world around me.

At five we headed to the pizza house, which wasn't too far from our camp. We arrived a little before six and signed up for a forty-five minute time slot, starting around seven since the first slot had already been filled. The place had the usual smells of red sauce, onion, ground beef, sausage, and pepperoni—all making me hungry. The place had a cheery feel to it with large store-front windows that faced a busy street of pedestrians, bicycles, and vehicles.

Our host, Mike, asked where we were from, our experience, did we do originals or covers and so on. He seemed to be a nice guy and happy we were there. Our pay would be free beers, a large special pizza, and any tips. Customers started to roll in, so Mike went to work. We found a table by the stage and ordered two iced teas and our free pizza. The first act was a solo guy, apparently a local, who struggled a bit, but received respectful applause from the clientele.

About fifteen minutes before seven, we got out our guitars and went to a side room to tune and warm up, and at seven sharp, we walked onto the stage to murmurs of, "Who are those two? Never seen them before ..." and so on. We looked at each other, smiled and winked, and began with a cover Hanna was sure everyone would know and like. Most everyone quieted down to listen. We ended to a nice round of applause.

She introduced us, telling everyone that we were traveling through to Glacier and then on home to San Francisco. Again she made no mention of Iowa, her words suggesting I was from San Francisco too. It was okay with me. It made me feel good that I was from someplace more important than "flyover" land. She started into one of her own songs.

Though only my third time playing in front of an audience, I enjoyed it more and more, feeling comfortable playing with her, and her music being easy to follow. I was still a baby guitar player, but I felt more confident the more I played with her.

The crowd loved her, and I had a good time putting in a few runs and additions other than just chords—though being careful not to get in the way of her singing and playing. I didn't know much about this, but I did know that my job was simply to support her, not get in her way. We finished our forty-five minute set and received standing applause with shouts of, "One more. One more."

We looked over and caught Mike's eye. He smiled and nodded to go ahead. Hannah finished with one of her best ballads. Everyone went stone quiet, listening to her enchanting lyrics. We finished and all remained silent. Then the place erupted into another standing ovation. We bowed, thanked them all, and walked off to put our guitars away.

A few minutes later, Mike came over and handed us a full tip jar. He thanked us and wondered if we could hang around town for a few days and play some regular gigs for pay: six to nine, plus tips, food and beer. We looked at each other, and as tempting as it was, we gratefully declined his offer, citing a tight schedule.

We sat and ordered beers to drink while we watched the next act, a guitar/mandolin duo. They were really good, both vocally and instrumentally. I fell in love with the way the mandolin player filled in spaces in the song with all his nice riffs and the way the higher-pitched mandolin sounded against the lower-pitched guitar.

On the way back to the campground, I said, "I loved the mandolin with those two that came on after us. I'd like to check out music stores to see what they might have tomorrow before heading out. I'd like to get one."

"I played with a mandolin player a few times," Hanna replied. "He was really good and added a lot to my singing. It'd be nice to have you play one with me, but I like your guitar, and a mando is a pretty steep learning curve."

"I don't know anything about them, but I'm a quick learner. Maybe we can just go see?"

* * *

On Saturday we rose early, had a bite, and went into town to look for the music store that Hanna had located on her cell phone. We pulled into a parking space almost in front just as the store was opening for business.

The store smelled of wood. Guitars, banjos, violins, and mandolins hung all over the walls, and strings, accessories, books and CDs sat on racks around the room.

I explained to the salesman—a guy about my age—what I was looking for. He asked me about my experience, and I replied that I had none.

He showed me several student models. I asked him the difference between those and more expensive ones, and he explained about the differences in woods (solid or laminated), manufacturing processes (how much hand work was involved), and price (solid wood being pricier). I asked if he could play some from the different price ranges. I found it easy to hear the differences: the student models were nice, but the more expensive ones definitely sounded much better, having a nice, woody sounding low end and less harshness on the higher strings. He played a number of different ones, and I asked Hanna what she thought. Interestingly, she liked the same one

I did, a Collings MT O Oval Hole A Style with a satin finish for $2,970.00 including a quality hard-shell case. The salesman recommended that I get a good humidifier for it.

Not understanding, I asked, "A humidifier? Why?"

"Where're you from?"

"Iowa."

"Well," he said, "it's pretty wet in Iowa, isn't it?"

"Yeah, it rains a lot, and it can be really humid, especially in summer."

"Our relative humidity out here can be really low, averaging maybe around thirty percent. Most wood instruments are now made in climate-controlled conditions around fifty percent. When the outside humidity is low, the wood dries out, warps, and can actually crack—usually the tops. Half our repairs are due to lack of proper humidity."

I thought about our guitars and looked at Hanna. I could tell she was thinking the same thing I was. So, along with the mandolin humidifier, I got two guitar humidifiers, some mandolin picks of various thicknesses, a shoulder strap, and two extra sets of strings for the mandolin along with two sets each for our guitars. I browsed the book shelves and found three books, one for beginners, one on accompaniment, and one of folk songs for mandolin, all with videos and sound tracks. I also bought another electronic tuner. I then found three folk type CDs with mandolin. The guy showed me a few things about care for the instrument. He threw in all our strings along with a polishing cloth and some polish. We walked out into Montana sunshine, and I couldn't wait to start playing.

The music store experience took over two hours, bringing us close to lunchtime, so we decided to stay in Bozeman for another night and just hang out and head for Glacier the next day. I'd long ago left my well-planned travel itinerary to the wind, and it didn't bother me anymore.

We strolled the main street, looking into various shops along the way, and found a small Mexican place for lunch. I wanted to start fooling around with my new mandolin, so around three we headed back to the campground.

Once back, we set up for the night, and I pulled out my new purchase and explored it until Hanna asked if I wanted to go soak. After the pools and dinner, I again pulled out the mandolin.

"Russell, you seem a little obsessed with this mandolin thing," Hanna said.

"Yeah, sorry, but I'm really loving this. Am I being too weird?"

"Sort of. You've hardly talked to me since you bought it."

"I'm sorry; I tend to go overboard on new projects. It's just that I want to incorporate this into our duo."

She smiled. "So, we're a duo?"

"Yeah. I liked the few times we've played out; it felt good. You're so easy and fun to play with. I really like it." Then I thought that maybe she didn't like me playing with her and was just being nice. I suddenly felt like I'd overstepped. "I'm sorry, it's just that I thought—"

"Russell, I really like you playing backup for me. You seem natural and don't try to overshadow my music, and I like that. So many have wanted to show how good they are rather than supporting me. I appreciate what you do, and you don't have to play a mandolin to impress me."

"I'm really not trying to impress you; I just like the way that mandolin sounded the other night and thought it would really work with our music. Just want to do what I can to help."

"Thanks, but I like your guitar playing. Take your time. We might be together a long time."

I pondered that last remark: did she mean music-wise or something else? I didn't pursue it. My mind had so much going on in it as it was. I was trying to figure out what the hell I was doing. Hanna was starting to mean something to me. I liked her free spirit, but how long until she found some other travel companion who was more interesting or a better musician? I didn't see me as a prize for someone like her. And then there was the sexual frustration.

"Hey, in there; are you still here? Still with me? Come on back now, Russell; I'm looking for you. I'm hungry. Let's eat something."

I blinked and looked at her smiling face, her head cocked, twirling a strand of hair. I melted. "I'm sorry. I was just lost in my thoughts."

"Care to share?"

"It's just; I don't know … I'm having a hard time, Hanna. I'm scared."

"Scared? Of what?"

"I'm afraid of what I'm doing, afraid of where I'm going, and … and, well, I'm afraid of what I'll do when you're gone."

"What? When I'm gone? I'm not planning on going anywhere."

"You will, when you get tired of me. Dammit, Hanna, I don't want to go back to Iowa. It'll never be the same. I don't know where I'm going. My parents think I'm nuts; my sister probably does too. You're the only person in the world who I care about, and when this is over, what will we have? Is there any future for us? And I can't keep on sleeping with you snuggled in next to me every night. It's driving me nuts … I don't know what it's like for women, but for me … I'm just goddamned sexually frustrated!" My voice rose. I was almost shouting.

After a long pregnant pause, Hanna said, "I'm sorry. I wasn't thinking about what you might be feeling. I liked it because I feel warm and safe with you. Sex aside, how do you really feel about me?"

"I don't know. It's ... it's confusing to me because I feel so alone, and you're there for me. I don't know if I'm just clinging to you because of that or if it's something more, something deeper. And I know you don't want a relationship right now, and I respect that. I have no idea what I want, and I think I'm saying more than maybe I should, and I should stop now." I couldn't believe I'd said all that; I'd just shared more of my feelings than I ever had before.

Another long pregnant pause followed my outburst. "I don't know where this will all lead either. I do know I'm starting to care for you; you're great to be with, and you have to admit we do pretty well together. I'm not planning on going anywhere else other than with you all the way to San Francisco. I'd like you to hang out with me there. I don't want to lose you either. You're a pretty special guy, and I may never find anyone as good as you, and I want to find out, see what happens. We really don't know each other, but let's keep going and find out where this'll take us. No one really ever knows where the road they're on may eventually lead to, even if they have a good map."

I sighed. "It's really hard for me. I've told you how I was brought up with strict structure in my life, and right now I feel so far out of my comfort zone, I can't even see it. I don't know how to handle it."

"I see what you're saying. I can't understand what you must be dealing with. I had such a different childhood ... and as it turns out, I might sometimes be more adventurous than I should be sometimes, so I appreciate your stability."

I was lost in this conversation and just sat there with nothing more to say.

Hanna continued, "I ... I'm sorry ... I just can't have sex with you ... not until I ..." She went silent, like she was trying to say something she couldn't. Then, "I'm sorry about your frustration; I'll move back to my tent tonight. I'll get my stuff out of the van."

She stood. I got up, put my arms around her, and held her, feeling her shaking in my arms. She nuzzled into my neck and whispered, "I'm sorry I can't be what you want, can't give you what you need. I can't ... please don't make me go away."

"I'm not going to make you go anywhere, and I don't want you out in your tent either. Having you close to me is better than nothing."

Her voice trembled: "God, I don't want to fall in love with you. I don't want a relationship. I don't know what I want."

"Me neither; so, let's just enjoy our moment. Okay?"

"Okay."

We stood holding onto each other for a long while. Looking back, though I didn't know it at the time, that was the moment I fell in love with her. We let go of each other only after we became too tired to hang on any longer.

It was late, so we each ate a Power Bar and got ready for bed. We crawled into our sleeping bags, and she grabbed my face and kissed me long and hard.

"Please don't hurt me."

"I could never hurt you." I kissed her forehead.

"You might when you know more about me ..."

I lay awake, hearing her breathing deepen into sleep. What did she mean by "know more about me?" What was that about?

And what she'd said earlier: "I'm sorry. I just can't have sex with you, not until I ..." I remembered again what John had said about her having some bad times. Then there were things she'd alluded to. I wondered if I should ask or try to pressure her into telling me. Maybe she never would. Could it be so bad that I'd actually leave her? The questions finally slowed, and I joined Hanna in sleep.

I dreamed of being in a tunnel searching for something that was close but kept eluding me whenever I drew near.

Chapter 16: Bozeman to Glacier

Another beautiful Montana day, clear-blue sky and an open road. After a quick stop at a grocery store, we headed north into the vastness of this very large northern state of rolling hills, mountain ranges, and pine forests to I-15 by Helena and onto Highway 287. All was quiet, as if last night had drained us of words and emotion and we had none left for the day. We came to a little wind-blown town of empty store fronts and grey, deserted clapboard houses. Hanna spotted an ice cream parlor amongst the otherwise empty shops and wanted to stop.

An older woman in a floral-print dress stood behind the counter and greeted us with a big, welcoming smile. We gazed at her few selections. She said they were all made right there on site. The ice cream was rich and creamy and delicious. It appeared to be the only business left in town, and I asked her how she was able to manage. She replied that the few folks still around supported her, and tourist traffic in the summer kept her almost busier than she cared to be. Winters were slow, and she was only open on weekends then, but she made enough to get by.

She wanted to retire and asked if we wanted to buy her business. For a moment, I actually considered it, thinking how great it would be to live so far away from everything and all the problems and expectations, but I graciously declined. I wondered what it would take to breathe life back into this apparently once-thriving town. But the life had faded too far, and soon the harsh winds of winter and the heat of the summer sun would melt the town back into the earth. Only the rubble of stone foundations would remain to fade more slowly, until time turned the area once again into rolling grassy hills.

Times had changed. People had moved to Great Falls or down to Helena. Those still left out here did online shopping for their needs, making a trip to the city maybe every month or so for groceries. I thought about Iowa and how so many small towns were drying up or turning into bedroom communities with maybe only a gas station-convenience store. Most of the folks that still lived in those places either worked in larger towns or cities where they could find work or else for minimum wages at the local grain elevator, hog-confinement operations, or seasonal farm work. Most were high school graduates or dropouts with families too early and dreams too late, suffering anger and alcohol to salve the sad and empty lives of faded expectations. A product of the times, there would be no resurrecting this little town or any others.

Moving on up the road, I thought of our talk last night, and as strong a free spirit as Hanna appeared to be, she suddenly seemed fragile. I realized also that I might be considered fragile as well, but in a different way. How many others were the same as us? Didn't we all have our own drama that we carried with us? From a Chicago banker to a minimum-wage worker trying to support a family, didn't we all carry our upbringing, our mistakes, our grief, our lost dreams, our singular perceptions of reality?

I tried starting a conversation several times, but other than the stop for ice cream, she seemed aloof and not interested. While we'd ridden in silence other times, I sensed something different today, as if she were somewhere else, staring out her side window. I thought I saw her wipe her eyes once.

"Is something wrong?" I asked.

She shrugged, not looking at me, answering like she was far away, "Yeah, I'm fine. Why?"

"Just wondering; you seem so quiet," I said dumbly, not knowing how to pursue it any further.

"So, I'm quiet. So?"

I shook it off and said no more.

Seeming like a millennium of icy silence later, we arrived at the St. Mary visitor center. After talking with the park ranger, we decided to camp in Many Glacier Campground, purchased our park passes, and booked a campsite for the next five days.

Grassy, rolling foothills, naked of trees, formed the landscape to our east, and the mountainous park sat to the west. We drove from the visitors' center along the east side of Lower Saint Mary Lake, and then into the park alongside Lake Sherburne. I felt as if we'd entered another world. I'd seen the Rocky Mountains from a distance on our travels, but this valley surrounded by high peaks and bordered by glacial lakes took my breath away. At Many Glacier Lodge, a number of cars had stopped, and people stood outside, looking up to the side of a steep mountain, some through binoculars.

We joined the other parked cars and looked up the side of the mountain but saw nothing unusual. Hanna asked a man what he was looking at.

"There are some mountain goats up there," he replied and pointed to some little white dots on the side of a sheer, almost vertical, wall.

The white dots—that's all they were to our eyes—moved about like some sort of comic-book-hero gnats that defy gravity.

Dusk was drawing near, so we drove on to Many Glacier campground and checked in at the ranger station. On asking how one got around the park, we were told that only one road went through it—The Going to the Sun Road. All other areas had to be accessed by hiking. We got trail maps, directions, and park information, along with other information pamphlets on bear and wildlife safety, trail preparedness, weather, and so on.

The camp area was clean with ample sites, most all sheltered by pine trees, occupied by everything from small tents to large motorhomes.

Warning signs told guests not to leave food or anything related to food outside other than when eating, to clean up immediately after, and store any food away. Steel bear-proof boxes were provided to store food, camp stoves, anything food related, even if it just smelled of cooking. Bear-proof trash cans were also scattered throughout, along with directions on safe trash disposal.

Grizzly bears lived in Glacier Park, and humans were no more than an inconvenience and a possible source of food to them. However, it was unlucky for the bear if they started invading campgrounds looking for human food; they would be tranquilized, collared, and relocated to a remote area. If they were found ever again being a nuisance, their fate was usually sealed. Bears didn't respect boundaries and could be very dangerous, especially if surprised by a hiker coming around a blind corner on a trail; sows with cubs were particularly dangerous. The park usually experienced around two bear attacks every year, and had had ten deaths from attacks since the 1960s.

We set up our camp and made a dinner of cold cut sandwiches, chips, and fruit. After securing all our food properly, we strolled around the camp and meandered towards the camp store and restaurant. Hanna was not her usual bubbly self, but was sullen, arms crossed over her chest, only going through the motions of being present.

The well-stocked store had everything a camper would need, including the usual camping necessities, t-shirts, and baseball caps. I asked a salesperson about trail books, the best hikes, what to see, and any supplies we might need. He showed us some of the guidebooks and more informative trail maps than the ranger maps. He also recommended bear spray (pepper spray) as a safety measure just in case we encountered a bear. He told us to check the message board for ranger-guided hikes, which were always good for first-timers. I ended up buying a guidebook, a good map, a warning whistle, a canister of bear spray, and a set of compact binoculars.

We checked out the message board outside on the porch. Along with all sorts of messages left for others, there were schedules for hikes and evening ranger talks. A guided hike, classified as medium to strenuous—due to the elevation gain, length, and some exposure to steep drop-offs—left at nine the next morning for the Ptarmigan Tunnel. A ranger was also giving a talk that night about the park, its history, the lodges, and back country.

Benches sat along the store on the porch so we each got an ice cream cone and sat, watching people file by, some with huge backpacks. We caught snippets of conversations about where they'd been, how many days they were out, what hike, or hikes, they'd been on, which they liked the best, and where they were hiking the next day. I found it interesting just listening to the adventures they'd had, and what they'd seen. It all sounded so foreign to me. I grew excited to do some hiking.

"Do you want to go on a hike?" Hanna asked dourly, sounding not the least bit interested. "It can be pretty strenuous. We're starting out at around 4500 feet and it's all up from here."

I always considered myself in fairly good shape, having gone to the gym to work out three or four times a week when I lived in Chicago. However, it'd now been a while, and I felt a little twinge of fear. What if I went too far and couldn't get back? The only real hike I'd ever been on was to Black Elk Peak back a few weeks ago, and I suffered on that one.

"Yeah, I think so," I said. "Maybe we should go on the guided hike tomorrow morning—see what this place is about— and let's go to the ranger talk tonight."

We followed the camp map a few hundred yards to a small outdoor area with wooden benches in a semicircle around a lectern. Folks already sat there, warmly dressed. No one used a cell phone because the area had no service. I realized I hadn't called my folks or Karen in a while and now I couldn't. Some of my usual guilt clutched my belly. Hanna's mood already caused me to feel tense, so I took some deep breaths and sat—in silence—waiting for the ranger talk.

After about ten minutes, a young woman ranger dressed in her green ranger uniform took the podium and told us about the history of Glacier National Park. Her talk, along with a slide show, told us how the mountains of Glacier Park were formed some 170 million years ago. Glacial activity had carved out the valleys and formed the moraines that dammed water, creating the over 130 named lakes in the park. In the mid-nineteenth century, the park had over 150 glaciers, but now only 25 active glaciers remained, and if the current climate patterns persist, scientists predict all will have completely disappeared by 2030.

The Piegan (Blackfeet) tribe of Native Americans originally inhabited the area, but they were forced to cede the land over to the United States in 1895.

After the foundation of the park, the Great Northern Railway built a number of chalets and hotels to lure eastern tourists via the railroad to the area. The fifty-mile-long Going to the Sun Road, the only road that goes from the east to the west side of the park, was completed in 1932. It crosses the continental divide at the 6646 ft. Logan Pass.

We learned that the park encompasses over 1,000,000 acres and is home for over 1000 different plant and hundreds of animals species, including grizzly bears, moose, mountain sheep and goats, wolverines, and Canadian lynx.

The park borders Waterton Lakes National Park in Canada, and the parks were designated as the world's first International Peace Park in 1932. Later, in 1976, the United Nations designated them as biosphere preserves and then as World Heritage sites in 1995.

Although at a lower elevation, it was still light out, being this far north and at the far western border of the Mountain Time Zone. By the time the talk finished at a little after nine, both Hanna and I were cold and looking forward to our warm sleeping bags. Hanna still seemed cold and distant, and didn't snuggle in as she had, maintaining as much space as she could in the small bed.

That night I dreamed I was alone in some mountain valley, lost, knowing no way out.

* * *

Up early, fed, our day packs ready with snacks and water, we arrived at the designated time and place to meet our ranger guide for our hike to Ptarmigan Tunnel. Five others gathered, all of us chilly in the early morning—frost still lay in the shaded areas, and we could see our breath. Everyone remained quiet, keeping to themselves. The same ranger who gave the talk last night appeared in her full ranger uniform.

"Good morning. My name is Rebecca Morgan, and I'll be your guide on the hike to Ptarmigan Tunnel this morning. Everyone have what they need? Plenty of water, snacks, warm layers, rain gear, good sturdy shoes?"

She walked around giving each one of us a quick inspection. She then asked us to introduce ourselves. The group included an older couple from St. Paul, Minnesota, a young woman from Bend, Oregon, and a couple, about our age, from Durango, Colorado.

"This hike is about eleven miles round trip with about a 2,000 foot. elevation gain, so it is a bit strenuous, but the trail itself is good. It's the length and elevation gain that make it hard. The highest we'll be is about 7,400 feet. above sea level, so those from lower altitudes may experience shortness of breath on the climb up. If you begin to feel dizzy, please let me know immediately. Drink plenty of water, which will help with the altitude. It's always important to stay hydrated anyway. Questions?"

Nobody said anything. I felt a little unsure about this hike, and I saw the couple from Minnesota whispering to each other, as if they also mightn't be too sure.

"Okay, no questions. Now, about bears. This park is their home, and we are their guests. Respect that and respect them. I see some of you have bear bells to warn them, which is fine, but the best warning is to be extremely cautious, especially going around blind corners or in heavy forest or brush where you can't see very far ahead. Make noise, talk loudly in these areas.

Generally, they don't want to encounter you and, if they hear you, will just walk off the trail. It's when they're surprised that they can be dangerous. Sows with cubs are particularly dangerous. I see a few have bear spray like I carry. Chances are we won't need it, but if we do, let me take care of it. Okay? Questions?"

The woman from Minnesota asked, "Can we turn around if we don't think we can make it?"

"You always have that option, and you'll then be on your own, but the trail is well defined and it would be very difficult to get lost. We'll take our time, so you should be fine. We'll be out for about for about six to eight hours. I'll stop now and then to give you a breather and explain a little about where we are, what to look for, and so on. And if you have any questions on the way or see anything, please feel free to ask or share. All set? Good, let's go."

And so we started.

Hanna looked at me. "Don't worry. You can always turn around." And she walked off by herself.

"Maybe we should have started with an easier hike?" I called to her.

Rebecca overheard and said, "There aren't really any 'easy' hikes here in Glacier, just some shorter ones. You'll be fine."

We trekked along in silence through high brush on a fairly smooth dirt and rock trail that was relatively easy walking. An hour or so out, coming around a corner, we came across what looked like a small plowed field, as if somebody planned to plant a garden.

Rebecca stopped. "This is where a bear was digging for roots."

"You're kidding, looks more like somebody used a plow," I said.

"Yeah, I know. Growing up in Iowa, I had a hard time believing it was bears, too."

"You're an Iowan?" I said. "Where'd you grow up?"

"Up north of Iowa City in a little town, Mount Vernon."

We began walking again, and I moved up beside her. "I grew up southeast of Iowa City. I drove through Mount Vernon a few times, I remember, with my parents."

We continued walking and reminiscing about growing up: me on a farm and her in town, one of two children of a college-professor father and a writer mother. I found myself so engrossed in talking with Rebecca that I lost track of time. She taught middle school in Missoula and worked here at the park during summers. We were the same age and had crossed paths many times in our early years. Finally Rebecca broke our conversation, needing to check on the rest of the group. Everyone was doing fine except for Hanna, who glared at me.

I fell back alongside her. "So, how're you doing?"

"Fine! Just fine!" she replied tersely.

"You're acting strange. What's bothering you?"

"Nothing!"

I walked along beside her, neither one of us talking. I wondered what was going on. Was she irritated that I talked with Rebecca? But this had all begun yesterday.

After a while, I said, "I'm sorry for whatever I did because I must have done something to upset you. I'm sorry."

"Fine! Why don't you go on and walk with your new friend?"

"What? We were just talking about growing up thirty miles apart, about some of the same people we used to know, same places we hung out sometimes. What was wrong with that?"

"Nothing! Just nothing!"

I let it slide and walked in silence up the trail that had now entered a pine forest. The scenery was stunning, and I elected to pay attention to my surroundings rather than the drama that seemed to be unfolding between Hanna and me. She dropped back and struck up a conversation with the woman from Oregon. So I walked alone—in a gathering funk.

As we gained altitude, breathing became harder, and I was almost panting. I noticed the couple from Minnesota were having the same issues. Rebecca saw we were having problems and told us we'd take a short break, have a snack and some water, and get our breath. A few rocks lay scattered around, and Hanna and her new companion sat down, talking intently. I stood aside, ignoring everyone, and looked out over the vastness of the park. Up ahead, the forest ran out, opening onto a stark-grey area walled in on three sides by mountains.

Up and going again, I followed along by myself. Everyone else chatted away with each other while my funk deepened. What the hell was going on with her? She was apparently having a good time, now engaged with the couple from Durango, acting like I didn't exist.

I noticed a movement on a rocky shelf above us to the right, and I caught up with Rebecca and told her. She stopped, got out her binoculars, and looked where I pointed.

"I think it's a wolverine; here, look."

I took her binoculars, adjusted them, and saw a black, slinky-looking form. "What's a wolverine?"

"It's rare and very hard to spot one." She turned to the others. "Hey everyone, check this out. I think Russell spotted a wolverine."

The couple from St. Paul had their own set of binoculars, and the others came up to share Rebecca's, looking to where she directed them, while she explained that it was a short carnivore resembling a bear, very solitary, and a nasty fighter, capable of bringing down much larger animals. It inhabited the northern climes but was rare due to trapping and loss of habitat.

"Good spotting, Russell. You have a good eye," Rebecca said.

I smiled and looked at Hanna. She glared back at me. I shrugged and turned away, focusing on the moonscape environment. The trail now clung to the side of a very steep slope and continued around several switchbacks, steadily upward. Rebecca explained that the tree line up here sat at around 6,000 to 6,900 feet. Above that elevation, trees couldn't survive due to the very short growing season and the harsh winters. She compared that to Colorado where the tree line would be around 11,000 feet.

As our party continued up the trail, breathing became more and more difficult, causing us to stop more often to get our breath. The couple from Durango and Rebecca appeared to be doing fine. The trail began to level out and a low man-made rock wall appeared immediately ahead of us. Around a little corner we came to the Ptarmigan Tunnel. We proceeded through open steel doors and through the 250-foot-long tunnel and were greeted by a view into the Belly River Valley, that went on seemingly forever north into Canada. We stood at dizzying heights above red-rock cliffs, a beautiful lake, and pine forests. The trail continued on to the right with a low stone wall on the edge of a sheer drop-off. Rebecca told us that the tunnel was built in 1930 through the Ptarmigan Wall to allow horseback tours of the park.

The group marveled at the view and took the requisite pictures and selfies. I wandered over to Hanna and asked her how she was doing and if I could take her picture.

She smiled. "Yeah, I'm great. Wow, what a hike, and the view here is so worth it. Let's get one of us together." She turned to the woman from Oregon. "Hey, Amy, will you take our picture?"

"Sure." She looked at me with a big grin and extended her hand. "Hi, I'm Amy. Hanna told me all about you."

I immediately wondered what "all about you" included as I extended my hand. "Nice to meet you too, Amy."

"Let's get one of all three of us," Amy said, and she went over and asked the woman from Durango if she'd take it.

The three of us stood with our backs to the emptiness as we and our big smiles of triumph were digitally recorded. I had no idea what was going on. Hanna was cold and had ignored me for almost four hours while we trekked up here. Now, it was like everything was all normal again. But on the way down, she again reverted to chatting happily with her new friend, Amy, once again ignoring me. I didn't understand what was going on. Had I done something? It occurred to me, had I ever really understood Dana? Or ever really paid her the attention she deserved? Was I doing the same with Hanna?

The hike down was much easier and faster. Excited from the experience, the group chatted with each other, already reminiscing about our adventure as if we'd scaled Everest. I walked alone behind Hanna and Amy, who talked non-stop. I felt alone and in a bigger funk.

Back at camp, I realized how weary I was and went to clean up in a pay shower behind the camp store and restaurant. The hot water washed away the tiredness, refreshing my body but not my spirit.

It was still light out and pleasantly warm when we returned to our camp. I asked Hannah if she wanted to go to the restaurant for dinner to celebrate our trek. She gave me an ambivalent shrug. Later when I asked if she wanted to play some music, she declined. When we crawled into bed, she stayed as far away from me as she could—no good night kiss or even a "good night."

The next morning, we left early for the Swift Current Lodge area for a hike up to Grinnell Glacier, named after George Bird Grinnell, an explorer and a strong advocate in the creation of Glacier Park. The glacier, like most in the Rocky Mountains, is receding and will eventually disappear.

The hike began in trees along Swift Current Lake, then along Lake Josephine, after which we started rising. My legs were tired from the hike the day before, but once we got going, the tiredness disappeared and we continued up the wide trail, bordered on the right by a mountainside and a very steep drop-off to our left. We hugged the rock wall, watching our steps, as we gained elevation and stopped often to take in the vista to our left, and to catch our breath.

We came to a waterfall and had to put on our rain gear to get through without getting soaked. Eventually we arrived at the last of several switchbacks that gave a view of the cirque surrounding Upper Grinnell Lake and the peaks and glaciers above. Several bighorn sheep ambled about the rocks. We proceeded up to the glacier above the lake. Looking back the way we'd hiked, I saw the deep valley bordered by craggy mountains, some higher ones still with snow, all under a clear blue sky.

I felt exhilarated. It all just kept getting better. Maybe it was like reaching enlightenment that I'd read about in the recent books on Buddhism. Then I remembered Hanna telling me, "After enlightenment, chop wood, carry water." I'd have to go back to real life at some point, but for now I'd dwell in this feeling of pure joy.

Hanna was in her mood from yesterday, not talking, seeming not aware of my presence.

"I'd just love to stay here forever," I said. "It's so wonderful."

"Fine. Stay, then. I'm heading back down."

"Hanna, what's going on? Did I do something else to make you angry? Can I do anything?"

"No. I'm fine. Just stay. I'll meet you back at the van ... whenever."

She turned and walked away, crushing my happy mood and replacing it with anxiety.

"Hanna, wait. Talk to me. Something's going on here, and I'm at a loss; I don't know why!"

She just hurried on ahead of me.

My heart sank, and I let her go.

We arrived back at the van and drove back to camp. We didn't talk on the way back. I felt nervous and didn't know what to say.

It was late when I got back from a shower, so I made sandwiches for dinner. Hanna returned, took a sandwich, and went off by herself.

She returned a bit later and said, "I'm going to set up my tent and sleep out here tonight."

"What? What's going on? Why are you acting this way?"

"I just want to be alone tonight. Please, just leave me alone! Okay?"

"Okay, then, but I don't understand ... but do what you need to do."

And with that she set up her tent, moved her things in, then climbed in without even a "good night."

After taking a sleeping pill, the first I'd had in weeks, I fell into a dreamless night, and awoke early with a headache, realizing Hanna wasn't there. I remembered she was in her tent, but when I got up and looked out, her tent was gone; her things were gone; she was gone. I went out and looked around, but she could've been anywhere in the campground. I dressed quickly and went out to look for her, then I noticed that Amy's camp, four spaces away, was empty. I noticed a piece of paper stuck under a wiper blade.

Russell, I'm very sorry, but I care about you too much to stay with you. You're the best guy I've ever known, and I'll only hurt you if we stay together. There are some things I needed to tell you, but did not have the courage to do. It'll be better for both of us this way. I'm getting a ride with Amy. All my best for everything you ever do. I love you. Hanna

I stood there in shock, staring off into space, not seeing anything. How could she just leave like that? *I love you …?* What the fuck did that mean when she just up and leaves like that? She said she wouldn't leave. She wanted to be with me. What the fuck was happening?

I sent her a text to her. *Where r u? Please tell me so I can see you and talk.* And then I realized there was no cell service. Dammit!

I took a folding chair and sat in the cold pine-scented air, closed my eyes, let my mind settle, and tried to figure things out, which proved fruitless. What's to figure out? She's gone. My chin quivered and tears welled in my eyes. I shook in panic.

I tried to eat something and have a cup of coffee. I needed to plan a course of action but hadn't a clue what to do. All I wanted was to leave this place, go find her. There was too much history in the three short weeks we'd been together. She'd shown me and given me so much, helped me realize that I didn't have to be in the life I'd been leading. I'd learned that I could do things differently, that I could be different.

After looking at the guide book for the park, not knowing what else to do, I decided to go over to west side to find a place to camp, thinking I might catch her somewhere. I packed up the van, let the campground host know I was leaving early so the spot was open, and drove out of the park and down to the St. Mary Visitor Center.

There was cell and WiFi service there. My text went out, and I checked my emails. I had several dozen. Most I just erased, but I read the few from Karen and my old boss in Chicago. I answered them both, letting them know where I was and that I was okay, and that I'd be out of cell service for maybe another week. I wanted to talk to Karen, but knew she'd be working. In my email, I told her to tell Mom and Dad that I was doing okay and missed them all.

I texted Hanna again: *WHERE ARE YOU? ARE YOU OKAY? I miss you and need to talk to you. I'm worried about you. You know I care for you. I need to know what's wrong. Please text me.*

I talked to the woman at the information kiosk and got information about camping on the west side of the park. Several spots were open at Apgar, so I reserved one for the next few days and headed up The Going to the Sun Road.

The road went for a number of miles along St. Mary Lake, then started up to Logan Pass. I took my time, enjoying the beauty of the place, trying not to think of Hanna, but she was always in the back of my mind. I wondered where she was, if she was okay, and if I'd ever see her again. I kept wondering what I'd done to cause her to leave like she did. She said she loved me. What does that mean when she left? My chest felt heavy and empty.

There were several view areas and pull-outs along the way, and I stopped at every one, taking my time, wishing Hanna was with me to see it and share the experience, and wondering if she and Amy had gone this way. I got to the pass and went into the visitors' center parking lot, but it was full. After a pass through the lot I headed down the west side towards Apgar.

I saw a parking spot at the Hidden Lake Trail Head, pulled in, and did the short hike to the lake. Again, the scenery was unbelievable.

I continued on down the precarious, narrow road by the Weeping Wall, where water seemed to come directly out of the rock face, then on down around a sharp hairpin and stopped at the Trail of the Cedars Trailhead. It was early afternoon, so I hiked up to Avalanche Lake, trying to calm myself. The trail wound through a dense forest of hemlock and cedar trees onto a boardwalk in an area of wetlands, much different from the arid east side of the park. Avalanche Lake nestled in a deep valley where families and kids played in the water and others just sat in the ambiance. I tried to enjoy it but sat there feeling sad, confused, and alone.

After the hike, I drove to the west end of Lake McDonald and found Apgar Visitor Center, Village, and Campground. I checked in, found my camping spot, and walked around the village and down by the lake. Several times I thought I saw Hanna, but it was never her.

Now late afternoon and not having eaten since breakfast, I went into a village restaurant for dinner. The hostess showed me to a table for two and gave me a menu. A young, well-trimmed waiter asked about drinks. I ordered a margarita and water and looked at the menu, deciding on a house-special ribeye steak with fries and salad. The restaurant filled quickly after I'd been seated and a line formed outside. The hostess came by and asked if I'd mind if another single customer joined me. I considered for a moment, not really wanting company, but agreed. The hostess returned followed by a tall, slender, extremely attractive woman who looked to be a little older than me, maybe mid-thirties. She had bobbed blond hair, turquoise-blue eyes, and a beautiful smile. Though dressed in typical Glacier Park apparel of hiking boots, shorts, and t-shirt, she had an air of elegance about her. A large turquoise-stone amulet at her throat matched her eyes.

She gave me a killer smile. "Thank you so much for sharing. I'm Cassandra, but everyone calls me Cassy."

"Nice to meet you Cassy, I'm Russ." *I never let myself be called Russ … ever.*

She jumped into the menu. "I'm starved. What're you having?"

"The ribeye."

"Sounds good. I've been out all day and only had a power bar and some trail mix. What did you do?"

I told her of my drive over the pass, not saying anything about Hanna.

"Where're you from, Russ?"

"Chicago," I said without really thinking. "How about you?"

"Boulder, Colorado, but originally from New York City where I grew up. I teach history of dance, as well as modern dance, in Boulder at the University. Are you on vacation?"

"Well, sort of in between jobs right now and taking some time off this summer. You off for the summer?"

"Yeah. Done for the semester and just got through a nasty divorce and needed time to be out by myself and get over all the shit."

"Well, the truth of the matter is that I went through a divorce a little over a year ago and am sort of exploring right now, trying to figure out my life, so I can understand." I wondered at myself for sharing so much information.

Our drinks came, and we continued sharing information about ourselves. Cassie's mother was a dancer in a modern-dance company and was now teaching. Her father was a renowned violinist, who played throughout Europe and America, both solo and with some chamber orchestras. She was brought up on dance, but due to an injury early on in her career she couldn't sustain the rigors of being a professional, so she went to school and got her Ph.D. in History of Dance.

Her pedigree both impressed and intimidated me. I went on to tell her that I'd been in finance and then about being raised on a farm in Iowa. She was actually impressed to meet a "real person", as she put it.

"I grew up surrounded by performers, musicians, artists, and such. Many were overly impressed with themselves. That's why I'm happy to have landed this job in Boulder. The people there are much more in touch with, well, I guess more important things, ah, like the outdoors, being fit, spirituality, you know."

Our food came, and I ordered us a bottle of wine. I found myself enjoying her company. She was smart and vivacious and self-assured. We continued talking about our lives as we ate. She kept looking at me, as if she were studying me; maybe that's what Ph.Ds did—never knew one before.

While she chatted on seemingly endlessly about herself, she also kept me in the conversation with her questions and acted interested about who I was. I never mentioned Hanna, and lied when I told her I'd been traveling solo.

Dinner ended and we sat, finishing the wine. The bottle empty, we paid our respective bills.

"Where're you staying, Russ?"

"I'm in the campground here; how about you?"

"Yeah, me too," she replied. "I'd like to walk down by the lake before going to my camper. Want to come?"

"Sure."

The long, narrow lake stretched up the valley, serene and peaceful, unlike my troubled mind. As we walked, I kept looking for Hanna. What if Hanna was there and saw me with Cassy?

"Are you okay?" she asked, maybe sensing my uneasiness.

"Yeah, just entranced by the beauty of this place," I lied.

After sitting for a while on a shore-side bench, we decide to head to the campground. Surprisingly, she took my arm. I felt awkward, but obliged her.

"Where's your site?" I asked.

"Right over here."

Her spot was directly behind mine. We both laughed at the coincidence.

"Want to grab a chair and join me for a while?" she asked.

"Sure, that'd be nice. It's fun talking to you. That's a nice rig you have," I said upon seeing her Mercedes campervan.

"It's not mine. I rented it for six weeks from a colleague, and he gave me a great deal. Very comfy. Want to check it out?"

"Totally." It was well appointed and much roomier than the Westy. I could even stand up in it without hitting my head the way I did in the Westy even after I'd raised my pop-up top.

"Go sit. I'll be out in a second."

After a moment she came and joined me, having put on a fleece top against the evening chill that had settled in. From her pocket she pulled out what looked like a pen and asked, "Want a hit?"

"A hit?"

"Yeah, it's a hash-oil vape pen. It's like highly concentrated marijuana in an oil form."

A little dumbfounded, I said, "I've never smoked marijuana before. What's it like?"

"It mellows me out, relaxes me. I'm careful not to do too much and get numb like when I used to get really stoned back in my younger days. This is much more potent but much milder than smoking actual buds."

I knew nothing about marijuana, but obliged her by giving it a try. I found it surprisingly mild and easy to inhale with only some minor coughing.

I was about to take another drag, but she took it from me, saying, "Just start slowly."

She took a nice long pull, put her head back and slowly exhaled. "I'm so happy this is legal in Colorado now. We used to smoke weed when I was in college, and even some in grad school, but you never knew what you were getting off the street, some good, some not so much."

A deep relaxation settled over me, and we both sat, not saying anything.

"I'm getting chilled. Let's go in the van," she said.

"Sure." I got up, feeling a little disoriented but clear in my head. *Interesting. Very interesting.*

She led me in and we sat next to each other on her bed. The next thing I knew, she turned to me, pulled me to her, and kissed me. It wasn't just any kiss, but a deep lingering kiss. I was surprised when her tongue went into my mouth. I did the same to her. All my built-up sexual frustration exploded. I went out of my mind with passion and desire. Immediately she undressed me, and I undressed her. It was like a movie I saw once. We were suddenly naked, and the next hour was amazing.

I'd never had such crazy, amazing sex. She did so many things to me I never knew women would do. She showed me things, told me what she wanted, where to touch her, how to touch her. So many things this woman wanted that I couldn't believe. I responded to everything with abandon. It could have been the wine, the marijuana, sexual frustration or all the above.

I released all the sexual desires I had with Hanna and then some. Our passion completed, we lay naked, wrapped in our post-coital bliss for, I don't really know, maybe ten minutes or maybe an hour.

While Dana was like a 1960's Volkswagen Beetle, Cassandra was like a Lamborghini. When Dana and I got married, neither of us had ever had sex before. Neither of us knew what to do, what we wanted, what gave us pleasure. It was mechanical at best.

"Russ, that was great. Thank you. I knew when I sat down with you that you were someone I'd like and want to make love with. Thanks. I needed that release."

"You're welcome. Thank you. I'm sorry. I'm really not that experienced."

"I know. But you were receptive to me. That's all I wanted."

I lay awake, feeling sexually inadequate and guilty as if I'd betrayed Hanna. But I told myself that it was she who'd left me. I didn't owe her anything. I never left Cassy's camper that night.

Still naked when we awoke, we made love again, more slowly and deliberately.

"So, what are your plans for today?" I asked.

"Hike the Highline Trail."

"Mind if I join you?"

"Not at all."

We dressed, had a quick breakfast, and were ready to go.

"I'll drive if you want," I said.

"Thanks. I'd like to ride and just enjoy the scenery."

We arrived early to find the parking lot at Logan Pass almost deserted. We headed out on the trail, deciding to go to the Granite Park Chalet, roughly seven-and-a-half miles. My legs felt fresh from an easy day yesterday, and we decided we could do the fifteen-mile out and back.

The trail followed the Continental Divide along what's known as the Garden Wall, a sheer incline covered with vegetation rising high above the trail, and with views on the other side far out to the west as far as one can see. We came to where the trail narrowed along a sheer drop-off on our left, only six to eight feet wide, which I thought less scary than the hike to Grinnell Glacier. Cassy, however, apparently nervous, kept to the inside and held onto the cable provided as a support.

We hiked in silence. All I could think of was Hanna. I felt guilty and a little uncomfortable with this strange woman. I'd become comfortable with Hanna's company. It felt strange and disconcerting being with Cassy.

At a steep section, which, I'd read, climbed about 300 feet to Haystack Pass, we rounded a corner and came face to face with a very large mountain goat lying on a large rock. We stopped and looked at him. He turned and looked at us, saying in mountain-goat body language that this was his rock, but he'd let us go on by, which we did after he posed for several quick pictures.

Some seven miles and three hours later, we came to a fork in the trail. I'd read that if we went up, about a 600-feet climb in a little over a half a mile, we would have a view overlooking Salamander and Grinnell Glaciers, so we decided to do it. At the top, we stopped to sit and rest on the edge of what seemed to be a thousand-foot steep slope to the glaciers below.

We were drinking water and eating snacks when Cassy said quietly, "Slowly, very slowly, look to your left."

I looked as she instructed. A large bighorn sheep glared at us from probably less than thirty feet away. Neither of us moved a muscle. All three of us stayed frozen for what seemed to me an eternity. Suddenly the sheep started to walk gingerly around us, and when he was directly behind about ten feet away, he bolted, kicking up rock and sand in his wake, scampering along the edge where we sat. On looking more closely, we saw a trail in the fine sandy soil. Apparently we'd been blocking his way. Thankfully he had the courtesy to go around rather than headbutting us over the edge with his huge horns.

After the incident, we both laughed, then left his trail and headed back down, getting to the chalet a short time later. The Great Northern Railway built this historic building, along with many other facilities, to provide accommodations to lure passengers from the East to visit the park. Guest rooms were available by reservation only, but with no amenities other than a common kitchen with a gas stove. One could purchase snacks and bottled water.

From the porch, views spread out to the southwest over forested lands and, as always, mountains and more mountains. After our respite, it was time to leave.

"Man, I'm not in as good a shape as I thought I was," I said as we headed back.

"Neither am I," Cassy said. "We can hike on down to the loop on the road and hitch back up to the parking lot. It's downhill and a bit shorter."

"I'm definitely up for a downhill. My legs are already thanking me."

The scenery on the hike down was less spectacular, so we hiked quickly and deliberately through the brush and trees bordering the trail, making it to the road in less than three hours. I was dead tired, thankful we'd not hiked the seven-and-a-half miles back on the Highline. At the switchback, we stuck out our thumbs and soon had a ride back up to the pass in the back of a pickup.

Back at the campground after a shower, we agreed to have dinner again that night at the same restaurant. I felt tired, but better after the hot shower and clean clothes.

After dinner we again strolled down by the lake. She took my hand as we walked, making me wonder where this was going with her.

"You realize, Russ, that this is nothing permanent with us. I'm heading out tomorrow for Yellowstone and the Tetons. What're your plans?"

Feeling relived that she'd answered my question, I said, "I'm leaving tomorrow as well … and, yeah, I figured we were only together for last night."

"And tonight?"

"And tonight, if you wish."

"I wish."

I really had no idea what or where I was going, but I knew I was ready to leave. "I'm thinking of heading south, down into Idaho and see where I might end up."

What? I don't have a plan? I always have a plan.

After another night and morning of great sex, we bid our goodbyes. "If you're ever in Boulder," she said, "look me up. Where are you going to land after your trip?"

I realized I had no idea where I'd land. "I really don't know, Cassy. I guess wherever I land."

We exchanged our cell phone numbers and parted. I knew I'd probably never see her again. A two-night stand. That's a new one for me. I felt like I needed a long hot shower.

Chapter 17: To Idaho

I left the park in the early morning and drove through the little tourist town of West Glacier into more open space. I enjoyed the open road, even without Hanna by my side. After electing to go down the east side of Flathead Lake, I came to the little town of Bigfork right at the north end—a quaint little place with interesting shops on the main street. They had an art fair on, so I found a place to park and strolled through the fair, looking at the various artists' and craftsmen's booths. I heard flute music coming from up the street, and as I got closer, I saw a booth with three sides lined with strange-looking wooden flutes. A fellow played the music that, like the Pied Piper, had lured me in.

"Hi, I'm Greg, the artist. Can I show you some flutes?"

"What are they? I've never seen flutes like these before."

"They're copied from the flutes that the Native Americans played a long time ago. They've experienced a revival. They're all over the gift shops out here now."

"Guess I haven't been in many gift shops."

"Well, while a lot of white folks make these along with a growing number of Native American artists, I'm probably the only white guy who's actually had an okay from two tribal elders. I taught school on the local tribal reservation for a number of years, so I knew a lot of the folks and got along very well. Made a number of close friends, and that's probably why I was given permission to do this. I also teach the kids how to make the flutes. Where're you from?"

"Chicago," I replied, thinking I wasn't going to San Francisco now.

Greg played a little for me, showed me several flutes, and explained his building process and how they work. He then pulled out a short piece of neoprene hose—for sanitary reasons, he explained—inserted it into the end of a flute tuned to a pentatonic major C and gave it to me to try. I noodled around on it for a few minutes and found it sweet and soothing to both play and listen to—plus, being in a pentatonic scale, it was also very easy. Greg had made a sale. I also bought a little buckskin bag to carry it in, along with two CDs of flute music by a Native American musician he knew.

I walked around the festival for another hour or so, had some food from Amelie's food truck, then continued my drive south along the eastern shore of Flathead Lake, a dense pine forest on my left and the lake on my right.

I started thinking again about where I was going and what I was going to do. I was tired of national parks. I wanted something, but didn't know what. The thoughts of going back to Chicago or back to my hometown turned my stomach. The fear of loneliness seemed to have faded a bit, and I felt more secure being by myself. Hell, it would be interesting to just be alone and see what happens, maybe see if I could even manage on my own.

I came to the end of Flathead Lake and kept on a southbound course, hit I-90 for a few miles, then turned off into Missoula. I pulled over in a shopping-center parking lot to check for campgrounds and found one south of town about halfway to Hamilton. I called and reserved a spot for the night. Still early afternoon, I drove around the town through older neighborhoods, eventually, by chance, running into the University of Montana campus. I parked and strolled the campus, now deserted for the summer but for a few summer-school students, a few grad students, and dedicated professors.

Remembering my undergraduate days, I felt a bit envious of the students and their freshness. I always worked so hard, I hadn't taken the time to really absorb what I was learning at the time. I could hardly remember most of the courses I took. What a waste.

I wandered into campus town and came across a bookstore. Along with the usual textbooks, they also had a good literature section. I found a Hemingway novel *The Sun Also Rises*, and though I remembered having read Hemingway in sophomore literature, I couldn't remember that title. I also found a book on the Native American flute. Then I found one in the New Age section titled *When You Wake Up, You Can't Go Back*. I remembered Hanna had used those very words with me, and a sharp pang ran through my heart. I bought all three and left.

I happened across a pizza house and, now hungry, went in, sat on the patio out back, and ordered a beer and a personal size pizza. I noticed a man and a woman setting up sound equipment on a little stage in the corner.

My beer came and I asked, "So, is there music tonight?"

"Yeah, we have music every Friday night, six to nine, even in the summer. Mostly local groups, folk-type stuff, ya know."

The male (guitar)/female (violin and mandolin) duo did a quick sound check and began playing a lilting instrumental, then into a song where the woman sang lead and her partner, harmonies. They were good, really good. I thought of playing with Hanna those few times and felt sad and empty, like part of me was suddenly missing.

The pizza came and I sat, eating slowly, listening. Food finished, I ordered another beer, thinking that it could be Hanna and me up there. I finished my second beer and pulled myself away, realizing that if I stayed, I'd get stinking drunk. I needed to check in at the campground.

Once settled in my pleasant, tree-shaded camping spot, I sat and wrote in my journal until dark, which at this latitude and at solstice time, was around nine-thirty. Before I crawled into bed, I checked my phone and discovered a text from Hanna. She sent the picture of us at the Ptarmigan Tunnel and a short message: *Miss you and love you. I'm fine.* That was it. I texted her back; *Please, where are you?* My heart pounded, and I lay awake, thinking about her, feeling an emptiness I'd never known. There was no response.

After a restless, dreamless sleep, I called Karen since it was Saturday and she wouldn't be working. She answered after several rings.

"Russell, where are you? I got your email from a few days ago. Are you heading home?"

"I'm in Missoula, Montana, and heading down into Idaho tomorrow. I've been out of cell service since we last talked, and I'll probably be in and out of cell service the next few days, but text me anytime, and I'll answer when I can connect. I'm not planning to head your way for a while."

"Well, we miss you and are worried about you. Please call Mom and Dad. They're concerned as always."

"I'm sorry, they shouldn't be. I'm really doing fine. I feel I'm finally being able to grow up. Do you know I'm going to Idaho and don't even have a plan? I have no idea where I'll end up. It's scary, but fun. I just love it out here. You and John need to come out here with the kids. It's so amazing."

"I'm sure it is, but I have responsibilities here, unlike some people," she said dismissively.

I didn't want to argue with her, so let the comment slide and said, "I have to go, Karen. I'll be in touch soon. Tell everyone 'hi' for me. Take care. Love you."

"Goodbye, and call your parents!" she said coldly and clicked off.

A latch on a cabinet in the Westy had broken, and when I drove by a recreational vehicle sales lot and store, I stopped and found a latch that would work. While looking around the store, I spied different sizes of solar panels for RVs. The smaller one I looked at could easily be hooked up to my battery. Then I could use my lights and charge my phone and computer without fear of draining my battery if I was dry camping—camping without the benefit of electrical hookups—so I bought the panel along with my latch.

I headed down south, passing by the turnoff to Lolo Pass where Lewis and Clarke had traveled back in the day. I'd had enough of historic sites, so I continued on down through Hamilton, over a pass, and on into Idaho. The road was mountainous driving for the most part, but in good shape, and I made good time. At the town of Salmon, I stopped for gas and a potty break, got some coffee, then continued on through the town, which sat on the Salmon River and provided rafting companies, fishing and sports outfitters, bars, and restaurants for tourists looking for adventure.

I continued on into a canyon along the Salmon River towards the town of Challis, then Stanley, seeing rafters on the river along the way. The still-snowcapped Sawtooth Mountains appeared to the west, living up to their name, looking like I felt: rough, craggy, dark, foreboding, lonely, empty, and cold.

Highway 75 turned south into an expansive valley of grass and sage that ran up the high, rolling hills to the east, with the Sawtooth Mountains on the right. I drove through Smiley Creek, by the headwaters of the Salmon River (a.k.a. the River of No Return), up over Galena Pass, and then downhill for miles, until I saw a National Forest Information Center, where I got information on campgrounds and trails in the area.

I decided to stay in a Forest Service campground north of Ketchum and found a spot for a week's stay. The next day, desperately needing to do laundry and get groceries, I went into the bustling town of Ketchum but saw nothing except sports stores, bars, galleries, and restaurants. After asking a local, I found a grocery store and laundromat. I laundered and stocked up with what I needed for a week, then drove north back to the campground.

I spent the next week alone, doing hikes, writing in my journal, reading, learning my neglected mandolin and my new flute. I couldn't pull out my guitar. Somehow it reminded me too much of Hanna. The campground had a number of visitors, but most tended to themselves and respected my privacy and I, theirs. My heart ached.

I engaged in a week of reflection about this trip and what I was discovering, both without and within. My sleep was off. I lay awake at night not able to doze off and realized I was slipping back into depression. I started back on my anti-depressants and sleep meds.

Mornings began with an hour's meditation as did the night with another hour before bed. I saw a number of people when I was hiking, but other than cursory greetings, I had no human contact—sort of a self-imposed retreat. The days passed slowly as if time itself had slowed.

I realized ever more strongly that my life would never be the same. Maybe I truly was waking up and could never go back. I resolved to call my folks. And I needed to check to see if I'd received anything from Hanna. I didn't have cell service at the camp, so on Saturday, I drove down to Ketchum.

Chapter 18: Ketchum

I'd received nothing from Hanna, so I texted her again. Then I called her, but the call went right to voice mail.

Sitting in the Westy, I hesitated, then called my parents.

"Hi, Mom. It's Russ; how are you?"

"Wondering where you are. And what's with 'Russ'? We named you Russell. That's your name. Are you headed home?"

"No, Mom. I'm in Idaho and not quite sure where I'm headed. Might hang around here for a while."

"Well, I think you've had enough gallivanting around and need to get home. I talked to Dana last week. She's not with that woman anymore. I think she regrets leaving you. You should call her. You can get back here and to your job in Chicago, get back to your real life. Not this irresponsible trip you're doing. I just don't know what is wrong with you."

I managed to break in when she took a breath: "You what? You called Dana? What's wrong with you? Really? How dare you! That's just wrong on so many levels!"

"Wrong? Wrong to realize how foolish you're acting? Wrong to want you to be a responsible child like your brother and sister? Wrong to want you to be the man we raised you to be?"

"Yes, Mom," I said as gently as I could, "it is wrong. You've tried to run my life forever, and it's time for you to let go. I'm sorry you feel this way, but I'm not coming back anytime soon.

I'm not getting back together with Dana, and I'm probably not going back to Chicago. I'm not your little boy anymore. I'm sorry, but I have to go now." I disconnected.

I took several deep breaths and let it go. Somewhere in my travels, I had maybe crossed a point of no return. I didn't want to return to my former life defined and confined by my family. But I hadn't a clue where I was headed. I was scared to death.

* * *

The trails around Ketchum were not nearly as rough and rocky as in the Rockies, and the hiking boots I had were heavier than I thought I needed. I wanted to get a lighter shoe and found a sports shoe store, where I explained to a young salesman what I wanted.

"You have two choices," he told me, "a low-cut hiking shoe, which is pretty much the same version of what you have. You'd save a little weight with those but not much. Or you could consider a trail running shoe which is much lighter, offer the same support and protection to the sole of your foot, and you can either hike or run in them."

"A trail running shoe?"

"Yeah, there's a lot of folks that like to run on our trails. There's a lot more opportunities than just the paved trail that goes down south. That can get pretty boring."

"So, do you run?" I asked.

"I do. Actually, I run ultra-marathons, which are anywhere from thirty miles and upward, all on trails; some can be pretty gnarly. But the new technology for the shoes is really amazing, Want to try a pair? What's your size?"

"I'm a thirteen, and yeah, I'd like to try a pair of those trail runners."

181

The salesman went to the back room. *Trail running? It sounds crazy, but might get me in shape.* He reappeared with three shoe boxes. I tried on all three and settled on a pair.

"These really are nice … comfortable, and light," I said. "What else do I need for trail running?"

"So you're interested?"

"Maybe."

"Well, first off, I'd recommend some running shorts." He took me to a display and showed me several pairs. I selected the pair he recommended and a light quick-dry t-shirt. He also recommended a running vest.

"I have a day pack," I said.

"Yeah, they're all right, but the vest fits snugger, not as heavy and won't bounce. It has a water bladder and pockets for energy bars and gel."

"Gel?"

"Like a liquid energy bar, and smaller."

I bought everything. Trail running? It would get me into better shape. "So, can I run on any trails? Are there some you recommend?"

"Tell you what, there's a group run every Wednesday night at six and one on Saturday mornings at nine. You should join us."

"Me, I never ran before in my life. I'd never keep up."

"There are all different levels, and you can start at the beginning and work up. It's a good group of both men and women. Some of us can help you with running, like style, form, stretching, things like that. Come meet us Wednesday or Saturday at the Whitney trailhead. Where are you staying?"

"I'm camped about ten miles north of town. Maybe I'll come on Wednesday."

"Great. Meet me here at the store around five-thirty and you can follow me out. Afterwards, most of us go out for burgers and beer. See you then. By the way, my name's Mike."

"I'm Russ. Good to meet you, Mike. I'll try to make it. And, hey, are there any campgrounds around with electrical hookups and WiFi service?"

"There's the one south of town between here and Hailey. You might try there."

"Thanks, I'll check it out."

I visited the campground, which was only a few miles south of town. There weren't any slots available until Monday, but I reserved one from then for the next four weeks. As I was leaving, I noticed a camper trailer and pickup for sale. I stopped and checked them out. The pickup was a newer-model Dodge diesel. The trailer looked to be new as well. My two nights in Cassy's luxurious Mercedes had been inspirational. I went back and asked the manager about them.

"It's one heck of a deal," he said. "Some wealthy guy up in Sun Valley thought he and his wife would like to be road warriors. His wife lasted two weeks, and that was that. He left them here for me to sell. Truck's hardly been broken in. The trailer is last year's model. Know anything about them?"

"Not a clue. Can I take a look?"

"Sure."

We walked out, and he showed me the trailer first. I followed him up three steps and inside. He pushed a button and part of the side opened up, making the room larger. I looked around the main level and took in two comfortable-looking reclining chairs, a nook with a booth and table, a small flat screen TV, a large fridge with a freezer, and a kitchen sink with a faucet. Up a short flight of stairs, I discovered a queen-size bed, ample closets and drawers, a shower, and a toilet.

We went outside and he explained how everything worked: electrical hookups, storage, propane and how to hook it up with the truck.

"This is the lap of luxury after living in my Westfalia for the last month or so."

He laughed. "They're making these fifth wheelers really luxurious and light. And they're really easy to tow. Want to see the pickup?"

"Sure."

The pickup had only 35,000 miles on the odometer and still had the new-car smell. It had a Cummins diesel with a six speed Allison automatic transmission. The leather interior boasted a state-of-the-art sound system.

"So, how much to upgrade to luxury?" I asked.

He looked at me, and I imagined him thinking, *this ratty kid in a Westy van and he's asking how much?* I knew I looked ratty: my hair was getting really long, my clothes were certainly not upscale, and I hadn't shaved in over a week.

"So, how much?" I repeated.

"Well, it's really a deal. This guy doesn't care, just wants to get rid of it. It's probably worth seventy-five or eighty thousand, but he's asking only sixty-five."

"I'll have to think about it."

I had no idea why I was even thinking about something like this. Hanna liked the Westy. I felt it would be betraying her.

"Thanks for showing it to me. It's more than I need right now. I'll see you Monday to get my site." I went back north to the forest service campground.

Sunday morning, I donned my new running clothes and shoes and went out on an easy trail. I tried a fast trot and found myself out of breath after about a quarter mile. I remembered I was still at around 5,000 feet. Maybe I should go a little slower to begin this running thing. I got my breath and started out again, much slower. That was better. I continued with a slow jog for about half an hour and returned to camp.

Monday, I awoke stiff and sore. Yeah, Mike did mention stretching. I meditated, then packed up my camp and went into town, where I got a haircut and shave. Then, still too early to check into the campground, I found a coffee shop. I struck up a conversation with the barista, an attractive twenty-something woman.

"So, passing through or a local?"

"Sort of passing through, but here for a while, maybe a month or so."

Through the usual where-are-you-from, what-do-you-do kind of small talk, I discovered that she taught at an elementary school and worked at the coffee shop for the summer. Her name was Abby Preston, and she'd moved from Wisconsin three years ago. Customers came in and she became busy. I finished my coffee and was leaving when she called to me, "Hey, Russ, I'm off at noon. I'll buy lunch."

She seemed nice, easy to talk to, so I said, "How can I refuse a free lunch? Where?"

She named a small cafe and said she'd meet me at twelve-thirty. I had some time, so I tried texting Hanna again.

I browsed a bookstore about a block away as I'd read most of the books I'd bought recently. I found two novels, one by a French author and the other by a British author. The bookstore had a used book section, so I traded in my already read ones, then I found a bench in a shady park and read until shortly after noon when I went to meet Abby Preston.

Lunch was fun and filled with lively conversation. Afterwards, she asked me, "So, what are you doing the rest of the afternoon?"

"No plans."

"Want to go for a hike?

"Sure. I'd like that. Any place in particular you want to go?"

"Let's go up Trail Creek. There's a nice hike up there I like."

"Okay. I can drive, if you want."

Abby directed me east of the town. We went by the upscale Sun Valley area and then travelled a few more miles into a low valley surrounded by sage-covered hills. The few trees in this part of Idaho lived on the north sides of the hills where the snow lasted and kept the soil moist longer. She directed me up a side road to a parking area and we proceeded out on the north side of a hill forested with shorter pine trees, unlike the tall pines in Montana.

We walked in silence for a while.

"So, Abby, what's the deal?" I asked. "Lunch? A hike? Just meeting me? I might be a serial killer or worse."

"She laughed. "I don't think so. Truth is, being a grade-school teacher, just finishing my first year here, I haven't met any eligible men, at least any that I found interesting. Most are ski bums, outdoor thrill freaks wanting to have a YouTube video of their exploits go viral so they can have a moment of fame. I'm not into that stuff. You seemed like a normal sort of guy and not from here, so I figured you might just be fun to hang out with while you're here.

"And Ketchum's a small town. I don't hang in the bars and mess around. A parent sees me doing something they might find 'not up to standards' and, just like that, you know …"

"How well I do."

We hiked in silence again for over an hour through sage and forest, different from Yellowstone and Glacier, but beautiful in another way. We shared some more small talk, but mostly, remained lost in our thoughts. We returned to the van and went back to town. I drove to her condo.

"Want to come up for a while?" she asked, flirtatiously— more than flirtatiously.

I hesitated a moment. "Thanks, Abby, but I just got out of a relationship and am not ready for … for anything right now. I need to pass. I'm sorry. I liked today and enjoyed your company. And thanks. I'm sorry if I gave off any impression that—"

"No, I was being a bit presumptuous. You're a nice guy. Maybe … maybe friends, then?"

"Friends. Yeah. I'd like that. I'll see you at the coffee shop. I owe you a lunch."

She chuckled. "I'll hold you to it." She turned and went in, and I drove back to my camp. She was nice, but I didn't need or want another "Cassy experience."

Stocked up with groceries, I settled into the campground, now with WiFi and cell service. I'd received nothing from Hanna, but I remembered that Hanna had told me that her stepfather, Frank, liked to hang around City Lights Bookstore in San Francisco. I went online and googled it. *Maybe I can find out from Frank or Meg if they've heard from her.* I got the number and, taking a chance that he might still hang around there sometimes, called:

A man answered. "Hello, City Lights."

"Hi, would Frank possibly be around?"

"No, he was in last week. He might be here tomorrow for a poetry reading. Why? Who's this?"

"My name is Russell. He doesn't know me, but I'm a friend of his step-daughter, Hanna, and I haven't been able to reach her. Would you please give him this message and have him call me when you see him."

"Let me get a pen and write this down."

He came back on and I repeated it all and gave him my number. *Now to wait.*

* * *

I spent a week in the campground south of town. A giant motor home on my left and an even larger fifth-wheel trailer on my right dwarfed my Westy. I soon discovered that many of the folks here planned to stay for most, if not all, of the summer. Most were my parents' age, retired, living somewhere south in the winter and migrating north to escape the summer heat. They didn't quite know how to deal with me in my little van. Plus the men expected me to be friends and hang out with them, talking about old times or playing cards and drinking beer. The women wanted to mother me and make me cookies. I had no privacy. After only three days, I escaped to another forest service campground far away from the madding crowd.

After several weeks out in the boonies, I began a routine of coming into town on Friday nights and renting a motel room for two nights. Since summer was busy time and rooms could be scarce, if not totally unavailable, I learned to book ahead.

I showered, did laundry, and went for the Saturday morning trail run. I also found a meditation group that met Sunday mornings and joined in. It was a chance to catch up on emails, financials, and phone messages.

I saw Abby for coffee, lunch, a movie, a hike, or all of the above. I found her nice to be with and smart. We talked a lot about books we read, about life and adventures. But though I enjoyed her company, we were just friends, as we'd agreed early on. Deep down, I think we both wondered if anything might ever develop further. She also knew I had no idea where I was going or would end up and that I most likely wouldn't become a permanent resident of Ketchum.

During the week, I found new places to explore. I camped and hiked out in the Pioneer Mountains, the Sawtooths, out by Redfish Lake, up out of Galena Pass, out Trail Ridge Road, and some trails closer to town. At first I found it hard, but I gradually became more comfortable with being alone and enjoyed my solitude more and more. I was getting to know myself.

After about two weeks of doing my motel routine, I'd just returned to my room to clean up after the Saturday run and meet Abby for lunch when my phone chirped—a San Francisco number. I took a breath and answered.

"Is this Russell Henderson?" a woman asked.

"Yes; who's this?"

"Hello, Russell, this is Hanna's mother, Meg."

"O-my-God, Meg! Thanks for calling me back. Do you know where Hanna is? Have you heard from her? She left me about three weeks ago, and I'm worried about her. I've called her. Texted her. Never heard back. I don't know where she is."

"Neither do I, Russell. Neither do I." She sounded tired. "But I've gotten a few texts from her assuring me she's okay and not to worry. I have a pretty good idea what's going on, though—she's in love with you and is scared."

"What? Scared? What do you mean? Why?"

"Russell, she's told me all about you: 'He's the best guy I ever met. He's nice. He treats me with respect. He's really special, Mom,' and so on and so on. You didn't know? She didn't say anything to you?"

"Well, I knew I really cared for her. I thought I might be more serious than she was, but didn't want to push it. Neither of us wanted a relationship, at least in the beginning. But that wasn't working very well, at least for me, anyway. I really miss her. Why would she be scared?"

"It's not for me to say. She'll have to tell you herself. She had a pretty rough time a few years ago, and I think she needs to sort out her feelings. She's done this once before, and she was at a Buddhist retreat center somewhere in Oregon. I suspect she may be back, but not sure. She reassured me that she's fine and not to worry."

"There can't be that many Buddhist retreat centers in Oregon. I'm going to get online and look."

"Russell! No! Please. Let her be. I know her, and she needs this time. I know she'll be in touch with you when she's ready. Please? Be patient. How did you how to get in touch with Frank?"

"She told me a little about you and Frank. I remembered she'd told me that Frank was a poet and hung around City Lights. It dawned on me to try there and—"

"I have to go, Russell. My agent is here—"

"Okay, great to talk to you, Meg. And thanks again for calling. Please let me know if you hear anything."

"I will. Have to go." She clicked off.

* * *

I called my parents and Karen once a week with unwavering results. Mom and Dad still thought I was a lazy bum, and I realized they were close to right. Even Karen felt I should come home and get a job. According to their standard, I was being a lazy bum, but I was making money doing nothing. Someday, I'd probably be a productive citizen again, but not right now. I needed this time, plus I had no idea what I wanted to do.

Now the middle of August, I thought about heading south. I knew Ketchum got cold in the winter, and there was no way I was going to spend a winter here living in the Westy. I was ready to move on, anyway. Where? Maybe down into Utah and Colorado in a few weeks?

One Sunday as I headed out of town to camp over by the little town of Mackey, I got a text—from Hanna.

Where R U? Got all your texts and calls. Thanks. Miss you.

I pulled over and immediately texted back: *I'm in Ketchum, Idaho. Where R U? Leaving in a few weeks for warmer climes. R U okay? I need to see you.*

A minute later, I got another text: *At a retreat center outside Ashland, Oregon. Would Ashland be on your way to warmer climes?*

Knowing she was at her phone, I called her. I wanted to talk, not text.

She answered. "Russell, hi—"

"Hanna, what's going on—?"

"I'm sorry, really sorry for … sorry for just taking off like I did. That was wrong. You deserved better. I couldn't … just had to …"

Her voice started to crack. Neither of us spoke. I sat there, not knowing what to say. I desperately wanted to go to her, to see her. Yet I was angry and wanted to scream at her for running away like she had.

"Hanna, why couldn't you trust me enough to tell me whatever you don't think you can talk about?"

"How do you—?"

"John mentioned something to me. Then I talked with your mother about a month ago. They both told me you'd had a hard time a while back. I knew something was wrong. Nobody would tell me. What could be so bad? Why couldn't you just tell me whatever it is?"

191

"Because you'd hate me." Her voice began to quiver. "You'd leave and I couldn't, I—"

"You couldn't trust that I'd understand. You thought I'd leave you. Nothing could be that bad. I care for you. I thought we were friends! You couldn't trust me?" I felt myself getting angry and I didn't want to, so I stopped and took some breaths.

"I told you I'm sorry," Hanna said. "I mean it. I had to get my head on straight. I didn't plan on you in my life. I wasn't ready for you to be in my life ... then you were ... there's just some things ... things in my past, that, that I'm so ashamed of. You are so nice and—" Her voice cracked again, and I heard her sniffle. "And I have to tell you face to face. Please come. Please?" She choked back another sob.

I didn't want to go to Oregon, but she was way more important than my stupid plans. I'd lost Dana thinking only of myself. I had to see her.

"I'll head your way tomorrow. I don't know how far or how long it'll take me. Text me the address or the name of the center."

"The Westy will get you here quickly," she said with a shaking voice.

"I'll check out routes and time and text you back."

"God, Russell, I can't wait to see you. I miss you. I miss you so much. Please hurry."

"See you soon. Bye." I clicked off. I had mixed feelings. It'd been almost two months since she'd so abruptly left. In some ways, I'd started to move on with my life. I thought I was starting to get over her. But, this call ... I needed to see her, if for nothing else, for some sort of closure.

I called the few friends I'd made with the running and meditation groups to let them know I was leaving. Lastly and regretfully, I called Abby.

"Who is she?" she asked.

"Who is who?"

"Come on, Russ, the girl you've been pining over. You told me early on you'd just gotten out of a relationship. You were never out of it. I knew she was still in your heart, and you were still in love with her," she said with a knowing chuckle.

"Was it that obvious?"

She laughed. "God, yes! All the time. You never said anything, but the way you acted when you were with me, like you were afraid of me." She laughed again. "I enjoyed being with you. I thought, and hoped, I might have a slim chance with you. But I saw from the first day we met that you were in love, so friends we were. I enjoyed knowing you, wish you the best, and will miss your company. Thanks for hanging out with me."

"Thanks, Abby. I'm going to miss you too. You'll find your guy. You're too great not to find someone good. Be well."

"Thanks. All my best." She disconnected.

* * *

I left in the morning and began the 600-mile, eleven-hour drive to Ashland, Oregon. I headed south to Highway 20, then west, hit I-84 at Mountain Home, and continued west through Boise and then north until I found Highway 20 again and kept heading on into Oregon.

I turned onto Highway 385 at the little town of Riley in the late afternoon and looked for a campground, finding one in Christmas Valley where I got a space and settled in for the night. I lay awake for a long while, wondering what tomorrow and seeing Hanna would bring. I finally had to take a sleeping pill.

I left Christmas Valley early for the final three-to-four-hour leg of the trip and entered pine forests with winding, slow-going roads. It was beautiful country, reminiscent of Montana, but without the high Rocky Mountains.

After Klamath Falls as I came into Ashland, I pulled over and texted Hanna that I'd be there shortly. Google Maps directed me south on Route 66 and then back east for about ten miles on another road. The Google Map lady announced that I'd reached my destination at a driveway to the left with prayer flags fluttering in the soft breeze.

I drove in and up a well maintained gravel road for a mile or so until coming to a building that looked like something I'd seen in a National Geographic article on Tibet. I parked and went in what appeared to be the main entrance. It looked like a small hotel lobby with soft chairs, hard chairs and tables, and one wall from floor to ceiling with books. I saw no one.

"Hello? Anybody around? Hello?"

A man rushed in. "Oh, hello. I thought I heard someone. Can I help you?"

"Ah, yeah, maybe. I'm looking for a friend, Hanna, Hanna Martin."

His face lit up. "Hanna. Of course. You must be Russell. She said you'd be coming today or tomorrow. I saw her a minute ago. I'll go find her. Make yourself comfortable. Do you want some tea or water?"

I declined and wandered over to look at the library. Though mainly books on Buddhism, it also carried a large number of books on other religious belief systems. I was looking over the titles when I felt her presence. I turned. She stood about five feet away, her eyes wet with tears and her mouth quivering into a weak smile. Neither of us spoke. We just looked at each other for a long time. A lump came into my throat and my eyes welled with tears.

God, she looks so good.

She wore the nondescript plain dress from the sweat back in Mission.

"Hi, you look great," I choked out.

"So do you." She took a step and literally jumped into my arms. I lost my balance, and we, fortunately, ended up in one of the soft chairs. She had both arms around my neck and started to giggle and kiss me. I couldn't help it. I just laughed. We hung onto each other, laughing, kissing, and crying all at the same time.

"God, Hanna, I missed you so much. I was so worried."

"I'm so sorry. It was stupid of me to do what I did."

"I'm so happy you're okay. I was so worried and—"

She let go and slid into the chair beside me, then looked up and pulled me down to kiss her, a long, slow, sweet kiss. Her lips were cool and she tasted like incense.

"How's the Westy?"

"The Westy is fine. Brought me all the way here to save my princess."

"Your princess? I think I deserve to be a queen."

"You can be whatever you want. But, please, don't ever run off again. Please promise?"

"If you'll still have me, I promise I won't."

She reached over and kissed me so warm and tender I felt tears come back to my eyes. I kissed her back and held her, sniffling into her shoulder, feeling her own tears wetting my neck.

"So, where do you want to go?" I said. "San Francisco? Let's head out tomorrow?"

"Russell ... ah, I can't leave here for another four weeks. When I came, I agreed to work for my room and board and made a commitment to fill in for a full-time resident while she visited her family in Georgia. I need to stay until she returns."

A month? I wanted to go, get her out of here, be together. "Can't go any sooner?" I pleaded.

"I can't break my promise, Russell. I can't. I owe Rinpoche and the people here too much. I can't leave any sooner without getting some bad karma."

"Bad karma?"

"Yeah, Russell, breaking promises is not a good thing. Especially when I committed and made a vow to do my work and continue on my retreat."

"Retreat? What retreat?"

"I not only committed to work, but also a rigorous meditation schedule, study, and silence."

"Silence? You're talking to me now. You texted me. We talked. I don't understand."

"I know. I know. I've broken my vow. But I had to talk to you. I talked to Rinpoche about it, and he encouraged me to contact you. Then to talk to you about—"

"Who's this? What? Rinpo ... who?"

"I'm sorry, Rinpoche is the head of this center. He's a Tibetan monk and teacher, incredibly smart and compassionate. I love him like a father. He's helped me before and is helping me now. I can't disappoint him."

"Sounds like a cult."

She pulled away and stood up, glaring at me with venom in her eyes. "Dammit, Russell! I thought you were over all that shit! It is not a fucking cult! When my retreat vow is over, I'm leaving with or without you. So you can fuck off if you want or be with me. I contacted you because he told me to."

I sat there wide-eyed, regretting what I'd just said. "I'm sorry. That was a really dumb thing to say. I'm sorry; really, I'm sorry. Please tell me whatever you want and I'll shut up."

"Promise?" *

"Promise."

"Okay, thank you for your consideration and patience," she said slowly and deliberately, letting me know to shut up and pay attention. "I have made a fucking vow and I fucking intend to keep it for One! More! Fucking! Month! Get it? You can stay or fuck off!"

The message came across loud and clear. I hung my head and nodded. A month? *I don't want to wait around here for a month. I could've stayed in Ketchum.*

"Hanna, I don't know. Can't you just leave now? I'm here. I was ready to get to San Francisco … looking forward to meeting Meg and Frank—"

"Oh, you're here. So? I'm happy you're here. Really. I didn't want to contact you until I was finished and ready to leave, but Rinpoche insisted I talk to you now. Now! I am finishing my commitment and don't give a shit what you do. So go and do whatever you think is so important."

"Hanna, be reasonable. What will I do here for the next month?"

"You could do a four-week retreat and maybe find yourself."

"What does that mean? Find myself?"

"Never mind. Do whatever you want, but I need to talk to you. Okay. Then you can leave. You'll probably want to anyway."

"Okay. I can hang around for a few days and see what happens. I want to talk with you too, but … you have a vow of silence? You're talking to me now."

"Rinpoche says that vows are taken, but can be given back. So I've given mine back until we talk. Okay? Then I'm retaking them."

"Okay, then, do you know if there's someplace where I can camp close by?"

"There's a camping area here on the grounds, a bit rustic, but you can use the bathroom and showers, and you can eat in the dining hall. I'm so excited you're here. I know Rinpoche will be happy to meet you. You need to meet him. He's, well, he's just been very helpful for me. Come on, we'll go the office, and you can register. She grabbed my hand and pulled me after her, almost running, into another building where a twenty-something man in shorts, t-shirt, and ponytail talked on the phone and a fiftyish woman in a colorful peasant-sort-of top and long grey-streaked hair sat working on a computer.

Hanna announced us: "Shelley, sorry to bother you, but my friend, Russell, is here and wants to camp for the next few days."

With an east coast accent, Shelley said, "Sure. No problem. Let me get you registered."

* * *

Once located and set up, Hanna and I went inside the van.

She looked around as if it were the first time she'd seen it. "Wow, it's so nice to be home. It really is. I missed our home. Can we talk?"

"Can't it wait? Later? Maybe tonight?" I was thinking of holding her, kissing her, enjoying being with her. I didn't think I wanted to hear whatever it was she wanted to tell me.

More pointedly than I wanted to hear, she said, "I think now would be good, unless you have something more important to do. I want you to know. We're either together or not. I can't deal with keeping this from you any longer."

"Okay, okay; I'm listening."

She remained quiet for a long moment, just looking at me with a blank stare, then she took a deep breath and said, "Okay … oh God, Russell, there's so much you don't know about me.

198

I'm so sorry. I wanted to tell you. But I didn't want you to hate me. I'm so afraid you'll hate me. I don't want you to hate me. Oh God, oh God." She started to cry softly.

"Come on, Hanna, don't cry. It can't be that bad. I can't imagine anything could be that bad. Please. Just tell me. I'll listen. I promise." I reached over and tried to comfort her.

She jerked away. "Don't touch me!"

I pulled back. "Please. Just tell me. It'll be okay. Promise."

"Oh God, this is so hard. Promise you won't hate me." She had another burst of sobs.

"I promise. I won't ever hate you," I said as sincerely as I could, now with my heart pounding.

"Okay, then," she took a deep breath. "Here goes." She sniffled.

I handed her some tissues.

Her eyes went blank and unfocused; her voice became lifeless. "About three years ago, I was pretty bummed. I was hot out of college and ready to make it big with a career in music, but, like I told you, I didn't get very far. I got down on myself, had low self-esteem. I moved out from home and lived in a room in downtown Sausalito. I was in a really dark place and depressed. This guy I met, Johnny, was no help. He just went along with my drama, encouraged it, made it seem like everything, everybody was against me. He brought me down even further. So I entered into his crazy world of sex and drugs.

"He was into S and M—sadism and masochism—weird sex play, bondage, other stuff I don't want to get into any more than that. Just know it wasn't very nice. I liked him and went along with some fairly weird stuff, some downright disgusting. Some with other people, group sex and stuff. I was high most of the time, mainly pot and hash. Then I started doing harder stuff sometimes.

"One night"—she shifted and blew her nose—"we were smoking some hash and doing some hard stuff. There were three others, two girls and another guy. I got more wasted than I usually got, stoned out of my mind … passed out, I guess … I couldn't remember. I woke up the next morning and felt awful. I was naked. I'd thrown up and was lying in my own puke. I felt like shit. My belly hurt real bad. I thought it was from vomiting. I called out, but no one was there. Then I saw the blood. I knew it wasn't my period; I'd just had it. I was bleeding heavily from my vagina.

"I panicked and managed to call my mother and told her what was going on. She was there in a heartbeat and, when she saw me, called 911. An ambulance came and got me to the emergency room. I was all bloody, and stunk from vomit.

"I had to tell the E. R. doctor everything. I was so embarrassed. My mother was there and heard it all. Oh God, it was so awful. The doctor examined me and said I had a bad tear in my cervix, that's where the blood was coming from. She cauterized it. Oh God, Russell, it hurt so bad. I was so ashamed and scared.

"My blood work showed that I had so much residual drugs in my system, the doctor couldn't understand why I was even still alive. They wanted to know what happened, and I had to tell them. The police came, and I had to tell them, too. They found Johnny and arrested him. I had to be a witness at his trial. I didn't know he was a drug dealer. But, all the same, I was found complicit, if nothing more, for using. I was placed under house arrest for six months, then put on probation. I had to do drug rehabilitation, mental health counseling, and community service. After two years, when I'd completed my time, I left on this trip.

200

"Then I found out he'd been shooting videos of all the sex parties and had posted everything on porn sites. I was told everything had all been pulled since, but I'm not sure that they're still not out there. People were seeing all the terrible things I'd done.

"A week later, I went in for a follow-up exam with my gynecologist. Things were looking better and healing, but then he told me I'd been so torn up, I may never be able to have children ... Oh God, Russell, I may never have children ... I'm sorry, Russell. I'm so sorry to disappoint you. I love you ... love you so much, and I'm so sorry. Please don't hate me. I'm damaged goods. Now you know ... now you know I'm nothing more than a dirty slut."

We sat there, just looking at each other, her with desperation in her eyes, me with confusion. The sex stuff and the drugs was way more than I could comprehend, but all that I'd heard just made me care for her more. I realized then that I was in love with her, how much I loved her. She was the most precious thing in my life. I wanted to hold her, comfort her, protect her, and never let her go.

After too long a silence, she said shakily, "Please say something. Please."

I pulled her to me and held her, like I was holding an injured bird. She didn't resist, falling into my arms. "I love you, too, Hanna, more than I could ever imagine, I love you."

I didn't even know if I knew what love was, but I knew I wanted to commit to her. For the first time in my life, I felt what that was all about.

Then it came, she started to sob uncontrollably, shook so hard I thought she might choke. She grabbed hold of my t-shirt and held on for dear life. Her tears soaked my shirt. I must have held her for almost half an hour before she finally managed to stop. She relaxed her grip but continued to whimper for a long while. Finally, she grew quiet and fell asleep. I gently laid her down on the bed and covered her.

This poor girl, holding all that in, worrying, scared about telling me while thinking she had to tell me. I'd read in the Dalai Lama's book about compassion, about forgiveness, about love. It was all making sense—compassion, love, surrender? Maybe this was a compassion test? I never wanted to be apart from her. I loved her so much my chest ached. I'd be there in four weeks when she'd finished with her commitment.

She slept all afternoon, and began to stir around five. "Russell? Russell, where are you? Are you here?" she said with panic in her voice.

I was sitting right next to her, reading. "I'm right here. You've had a good rest. How're you feeling?"

"Drained. Did you mean what you said? That you loved me? What I told you? You know I'm a dirty slut. You know I'm damaged, how pathetic my life is."

I gave her an incredulous look. "Now you're being stupid and self-pitying. What happened, happened. You can't change that. It's in the past. You talked to me about our 'moments'. Well, that 'moment' passed a long time ago. Now it's this 'moment', our 'moment', right now."

"I know that, but it remains that I probably will never have children. You want a family? I can't give you one."

"Slow down here; I've never said I wanted a family. And you seem to be projecting that we will someday want a family."

"I've been dreaming of us being together. I'm sorry. I was spouting my own fantasies about having children, being a family. I shouldn't have. I'm being stupid."

"No, you're not stupid. I think I told you one time, I don't know about love. I don't understand it. I don't know if I ever loved anyone or anything, ever. Everything in my life has always been so planned, so regulated, so sterile. But all I know is what I'm feeling for you is something different from anything I've ever felt before about anyone. It's a new experience, a new feeling, and I like it. I'd like to see where it takes me … us, I mean."

"But you'll always know … and children. I've always wanted to have a baby. Now—"

"Hanna, I think two people can be together without procreating. I like children, but they're not a necessity in my life. We could adopt someday."

"You mean, you want to be with me?"

"What don't you get about what I just said? I'm committing to you. I'm in love with you. Please understand." I reached over and kissed her, hugged her, felt her shaking. She felt good. She was good. She was genuine. She wasn't Dana. She wasn't my family. She was precious.

Breaking away, I said, "So, do you want some wine? I'll make sandwiches for dinner."

"I can't. I have to get back. I'm up for kitchen duty tonight, and I'm already late. I need to go. I really have to get to work."

"Let's get together later. Come by for a while? I want to know what happened after you left. I want to talk."

"I can't. I'm going to continue my vows for the time I'm here, and alcohol isn't allowed. If Rinpoche found out, he'd … oh, he'd probably just laugh. He's a great teacher. You have to meet him. You'll stay … a few days? You could do a retreat? And we'll be together after and go to see Mom and Frank. I want you to meet them. Please?"

"So, what do I have to do to stay here? Like do this retreat thing, I mean?"

She looked at me with the most loving look, melting me to the core. "You'll stay? For how long?"

"Four weeks, I guess. Until you're a free woman."

"Oh my God!" She jumped at me and hugged me so tight I could hardly breathe. "I'm so happy right now. You have no idea! No idea! See Shelly tomorrow, at the front desk. Gotta go."

She gave me a lingering kiss, and, like that, was gone. They were the last words we'd share for the next four weeks, during which time we would only see each other like the proverbial "ships passing in the night," usually at group meditations and mealtime.

I sat there, wondering what had just happened. I had four weeks to think about it.

* * *

The next morning, Shelly said I could live in my camper and eat in the dining hall. Or, I could simply check into the dorm. She quoted me the suggested donations, which I thought were more than reasonable.

The dorm would be convenient. Single room. No distractions. Nothing to do but meditate and think.

"I'll do the dorm. Do you want a check or a card?"

"Either will do. But you'll pay at the end of your stay. You may not think it was worth anything. Some people have simply walked away."

"What? That's not right."

"Some people just … you know … And you can request a conference with Rinpoche if you wish."

"Who is this 'Rinpoche'?"

"He's the head of the center. He's a Tibetan rinpoche, which translates to 'Precious One'. It means that he has achieved enlightenment in a past life and wouldn't have to have any more rebirths. A rinpoche is regarded as one who has great compassion and has elected to come back in human form to another life, or lives, in order to teach us how to attain enlightenment.

"As a member of the Mahayana School of Buddhism, he has completed rigorous studies in philosophy. He has the equivalent of probably two or three Ph.D.s, really smart. Anyway, 'Geshe' is a scholastic degree he was awarded. It's a long history. It's all about Tibetan Mysticism and … just check out the book *Tibetan Mysticism* from the reading room, dry reading but explains it all, sort of …. pretty esoteric stuff. That all make any sense?"

"Not really, but I'll look for the book. Thanks."

She laughed, gave me a key, directions to my room, and a pass to the dining room. I found out there were twenty-three other people there, some for a few days, some for a year or longer. I'd been alone during the weeks in Ketchum, but always had weekends with Abby and others I knew, eating, drinking beer, laughing and talking. I wasn't sure I wouldn't go bonkers after a week, much less four weeks of not talking to people. Shelly told me that most, if not all, were, like Hanna, practicing silence. No talking? If nobody was talking, then there would be nobody to talk to anyway.

I got what I needed from the camper and locked it up—like I need to lock things up here. I found my room. It took "austere" to a totally different level. A single bed, a wash basin on a table, a straight-backed chair, a cushion to meditate on, and a window. No TV. Computers and cell phone weren't allowed. Communal bathroom was down the hall.

I made one last call to Karen to let her know what was going on, but the call went straight to voice mail. I left a message saying I'd be out of communication for probably four weeks and left the emergency number at the center with orders not to call unless a matter of life and death. I turned off my phone ... for four weeks.

I had the day. For a long while, I sat and thought about yesterday. Did I really love her or was it only the drama of that moment, the trauma of her story? Was it simply a sympathetic reaction on my part? I felt I was sincere with what I'd said, but it frightened me all the same. What if after four weeks I didn't feel the same way? My stomach knotted up. I took a breath and pushed my doubts away.

Later, I found the reading room and the book Shelley had told me about. I curled up in a chair and read until I was bored, then decided to go for a run. I checked the site map Shelley had given me and saw trails in the forest. I found running through a pine forest exhilarating and went for miles, running, walking, resting, but it felt free.

The first days I spent settling down, settling in. I decided to try to practice silence. There wasn't anyone to talk to, anyway. I tried meditating longer. Then the days started to go by more quickly than I would've guessed they would. I went for a run every day. I read. I thought.

One-hour group meditations happened every morning before breakfast and again in the evening after dinner. They were held in a large room with dark wood floors, off white walls with tapestries of various entities, and an altar at the front with a giant golden statue of the Buddha dominating the space. The room smelled of incense and candles.

After morning meditation, Rinpoche gave a talk. He dressed in maroon and yellow robes, was taller than I'd imagined, neither heavy set nor thin. I guessed him to be somewhere between thirty and fifty years old. He was some sort of enigma and an imposing character.

It took me a few times to grasp what Rinpoche was saying. But after a while both his accent and his message became clearer. He spent a lot of time with esoteric ideas and funny anecdotes—many of which only he got the joke. He laughed and laughed, while his audience snickered—most likely at how he enjoyed himself. But what I understood was that it was important to simply lead a good life, be kind and loving to all sentient beings, and, lastly, meditate a lot to quiet your busy mind. He seemed so happy and so satisfied with his life, a life of being a monk, a life of austerity, a life separated from his country and his family.

I signed up for meditation instruction with one of the long-time residents. With him I started to really learn the nuts and bolts of the practice.

I usually saw Hanna once or twice a day, mainly in the dining hall. We made eye contact, but never spoke. She mouthed, "I love you," her eyes confirming just how much she did, and I mouthed back the same, "I love you," to her.

On around the third day, a twenty-something man in morning meditation asked Rinpoche about praying to the Buddha for salvation. Rinpoche took a moment, then said in his quiet manner that the Buddha was not a god; he did not ever want to be worshipped, and he would not come and save you. The only person who can save you is yourself. That's why we simply respect and honor the Buddha, the dharma (the teachings), and the sangha (the community). Buddha was a great teacher who achieved enlightenment in his lifetime, but no more than that.

At the end, he asked the young man, "Does that help?"

Silence.

I lay awake that night considering what I'd heard. Being brought up Christian, it was engrained in me that there was a savior, and if you prayed hard enough and were good enough, he would come and save you at the end. If what Rinpoche said was true, then there was no safety net. I was on my own. It was disturbing and a difficult concept for me to grasp. I thought about that enormous responsibility, and it scared the hell out of me.

I set up a time for a meeting with Rinpoche for the next day at ten in the morning. Precisely at ten, I hesitantly rapped lightly on Rinpoche's door.

"Come in. Come in."

I entered and found him sitting on a cushion behind a very low table.

Laughing, he said, "Sit. Sit. Please sit," as he motioned me to a cushion.

I didn't do well on the cushions. I liked chairs, but I clumsily got seated.

He laughed at my effort. "What can I do for you? You have questions, Russell?"

He knew my name? Probably from a list of his appointments Shelly must've given him, I thought. But I found out later that he never had appointment lists.

"Thank you for seeing me. I'm not sure what questions I have. I don't really know much about Buddhism."

"What is there to know? Know, know, know? Just practice, practice, practice. That's all." And he laughed and laughed.

"One thing I do want to ask is, why are you always laughing?"

"Laugh? Laughing is good for you. You should laugh more. Laugh a lot. Don't be so serious. Americans are so serious: work, work, work; hurry, hurry, hurry; busy, busy, busy; more, more,

more. Nobody enjoys life. What do you gain? Soon it's all over; you die, then all those possessions you worked so hard to accumulate, how important are they?

"You see, Russell, life is an illusion, like … like a hologram? Is that right? Yes, a hologram. In our desire for things we lose our true nature. Our true nature is loving kindness, it is compassion. It is not possessions. Americans need to, how do you say … 'chill'? Spend time with family and loved ones. Then you be love, be love to everyone and everything. Then you will understand.

"Go see your family. Marry your young woman, Hanna. Be happy together. But see your family. They miss you and worry. And meditate."

I sat there, speechless, for a while, then blurted out, "Rinpoche, how can you know all this about me? Did Hanna tell you?" I was embarrassed and knew I was flushed.

"Hanna came to see me when she first arrived and many times since. I told her you would come. You would come soon."

"You told her I would come? Soon? You thought you knew I would come … soon? I don't—"

He laughed. "I knew from what she said that you would be together. You both love each other very much. You are destined from your past karma."

"What? We're destined? But …" I couldn't say anything, considering this voodoo stuff he was saying. "But what did Hanna tell you about us?"

"I cannot say any more. You understand?"

I did understand; he'd probably already said more than he should have. "But how do you know about … about my family?"

He laughed again.

I started to feel giddy as well, just being in his presence. It was hard not to feel light.

"So easy, Russell. I see; I observe; I see your troubled face, and I see you have problems. I guess it may be family. I was right? No?"

I didn't reply for a few moments. "Yes, Rinpoche. You are very right. My family thinks I'm ..." and I went on, telling him about my life and my struggles to let go, how much this road trip was changing my thinking, shattering many of my beliefs, and how alone and confused I felt. Then about my failed marriage, and lastly Hanna. I unloaded everything on this poor man who seemed so nice.

"Russell?" He said my name like he enjoyed saying it. "Are you aware of the law of karma?"

My blank look must have answered his question. "Very simple. Everything we do in our life has a karmic effect. If we hurt others, sometime we will also be hurt, whether in this lifetime or the next. It doesn't matter. Many things we suffer in this present form may be the result from something in a past life. When we do kindness, we are rewarded with kindness. That is why we practice mindfulness, loving kindness, and compassion. We practice so that we might attain Buddhahood for the sake of all sentient beings. We have lessons to learn and work to do to erase bad karma whether from this life or past lives.

"Your parents struggle to control you. Your brother does not like you. Your sister is sometimes being cold to you. Your wife left you. They are the ones struggling, Russell. They struggle with their strict beliefs about what is right and wrong. They are attached to their strict beliefs. No middle ground. Don't suffer like them. Help them not to suffer."

"But, Rinpoche, what can I do? I've tried to talk to them, and they just get angry with me."

"Practice mindfulness, loving kindness, and compassion. Wear them down with love." He laughed as if it were the biggest joke in the world.

"I don't understand. Loving kindness? Mindfulness? I think I understand compassion. It's like caring for others?"

"Yes, compassion can translate as 'with love', which is caring for others. Loving kindness is holding doors for people, smiling when you meet a stranger on the street, helping a wounded animal, driving your car with respect for others, you know, simple everyday things? When we become mindful, loving kindness becomes easy. Like when you throw a pebble into a quiet lake, you see those ripples radiate out from where the stone landed. Right? Well, practicing loving kindness towards all sentient beings does just that, it radiates out love. You be that stone. How do you feel when someone is kind to you?"

"I feel good. I think I understand what you're saying."

He then remained silent for a long time, maybe to let that all sink in. It got to the point where I began to feel uncomfortable. I fidgeted and looked around, trying to distract myself from the silence.

"Russell? How did that feel?"

"What?"

"My silence."

"Well, it made me a little uncomfortable."

"Embrace silence, Russell. It is a time for our mind to rest. I see many who cannot be with silence, but must always fill that space with idle chatter. Or cell phones like this," he pulled out a cell phone from somewhere inside his robe, "or some other distraction from that empty space."

I found it hard not to laugh at the cell phone, but I contained it. But he blew my mind with this new concept, silence. I considered it. I hated vacuums. Time, space, whatever, should be filled, utilized; time was money.

"But people need to be productive," I said. "I always tried to plan and consider any decision carefully for the best outcome."

"But life can't be planned, Russell. I could die in the next moment." He laughed. "Then you would be upset." He laughed again like his dying was a big joke. "A heart attack … you could have a heart attack." He laughed as if me dying would be a big joke. "There could be an earthquake and we could all fall into the ocean." He laughed again. "There could be any hundreds of things that might end this conversation right now. Yes, we plan. We create objectives for ourselves, but do not get attached to them. Life is here, and life is gone. Just like that!" He snapped his fingers.

"Use your life well. It is precious. Be flexible. We have to bend like the tree in the wind. Sway with good and sway with bad. Be mindful. Mindfulness … mindfulness is very important. We need to be aware of where we are and how we are acting towards ourselves, to others, and to animals, the environment. We become mindful through meditation. Did you meditate, Russell, before you came here?"

"Yes, a yoga lady showed me a few months ago, and then Hanna and I would sometimes. I did a lot in the last month. And I'm working with Roger now."

He laughed again, and all I could do was to sit and grin. He was contagious.

"I like Roger. He is a good teacher. I taught him." He roared with laughter.

I lost control and started laughing with him.

"Good, Russell, it is good to laugh. You are so serious. You are too serious. Laugh, Russell, laugh. One thing, Russell, that is important is to become at one with peace and silence, to be at peace with yourself, to stop judging yourself. Then stop judging family, friends, anything. Be at peace with yourself. Trust yourself. Then you will find peace in all you do. And laugh."

"With all due respect, I don't want to be a monk in some secluded monastery."

"Why not?"

"There's so much to do, work, food, shelter. So much to do, I just—" I stopped and thought about what Rinpoche had just said to me. "Okay, I know what you just told me, but I'm confused, how can someone lead the life you described without being totally secluded, like in a monastery?"

He chuckled. "Russell, you do not have to live in a monastery. There is nothing wrong living a normal life in the world, with having family, possessions, or work, or play, nothing wrong. What is important is that there is no attachment to possessions, or work, or whatever. Attachment and desire, they make us suffer: 'Oh, I don't have enough. Oh, I should work harder so I can get more things I think will make me happy.' But happiness does not come from possessions, but from letting go. When you let go, you can be happy. Change can be hard. We are always evolving.

"And meditate. Keep a steady meditation practice and remember, it is practice. Listen to Roger. Come back and talk to me. I like talking to you. You need to laugh. Not be so serious."

I didn't say anything, already lost in trying to figure out all I'd just heard.

He continued, "The trick is to direct our evolution toward the goals of a mindful life, not goals being dictated to you from outside sources, but from your own heart. Call your family. Tell them you love them. Wear them down with love. Take good care of Hanna.

"I know you have questions, questions maybe about karma and past lives." He handed me a list of three books and smiled so warmly, I felt my heart melt. He gave a little bow, letting me know I was dismissed. I bowed back, got up, backed away, thanked him again, and exited the room.

"I will look forward to our next talk," he said as I left.

Next time? This was enough for me.

I stopped on the way out and had Shelley schedule me again in two days.

The next time, he led me into a meditation. "Follow your breath, breathe in and breathe out. Be conscious only of your breath. Breathe in; breathe out. Breathe into every cell in your body Now exhale from each cell of your body."

Then he became silent for a long time. I felt uncomfortable with my eyes closed and him there. Was he watching me? Judging me?

"Where is your mind?" he said. "Is it present? Is it following your breath?"

That brought me back from my concerns, and I again focused on my breath. Then, another long silence. I became aware of my mind. No thoughts. Somehow I knew there were no thoughts. So I simply stayed there in that 'no thought' place. This was what Roger was trying to get me to focus on, without much success. But somehow sitting here …

I heard a little bell gently ring: once, pause, twice, pause, then a third time. Jolted back from wherever I was, I opened my eyes slowly, looked around, and saw Rinpoche still sitting across from me, doing the same, opening his eyes. He turned to me and smiled. I smiled back and took some deep breaths. "Wow,

Rinpoche, that was the deepest meditation I've ever experienced."

"Good. Now, you do that every day from now on, morning and night. Twenty minutes is good. If you are too busy to meditate twenty minutes ..." he paused to laugh, "then meditate for an hour." And he laughed again. His meaning was crystal clear.

"So, Russell, tell me, where was your mind?"

"I don't know. I was thinking about meditating, about Roger, and then, I realized there were no thoughts, only the realization that there were no thoughts, actually that there was nothing. I knew I was present, but I wasn't there. There were no sensations. I saw my breathing, but there was nothing else. It was a little weird. Like I was observing my own mind. Was that thinking? Was that in itself a thought?"

"What do you think? Who do you think the observer was, the observer who observed your empty mind?"

I sat there, first trying to understand the question. I had no answer. He looked at my blank stare and laughed. I looked at him and laughed along with him. My time was up and I bid goodbye.

"Think about that question, Russell. Have an answer for me next time."

I made another appointment on my way out.

The first week passed. Other than talking to Rinpoche, I hadn't used my voice. In many ways it was a relief. I never had to think of anything to say. Anything I needed, I could usually manage by gesturing. Sometimes I had to resort to writing on a notepad I'd learned to carry with me. I got into a rhythm—an ease of being, for lack of better words—and experienced new inner peace and happiness.

Prior to my next meeting with Rinpoche, I pondered his question and did some research, but I still felt confused. Since meditating with Rinpoche, I'd not encountered the same experience again. I'd rather enjoyed those moments of whatever it was I was doing and wanted to recreate it.

I entered his office and sat, and his first words were, "So, Russell, do you have an answer for me?"

"I don't. I've done some reading and have tried to find information on 'the observer' but I either couldn't find anything or didn't understand what I'd found."

He laughed. "Russell, you are a beginner. You have been instructed to meditate by observing your breath, your emotions, your thoughts. Right?"

"Yes."

"But you still deal with ego. You are still engaged in doing. You are the observer of all this commotion going on. But the other day, you said you were observing the observer. You only meditate three months, maybe? You have some way to go, but you do have that experience. That is good. You have it again, then again, and then you have it most all the time, then you even have it even when you are not meditating.

"You spend all this time meditating and getting comfortable, and it becomes a habit, which is just ego letting go and becoming comfortable with not being so important. But then you move beyond, totally get rid of ego, you begin observing the observer, like you did. You watch yourself watching yourself. Then you will understand." Rinpoche laughed. "Then, where is the observer observing? Your brain? Your eye? Your left foot? Your little finger?" He laughed again.

I had nothing to say. All I could do was sit in confusion and stare at him with what I knew was a silly grin.

"Russell, you will work to find this. You will meditate on this and will study this."

My face was blank. *Like what am I supposed to say?* My head hurt, like it might explode. I simply nodded, then managed to say, "Thank you, Rinpoche. Thank you. You have again given me much to consider and think about."

Of course he laughed. "Russell, don't think about it. But do. Do by meditation, much meditation. Then you will know." He bowed, excusing me, and smiling the nicest smile, as always.

I had many more meetings, teachings, meditations, as well as my instruction with Roger. I never did understand the "observing the observer" thing.

I meditated morning and night with the group and times in between. It consumed a lot of time. I thought I should be doing something else, like journaling, running, reading, checking emails, and whatever. I didn't have access to the internet so that wasn't a problem, but I wanted to go into Ashland to a coffee shop, have a chocolate mocha, check my emails, make phone calls.

I met again with Rinpoche. Sitting in his presence was addictive. He was like a drug, a happy drug. I loved being in his presence.

"What is on your mind today, Russell? You have deep thoughts? Deep questions?" He laughed at his inquiry.

"I've been meditating a lot, as you directed me to. I spend a lot of time every day meditating, but I'm leaving next week. I won't have the time like I have here. I want to continue to practice, but I'm not sure I'll have the time."

He looked at me for a moment, then, without his usual laughing, said, "Russell, this almost, what, four weeks I have seen you was a gift you gave yourself, to be here and do this. It was precious time. You learned. Now soon it is time for you to go back to your world. What will you take with you when you leave?"

I thought for a moment. "All the good memories, what I learned from you, I guess."

"Yes, Russell, you have those, but you now have a foundation. You know what to do. You know how to do it. You know how to practice. Now you meditate twenty minutes in the morning and twenty minutes at night. Longer when you can. Maybe you find a sangha where you can go. Be with others. Meditate with others when you can. That is good.

"Time? Time? What is time? Time is meaningless.' He held up his wrist, showed me his Apple Watch and laughed. "This is a good watch. It tells me many things. It even tells me what hour it is. Good to know when I need to meet with Russell." He laughed at his little joke, of course.

"But there is no time. The sun and moon do not know time. The animals and birds do not know time. Everything goes on very nicely without knowing what time it is. Everything but us humans do not know time. But we humans run our lives on thinking we know time. What is the point?

"The point is that time helps us to give some order to our lives in this world. Our early ancestors did not know time, but they didn't have to keep an appointment with Russell at one o'clock today. So time is useful.

"Like all we discussed about possessions and attachment, time is the same. Keep your appointments, but do not become attached to time. It is only constructed for our convenience. Maybe not?" He laughed again at his usual way of making our crazy lives sound absurd. I laughed with him, thanked him and was excused.

I had my last meeting during my last week at the center. As always, he asked me what was on my mind. I think he already knew what I'd ask. "Rinpoche, I have two questions; can I ask, do you have a name other than Rinpoche?"

As always, he preceded any answer with a laugh, which now made me laugh as well. I was learning. "Of course; no one ever told you? I will talk with them." He laughed.

I laughed, too, knowing he'd be really brutal. "My name is Tenzin Lhundup Karma. Thank you for asking me. What is your other question?"

"Early on, you mentioned 'karma from past lives'? Isn't this our only life? And Shelly told me you were reincarnated and have come back to teach us. I don't understand."

"Good question, Russell. I'm sorry I didn't explain, and I will now: our bodies we presently inhabit will eventually die and go away back into the earth, but our consciousness will continue on. Our consciousness will move into the bardo realms where it realizes the goods and bads of its lives, understanding what good and not-so-good things have been accomplished. Our consciousness looks for rebirth into another realm, maybe this one again to work on what was not so good, on doing good to erase all bad. There is a book I recommend for you that explains all this in greater detail than what we have time for, *The Tibetan Book of the Dead*. There are several copies in our library. I'm sorry we don't have more time since I know you're leaving. But you will come back, and I will have many more discussions with Russell. And you will be a great meditator the next time we meet."

"Thank you, Rinpoche. I'm always honored to be in your presence."

"Russell, I'm also honored to be in your presence. You are a good student. I like you very much. I would like you to take refuge with me."

"What does that mean? Refuge?"

"Simply means, you take refuge in the Buddha, the Dharma, and the Sangha. It gives you a place of refuge from the suffering of the world. When a devotee takes refuge, they get a new name. Do you want to take refuge? You are ready. If you want? I would be honored to have you."

For some reason, I choked up and couldn't speak. I pulled out my handkerchief, blew my nose, and, as discreetly as I could, wiped my eyes. When I left him that day, my new name was Jampa (loving kindness) Dhargey (progress, development, spreading) Yonten (good qualities). I was overcome with emotion and went out into the forest and cried my heart out until I was exhausted. I never knew I could love a man as dearly as I loved Tenzin Lhundup Karma, Rinpoche.

* * *

The month was over, almost too soon. I felt apprehensive about re-entering the world of busyness. The peace and quiet I'd experienced at the center was extraordinary. Deep down, I didn't want to leave. Things had simplified, simplified to absolutely nothing. I even found my desire to speak again other than to Rinpoche somewhat intimidating. Not speaking freed up so much. Daily activities had been reduced to complete minutia. Maybe monastic life wouldn't be so bad after all.

The day came for my departure. I assumed Hanna would be ready to leave. I hadn't talked to her in four weeks.

I went to see Shelley to settle up as I was scheduled to leave tomorrow. She said that any donation was welcome, then told me of the expected donation for food and lodging plus any dana (direct donation to the teacher) I might want to make to Rinpoche. I got out my checkbook and wrote a check for a sum much more sizable than what she suggested. Then I wrote another large check for Rinpoche. Shelly took them, saw the total, and took a deep breath. "Oh my, this is very generous of you, Russell. It will be greatly appreciated. Thank you."

"No, thank you and everyone for this time. I'm really sad to leave. Hopefully, someday, I'll be back. Thanks again, for everything."

That night at dinner, I saw Hanna. I'd already sat and started eating when she got her food and sat across from me. I felt clumsy after not talking to her for the four weeks.

She looked at me and said, "Are you ready to leave tomorrow?"

"No, not really. I like it here, learned a lot. It was peaceful. Thank you for talking me into it. But the world now awaits. Are you ready?"

"Same as you, not really, but to Sausalito, then?"

"Yep, I'm looking forward to meeting your parents, but I thought you were from San Francisco?"

"Sausalito's right across the Bay Bridge. It's simpler sometimes. Most folks know where San Fran is, but Sausalito, not so much, especially people from out of state."

"Okay, Sausalito it is, then. We're just a bit north of San Francisco, so it'll be an easy jaunt."

She looked at me and smiled. "It's a long way, Russell. California is big. I'd like to take our time, re-enter, get to know ourselves again, take it slow, the Coast Highway. I want you to see the ocean. It's so beautiful. I went with Mom once about six or seven years ago when she drove to Portland for an opening of her work at a gallery there. We drove that road. We had so much fun, the two of us. I miss her."

"I'm open to anything. Let's leave right after breakfast, then. Oh, one thing I need to tell you, when I was in Ketchum, everyone there knew me as Russ. I liked it, so, I guess I can be

221

Russ, like you first called me back in Iowa, and I had a little snit. Remember?"

"Huh? No, I really don't remember, but, no, I don't think so. You're Russell and always will be. You are definitely a 'Russell'." She gave me a lingering look, like she wanted to ask me something or say something more. Then it faded and she said, "I'll see you at breakfast." She got up, picked up her dishes, and left.

I lay awake, wondering about re-entry into a world I'd been away from for a month, about what it'll bring, about my parents. Then I drifted to Dana, wondering where and how she was. I thought of Karen and her family. I even wondered about Donny. And then Raymond, and John, Manuel and his family, all the people I'd encountered on this journey.

I reflected on Rinpoche, what he'd taught me, his kindness, his laugh. I fell asleep smiling with a lump in my throat.

Chapter 19: Heading South

Morning came, and we headed north through Medford, then west over Grants Pass, towards the Pacific Ocean. The road wound through the mountainous Coastal Range. Though slow going, the scenery of the forested wilderness made up for it. Hanna remained quiet, her normal bubbly attitude missing, like when I'd first given her a ride back in Iowa. I tried to start a conversation several times with no results. So I just drove.

Somewhere we entered California, and at Crescent City I picked up Highway 101 and turned south. Soon the Pacific Ocean spread out before us. I stopped in a pull-out area, and we got out to just look. Having never seen an ocean before, I felt very small. The vast expanse of water, the salt air, the sound of surf pounding the shore, and the power and strength of that endless body of water was overwhelming. It was so much more than Lake Michigan, which, up until then, I'd thought was big.

Hanna stood beside me, took my hand, and turned to me. "Kiss me."

We kissed, then stood embracing each other.

She broke away, holding both my hands and looking directly at me, "Russell, I want you to know you are the most wonderful man I have ever known. I talked to Rinpoche early on. It was so hard. I was so embarrassed. And after I told him everything I told you, I felt like I was going to throw up, but he just looked at me and smiled, smiled his warm loving smile, and said, 'That must have been an awful experience. What lesson do you think was there for you?'

"'Lessons?' I shouted at him, 'Lessons!' I was livid, angry. Being hurt like I'd been—shamed, ruined—and he asked about fucking 'lessons.' I was really upset when I left the interview. The next time I was with him, he talked to me about the choices we make and taking responsibility for those choices. Good ones bring us happiness; bad ones, we suffer consequences. Our choices are our responsibility. We need to make our choices mindfully. I knew I'd made bad choices and my problems were of my own doing. I had to make amends to those I hurt and move on. I had to forgive myself."

She moved in and I held her. She stayed quiet for a long time.

I thought of what Rinpoche had said about karma, then I drifted to my family. I thought of my own issues, about being always uptight, always thinking of risk assessment anytime I did anything. But isn't risk assessment another way of being mindful about our choices? Maybe I wasn't so far off.

I pulled away from her. "I can't stand it. I'm going crazy. It's all nuts. Everything is crazy fucking nuts!" I shouted. I looked around, relieved to see we were the only ones there.

She looked at me with wide-eyed fear. "I'm sorry. I know. I'll leave. I'll get my stuff. I'm sorry. I'm—"

"No! No! It's nothing to do with you, Hanna. No! Right now, you're the most stable thing in my life. It's everything else, everything with my parents, my brother, my sister. What Rinpoche told me, what we talked about. I felt so calm and happy when there at the center. Now … now I don't know. There's so much I have to deal with. I wish I could erase everything about my past up until three months ago ... when I met you."

She didn't say anything. She came back to me and held me.

"Let's go," she said after a moment. "Let's see if we can find a place to camp down by the Redwoods."

We found a grocery store and stocked the cooler and cupboards with food for a week, then she got on her cell phone and made arrangements for us at a campground close to the Redwoods National Park, a few hours' drive away. We rode in silence. I was in a funk.

The drive along the coast and through the edge of the Redwood Forest was, again, different from anything I'd experienced before. As other times on this journey, the land, the scenery, and now the ocean seemed to drain away all my fears and worries. I reveled in the beauty and the mystery.

After checking into the bare-bones campground, Hanna perked up; my funk started to lift, and we got things set up for the night. We made dinner together, still not conversing other than what was necessary.

"Can we have some wine?" Hanna asked.

"Of course." I got a bottle out of the cooler.

We ate our meal quietly. Hanna seemed pensive, but we made small talk about the center, the drive down, the scenery.

Dinner finished and cleaned up, the air around us started to get really heavy.

"Russell, I need to talk," she said. "We need to talk."

I remembered Dana saying those words, and it was never good. "Okay, let's sit."

We each got a cup of wine. Neither of us said anything. I waited for her to start, and, I guess, she was waiting for me. Neither of us made eye contact. Finally I blinked and said very feebly, "So ... what's on your mind?"

"Russell, we're playing games. I'm uncomfortable. I'm not sure what I'm doing, what you're doing. I … I'm scared, scared of where I might be going, scared of where you might be going. You're scared of commitment."

I didn't say anything, trying to think. My head felt dizzy.

"I don't know where this is going," she continued, "but I know where I want it to go. And I'm not sure you want the same—"

I took a deep breath. "Hanna, here's what I am feeling. Yes, I'm frightened. But … but I don't want to lose you. I don't know … I don't know how to love someone. I know I said I love you. I want to love you. You deserve to be loved and cared for. I couldn't do it before with Dana. I don't want to hurt you. I … I …" I put my head in my hands. It was too much for me. Tears started to flood my eyes. "What can I do?" I blubbered. "What can I do?"

I felt her arms around me. "Just let it go. Let it all go."

I buried my head in her breast and cried. Was this becoming my new norm?

Hanna held me gently, rubbing my head.

I looked up, drying my eyes with my sleeve. "I was around four or five, and my older brother, Donny, had teased me and pushed me down. I got up and went after him, and he, being bigger, gave me a beating. I was crying and went to my mother. She grabbed me, spanked me, and called me a tattle-tale and a crybaby. Don't ever come crying to her. I never cried again, until I met you, and now … I'm sorry. I'm so embarrassed. Please don't think I'm a crybaby."

"A crybaby, like your mother told you? I've told you that's old parent talk. You have a lot of sadness to make up for. There's nothing wrong with crying. It makes you more human … and more lovable."

By now it was around eight in the evening. My crying jag had worn me out. I felt drained, but also good—relaxed. "I'm wiped out," I said. "How about you?"

"Yeah, me too. What are our sleeping arrangements going to be? I can sleep in my tent."

"There's a perfectly nice bed which has accommodated both of us before and will do again. I want you close to me."

She hesitated. "Separate sleeping bags to keep us apart?"

"What makes you think I want us apart? Why don't you go get ready first, and I'll crawl in when you're done?"

She called, and I slipped into the bag, avoiding any contact.

"Russell, this is a little hard to say. Please don't laugh at me. But I'm so much in love with you I think I'm going to die. Please, can you love me back?"

"Love? Does love mean commitment? I missed you and worried about you. I came to you as soon as I knew where you were. I like being with you, want to be with you. You make me feel good and happy. You challenge me, push me, make me think. You're supportive. I can't imagine ever being without you. Is that love? I like holding you, kissing you and … and I want to make love to you. If love is all that, then, yeah, I love you more than anything ever. I want to love you back, and I will be committed to you as long as we can stand being around each other. I … I do love you, Hanna. I love you, love you more than I could ever imagine loving someone."

She didn't say anything in response for a few moments, as if trying to digest something bigger than she was. "You've just made me the happiest girl in the world! Oh God, Russell, I love you so much."

She came to me, and I reached to hold her. We kissed and kissed. Soon our hands were exploring each other's body. Quickly, as if by magic, we were both naked. I entered her. It

227

was the sweetest, most wonderful sexual experience of my life. I became one with her. I realized love, what love really was. I knew love. I was thirty years old, and for the first time ever, I knew love. I was in love with this woman. I loved her, loved her more than life. Rinpoche talked about nirvana. I could only imagine that this was it.

We lay in each other's arms for a long time after, giggling, talking, sharing more of our secrets, desires, hopes, dreams. We fell asleep and awoke, still in each other's arms. My right arm had fallen asleep. We made love again. I could have stayed like this forever, lying with her, naked, enjoying an intimacy I never could have imagined.

Once we fed ourselves, Hanna suggested we go down to the Redwoods. She found a place in Prairie Creek Redwoods State Park and reserved a spot.

* * *

We spent a week there, slow days, taking our time together, driving and hiking through magnificent redwood forests. Some of these huge trees were over 2,000 years old and 300 feet tall, the tallest trees on the planet. The trunks were enormous.

We saw deer and elk grazing in fields of grass, and one day we went down to the coast and spent the entire day walking on the beach.

So this is what happiness is.

Hanna told me about why she'd left me in Glacier. After the night in Bozeman, she knew she was falling in love with me and it freaked her out, so she decided that if she could push me away by being a bitch, I'd pack up and leave her.

"That would've been an easy out for me," she said. "But you didn't. All I did was make you more concerned about me, about what you might have done to upset me. When I met Amy on that hike, I told her what was going on, and she was understanding and supportive, but was reluctant to help me leave you, not being that sure of the situation. I convinced her, and she offered to take me with her on her way home to Bend. Then you sent me all those texts and voice messages, and I knew you were having a hard time. I felt terrible and cried all the way.

"I was a basket case, but she was so nice, putting up with me, consoling me. I spent three days with her and decided to call the retreat center. I'd stayed there before for a few weeks back when I was waiting for my trial. They needed someone to fill a space for a woman who'd left for a few months to be with family, so I volunteered. Amy drove me down two days later. I'll be forever indebted to her for all she did for me. I realized how much I loved you and missed you. I needed to be with you, but needed some time to get myself together, and with Rinpoche's help and a loving community there, I was able to drum up the courage to talk to you and share that terrible part of my past.

"And that's about it. Right now, I'm so happy. You can't know how happy I am."

"Probably about as happy as I am right now. Thanks for telling me, it makes me sad, knowing the pain you must have been in. I'm sorry. I wish I could have done something, but—"

"I think it all worked out for the best," she said. "I needed that time. Without it, I may never have been able to really say what needed to be said and we'd still be stuck. The main thing is that we're now together, and the air is clear, and I know you love me."

* * *

On the second night, Hanna said, "Hey, let's play some music. Have you been practicing? I wrote three new songs while I was at the retreat center, and I'd like to work them out with you."

"Sure, let's do it, and yes, I've been practicing mandolin and the little flute I bought." I told her about the flute and the night in Missoula at the pizza place, seeing the male/female duo and how it reminded me of us, of our fun times, and how sad it made me feel.

She was quiet, her head down, but after a long moment, she set down her guitar, came over and hugged me. "I'm sorry, Russell. I'm so very sorry." Then after another long pause, "Let's play."

We played together for a straight two hours. Some other campers came by for a while. I showed her some of the new licks—musical phrases—I'd learned. She liked what I was doing. It was like we'd never stopped playing music together.

"So why not get your guitar?" she asked.

"I haven't played since you left. It reminded me too much of playing with you. It was too hard."

She looked away for a while, then rubbed her eyes with her sleeve. "Russell, I can't say I'm sorry enough. I thought you'd just write me off as some crazy woman you picked up along the road one day. I thought you'd just forget me … I'm happy you didn't."

* * *

The next few days were unbelievable. We made love at least twice a day, never seeming to satiate our desire for each other. I guess it was what a honeymoon was for married couples. I thought about my first honeymoon when Dana spent her time studying for the Illinois bar exam and, me, studying all the information Americo had sent. I think we maybe made love twice the whole time.

Marriage never entered our conversation. It never seemed like anything important. Although we knew each other, we really didn't know each other in so many ways. I became more aware than ever of little things she did, how her behavior was so much different from mine. I loved just watching her, the grace with which she moved. I absorbed everything she did, how she did it, paid attention to the way she thought, reacted, responded, her need for reassurance, her wants and desires, her needs.

I realized how ignorant I'd been with Dana. I thought Dana should be like me. I couldn't remember ever responding, or even listening, to her needs or desires, and I couldn't remember her ever expressing any. No wonder she left me. I would have left me.

* * *

After experiencing as much of the Redwoods as we wanted, we moved south to Fort Bragg. Not being the busy summer tourist season, it was fairly easy to book camping places, and we found one close to the harbor right south of the town.

That night, we enjoyed a delightful dinner at a seafood restaurant overlooking the harbor decorated in sea-faring fisherman chic. Afterwards, we found Noyo Headlands Park, where we went for a walk, hand in hand, hearing the sound of ocean waves crashing on the shoreline rocks. We stayed to watch the sunset over the ocean, then went back to the RV park and bed.

"Let's stay here for another day. I'd like to explore the main street and go back to that park again," Hanna said before we dozed off.

"Okay with me … thought you were in a rush to get to see your mom."

"Another day won't hurt. I love you."

She kissed me goodnight and rolled over. Her breathing deepened into sleep. I lay awake, thinking how much I liked this little town and was happy to stay for a day, or possibly longer, maybe even live here.

The next morning, Hanna wanted to call her mother. It suddenly occurred to me that I'd not turned on my cell phone since I went into the retreat center over five weeks ago. I'd completely spaced off both phone and computer. I tried booting it up, and seeing the battery was drained I plugged it in. In a few minutes, it came to life and notified me of a number of phone calls, seven messages, and many emails. First, I checked messages: two from my parents; three from Karen, and two from Gordon, my boss from Americo Finance in Chicago.

I needed to call him back but wanted to avoid a decision I knew I'd have to make sooner or later. It was Saturday, and Karen would be off work, so I took a breath and decided to call her.

She answered quickly with the usual, "Russell, where are you? We haven't heard from you in weeks. We're all worried sick about you and—"

I interrupted: "I called and left you a message that I would be off my cell for four weeks. Didn't you get it?"

"Well, yes, but we didn't know where you were and that number to call only if it was a life or death matter. What was that about? Where have you been?"

"I'm in Fort Bragg, California. I turned off my cell when I spent four weeks at a Buddhist retreat center in Oregon. I've been traveling and exploring the redwoods this last week. I know I should've called when I left Oregon, but I didn't even think about my phone. I just turned it on and—"

"Well, thank you very much. Mom and Dad are worried to death and you turn off your cell phone?"

"I'm really sorry, Karen. I apologize, it was thoughtless of me. I'll call Mom and Dad and let them know I'm okay."

"Well, I hope so," she responded coldly. "You out running round by yourself. Anything could happen. You could be murdered or something and we'd never know. And what kind of center? Buddhist? Have you totally lost your mind! God, Russell, you weren't raised like that, doing some pagan thing!"

"I'm fine, Karen. Truth is, I've never been happier in my life. It was a good four weeks there. I learned a lot. I feel more alive every day," I said with elated enthusiasm.

"Slow down. What? You sound like you're in love or something."

"That too. Yes, for the first time I think I understand love, and I'm in love and committed to the woman I met hitchhiking back in Iowa, Hanna, she's—"

"Committed to? You got married! You really have lost your mind! What'll Mom—"

"We're not married, have no intentions of marriage … yet."

"You need help. Are you drinking? Is that it? You've turned into a drunk. Or drugs? God, Russell. Please. You need help!"

With that, I couldn't help myself; I started laughing, just as Rinpoche had laughed at what he saw as the absurdity of life. "I'm not drinking. I'm not drunk, not on any drugs. I'm just happy. Please just understand. People can be happy, you know."

233

"I wish that were the case; I … I really wish that were the case."

"Karen, what? What's wrong? Is something going on? Is everything okay?"

I heard a sniffle. "No, it's not. It's John … we've been going through some bad times. He wants a divorce." The sniffles increased. "I can't fail, Russell. I just can't. First you. Then me. Then … then what'll I do … the kids? He took the boys."

"Holy crap! No! How can this be? You both seemed so content and happy when I stayed with you. It made me jealous. What happened?"

I heard her blowing her nose. "Everything was bad before you came. With you there, it broke the spell of the problems we were having. But after you left, it fell apart again, really fell apart. That's when he told me he was having an affair. I don't understand. He's moved out, to Iowa City, and he took the boys. I feel so bad for them. They were like my own kids and now—Mom and Dad don't know. I'm scared, Russell. Now I understand how you felt. I don't know what to do."

And then I heard full-blown sobbing. My heart ached for her. Now I understood her recent coldness towards me. I'd offered structure to a crumbling marriage when I'd stayed with them. I struggled for something to say and remembered Rinpoche's words about suffering and attachment. In the kindest way I could, I tried my best to talk to her about suffering, about attachment, about letting go. Her crying slowly abated.

"Thank you. Those were nice words, but I'm not sure I can just let go like you say. There's so much involved, so much history."

I talked to her about being present, being in the moment, being aware, taking charge of your life, and, repeating, to let go.

Here I was, some novice trying to be a counselor, but I'd learned some things this last while, valuable things that were becoming clearer each day.

"Thanks, Russell. I know you're trying to help, but I really don't understand what you're talking about. Are these things you learned at that retreat center?"

"Some, but a lot from Hanna and a lot from reading. Just think about these things. It took me a while, but this stuff started to make sense to me. It's hard and still sinking in. Is there anything else I can do? Do you want to come out here for a while? We have a tent. You'd be welcome. Getting away for a week or so might help. I'll send money for a plane ticket. I'd love to see you and have you meet Hanna. Take some time, Sis."

"Thanks, Russell. That means a lot, but—"

"But what?"

"What would Mom and Dad think? Then they'd suspect."

"They're going to find out anyway, sooner or later. I'm surprised they haven't already with small town gossip and all. You said John's left, taken the boys? They're going to find out. You need to get out of there. We're heading to Hanna's mother's in Sausalito. You could fly into San Francisco. We'd come and get you."

"Give me some time, Russell. It sounds tempting. I'd love to get away. Give me a few days. I do have a lot of accumulated vacation time. But then there's Mom and Dad."

"Karen! Mom and Dad will be Mom and Dad. They haven't gotten over me, so no matter what happens, they'll be who they are."

"I know; I know," she said wearily.

"I need to call them, but I won't say anything about what we talked about. Promise. Been there, know the consequences."

"Thanks. I'm sorry for being so, I don't know, cold to you. You said you loved me; you never said that before; I didn't know how to respond, but, Russell, thanks. I love you too. Gotta go."

"Love you too, Sis. Talk to you soon and think about everything I said. Okay?"

"I will. I promise. Bye." She clicked off.

I sat there, thinking, wondering how weird life can be. I thought Karen and John were the perfect family while everything was shit. How long had my own marriage been shit before I even knew? It hit me how much Karen and I were alike. I knew I loved her like the only real family I had.

Hanna returned all bubbly and excited, telling me about her call to her mother: how excited she was in looking forward to meeting me; that they wanted us to stay in the house; how Frank wanted to meet me; how happy they both were for us, and that they already loved me.

I must have sat there acting disinterested because, sounding annoyed, she said, "What's wrong with you? Are you listening? Do you even care what I'm saying?"

"Yes, yes! I'm sorry. Yes, I'm very excited to meet your folks; really, I am. It was my call to my sister." I told her of the conversation.

"Oh, shit! I'm sorry. Do you think she might actually come out? That would be so exciting. I'd love to meet her. I'm really sorry for her. So sorry." She gave me a reassuring hug, "Come on, let's go to town."

Hand in hand, we strolled down the main street lined with the sort of quirky little shops that cater to the tourist trade. The smell of incense wafted out the open door of one shop as we walked by. Hanna pulled my hand.

"Let's go in here to look around."

I glanced at the sign in the window as she dragged me in. It read, *Incense, Crystals, Tie Dye, Meditation Supplies, Metaphysical Books, Readings, and More.* Tapestries hung on the walls, and Buddhist statues, candles, beads, jewelry, scarves, clothing, and so on filled shelves to overflowing.

A pleasant-looking woman wearing a colorful, flowing dress greeted us. Gray streaked her long, once-dark hair. "How can I help you? Looking for anything in particular?"

I was about to say, "No, just looking," when Hanna said, "Tell us about your readings."

"My name is Mariah Morning Star. I do aura readings, chakra clearing, and palm readings. Are you interested?"

"We are," Hanna replied gleefully.

I tried to pull Hanna away, but she pulled back, and asked this Mariah Morning Star about cost and scheduling us. *Us? Us!*

"Things are so slow right now," Mariah said, "I could do both of you right now. Do you want to be together or separate?"

Hanna said, "Together," just as I said, "I decline."

Hanna shot me a look. "Come on, Russell. Don't be such a poop. It'll be fun. I'll go by myself if you want."

"Go ahead. It's not something I want to do. I'll wait. How long will you be?"

Mariah answered: "Oh, usually half an hour or so for a basic reading, depending on how far the client wants to go. Some want an aura reading and a chakra cleanse. It all depends on what you want."

They discussed prices, and Hanna gave me her I'm-doing-this-and-so-are-you look. I smiled weakly and said, "Go ahead. Take your time, and I'll think about it. I'll wait here or browse the bookstore we saw."

Mariah gave me a key and told me to lock up if I left. She then locked the front door and led Hanna into a back room. I browsed the store and found myself drawn to a bronze statue of the Buddha, similar to the one I'd seen at the center, but smaller, about eight inches tall. I set it on the counter by the register, then I looked at a display of different-colored stones and crystals. One about six inches tall had a tag that specified it as a quartz crystal. It also called to me. I picked it up and felt a tingle run up my arm and into my body. I'd ask Mariah about that. I set it on the counter along with the Buddha.

I continued looking through the assortment of items. They seemed odd to me, but interesting all the same. I found some incense I liked and a little wood bowl to catch the ashes as it burned. The books had topics such as angels, crystals, energy healing, and things I had no clue about. Engrossed with my browsing, time flew by.

"Hey, Russell, you're still here. I thought you'd be at the bookstore." I looked over at a beaming Hanna and a smiling Mariah. "You really need to do this, Russell. Mariah is amazing," Hanna said with big sweet eyes. "Come on! You have to do it. Please. Please do it; do it for me. Please."

"I'm sorry, but I don't think so. It's just not something I'm ready to do."

"That's okay," Mariah said. "Not everyone wants to or needs to do this woo woo stuff, and I can perfectly understand. It can be weird."

Hanna shot me a mildly disgusted look. "Russell? Come on."

"Sorry, but no. Maybe another time," I said firmly, and the subject was dropped.

"Are you wanting to buy these?" Mariah asked, pointing to the items I'd placed on the counter. I nodded.

"That's a nice crystal. Leave it out in the full moon whenever you can to cleanse it, or bath it in salt water every month or so.

It'll help you on your journey. And the Buddha … it's nice. I'm able to get these from India."

"Tell me about this crystal," I said and related the sensation I'd felt.

"Many semi-precious stones, especially crystal points such as this one, are sources of energy," she explained. "It's said that crystals are able to project the energy of the sun, moon, earth and oceans. There's anecdotal evidence that stones have healing powers." Mariah gave me a questioning look to see if what she'd said made any sense to me.

"I don't understand how an inanimate stone can have energy."

"Everything has energy; inanimate objects, such as stones, manifest it in more subtle ways than we, as animate humans, understand. Everything is essentially constructed of the same atomic matter but have different forms. Our subtle bodies are made up of the very same elements as that crystal. More sensitive humans can sense the more subtle energies like you apparently just did.

"For instance, there have been experiments done on water by a Japanese researcher by the name of Masaru Emoto who demonstrated that water crystal patterns can be changed simply by intention. He placed water into various vials from the same original source. He then taped notes of different intentions, both positive, like love and peace, on some vials, and negative, like war and hate, on others. Later, he froze the water and examined the frozen crystals under a dark field microscope that has photographic capabilities. Come over here and I'll show you his book."

I went with her and she pulled out the book. I saw exactly what she'd told me: the water picked up the positive intentions and the frozen crystals were bright and beautiful while the ones with the negative crystals were misshapen and dull-colored. He'd also experimented with music and gotten similar results.

"Okay, this looks impressive, but what does that have to do with crystals?" I asked.

Mariah took me over to where I'd found the crystal and said, "Here; let go and close your eyes, and I'll hand you different stones. Tell me if you feel anything from any of them. Now, don't peek."

I played along with her little game. One at a time, she placed stones in my hand until I felt a tingle from one. I looked. It was the same one I'd picked earlier.

She laughed. "See; what did I tell you? Let's try some more."

I closed my eyes while she placed several more of different sizes and shapes in my hand. I felt another tingle and peeked. This one was smaller, rose-colored, and polished smooth into the shape of a heart.

"Interesting," Mariah said. "This stone is about love, about the heart. It draws love, plus it can heal a heart if it's been deprived of love."

I found that interesting given my past and present circumstances. Maybe there was something to all this crazy stuff she was telling me.

"Thanks, Mariah, while this all seems weird, I have to say, it is interesting. I'd like this stone also."

"Take it as a gift. It likes you. Carry it with you in your pocket. Some folks say that a stone actually chooses you, rather than you, it. I think these two have chosen you. And the quartz crystal you've chosen is a master healer and will raise your energy and awareness. Place it in your meditation room or anywhere you choose."

She looked at Hanna, who'd been watching patiently, and said, "Drink lots and lots of water today, lots of water. Okay?"

"Of course," Hanna said.

With that I paid for Hanna's reading and my purchases, thanked her, and went to find lunch.

"So, what did she tell you?" I asked.

"It was interesting. I've had readings before where I'd be asked a lot of questions, and the reader would build off my answers. I always thought that they just told you what you wanted to hear from how you answered. But Mariah just took both my hands in hers and closed her eyes, not saying anything. Then, after a few minutes, she started by saying she saw some past trauma, a dark time that occurred a while ago, that I'd shed some karma and my path was now cleared of a shadow from a past life. She went on to tell me that I'd have some success with the career I wanted, that my past struggles with finding success had been removed, that a new partnership would emerge. She didn't mention anything about us."

"So what do you think about all that?"

"It was interesting that she focused in on what I'm guessing was what happened three years ago, and then her response about a shadow from my past life being cleared. And my career? What career? I asked her and she responded with, 'you'll know'."

"Music, silly. What else could it've been? That's what you want."

"You think so?"

"I know so … and I'm not a psychic reader."

"I really wish you would have done a reading too," she said.

"I know, but right now, I have enough to deal with."

"Maybe it would've given you some better insight into your life."

"Maybe, but it's not something I wanted to do. Rinpoche gave about as much insight as I can handle right now."

The rest of the day we spent with a light lunch, browsing through bookstores and shops, and another evening walk in the Noyo Headlands Park.

That night, I lay awake, trying to wrap my head round the strange events in Mariah's little store. We left for Sausalito in the morning.

Chapter 20: Sausalito, October 1

We stayed on the Coast Highway, which was slower, calmer, and more scenic, as well as being gentler on the Westy than Highway 101 or I-5. I wanted to pull over every time an opportunity rose to just look at the ocean with all its mysterious expanse—nothing but rolling, roiling water between Hawaii, Japan, China, and so many other exotic places. I thought about getting a sailboat and sailing to all these places. When I told Hanna these thoughts, all she said was, "Dream on, Sailor."

Miles later, we left the ocean and went inland, along Tomales Bay, then inland again onto the 101, and arrived in Sausalito, which is built on a hill overlooking San Francisco Bay.

We didn't go into the town. Hanna directed me off 101 to the right and through some winding streets. She told me to slow, then turn up a narrow driveway.

Hanna, eager to see her folks, jumped out before I'd even stopped. "Come on, Russell. Come meet my family."

I got out and saw an older version of Hanna coming to greet us—same green eyes, auburn hair, only much longer and with strands of grey, braided into a plait. She had an air of grace and elegance about her, like a dancer I'd recently known briefly. I immediately sensed her as a woman to be reckoned with.

She ran up and gave Hanna a long hug, then turned to me, gave me a once over and said, "Hi, Russell. Welcome," then gave me an equally long embrace. "Thank you for bringing her home. Come, let me show you around our humble abode."

She took my hand and led me towards what, I would find out, was a Spanish-style house. The "humble abode" was a sprawling one-story, white stuccoed palace with a red-tile roof and a covered porch with arches supported by round columns over a glazed red-tile floor. The dark-stained, solid-looking, wooden entrance door opened into an arched entry leading into a large room with a dark-wood beamed ceiling and multi-paned windows. The interior walls were soft off-white stucco hung with tapestries and modernist artwork.

She led me through the comfortably furnished room to wide double doors and out to a back yard enclosed by thick shrubbery, then onto a flagstone patio where chairs and benches surrounded a fire pit. A large hot tub sat on the right. An outbuilding turned out to be Meg's studio, and Frank's woodshop sat behind the two-car garage.

Meg chatted all the way, asking me questions, while Hanna tagged along behind. After the quick tour, Meg took us to a large bedroom with a king bed and an attached bathroom with double sinks and a walk-in shower. Large doors opened onto the back patio.

"You and Hanna will stay in here," she said. "Bring in what you need, and make yourself at home for as long as you want. Excuse me, I have a phone call I need to make. I'll see you shortly. Frank should be home anytime."

She turned, slid by Hanna, and flitted out of sight down the corridor. I felt a little uneasy and overwhelmed by these accommodations. I turned to Hanna. "I feel strange sleeping with you in your parents' house. Maybe I should have my own bedroom? Or I could stay in the camper."

"God, Russell, you can be so dense sometimes. She knows we've been sleeping together. I've told her we were and everything else. Let's get our stuff." She grabbed my hand and led me out, mumbling something about prudes.

I stood there, beet red, knowing that her mother was fully aware of our intimacies.

Outside, I asked, "How long are you planning on staying here? A few days? A week?"

"Oh, as long as we want. Mom is hoping we'll be here for a while. I don't know, probably forever if it was up to her. She likes having me here, and this house is so big. We've actually gone days without hardly seeing each other. Do you have someplace else you need to be?"

"It's just, like … well, I don't want to be a freeloader."

"You won't be a freeloader. Trust me."

We got everything we needed from the camper, which really wasn't much. I'd hardly increased my wardrobe since I'd left Iowa, and Hanna had everything she owned in her backpack. We had the few books we'd bought and our instruments. That was it.

"Oh, I think I hear Frank. Come on and meet him."

I followed Hannah to the big room, where I saw a tall man with narrow hips, broad shoulders, blond hair, and blazing blue eyes set into a square-jawed, chiseled face. He wore a sleeveless t-shirt exposing his muscular, tattooed arms, khaki cargo shorts, and flip-flops. Hanna ran to him, and he swept her up into what appeared to me to be a bone-crushing hug.

"Hanna! So good to see you! You're back. I can quit worrying now. Man, you look more beautiful than ever. Traveling must suit you." He grabbed her again for a long hug and kisses on her cheeks. She giggled in delight. He let her go and turned to me. "And you're Russell …"

He walked towards me, and I felt completely intimidated by him. He grabbed my hand and pulled me into a man hug, something I'd never experienced before. Men in my family and in my hometown did not hug. You shook hands at proper arm's length and that was that. Having never been hugged by a man before, I was taken by how hard his body felt, unlike Hanna's, which was all soft and snuggly. As I thought about it, I realized that where I came from men and women didn't hug either, unless it was women and their husbands, and even then never in public.

"Damn, Russell, good to meet you. Hanna's told me about you, said she likes you. I guess if she thinks you're okay, maybe I will too."

I tried to be brave and put on my best financial bank poise. "Frank, nice to meet you. Hanna's told me you're a poet, recently published."

"Yeah, the third book, a small book, is just out. I'll get you a signed copy. Have a few around somewhere." He turned to walk away, and I noticed the ponytail that hung down to the middle of his back.

This guy is like a Hell's Angel guy on steroids. And he's with Meg?

I spoke quietly to Hanna so he wouldn't hear me: "This is Frank? I expected some sort of scholarly guy; he scares me. Seriously, he's like scary."

She just giggled. "He's. Not. Scary. He's a real pussy cat. He's the mildest, nicest, most caring man I've ever known … except for you, of course. You're even more so in all categories." She looked at me with those soft, loving eyes, took my hand, and pecked me on the cheek. I melted.

Frank returned and handed me his book. "For you, Hanna's friend. Hope you enjoy."

I took the book. "Thanks, Frank. This is really nice of you."

"Hell, man, you're family, unless you fuck up. Until then, want a margarita or a beer?"

"Go ahead," Hanna said. "I'm going to put in our laundry."

"I'll have whatever you're having," I said.

"Then let's do some margs. Com'n and follow me to bliss." He headed for the kitchen. "So, she's doing your laundry, eh? That's serious shit, my man, serious. Especially when she sends you off to drink with me." He laughed with a big booming laugh—like I would've expected any less? "So, Russell, what's your gig? Just out roaming around in that nice lookin' Westy?"

"At the moment I'm sort of on sabbatical from the bank where I work in Chicago. Yeah, guess I'm just out on the road, until now, anyway." *Dammit, I have to call my boss.*

"Good for you, my man. Don't go back to that shit. Stay here in sunny Cal. I've lived here all my life, and I'll never leave. I have so much. Dude. I have a wonderful woman, who I love more than life itself. I love doing woodwork, and people pay a lot of money for what I do. I write poetry for my mind and spirit. My body I work out other ways. Want to go to the gym with me tomorrow morning and do some lifting?"

"Maybe another time? I need to settle in and just be off the road for a bit. When do you go?"

"Oh, I go about every other day or so for around an hour. I'll let you know. It'll be fun. Then we'll go for breakfast." He handed me a frosty margarita. "Let's go sit outside."

We went out by the fire ring to enjoy a beautiful afternoon. I sat back into a chair and basked in the sun. I felt good. I liked "scary" Frank, only worried about trying to keep up with him.

Neither of us spoke. I savored my excellent margarita and the quiet of the Californian afternoon.

247

"Hey, guys, we're heading to the hot tub," Hanna called. "Come join us."

Frank called back, "We'll be right there. Save us a seat."

I never knew anyone that actually had a hot tub. The gym I went to in Chicago had one, but I'd never used it. After doing the sweat lodge, this couldn't be all that bad.

"Give me your glass and I'll refresh it for you," Frank said. "Go get ready and I'll bring it out."

Hanna came out with a towel wrapped around her as I went in to change. She stopped, pecked me on the cheek and said, "I put a towel for you on the bed. See you in a minute. I love you."

I fumbled around looking for my swimsuit, which I couldn't locate. Then I remembered I'd left it in a cubby in the camper. I went to get it and saw Frank heading out wrapped in a towel and carrying two drinks. I hurried and got my suit and headed to the tub. Hanna motioned me to sit in beside her. Meg and Frank sat across from us, and I noticed quizzical stares from all three as I got in. Frank motioned me to my margarita, now in a plastic glass. Hanna and Meg both had wine.

I slid into the hot water which seemed really hot, but mellowed as my body got used to the heat. I relaxed in. The jets gave a slight massage to my back.

This is living. Sure isn't Iowa. God, I'm already loving California.

We didn't talk, everyone just lay back and enjoyed the warmth and the ambience. The jets stopped and the water quieted down, and I saw, for the first time, that everyone was naked, but for me. I diverted my gaze. I know I turned beet red.

Meg saw me and—I will love her forever—reached around and pushed the button for the jets. "Ever been in a hot tub before, Russell?" she asked.

"My first time. It's nice. Relaxing and, uh, interesting."

"We're out here almost every afternoon, sometimes in the evening before bed. It is relaxing. We're doing steaks tonight for dinner with sweet potatoes and green salad. Do you have any dietary concerns?" she asked, looking at me.

Dietary concerns? "I don't think so. I just eat what's available."

"Good to know. So many are gluten intolerant, or vegetarian, or vegan, or whatever, these days. I always need to ask. We're pretty much paleo: meat and lots of veggies. But we cheat every so often."

"Yeah, like all the time," said Frank, laughing.

"We do not … well, more than we should," Meg answered back, laughing, giving him a peck on the cheek.

I'd never seen my parents show affection to each other. I felt a little embarrassed, but warm and happy to be there.

The mood was quiet. Paradise. Meg and Frank seemed nice and gracious, and I was with Hanna, and in love. It was a perfect moment, except everybody was naked.

I got up to leave before anyone else. "I think I've had enough. I'm going to take a quick shower. See you all in a bit." I jumped up and out, grabbed my towel and headed the house, not looking back as I heard the others getting out.

I went in and showered off quickly and was just coming out when Hanna came in.

She looked at me, almost choking, trying to keep from laughing. "Russell, I'm so sorry. I should have told you, we always hot tub naked. I'm sorry. I saw you were uncomfortable. Meg and Frank feel bad too. But, actually, seeing your look when you saw us—" She was burbling, couldn't hold it any longer and fell onto the bed laughing so hard I had to get her a tissue to dry her eyes.

Acting faux indignant, I said, "Hope you all had a great time running around naked in front of this innocent, embarrassed boy."

She grabbed me and pulled me onto her. "I love you so much it hurts."

Sometime later, we arrived in the kitchen where Meg was making salad and Frank was readying the steaks for the grill. Meg shot us a look with a knowing grin. I knew she'd heard our lovemaking, and now I felt really embarrassed. Hanna grabbed my hand and pecked me on the cheek, letting me know it was all right. I squeezed her hand, letting her know that I was all right.

Hanna left to help Frank with something at the grill, leaving me alone with Meg. "Can I help with anything—salad or set the table?" I asked.

"No, just sit and relax."

I took a stool from under the counter.

"Russell, I'm really sorry. We should've—"

I laughed. "What? Sorry you didn't know I was a prude?"

I told her of my first encounter with Hanna back in Nebraska, and we both laughed.

"Meg," I said after we quit laughing, "I'm learning. Hanna has exposed me to so much. She's showing me a whole world I never knew existed. She's the best thing that ever happened to me. She really is. And I'm very much in love with her."

"Serendipity is an interesting concept, isn't it?" She came around from her salad-making, pulled me to her and hugged me. "I'm happy she found you. I haven't seen her so happy and so centered in a long while. She told you about what happened, didn't she?"

"Yeah, she did. I'm really sad and sorry."

"Are you okay with it? Please don't lead her on if you're not."

"I'm perfectly okay with it, and my intentions are all good. I can't remember ever feeling so strongly about anyone. She's the most important thing in my life. I truly love that woman … truly, truly love her." A lump choked off anything more I might've wanted to say. I couldn't believe I had said all that I just did.

She looked at me. "Then we all love you just as much. You are now officially part of this rather wacky, wicked family. It might be a wild ride."

I laughed, then became serious. "Thanks, Meg. You have no idea how much that means to me. You have no idea."

When the food was ready, we gathered at the outside table. Frank said a blessing, giving thanks for the food and for Hanna being back and for me being there. I basked in the feeling of warmth and inclusiveness. Right then, I felt more a part of this family than I ever had with my own.

Conversation went on after the food was cleaned up, and another bottle of wine was opened. Frank lit the gas-fired fire pit, which we sat around, enjoying the warmth against the oncoming night, and, for me, a new sense of closeness. Frank lit a joint and passed it around. When it came to me, everybody looked at me, and Hanna said, "Have you ever smoked weed before?"

"No, never have," I lied. "What's it like?"

"It just mellows you out. But only take a little puff. It's seriously powerful."

I noticed everyone else had only taken a little "hit", so I took an even smaller one, sputtering and coughing. Soon I felt that nice quietness come over me as it had with Cassy back in Glacier. I quickly wiped away that thought.

"Russell," Meg said, "Hanna tells me you're a good musician. Will you play something?"

I turned red. "First off, I'm far from being very good. I admit to having backed up Hanna on occasion, but I'm certainly not a solo performer, not even close to how good she is."

Hanna smiled at me. "Then let's play together, and you can show your stuff."

I had no argument, so we got our instruments, tuned up, and played several of Hanna's songs, then did some old folk songs everybody knew. Frank got out his banjo and joined in. He was really good. Now I had to stay out of the way of two people. I did what I could on the mandolin.

It grew late and chilly, even with the fire, so we called it a night.

"I'm going in for yoga in the morning," Meg said as we walked towards the house. "You and Russell want to come? I think Frank's got an early meeting in the city with the contractor to discuss the door he's working on."

"Is it Star's class?" Hanna asked. "Then I'll go for sure. Russell does yoga—"

I interrupted: "Ah, once, and it wasn't pretty. Maybe not."

Both women at the same time said, "Oh, you're coming. We'll kidnap you."

After another session of beautiful sex, I remembered nothing until Hanna said, "Get up, sleepyhead, we're leaving in a half hour."

I opened my eyes and saw her standing over me, dressed in yoga pants and a tight black tee that read "Yoga Bitch" in pink on the front.

"What time is it? I was really asleep. How long have you been up?"

"Not long. Coffee's ready. Mom made some killer muffins."

"I'm going to have to pass. I have a phone call to Chicago, and it's already eleven thirty there. I've put it off too long already. I have to let them know what's up. Next time?"

Hanna looked at me. "What? You okay?"

"Not really. I have to call my boss at Americo."

"Wow, what are you going to do? You're not going back, are you?"

"I don't know. Maybe this is all ridiculous. I can't drive around, living in a camper. I have a good position and make good money. It really wasn't that bad. I feel better about my life. My parents would be happier. Maybe things would be better—"

Hanna gave me an incredulous look. I couldn't tell if it was a look of surprise, dismay, anger, or all three rolled into one.

She turned away and started toward the kitchen. "Let's go, Mom. Russell's not coming. He's going back to fucking Chicago."

"But, Hanna, we could—" I started to go after her, but I was still in my birthday suit. I hurried to get some clothes on, but heard the front door slam and a car leaving. "Awe, shit! What just happened?"

I heard Frank say, "I think you royally fucked up, man."

"Shit! You scared the hell out of me. I thought you were gone for your appointment."

"Sorry, couldn't help overhearing. Leaving in a few. Want to come? I'm going into the city to meet with the contractor for this door I'm building and get some more accurate measurements now that the opening's framed. Won't take me long. I'd like the company. Obviously, you're not going to yoga."

I grabbed some coffee and a muffin, happily blew off my Chicago call, and joined Frank in his pickup. He went to his

253

meeting in shorts, a Grateful Dead t-shirt, and running shoes. At the bank, I wore a three-piece suit to meetings. I found it hard to get my brain around his way of doing business.

After a few miles of silence, Frank asked, "So what's this about you going back to Chicago? Hanna isn't too wild about that idea from what I saw."

"Truth is, I took a sabbatical to get over some depression issues. I guess, my boss thinks it's time to be over my depression and come back to work. I stupidly hadn't talked to Hanna about any of it. God, I'm so stupid."

"Yeah, man, you've got to talk about this stuff. You're not the lone ranger, if you're at all serious about her. So, are you … over it, the depression, I mean?"

"It's a long story …" I told him about my position at the bank and the conflict I felt because I had to make a decision, either resign or get back to work.

"So, Russell, do you like working at a bank in Chicago? Is that what you want to do with your life?"

"I don't know—no, I don't. I don't. But there's my parents and their expectations. What'll I do? I haven't a clue what else I could ever do."

"How's your cash? Do you have to work right now? You have your van. Hell, I'd stay on the road for a while if I could. Or stay here. Enjoy. Chill. You're young. You'd be able to find work."

"I'm okay money-wise, but it's not very responsible to just not work, to just travel around."

"So, who gave that information? Your parents?"

"Well, yeah. They … they raised me to be responsible and hardworking, and lately I've been really slacking off."

He laughed. "Well, that should make you feel guilty as hell. Take your time, man. Enjoy your life. It's all we got. Ya know,

I grew up in Oakland. My father was a hippie and a carpenter. Smoked dope, drank tequila, and was hard as nails. My mother? Never knew her. She left when I was around three. So my dad, Ray, raised me by himself.

"He taught me to be independent, to think for myself, to reject the usual bullshit. I was a bit of a rebel in high school, in and out of trouble, expelled once for two weeks. I did graduate, though, somehow. Dad lined me up with a woodworker he knew, and I started an apprenticeship of sorts. I liked it and still do; it's been good to me. Meg's an artist in oils on canvas; I'm an artist with wood.

"What I'm trying to say here is that conformity sucks, and you seem totally caught up in the conformity game and what others think you should do rather than thinking about whatever it is you want. Am I close?"

I didn't say anything for a few miles, then admitted, "Yeah, pretty much sums it up."

He didn't say anything more, and I just rode along thinking, trying to figure out just what the hell it was that I did want. I had money, more than I'd ever need. My portfolio was growing, and I wasn't spending anything hardly, except for food and fuel. I was used to shelling out over three grand per month for the Chicago apartment, plus utilities. Dana and I always ate out. And I spent on clothes, laundry, dry cleaning, and taxis. Summing it all up, our cost of living was probably close to five or six grand a month. Now I was living on less than five hundred a month.

We drove across the famous Golden Gate Bridge where the city of San Francisco spread out to our left from the edge of the bay to the hills to the east. Frank navigated through the city traffic into a quieter neighborhood of Victorian-style houses on one of the famous San Francisco hills. He pulled in behind a dumpster in front of a house with plastic sheeting in place of windows and a piece of plywood for the front door. A few workers went about their business on the property.

Frank got out. "Come on in, Russ, and see this. It's a huge restoration of an original, built right after the fire. It's going to be an amazing house when done. I have several parts that I'm restoring or building new like the fireplace surround and mantel, several interior doors, and the front door. I'm also making some base and crown moldings to match the original as well—fun job."

I followed him inside. He found the head carpenter, and they went over some construction drawings. Frank took some notes, then went to do some measurements. He caught my eye, motioned that it was time to go.

Back in the truck, Frank said, "I know a great place for some coffee and pastries. I'll buy."

We drove through several city blocks, and he found a place to park about half a block away from a small bakery with mouth-watering smells—and that's before I even went in. We ordered, found a table.

Frank asked, "So, what are you going to do? About Hanna and this Chicago thing?"

"Obviously I need to talk to her. Chicago? It would be the responsible thing to do. It would certainly make my parents happier about me than they are. Except they also think I should get back with Dana, my ex-wife, who divorced me. I need to make a decision about the job. I should've called this morning."

"It appears that you are more concerned about pleasing your parents than yourself," he said. "You know, you exist as an individual. You have freedom and choice. We humans define our own meaning in our life, trying to make rational decisions in an otherwise irrational universe."

256

"I'm not sure I understand. I think I owe some responsibility to my parents. I mean, they raised me and put me through college. And they took me to church. That gave me some basis."

"Yes, they did all that … and now? Now what? You're a grown man. They should trust that you can make your own decisions with your life. Like, you made a choice to go on this journey. What have you discovered?"

"That I like it out here, I guess. I'm happy I met Hanna. I don't know, sometimes I get scared. I sometimes wish I never did this. I had a decent life, a great apartment in downtown Chicago, made good money. I would've eventually gotten over my depression about my divorce if I'd stayed there. Sometimes I think it'd just be easier to go back."

"Maybe all that might be true; you could go back, but back to what? Once you start to wake up, it's really hard, if not impossible, to go back. And I seriously doubt Hanna would want to embrace the lifestyle you've just told me about. What about her?"

I shrugged. I had no idea.

"You have to understand," Frank continued, "that our traditional religious and secular rules are arbitrary, made up by folks who want to control us, folks who think they have all the answers, know better than we do about ourselves. Trust me, they don't. You're best when working with your own nature, struggling for your own life. We choose our own self through our choices and our choices alone. But there're lots of folks who choose to live by the rules because they're afraid what might happen if they don't. Know what I mean?"

"I'm trying to grasp what you're saying, but don't we need rules?"

"Sadly, for the majority, we do need rules. Why? Because thinking for oneself is difficult and can be downright damn scary. In order to be free, personal responsibility, respect, and discipline are crucial. We have to be responsible and respectful, not only to ourselves but also to society at large. Just imagine if every single human being on this planet had the utmost respect for everyone else, every creature, every plant, everything."

This sounded like what Rinpoche had told me—compassion towards all sentient beings. I hadn't touched my coffee or my croissant. Frank's words were hard for me to grasp—scary.

He continued. "Personal responsibility and discipline are crucial to a balanced society and very difficult … can be frightening and overwhelming. It can be a lot of work. It's our responsibility to be aware of ourselves and how we move through this life."

"I think I know what you're getting at. Who runs my life? Society, expectations of others, my parents, or me?"

"Exactly. The point is, you made a decision to do this trip, to try to see some different parts of the country, have new experiences. But what've you truly experienced? Good things, bad things? How has your decision impacted your life?"

I didn't say anything, just sipped at my now-cooling coffee and munched on the sweet, flaky almond croissant. "Getting right down to it, you're right," I said eventually. "It is hard trying to live up to everyone else's expectations, and I guess I've been living my life for everyone else except me. I made the choice to marry Dana, then work seventy or eighty hours a week, thinking I'd impress her and my parents. That didn't turn out very well. I made the decision to do this journey against everyone dismissing it as some stupid fantasy. It's opened my eyes to a lot of things, and a lot of it has been very uncomfortable."

"Facing yourself can be very difficult," Frank said. "Downright terrifying at times. But it can be a blast, if you quit taking everything so damn seriously."

"So, Frank, how do you know all this shit? I mean, you just laid some interesting stuff on me."

He laughed. "Sorry, but if Hanna likes you, so do I. She and Meg are the most important and precious things in my life, so I wanted to tune you in. But, ya know, I never had a college education. I learned everything from reading: philosophy, poetry, historical fiction, and history. I was lucky enough to meet Meg, man, like twenty years ago. She was a single mother with Hanna in this artist commune. I was working for the woodworker that I apprenticed with. We hardly had a dime between us. Meg's parents were supporting her and her art, so we managed to hang on.

"A few years after we met, she got a showing of her work in a fairly decent gallery here in the city. Her work was well received, had a good turnout at the opening, selling half her paintings. The newspaper gave her a good review, and the rest of her work sold out in a few weeks. It was instant success for a young artist. Now her work is easily sold before she's even completed it. People are now looking at her work as collectable, rather than decoration.

"Shortly after all this, old Harry, the guy I worked for, decided to retire, and by that time, we had enough money that I could buy his business. And here we are. I never looked back. Hey, let's go. I want to go by City Lights before we head back."

On the way I saw my first red cable car. It rattled and clanged down the middle of the street, loaded with riders. Frank told me they're mostly a tourist attraction now, but a few locals still ride them to and from work or whatever. They're a San Francisco icon and the only remaining cable car system in the world.

Lawrence Ferlinghetti and Peter D. Martin established City Lights, another San Francisco landmark, in 1953. The store specializes in world literature, arts, and progressive politics. The signs in the upper four windows read, "Open Door, Open Books, Open Mind, Open Heart."

Inside, Frank went to talk with the manager, and I roamed the main floor, then the upper, and then discovered a basement. I wanted to read everything here. Frank found me downstairs.

"Hey, Frank, what do you recommend? Anything about what you talked about earlier?"

He motioned me to follow him to the philosophy section and pointed out several books on Existentialism and Deconstruction. "I have these back at the house, and you're more than welcome to read them—if you're going to be around, that is?"

"Thanks. We'll see. If so, I'll take you up on your offer." I'd already picked up a novel and another book on Buddhism.

We left and drove back to Sausalito without talking. I sat back, enjoying the city sights and the return trip across the Golden Gate Bridge.

Meg and Hanna weren't home when we returned to the house. Frank said, "Come on, and I'll show you my shop."

He led me into the large room behind the garage filled with machinery and the musky scent of wood from neatly organized stacks of various woods against one wall of the shop. He explained all the machinery, tools, and woods to me with great pride, then showed me what he'd completed so far for the door for the remodel. His work was impressive with precise detail.

We chatted a while, and I took my leave as it approached mid-afternoon. I wanted to call Americo Financial before they closed. The receptionist quickly patched me through to my old boss, Gordon.

"Russell. Good to finally hear from you. When are you coming back? I'm under a lot of pressure from above. They lost patience about two months ago and want your office with someone permanent in it. We have a temp, hoping he'd come along, but he hasn't. We need you back."

"I'm sorry, Gordon. I really am. I should have called you sooner, but—"

"Where are you? Are you in Iowa? Can you be here Monday?"

"No, I'm in San Francisco and plan on being here for a while."

"But, Russell, what's going on? You really need to get back here or I'll have to let you go."

"Understood ... truth is, Gordon, I want to tender my resignation. I'm sorry, but a lot of things have changed. I appreciate all you've done for me and for your patience, but coming back to work at Americo just won't work for me right now. I don't think I'd do you any good either. I'm sorry and grateful for your faith in me and for all your support."

"I'm shocked, Russell. You were one of our main employees. You did great work. Did you find another institution out there? Something better? More money? We'll match—"

"No, it's not that at all. I've been living in a camper since last May, traveling out west, trying to get over my depression, and I ended up here and like it, going to hang around here for a while. Anyway, I can send a written letter of resignation, or email you if that would be okay? Whatever will work for you."

"Are you sure about this? Really sure? I might be able to buy you more time. Think it over for a few days. If you're serious about resigning, we'll have to decide what you want to do with your stock options."

"Thanks, Gordon. I appreciate it, but no; I've made up my mind. Stock options? I forgot about them. Can I cash them out?"

"We can cash them out if you want. I'm really shocked, but it's your decision. You seem sure about it. I just can't understand why; I thought you appreciated being here, would be in my office someday. Anyway, I'll have my secretary get everything in order and email you the forms, plus I'll also send everything regular mail as well. There are some things you'll need to get notarized. One last time, are you sure about this?"

"Yes, Gordon, I'm sure. Again, I want to thank you for everything. If I ever get to Chicago, I'll buy you a drink."

"I'll hold you to that."

We said our goodbyes and disconnected. An immense weight had been lifted from my shoulders. It was a relief.

"Russell? Where are you?" I heard Hanna call.

"In here."

She came into the bedroom. "I thought you'd be on your fucking way to fucking Chicago by now. Better get your ass going. Time's wasting." She turned and walked out.

"Hanna! I resigned. I'm done with it. I'm sorry. I'm so sorry. I should've talked with you. It all blurted out, and I was thinking out loud. I'm really sorry. I just got off the phone, and other than paperwork formalities, I'm done. Period. I'm free."

She stopped, paused, and turned. "You what? You did it?"

"Yeah, I did. It was a hard decision, but it's the right one. Hell, Hanna, we can live forever on my investments. We can't be crazy, but I'm really well off. I want to share it with you. I love you, girl. I can't imagine ever being without you."

I happened to be sitting on the bed when she attacked me, and an hour later, we showered together, then went to the kitchen to help with dinner.

Meg and Frank were already there having cocktails and prepping something with lamb chops, asparagus and sweet potatoes. Meg gave me a look. Frank smiled and winked. I felt at home.

Next morning, I begged out of going to the gym with Frank, and Meg asked me to come and see her studio. The room was spotless, painted completely white and flooded with good natural light. A bounty of brushes and a large tray of oil paints sat on a table, and several different-size easels and a number of canvases leaned against the walls—some bare, some apparently in progress and some finished. A large painting sitting on a table against one wall dominated the room.

"This is my latest canvas, already sold."

I saw nothing recognizable in all the colors and meaningless shapes. I'd gone to the Chicago Art Institute with Dana a few times, but found it boring.

She saw my confusion. "What do you think?"

"I'm not sure. I don't know what to … or …" I stammered. "I guess I don't understand it."

Meg smiled. "It's abstract art. There's no recognizable image, and it isn't meant to depict anything other than to illicit emotion, feeling. Don't try to see anything representational. Most people see a painting and expect a recognizable scene, or person, or something they can identify. Just look at this and let go of preconceptions.

"Early painters up through the late nineteenth century worked on portraying the world as it was, realistically, many times incorporating fantasy, mythology, religious icons, and such. The French Impressionists felt that representing what they painted as reality, like what everyone was doing, was not what they wanted to do. They were the first to start abstracting reality. Then Pablo Picasso and Georges Braques pushed abstraction

263

even further with what they called Cubism. Then there were the Dadists. And now we have total abstraction that elicits pure emotion rather than any representation whatsoever. There's still representative art and always will be. But I chose this genre and have done well with it. Sometime I want to move away from this pure abstraction and to something else, but for now, this is what I do. It's served me well."

She faced me, and I noticed how she cocked her head and twirled a loose strand of her hair, exactly as Hanna did. It was very sexy.

I stared at the painting again for a while, and I did start to feel it. It was like meditation—not anything, but everything. "I have to admit, I'm not very astute as far as art goes, but I think I understand what you're saying. It might take a bit of practice for me, though. "

She laughed. "You aren't alone. We're so used to identifying what we see, categorizing things into this or that. Our brain has been taught to quantify what we see hear, touch, smell. We perceive things as we've been taught. When we see something, we immediately try to understand it, put a label on it, like, 'Oh, that's a cat,' or 'Oh, that's a car,' or 'Oh, that's a mountain sunset,' and so on. In my work, I try to have the viewer feel quality of the shapes, forms and colors, to move away from quantifying.

"When faced with something that challenges our perception, we can either try to understand it, learn about it, embrace it or, as many do with something unfamiliar, challenge it, dismiss it or, in a worst-case scenario, destroy it. Change and the unfamiliar can be very frightening for some people, and it can be much safer and easier for them to stay in their own narrow place. Closed minds are sad."

I stood, looking at her painting, absorbing all she'd just said. That was me, closed-minded, scared. I'd just made another major change in my life, and I was scared shitless. "I'm not sure what I feel, but I do like how the colors seem to want to work together and how it all goes together. Thanks for showing me. Can I see some others?"

She showed me about a dozen others, all large canvases. The more I saw, the more I understood what she'd just told me and what she was doing with her art. I couldn't say I liked it, but it started to grow on me.

Back at the house, Frank was taking a break and having a cup of coffee. "Russell, follow me. I'll show you the library."

He took me down a hallway to a part of the house I hadn't been in before, and we went into a small cozy room with a window facing to the front of the house, dark-wooden bookshelves on walls opposite each other, and two comfortable leather chairs. Soft creamy white walls and light brown carpet made for quiet, privacy, and reading.

"Help yourself to anything here." He pointed out the various categories of subject matter. "Here, there's one more room I want to show you." He led me to a room across the hall. "This is our meditation room."

I peered into another relatively small room. This had quiet, warm-gray walls with a darker gray carpet. A large window opened into the backyard where a large, maybe four-foot-high, concrete statue of the Buddha sat hidden under a canopy of well-trimmed bushes, only visible from here or if one walked to a certain place in the yard. Four meditation cushions faced a small table on which sat a twelve-inch-high bronze statue of the Buddha, candles, and a little bowl for burning incense.

"Meg and I meditate every morning," Frank said. "Please feel free to use this as well."

"Thanks, Frank. Thank you for everything, for all your kindness."

"We're happy you're here, man. We're hoping you and Hanna will stay for a while."

"I'm not sure. We haven't talked about any other plans, so, for the time being, I guess we're here."

* * *

The next days and weeks floated by. I remembered Meg was in a commune and Frank wasn't far behind, so I thought of this as our little commune. I tried to pay some rent, which was refused, so Hanna and I insisted we buy all the groceries, tequila, beer, and wine. I couldn't ever remember being so at home and happy.

Hanna worked on more songwriting, and she and I practiced together a few hours every day, sounding better and better. Her voice seemed more beautiful than ever, and I learned more and more about accompaniment. I started back with the guitar again and also kept up the mandolin.

I finalized my resignation paperwork and stock option business, and now had a whole lot more money in my portfolio. It was nice not worrying about a real job. My real job now was Hanna and music.

We meditated together morning and night, and I started trail running again on nearby routes. I also went with Hanna to yoga once or twice a week, and to the gym with Frank once or twice a week. I met some of her friends, mainly women, at yoga classes. Suddenly, it was the last week of October.

One morning while we were all having coffee, Hanna said, "I think we should have a party. I haven't seen much of my friends since we've been here. I'm guessing most don't even know I'm back. I'd like them to meet Russell."

"Sure, why not?" Meg said. "We haven't had a function in a long time. There are some people I'd like to invite, too. Frank?"

"Yeah, I'd be up for it. Maybe next Saturday night?"

So calls were made, liquor and beer stocked up, a caterer hired, and the cleaning person came. I felt both excited and apprehensive about meeting Hanna's friends.

It was a perfect, balmy California day, and people started arriving around three thirty. I made myself a vow to behave and watch my alcohol consumption. Hanna pulled me around to meet everyone. She'd told me that she had an eclectic group of friends, and they were all there. I met Mike and Ronald who were planning their wedding, then an older couple, friends of Meg and Frank, who were from Turkey. He was an artist and she taught international economics at Berkley. I met Chloe and her partner Nadia, who both arrived on their Harleys. The house filled with people of color, artists, musicians, writers, designers, all creative types—a group of people I'd never have imagined ever being with. I found them all super nice, and they made me feel like a long-time friend.

Mike and Ronald were funny and two of the nicest guys I'd ever met. "God, Russell, you are so cute," Ronald said. "Hanna is so lucky, and I'm so jealous." Mike shot him a dirty look, and Ronald just laughed. "I'm getting another drink, Russell. Your hands are empty; what can I get you?"

"Ah, nothing. I'm trying to behave and act sensible tonight."

"God, Russell, don't be such a tight ass. Enjoy. It's a fucking party. Let it go."

I got a little defensive, and my response came out sort of whiney: "I'm not a tight ass. Really, I can have fun. I'm just—"

"Oh, stuff it. I'm getting you a beer, so just lighten up." He walked away.

Mike laughed. "Gotta get with the program, dude. Ronnie won't let you get away with being a non-partier."

Ronald returned with three beers. We continued to chat away. I liked these two.

Time passed, and the smell of marijuana permeated the air. Things grew mellow. Around five, Frank called out, "Come on, folks, food's out. Let's eat."

The caterers had laid out a spread on tables on the patio. People casually filled plates and wandered off to tables set about the yard. I sat with Hanna and another couple who were both software developers, both smart and interesting to talk to, and avid outdoors people when they had time.

People were finishing eating when a man, who I hadn't met, appeared with an upright bass and hollered, "Hey, let's play."

Several people got up and headed to the house. Hanna grabbed my arm. "Come on, let's get our instruments."

"What? What's going on?"

"We're going to jam. It'll be fun."

"But I've never 'jammed.' What do we do?"

"Play music, goofy guy. Come on. It'll be fun. Just play like you always do."

"But what if I don't know the songs?"

"There'll be other guitars there. Just watch and play what you can. You'll do fine."

"But—"

"No 'buts,' just come!"

Hanna got her guitar; I found my guitar and mandolin, and we went to join the gathering group of musicians. Two more guitars, a violin, another mandolin, a recorder, a large mandolin (I found out was an octave mandolin), Frank with his banjo, and a harmonica player joined the bass—a raucous group. We played a bunch of old chestnuts that everybody knew and sang along with, giving instruments a chance to take a lead break. I got into it and found it fun.

Then Mick, the bass player, said, "Hanna, sing one of your songs."

She looked at me. "Let Russell and I start it out until after the first chorus, then join in whenever."

She told me what she wanted to do, and we started out with one of her more sensitive ballads. No one else joined in. At the end there was silence, then everyone started clapping.

"Shit, you two are great," Mick said. "I'm totally blown away. It sounds like you've been together for years. Russell, good job, man. Good job."

Others echoed his comments. I felt good, real good. I had an idea.

The party went on. We played until everyone was literally played out, plus it grew cold, even under the heaters. Sometime after two when people were slowing down, I told Hanna I was done and going to bed. She felt wiped out, so we bid good night and went and crashed, literally. I fell asleep in a wink.

The next morning I awoke to find Hanna still asleep. I lay there thinking: *Was I really a tight ass? Everyone I met last night was so excited about life, about their work. Did I have fun? Did I let go?*

Hanna stirred. "Good morning, love of my life. Sleep well?"

"Never better." I kissed her, and one thing led to another and …

We showered together quickly, then headed to the kitchen to the welcome smell of coffee. Bodies of people too drunk, tired, or stoned to go home were strewn about like there'd been a biological warfare attack and everyone had died where they were. Some curled up in chairs; two lay on the couch, and others sprawled on the floor with couch pillows or jackets under their heads. A few began to stir. Frank was making coffee, Bloody Marys, and mimosas. Leftover food already lay on the counter, along with fresh plates, silverware, and napkins. Hanna and I went for the coffee. Some started all over again with the alcoholic beverages; others staggered for coffee. People hugged and laughed and carried on as if there'd never been a break from last night.

Around noon, folks started drifting out with more hugs and kisses. Ronald kissed me full on the lips, which made me feel uncomfortable and completely out of my element.

He noticed and said, "Sorry, Russell, shouldn't have done that, but you're so darn cute."

Mike took him by the arm. "Come on, you flirt, time to go home." He turned to me, smiled, shrugged, rolled his eyes, and they left.

After a few moments, I recovered from the shock of his kiss and realized it'd been a nice gesture. I liked them both.

I felt part of a huge extended family of crazy, wonderful people, the freest people I could ever have imagined. I wanted to be one of them—free, unburdened, loving, kind, and sharing hugs and kisses.

By one in the afternoon, everyone had cleared out and the cleanup began. The house was back in order by three, and we were all exhausted and in bed by eight.

* * *

Thanksgiving approached. I had to call Karen, and Mom and Dad. I'd only talked to Karen twice since she'd told me about the break-up. I kept urging her to come for a visit without any success. As always, I dreaded talking to Mom and Dad. I knew what it'd be like, but I took a deep breath and called my parents first.

"Hi, Mom. Sorry, I haven't—"

"You ungrateful little shit. What is wrong with you? Do you know about your sister? She's being divorced! Just like you! I'm so embarrassed, just ashamed. How could you both make such shambles of your lives? You both failed us. How could we have raised two such ungrateful children? Donny makes us proud, but you two—"

"Mom, please, just listen! For once, just listen to me, damn it! This is not about you. This is about Karen. This is about me. What don't you understand? Screw it! When you figure it out, we'll talk. Goodbye!" I disconnected.

I sat trembling, taking deep breath after deep breath. How can my mother be that way, as if she's the one who needs some understanding? Poor her. Cooled down, I called Karen.

"God, Russell, Mom just called," she said. "What did you say? She was almost crazy. She screamed that both of us were ungrateful horrible children who would burn in hell. What happened?"

She remained quiet while I told her the conversation, then she started giggling; the giggle broke into an outright belly laugh. "Thanks, brother. I needed a laugh. I've been wanting to tell them that for a long time They've been unbearable ever since they found out John and I were getting a divorce."

"Oh my God? She said you're doing it. No wonder Mom was so ballistic."

"Yeah. I did some deep thinking about what you said last time and found a meditation group in Iowa City. I talked to several women there and they were really supportive and helpful. I've been meeting with them a few nights a week. They've been giving me a crash course. It's really hard and I'm scared, Russell. Really scared. John's taken the boys, of course. I know I'm not their real mother, but I've raised them for the last five years. They know me as their mother. They must be confused and scared. I don't know what to do. It breaks my heart when I think about them. He's such a bastard. I don't know what I ever saw in him."

"Karen, I've asked you to come out before, and now I'm going to just go ahead and get you a plane ticket. Get out of there and come out for a few weeks. I know things are slow with work right now, so take some time. Please. You're welcome here. Everyone knows what's going on. We would love to have you. Please?"

"I don't know. There's too much, just too much to do."

"What is there to do? Mom and Dad are out to lunch and no help. John's taken the boys. You need time with people who will love and support you."

"Thanks. Really; thanks. Let me think about it. Okay?"

"I'm getting a flight for you to San Francisco. It's Sunday. I'll try to get you a flight for Wednesday. Be on it. You don't like wasting money. I'll send you the details. See you Wednesday."

"Russell—"

"Get packing. Wednesday." I clicked off and went online. I got her a business class flight leaving Cedar Rapids at ten thirty in the morning with a one-hour layover in Denver. She'd be in San Francisco at two-thirty on Wednesday.

* * *

Hanna and I waited outside security for Karen's flight to come in. I spotted her and waved. She saw me and ran into my arms, hugging and crying. We finally let go, and I introduced her to Hanna. They looked at each other, then Hanna grabbed her and gave her a hug.

"Welcome to San Francisco, Karen. I'm so happy to meet you, so happy you're here."

Karen started crying, and Hanna held her until she'd finished, then she gave her a pack of tissues.

Karen didn't look well. Her hair looked stringy and colorless. She'd always been a little heavy, but now she was really puffy, and she had dark circles under her bloodshot eyes.

The house had one more bedroom available, and it was Karen's for however long she wanted. Tired and hungry, she had a snack, then went to lie down. At five thirty, Hanna went in to wake her.

When Karen came out, she looked a little better, but seemed nervous. She met Meg and Frank, then we went to the patio for cocktails and tried to engage her in conversation. She stayed aloof and quiet, so the rest of us talked and kept on trying to include her. After dinner Karen excused herself and went to her room.

With everything cleared up and put away, we went to the hot tub for a soak. Did I go in naked? Yes, but I wore a towel until the last minute and kept it close by for when I got out. Embarrassed? Yeah, a little.

"She seems uncomfortable," Meg said when we'd settled in the hot tub.

"I think it's good she got away," I said. "She needs some support, and I know my parents and brother are no help. I can attest to that after my divorce."

"Let's take her to the day spa tomorrow," Hanna said. "We can all get the full treatment."

Meg nodded. "Good idea. I'll call first thing and see if they can schedule us in."

We soaked for a while longer in silence, just enjoying the evening.

After showering off, I prepared to sit and play some music with Hanna, but my phone chirped.

"Awe, crap; it's my parents. This won't be good."

"Should I leave?" Hanna asked.

"Only if you want. It should be interesting." I accepted the call. "Hello?"

"Russell!" Mom said. "Have you heard from Karen? We tried calling, and she doesn't answer. We drove out to her place, and her car's gone. We're worried. You know she's getting that divorce, just like you. I thought we raised you two to be more responsible. We are so disappointed—"

"Mom! Please listen to me for a minute. I'm really sorry you're disappointed, but this is not about you! Please understand that. This is about Karen. Please! Karen's here with us. She needed to get away, and I sent her a ticket. She flew out today so she can get herself together. She's a wreck and needed someone to give her some love and support, and she wasn't getting any from you. It's certainly not her fault that John left her for another woman after what? Five years? It's not her fault that he took the two boys she'd bonded with. It's not your fault or about how you raised us. It is not about you. It has nothing to do with you. What don't you get about that? We are two adults and are doing the best we can, trying to make our own decisions. That's what you taught us. Sometimes the decisions we make don't always turn out the way we want, but they are ours, and we have to live with them. Not you."

"But, Russell, Donny—"

"Mom, I don't care about Donny. I'm happy he's doing well and is making you happy or whatever."

"But you and Karen need to come home and straighten out your lives. You're out in where? California? What are you doing out there, anyway? You can't straighten out your life out there."

"Mom, that's exactly what we're doing. Karen needs some peace and quiet and be around people who can help her."

"What, all those California Beatniks and Hippies? Are you still with that slut you picked up along the road? I suppose she wants your money. They'll lead you to hell and depravity—"

I'd had enough. Through with trying to be nice and keep my voice even, I lost my cool. "Mom! Don't! You! Ever! Call! Hanna! A Slut! Ever! That is rude and abusive. You don't even know her. You're just being horrible, and you're wrong about everything. I'm done trying to justify my life to you. You'll never understand. I can't talk to you anymore. I won't talk to you anymore. I'm done! I'm sorry. I'm sorry you can't understand. I disown you as my mother!" I clicked off.

A few seconds later, the phone chirped again—my mother. I blocked their number and turned off my phone.

"I'm sorry, so sorry," Hanna said.

"No, I'm sorry. I'm sorry you had to hear all that. She, she's … she's impossible. Screw it, let's make some music."

I struggled to concentrate and finally gave up, and we went to bed. I finally dozed off sometime after two.

The next day, the three women went to the spa. Feeling guilty, I unblocked my parent's number, then helped Frank in his shop. He showed me how to use tools and be helpful. I liked working with him. We talked about philosophy, authors he liked, authors he knew, poetry, and life in general, opening my mind to new ideas and new possibilities. Over time, he became a teacher, a mentor, and a father figure. While my own father taught me discipline and rigidity, Frank taught me about life.

The women came home around five. All three looked radiant, including Karen who was all smiles, apparently imbibing in some spirits along the way. They laughed and chattered away, oblivious of Frank and me.

"Come on, let's get a beer and go to the hot tub," Frank suggested.

Shortly after, the three women joined us outside the tub. They'd been massaged, mud-packed, pedicured, finger-nailed, sauna-ed, coiffed, and were giddy and looked beautiful. Over their wine drinking, we heard all about it, every detail. All Frank and I could do was listen and smile.

* * *

Some friends of Meg and Frank's invited us to Thanksgiving dinner. Hanna and I spent several days taking Karen around to see the sights, plus a ride on a cable car. She began to feel more alive, and the stress she'd been feeling began to melt away. It took some convincing to overcome her reluctance to go to the dinner, but she finally agreed.

Thanksgiving dinner wasn't like the normal holiday dinner we'd experienced in Iowa. The festivities began at noon at a house nestled in trees outside of town. Contemporary in style, the house had lots of glass looking out onto a professionally landscaped exterior. Modern furniture with abstract art on the white walls decorated the interior—stark, but inviting all the same.

The first person I recognized was Mick, the bass player, who came running over. "Hey, Hanna, Russell, I was hoping you guys'd be here. Bring your instruments?"

"Yeah, we did. This is my sister, Karen. Karen, meet Mick."

He looked at her, and a broad grin spread across his face. "I'm very happy to meet you, Russell's sister, Karen ... so very happy." He took her hand and kissed it. "Where are you from, beautiful lady? How long are you staying? I hope for a long time."

Karen grinned so wide I thought she might hurt her jaw.

"I'm visiting from Iowa, for two weeks. I have to go back next week."

"Why? What do you have there that you can't have here? Like me, for instance? Come and let me get you a drink." He took her arm and placed it in his, then led her towards a bar in the back of the house.

She glanced back over her shoulder, smiled and winked, then turned and began talking to Mick.

Hanna looked at me. "I've known Mick like forever, and I've never seen him like that. I'm going to get her. She's vulnerable right now."

"Let her go. She needs to meet some people and have fun. Mick seems harmless enough."

"He's probably one of the nicest guys I know, but I'm still going to keep an eye on her."

We joined in the growing crowd. I saw a number of people from the last party, including Chloe and Nadia, and I ran into Mike and Ronald.

Hanna and I both kept an eye on Karen. Mick introduced her around to others, talking briefly, then moving on. They got drinks, sat at a garden table facing each other, and had an animated talk. I saw Mick hand Karen a handkerchief, and she dabbed at her eyes. Then they held hands across the table, still talking intently. She spoke and Mick listened, then Mick spoke and she listened.

Hanna and I gave up watching and mingled with the group. A long, white-linen-covered table had place settings for thirty people—white china plates, wine and water glasses, and lots of silverware.

We hadn't eaten much earlier. I grew hungry and had to slow down on the beer or I wouldn't make it to dinner. At three, we were called to sit. Hanna, Karen, I, and, of course, Mick sat together at the long table. As soon as we were seated, the host called us to attention, reminding us that it was Thanksgiving. She said that each of us were to take turns giving thanks for at least one thing in our lives. When Hanna's turn came, she looked at me, smiling, gave me a peck on the cheek, and said, "I'm thankful Russell picked me up along the road somewhere in Iowa sometime last summer."

I smiled and took my turn. "I'm thankful I stopped and picked up this beautiful, amazing woman back in Iowa sometime last summer. And I thank Meg and Frank for giving us shelter for these last few months. It's been an incredible journey."

At Karen's turn, she said, "I give thanks for having my sweet and loving young brother who got me out here to this beautiful place … and for my new friend, Mick."

Mick said, "I give thanks for meeting Karen here. And I extend a big thank you to Russell also for bringing Karen to us."

Karen blushed, and, despite her smile, tears ran down her face. I noticed they held hands under the table.

Immediately after the last person had given their thanks, a bevy of waitpersons appeared as if from nowhere, pouring wine, serving enormous amounts of the traditional turkey, mashed potatoes, dressing, gravy, vegetables, cranberry sauce, rolls, along with vegan and vegetarian dishes. Unlike the Thanksgiving dinners I'd attended, this passed with slow, deliberate eating, talk, toasts, cheers, and wine. The meal lasted close to two hours. When everyone had finished, the waitpersons magically appeared again, sweeping all dirty plates, utensils, leftover food, and glasses from the table. A further waitperson assaulted us all with pumpkin pie a la mode and dessert wine.

By six, people began getting up and moving about. Appetites satiated, they moved towards more after-dinner wines and continued conversation.

Mick said loudly, "Let's play some music."

From nowhere, guitars, fiddles, mandolins, banjos, whistles, flutes, and Mick's bass appeared. Tuned up, we launched into music, singing, and dancing. By nine, the temperature was dropping and we were slowing down. The food, drink, and copious marijuana had everyone pretty mellowed out. We arrived home at ten thirty to welcome sleep.

* * *

Over the next few days, Karen and Mick hung out together constantly, out somewhere by themselves, hanging around the house, or with Hanna and me. One day, Mick took us to a deserted beach. We took a cooler of food and drink, and swam in ice cold water, and drank and ate all day. We gathered driftwood and lit a bonfire as evening approached. Mick fired up a joint, and we all got mellow. I was surprised to see Karen indulge herself. I'd never seen her so happy.

The night was warm and balmy, so Mick decided to go back in for a swim. He and Karen got up, and they ran whooping and hollering, like two kids, into the lazy surf. I sat, shaking my head, with my jaw dropped onto the sand.

"She seems to be having fun," Hanna said. "Let's go join them."

* * *

The Monday before Karen's departure date on Wednesday, she took me out to the patio and said, "Russell, I don't want to go back, but I really have to. I have my job, and I have to get the house ready to sell. I haven't talked to you about this, but the divorce is scheduled to be finalized before Christmas. A part of the agreement was that we'd sell the house. I can't afford it and don't want it anyway, and John has a new place in Iowa City. I dread seeing Mom and Dad. And Donny, he's just a pompous ass. He acts so self-important, so smug, thinking he's so much better than we are, especially now that I'm going through a divorce. He's so convinced he's the perfect child.

"Then there's Mick. God, Russell, he's so great, so much fun, so considerate. I've never met a guy like him, and I don't want to be away from him. I have no idea where it will go with him, but he makes me laugh. He makes me happy. He makes me feel safe."

"But what does he do for a real living?" I asked. "I know he bartends down town."

"He has a Ph.D. in macro-economics. He taught at UC, Los Angeles, for a while … hated LA, so he resigned and moved up here. He does some consulting work in Silicon Valley and other places, but likes tending bar and enjoying life."

"Wow, I didn't know," I said. "I just know him because he plays bass and is a nice guy. What do you have to clean out of the house? What about John? Can't he help?"

280

"He's already taken everything he wants and left the rest for me. It's mainly stuff I don't want, but somehow John thinks the rest's up to me to clean out."

"Why don't I go back with you and help? How much is there?"

"I don't know, a few pickup loads. Most of which I just want to give to Goodwill and be rid of. I can pack what I want in my car. But there's Mom and Dad. I don't want to have to deal with them."

I thought for a minute. "Here's what we'll do."

Chapter 21: Back to Iowa on a Stealth Mission

All four of us landed in Cedar Rapids late Wednesday afternoon. Once Hanna and Mick knew what we were up to, we couldn't hold them back. The rental cargo van was waiting for us. We drove to Iowa City and got motel rooms. I felt a little shocked when Karen and Mick got a single room with a king bed.

After an early dinner, once it grew dark, we drove out to Karen's, shutting off the van lights when we turned up the drive to avoid any neighbor gawking and gossiping. We filled the van. Mick and I went to Iowa City to the Goodwill and made a drop-off, then we went back and got another load before they closed.

The next day, we drove to Cedar Rapids so Karen could see her lawyer and sign the papers. We celebrated with lunch at a local craft-brew pub.

That night, we managed three loads to Goodwill and got the remaining stuff loaded to deliver in the morning. Karen put what she wanted into her car. The next morning, we dropped off the last load and turned in the van, our mission complete. Karen had moved out, and no one either saw us or paid us any attention. The four of us piled into Karen's car and headed west on Interstate 80 for nights in Ogallala, Salt Lake, and Reno, and four days of listening to music, singing ourselves silly, laughing, and enjoying the road and friendship.

Back in Sausalito, Karen and Mick became inseparable. I'd never seen her so happy. I still worried about her, but that slowly passed. Mick joined us for music every day when he didn't have a consulting job. He sang well and performed harmony with Hanna much better than I did. We worked up several long sets.

Tuesday afternoon a few weeks later when Mick came by to play, he said, "Hey, I can get us a gig at the bar where I work. My boss is up for it. Friday night if we want. You up for it?"

Hanna spoke first: "How long and what time?"

"We could go on early, five for the after-work crowd. Play until nine?"

Hanna nodded. "I'd be up for it. I think we have enough material. I'll do a set list. Maybe three sets with fifteen or twenty minute breaks … it should work out. What about you, Russell?"

"Why not? Sounds fun. Sure. Let's do it."

"Perfect. I'll let him know tomorrow. He said he'd pay according to turnout. I've known him for a while, and he's fair. Any tips are ours to keep. There's a decent sound system, but I suggest we get our own mikes. The ones there are pretty scuzzed up with beer and slobber from some others who, well—I suggest we get our own. Russell, do you have pickups in your guitar or mando?"

I didn't, so the next day we went to a music store in San Francisco. I had pickups installed along with new strings and bought several sets of extras. The three of us bought voice mikes and stands, and some extra patch cords just in case. Karen would be our roadie and support.

Hanna worked up four set lists. I felt nervous, excited, and eager. We spent the rest of the week going through the sets until we were tired of it. It was becoming work, but we wanted to get it right.

Friday afternoon, we loaded Mick's truck and headed down to the bar, across the street from the bay. We arrived a little after three, took our gear in, and set up on the small stage.

The bar was long, dark, and cool with a ceiling of stamped tin and a dark polished-wood bar running about halfway down. The dull-colored walls above dark-wood wainscoting carried grainy pictures from a bygone era under, all carrying years of tobacco smoke, sweat, and dirt from those who'd drunk their fill. Maybe twenty stools sat at the bar, which had a brass footrest; the only thing missing were spittoons, men in frock coats with pistols in their belts, and ladies dressed in red and black short crinolines and uncovered matching corsets. Several patrons already sat or stood at the bar, nursing beers. Around twenty small tables scattered about the room in some random order.

Roy, the owner, helped us do the sound check on a low stage towards the back. We played parts of several tunes from ballads to lively, and the patrons at the bar rewarded our sound check with energetic applause. Satisfied, we went and had some ice teas.

At five o'clock, show time, when Roy came to a mike to introduce us, we realized we didn't have a name. The three of us looked at each other dumbly.

"We're the Stealth Movers," Mick said.

Hanna and I laughed.

Hanna counted off, "One, two, three, four … and we jumped into a lively old folk song. We played solid and ended to wild applause from the gathering late-afternoon crowd. Hanna chatted for a minute, and we did one of her ballads, then more standard folk tunes. Then Hanna announced we were taking a break. The set had passed quickly. We joined Karen, Meg, and Frank at their table.

"You all sounded great," Meg said. "I'm impressed. Hanna, I'm so happy for you. Your voice was just—What can I say? Just amazing."

"Thanks, Mom. These two really make me sound better."

Mick and I just "awe shucked" and smiled. Karen and Frank also sang our praises. Customers came up and complimented us, wondering if we were on Amazon, social media, or had any CDs for sale. We weren't and we didn't.

The rest of the night went great. Frank sat in with his banjo on a few tunes. We tried to stop at nine but kept getting called back for encores and could've played all night, but at ten, Roy gave us the sign to cut it. We thanked the crowd and promised we'd be back. We were a success, at least at Roy's Bar in Sausalito.

* * *

Not only was my birthday coming up, but also the anniversary of Dana's leaving. Was it only a year ago that she'd left? Reflecting on that past year again made me feel unsure of all I was doing, of everything I'd done. All my old demons reared their ugly heads again, stronger than ever. My insecurities howled in my head like the banshees I remember reading about in some lit class I'd had to take in college. I told Karen to not mention my birthday to anyone as I didn't want to celebrate anything while feeling that way.

Chapter 22: Solstice

Hanna, Meg, and Frank didn't celebrate Christmas; instead, they celebrated the Winter Solstice along with most of their friends. Of course there was a party, this one at a house overlooking the ocean. We all arrived, including Karen and Mick, around four-thirty for cocktails along with others who I now knew. The potluck made for copious amount of foods and hors d'oeuvres. As usual, marijuana smoke floated in the air. We chatted, ate, and drank until after dark when everyone filled their glasses, got fresh beers, and headed down a flight of wooden steps to the beach, where a huge pile of wood had been stacked for a bonfire. It would be lit to welcome the new light and the longer days beginning tomorrow, which would take us to the summer solstice in June.

The solstice had never seemed too important to me. I knew it was the shortest day of sunlight of the year, but these folks seemed to take it much more seriously. Everyone gathered in a circle around the soon-to-be-lighted wood stack. Some had brought drums and noise makers, and they created a rhythmic background as the circle began to sway back and forth. Someone lit the fire. As it grew, so did the excitement of the drummers and dancers. The circle broke into groups. Some people began tossing off clothes; some were already naked, dancing ecstatically. I saw Karen and Mick, both naked and lost in their revelry. My sister? Dancing naked? Having lost Hanna in the milieu, I slid into the background, into the darkness beyond the fire light. My head spun like the dancers. I began to feel nauseated and sweaty. I had to get out of there.

I slipped away and back up to the house, then got a fresh beer and sat and wondered what I was doing, feeling as if maybe I was in something I couldn't handle. I'd had a few beers and hits of weed and started to feel paranoid. All my past "shoulds" and "ought tos" reared up inside me. What was I doing here? What was I doing with my life? I was wasting time. All this sweat lodge, Rinpoche shit was crazy. I was doing exactly what my parents criticized me for doing. Maybe they were right. These were not my people. I don't know them. My people are back in Iowa. What had I gotten Karen into? What was I going to do? I hadn't worked in over six months. I'd quit my job. Maybe Gordon would take me back. My parents would be happy. I could try to be more like Donny. Then they'd like me more.

I felt fingers in my now-long hair and a kiss on my cheek. "Hey, you; here you are. I lost you. Are you okay?"

"Hey. Just a little overwhelmed by the night and the bacchanal on the beach."

"Once again, my bad," she said. "I should've told you what usually goes on at the solstice party. You sure you're okay?"

"I don't know, Hanna. What're we doing? Really? We're just hanging out at your parents. What are our plans? Where are we going? I'm sorry, tonight sort of shook me. I thought I could be part of this scene, but I'm not sure I can be."

I told her of all my doubts, about all the old stuff she'd already heard ... too many times. Hanna listened, twirling her strand of hair like always, but there was no sexiness in it tonight. Her look seemed hard and cold.

Abruptly, she stood. "Russell, we've been through this shit before. I know this is hard for you. I have no idea what more I can do to help. I really don't. I'm really tired of your pathetic, self-pitying, poor-me bullshit." Her voice and anger rose. "I'm sick of it. Maybe you should go back and spend your fucking life trying to please mommy and daddy. I'm starting to think you deserve each other. Go back to fucking Chicago. Wallow in your own shit. I'm so tired of listening to you whine. Get help! You need to get over your fucking mommy-daddy issues! Until then, I'm not sure I can be around you. So just please leave. Go away and wallow in your shit. Please just get the hell away from me! I want to try to salvage this night and have some fun with my friends. Just go! I'll find a ride home."

I looked at her. "But—"

She screamed at me with fire in her eyes. "Just fucking get away and leave me alone! You're nothing but a huge pain in the ass! I want to enjoy the rest of this party. You've already fucked it up enough. Now GO THE FUCK AWAY!" She turned and joined the partiers starting to come up from the beach.

I sat there stunned by my own stupidity. She was right. She'd tried. and I was a pathetic idiot. I got up to leave and glanced over my shoulder. Hanna joined with a group giving hugs and kisses to everyone. She turned and shot me an icy glance, then turned back to her friends.

I walked by the bar table, grabbed a bottle of whiskey, and took some long pulls. I stood watching the revelry for a while, taking more pulls on the whiskey until I started to sway.

I managed to get out to the front of the house, where I stopped and screamed to the heavens, "Mom! Dad! I fucking hate you! I hate you! I hate everything!"

I staggered towards the van, feeling like a whipped feral dog. I ran to some bushes, fell to my knees, and vomited until I thought my insides would come out. Too weak to stand, I crawled over to the van, got in, locked the door and lay down, pulling a sleeping bag over me before I passed out. I woke to banging on the window. I peered out from under the sleeping bag. The sun was up. It was so bright. My watch told me it was nine thirty. My mouth tasted like I'd eaten a dead skunk, and I was thirsty. My eyes felt scratchy and dry. My head hurt.

"Russell? Russell?" a female voice called. "Are you in there? Open up."

The best I could do was mumble a shout, "Go away!"

"Russell. Open up! Are you okay?"

"No, I'm not. I feel like shit. Go away. Leave me alone!"

The banging moved to the side of the sliding door and became louder. *Please, God, make it stop.*

I heard someone say, "Wait, I remember. I have a key. Just a minute."

I heard the key in the lock and the door open. Karen and Hanna stuck their heads in and started to laugh.

Karen finally stopped long enough to say, "God, Russell. You look like death warmed over. Do you feel as bad as you look?"

I just glared at them. My head hurt terribly, but still the conversation with Hanna came rolling out of the depths of my fried brain. Now I really felt awful. But here she was laughing and smiling at me as if nothing had happened.

"Thanks for all your sympathy. I feel sick. Just leave me alone."

"How much did you drink last night?" Hanna asked.

"I don't remember. Too much, I guess. God, I'm so thirsty."

"Can you get out and come into the house. We can get you some water. Coffee is going and mimosas are made. Come on."

I suddenly had to heave again. I jumped up, pushing them aside, and ran over to my vomit bush and dry heaved. I felt a hand on my back.

"Come on, Russell. I'll take you home." Hanna helped me to the van and drove. She got me into the house and found some water and aspirin, which I managed to keep down. She took my vomit-stained clothes off me and put me into a cold shower. It felt good. By the time I got out, dried off, and dressed, I was starting to revive.

Hanna brought me more water, some coffee, and dry toast. "Can we talk?"

"Why? I think you said it all last night. Why do you even care? What more is there to say?"

"Russell, listen, first I want to apologize for going off on you so hard last night. But do you realize how hard it is to listen to the continuing bullshit about your parents and your sad life? I'm serious about you getting help to deal with your shit. As much as I love you, I'm really tired of hearing about it. It's wearing thin, real thin. Do you understand?"

I sat staring straight ahead, not able to meet her gaze, not able to respond. I took a reluctant bite of toast and sip of the hot coffee. I didn't know what to say.

"Don't you have any response?" she asked.

"I thought you were done with me. But you're right. I am a pain in the ass. I'm sorry. I'm so tired sometimes. Last night— the dancing, the crazy wildness—I was a little stoned, and I couldn't deal with it. Then all the old shit was just there. All the guilt, the fear, my parents' voices running around in my head, everything. I'm sorry. I can understand why you want me to leave."

"Russell, I don't want you to leave. I just want you to be free of your past and to grow up and be with me. Haven't you learned anything over the past few months? Anything?"

"I thought I had. Guess it doesn't go away quite so easily."

"Karen and I talked a lot last night. I told her about our episode. She is having some of the same issues popping up in her as well. Mick's in love with her, and she's scared. She wants to find a counselor and do some therapy work. Would you consider going with her? I'd like it if you did."

"I did some counseling in Chicago, but cut it off when I moved back to Iowa to Karen's. My doctor insisted I find someone in Iowa, but I never did, just found a guy so I could keep my depression and sleep med prescriptions. I thought I was all better, that I didn't need any more therapy, but guess I still do. I'm sorry, really sorry for being such a pain. I'll talk to Karen."

"Thanks. It'll be good for you. I know from my own therapy it can really help. Please believe me when I say I love you. If I didn't think you were worth it, I truly would kick your sorry ass out. But I know you're worth it. We'll make it. Plus I need your guitar and mandolin skills so I can be at my best when I perform. You're not getting off so easy." She slipped over and gave me a hug and a kiss.

I lost it and broke down and cried.

"Let it out, sweetheart. You need to let it go." She held me and stroked my head, kissing my tears away.

"I'm sorry, so sorry," I blubbered.

"I love you, Russell. I do. I want to be with you. Please. We can work it out. Okay?"

"Okay. I love you, too, so much it sometimes hurts."

We sat for a long time, her head on my shoulder. I felt her breathing. It felt good.

"I was going to give you this last night as sort of a Solstice present," I said, "but, well, anyway, I got this for you." I found my billfold and gave her a folded piece of paper. She opened it, looked at it, and read it, looking puzzled, then read it again. I watched her puzzled look turn into a huge grin, and she flung herself into my arms, showering me with kisses, then it was her turn to cry into my neck.

"God, Russell, how did you …? When? This is just … just so amazing. A week of studio time. Five hundred CDs! We can record everything we have. God, I love you. When can we get in?"

"I scheduled us for mid-February, but we can maybe get in earlier, whenever you feel we're ready."

"Thank you! Thank you! How can you afford this? It must have cost a fortune. This is one of the best recording studios in the Bay Area."

"Not to worry. You need to get your music out there. Mick may have helped direct me a bit." I smiled.

"This so perfect. We need to get *our* music out there. You are just as much a part of this as I am. We'll have quality stuff to get onto Amazon and other places and maybe sell some. We'll be professionals. Wait 'til I tell Mom."

Her excitement was well worth my investment. Professional? That aspect of my playing never crossed my mind.

It was a quiet day. Everyone felt a little worse for wear after last night. Mick brought Karen back around four.

"Look what Russell got us," Hanna said, showing Mick and Karen my present. "Mick, we want you to be part of this."

"Awe, no, that's for you and Russell to do."

"No way! You're going to be part of it. We need you. No discussion."

It was set. We were a trio with a purpose: The Stealth Movers.

* * *

Neither Karen nor I had talked to our parents for a while, but I received a call on Christmas Day. I reluctantly answered.

"Merry Christmas, Mom. How are you?"

"Not very good. Donny's in jail."

"What? In jail? What—"

"He started drinking again a few months ago. He'd quit for a while after his last DUI. You know he can get real mean when he drinks. Well, he came home and beat up Alice pretty bad. Put her in the hospital. I guess she'd been in the emergency room other times, too, that we'd never heard about. This time they had to admit her. She's pretty beat up. Anyhow, the hospital reported him to the sheriff. I guess it's spouse abuse, something like that."

"How's Alice? Where's Zoe?"

"He's not doing too good in jail. He's not being too nice to anybody there. We got him a lawyer, but he don't pay no attention to him. Just keeps mouthin' off to the guards and stuff."

"I'm sorry, Mom. Really am, but what about Alice and Zoe?"

"Yeah. I'm sure you are … like everything else. Your father and I are worried sick about you two. We never hear anything from you. Where's Karen? I try calling, but she never answers. I'm worried. I heard her house is for sale. Is she coming home?"

I stayed on point. "But what about Alice and Zoe? Is Alice out of the hospital? Where's Zoe?"

"Zoe went to stay with her grandparents in Cedar Rapids. I think Alice is there now. She was only in overnight, a broken rib, black eyes, a few stitches and a lot of bruising. He really beat her up bad. We don't know about Donny. His lawyer says it's pretty serious. He'll probably go to jail. I guess it just depends on how long. I guess this isn't the first time, you know."

"No. I didn't know, Mom. I know he had a problem with his drinking, but wife-beating? I don't know what to say."

I could hear her starting to cry.

"Mom, I'm sorry, truly sorry."

"Oh, Russell, I'm so damn disgusted and mad at that boy. I've tried to teach him respect, but I failed miserably … and now you and Karen hate me and left for California. I screwed up everything … everything so bad. I'm sorry. He was so much to handle. I spent so much time with him. It was so frustrating. I know I neglected you two, took out my frustrations, and now look. All I wanted for you kids was to be successful and be happy. I know I was hard on you kids. And now you're both gone."

I didn't say anything for a moment. Then she asked, "How's Karen? Is she all right?"

"Karen's fine, Mom. The reason she probably doesn't answer your calls is because she knows how you'll act. She's struggling to come to terms with her divorce and is scared. She has a lot on her mind right now and doesn't need criticism or the guilt trip you try to put on me and her. She needs some time to get herself together."

"Well, we know someone moved all her things out of her house. Do you know anything about that?"

I didn't know if she knew about our escapade and was baiting me or if she truly didn't know. I didn't know if I should lie or tell the truth. I took a chance and lied.

"I have no idea, Mom."

"Well, I heard there were some strange goings-on there a while back. Then all of a sudden, there's a 'For Sale' sign out by the road. I know she came back because I heard she signed the divorce papers in Cedar Rapids with that lawyer woman. Never came by to say hello. I just don't know what has gotten into you two kids."

"It's called life, Mom. We're both doing what we can to be happy."

"Why couldn't you be happy and be closer by? Are you still with that … woman?"

"Yes, I am, and 'that woman's' name is Hanna."

"Where are you living? Surely not in that dreadful little car."

"I'm living with her at her mother's house outside of San Francisco."

"You are what? What kind of woman would let a boy stay in the same house as her daughter? You haven't gotten married, have you? I sure hope not! What about Dana?"

"No, we're not married. And, Mom, Dana is history. She and I will never get back together. Please accept that."

"I was hoping you might make up and get back together. I feel so bad about you two. Never did care for that John who Karen married. He was too slick, that one."

"As I was about to say, we're staying here because her mother wants us to. She likes me and is happy Hanna and I are together. She's a wonderful person, as is her partner."

"Partner? What does that mean?"

"It means she and Frank live together, as they have for the last twenty years, without being married."

Kaboom. That set her off on a tirade about hippies, bohemians, antichrists, Satan worshipers, hell and damnation, fire and brimstone, and on and on. I set the phone down and listened from a distance until she calmed down. Actually, a lot of what she was saying was true. I smiled to myself.

"And what about you, Russell? I sure hope you aren't 'partnering' with that woman!"

She tried to push all my buttons, and since I didn't respond, it probably made her even more agitated. "Ah, you mean Hanna? I guess we are partners. We do everything together: we sleep together, play music together, eat together, have fun together, and so far I'm enjoying and loving every moment I'm with her. I am in love with her and plan on being with her for as long as she can stand me."

Silence. I could almost hear her mind churning, trying to digest all this information.

Eventually, sounding defeated, she asked, "What about Karen? Is she working? Where is she living? Is she eating and sleeping okay?"

All of a sudden, I felt an overwhelming sadness for her. This was way out of her league. She sounded like a mother asking if her ten-year-old was all right.

"Mom, all I can say is that Karen's fine and will talk to you soon. I'll tell her about Donny. All I ask is that you be kind towards her. She needs your love, not any criticism."

She didn't respond.

"How is Dad, by the way? You never mention him."

Her mood brightened. "Oh, he's busy. He and Donny were trying to rent some more land, but prices are high. It's getting harder and harder to keep going. Then this awful thing with Donny."

She told me the same old story of gloom and woe I'd heard from the time I was old enough to understand words. Again, I smiled to myself, knowing deep down that they were fine. It seemed to be the same story from every farmer I ever talked to.

There were never any good times, according to the common story, even when corn and bean prices were sky high. I wondered if doom and gloom was part of all farmers' DNA.

When she started to wind down, I said, "Mom, I have to go. Merry Christmas to you and everyone there. I hope you have a wonderful day. I wish we could be with you."

"Thanks, Russell. I wish you could be here too. Will you and Karen come back and visit? Will we ever get to see you again? Soon?"

"I'm sure we will, Mom. Maybe this spring or summer. Promise. It was good to talk to you. I love you."

She didn't respond, simply disconnected.

I sat with a lump in my throat, thinking about our conversation. She sounded so defeated and sad. I started to realize that my parents also had struggles and choices to live with. I made a note to myself to schedule a trip back to see them sooner rather than later.

I told Karen about the conversation. She was as stunned about Donny as I was, although not as surprised, having lived closer for those years and knowing more of his recent history. She called Mom as soon as we finished talking.

Christmas and New Year came and went with the usual celebrations—parties with our extended family, but lacking Christmas tree, decorations, or presents. I felt better about life. My angst settled down. We didn't hear any more from our mother about Donny, and we hadn't called to check in. The day after New Year, Karen moved in with Mick at his cabin north of town.

Chapter 23: To Counseling

A few weeks after New Year, Karen called me one morning. "I need to talk. Can you come over? And come alone."

"Sure. I can come. What's going on?"

"Just come over, alone; don't bring Hanna. I need to talk to you alone."

"Okay, give me twenty minutes."

I explained to Hanna and left.

Karen waited for me at the door. I gave her a hug. "So, what's going on? You and Mick have a—"

"No. No, that's not it. Mick's great. Totally love the big guy. But, truth is, I'm feeling totally confused about ... about everything. I know we talked about counseling. I think I need help. Mick's been gone now for a few days on a consulting job, and I've had a chance to think ... and I don't know, I feel like I'm treading water, just barely staying afloat. I'm not sleeping. I'm nervous. I don't know where I belong. This whole thing here is like a dream, and now I'm waking up, and the reality is hitting me.

"I mean, what am I doing? I miss those two little boys. I miss the crew at the dealership. I miss my house. I miss the stability of being married. But I don't want to go back there. I'm somewhere in limbo land. I love it here. I think I'm really in love with Mick, but sometimes he feels like a stranger.

Everything all of a sudden feels so strange. As much as they make me crazy, I want to see Mom and Dad. But I know I'll just want to leave as soon as I get there. I'm scared. How do you manage so well?"

I didn't say anything, absorbing what she had said, then, "I understand how you're feeling. I've been there. I'm not doing all that well, either. Yeah, we talked about counseling after my meltdown at the Solstice party, but I've sloughed it off with holidays and everything. Maybe now is the time. I promised Hanna. I know I need to do something."

I told her a lot of what I went through and was presently going through.

"So, when's it ever over?" she asked.

"I don't know if it's ever completely over. When we're so involved with someone, intimately in mind, body, and spirit for as long as you and John, as long as Dana and me, I don't think it ever ends. Let's see if we can find someone who'll see us."

We googled "counseling," sorted through the many listings, and selected a few we thought would work for us. I called them, explaining that we were a brother and sister, both who'd recently been divorced. I also mentioned family problems. Most calls were answered by a receptionist who could schedule us anywhere from two to six weeks out. Some weren't taking any new clients, and for others, our call went to voicemail. One answered the phone himself and told us he was just starting his practice and had openings the next day. He sounded eager and asked each of us a few questions. We decided to schedule an hour each the next day.

"I'm scared, Russell," Karen said. "I'm not sure I want to do this."

"It'll be fine. I'll be there. Don't worry."

"Maybe I should talk to Mick about this?"

"I'm pretty sure he'd agree with what you're doing. Don't worry. Do you want to come and stay with us tonight?"

She thought for a moment. "Yeah, I'd like that. Thanks."

On our way back to the house, I attempted to explain everything Rinpoche had taught me. She didn't understand or couldn't accept most of it. I talked about meditation.

"I started to learn about meditating before I came out here and sort of forgot about it with everything else," she said. "Does it help?"

"Yeah, I think it does. Rinpoche was a good teacher. We should check and see if there is any place for group practice around here. He said that being with a group helps a lot.

"Also, I think exercise helps. I know Hanna and Meg would love to have you join them for yoga sometime. I even go with them once in a while. It's fun and usually a good workout."

Karen snorted. "So, great. Just give up everything I like? And what? Meditate and do yoga? Really? You gotta be kidding."

"There's more, just hear me out. First of all, nothing happens overnight. This thing is not called a 'practice' for nothing. It's work and commitment like everything else."

She shook her head. "All meditation ever did for me was make me bored and fidgety."

"It helps to calm the mind and bring one into an awareness of self and others, of the world around you," I explained. "You begin to realize everyone has their own struggles, their own suffering. I find I tend to be more open with people, smiling more, saying hello to strangers. As I said, it's a practice. It takes time and commitment."

We arrived at the house and sat in the car while I pulled out my cell and did a Google search for meditation groups. I found three, easily narrowed it down to one—a Mindfulness Meditation group downtown—and went to their website. They had several meditations a week and had ongoing beginner classes. I showed it to Karen.

She looked at me. "Sounds too voodoo to me. When I tried it in Iowa City, it didn't do anything for me other than make me want it to be over."

I didn't mean to let out my chuckle. "Sorry, but it takes time, and practice. All our society wants now is instant gratification. Everything needs to be immediate. This is not immediate gratification. It takes—"

"Yeah, I know, 'time, commitment, and practice.' I'm not sure I want to get into something like that."

"I know. It's your choice. Do the work, move on, or not. I'll go with you if you want."

"Let me think. The other thing is I'm unemployed. I'm freeloading here at Mick's. I don't have much of a resume. Office manager in a John Deere dealership. Lots of demand for that out here, I'm sure. I feel useless, like a slug, like I can hardly move. I know I could find work back home."

"Have you given any thought as to what you might want to do? Have you tried to put a resume together?"

"No. Mick keeps pushing me to do it. But I feel so useless. I'm afraid I'd just be laughed at. God, what am I thinking?"

"Just think about starting a meditation practice, Karen. Give it some thought. You apparently aren't doing real well the way you are. Let me help any way I can. Let us all help."

"Thanks." With that, our conversation ended, and we went into the house.

The next day, Karen and I went to meet Robert, our young, soon-to-be long-term therapist. The three of us had a brief discussion centered on our family issues. Karen went first. She came out later with red eyes, but smiling. I gave her a quick hug and followed Robert into the inner sanctum. I told him about everything, including my earlier aborted counseling.

I quickly liked his laid-back but direct approach. I gave a brief overview of what I'd discussed with my first counselor back in Chicago, mainly about my parents' reaction to my perceived failure. I talked briefly about my journey and my relationship with Hanna. That took up most of the session, so other than taking copious notes, he didn't have much time to give direction other than encouraging me to get back to my journaling that had fallen by the wayside after I left the retreat center.

"When you write your thoughts and feelings down in black and white," he said, "they become real, concrete; we can look at them as more real than simply internalizing them. It truly helps us to understand ourselves better."

"I never thought of journaling in that way. Thanks."

"So, that's your homework. Also, bring questions. From what you've told me, you seem to have moved on a lot, but there are some family things we need to talk about. Can you come next week same time and day?"

"Sure. I'll be looking forward to it."

I found Karen reading a magazine in the small waiting room. She, too, had rescheduled for appointments the next week. Neither of us talked on our way to her house.

Once parked, I asked, "So? How was it?"

"It was like you said, hard. He began asking questions about my marriage, then … then there was something that got dredged up that … that I thought I'd tried to forget about."

"Like what?"

"Just family stuff."

I didn't say anything.

"It's not only my marriage, but something that happened when I was fourteen, something I wanted to forget, but this thing with Donny—"

"Want to talk about it?"

"Not really, but now that it has been resurrected, I'd like you to know. I think you need to. It was one night when Donny sneaked into my room and slipped into my bed. I woke up and he was fondling my breasts. I stirred, and he pulled my hand to his hard cock. I broke away from him, grabbed my softball bat, and hit him as hard as I could.

"It was dark, so I didn't see where I caught him, but he howled in pain. I told him to get the hell out and swung at him again; this time I know I hit him hard on his shoulder. He howled again and threatened me. I held my bat over my head and was coming down with it when he squirmed out of the bed and ran out the door.

"I was so scared and so angry. I wanted to kill him. I closed my door and wedged my chair under the door knob like I did every night from then on for two years until he left for college."

"Did you ever tell Mom and Dad?"

"Hell, no! I was too ashamed. And I knew Mom probably wouldn't believe me or would take his side, put the blame on me, like she always did."

I was too dumbstruck to say anything.

"Robert thought that most likely my relationship with John, as well as with other men, of whom there were only two before John, were hampered by that incident. That I probably had a lack of trust that manifested, especially, with any intimate relationship. Maybe John moving on was my fault. I know I wasn't very responsive to him sexually. I guess I don't know what it was that ever attracted him to me. It surely wasn't because I was a hottie in bed."

I didn't say anything.

"So, my loving brother, what do you think of all that. Creep you out?"

"Shit, Karen. I'm so sorry. Donny was always an asshole. He always picked on me. Mom always sided with him. Dad never said anything. Now this. I ... I don't know what to say."

"Don't need to say anything. Robert also told me pretty much the same things as you told me. I was surprised about how easily he got into that issue. I really like him. Thank you for making it happen for me. Please don't tell anyone about what I just told you, even Hanna. I'm still so ashamed."

"It is nothing to be ashamed about, but I promise. Not a word. You okay?"

"I think so. Mick works tonight, so I'll have time to think. I need to tell him. It'll be hard, but he needs to know. It's interesting that I feel so different with him, much more open emotionally and"—she paused and looked down, and I saw color creep into her cheeks—"and sexually. It'll be interesting to see how he feels when he knows." She opened the door to get out.

"You might be surprised about Mick," I said. "Are you sure you're okay? I can stay for a while if you want."

"No. I think I'll be fine now. Thanks. This first time was scary. But, actually, it felt good to talk about these things. Sort of looking forward to next week." She leaned over and kissed me on the cheek. "I love you, little brother."

"I love you, big sis." She turned and went into the house.

Chapter 24: Music Becomes Serious

I started taking mandolin and guitar lessons from a guy Mick knew. He helped me with a lot of chord theory as well as general music theory. Hours and hours of scale and chord practice became another form of meditation. I learned how to throw in some new chord progressions to my background rhythm work. And I learned different riffs and fill-ins on the mandolin. I figured out how to translate what I learned on one instrument to the other. I never knew how much fun making music could be. I'd always thought of music as a hobby, something to do in spare time from a real job, from real work. I found out that music could be real work, work that I liked.

The three of us practiced until we were bleary-eyed. We fine-tuned, we honed. I kept working on new licks and rhythm patterns. We became a true unit, feeding off each other, commenting, criticizing, encouraging, and growing.

We invited some others, the violin player and the whistle player from our jams, and, of course, Frank, to sit in on various tunes. They were eager, and we worked out those tunes as well. Other than Frank, the other two played professionally and had recorded before. Frank was a novice, like we were, but was up to his part.

Our session date arrived. Hanna and I packed up our gear, picked up Mick and Karen and headed to the studio, which was in a nondescript building in an industrial area of other nondescript buildings. A twenty-something woman with green hair and numerous tattoos and piercings greeted us, introducing herself as Bobby. She led us to an office where we met our recording engineer, Johnny. Aged somewhere north of forty but south of sixty, he was a heavy-set man with droopy eyes and the requisite ponytail. Initially I found him professional to the point of being standoffish, but he turned out to be a really nice guy.

He asked about our style of music: acoustic or electric? Did we have pickups? What were our goals? And had we ever recorded in a studio before? Hanna, our only true professional and spokesperson, answered for us. He explained that we could each lay out separate tracks individually or do it together as a group. If we chose the latter option—which we did—we'd record in separate recording booths with Hanna in the center where we could see her. At the end, we signed a bunch of paperwork, including the contract.

Before we separated, we got in tune, then we were ready—as ready as we'd ever be. Bobby led us to our separate, soundproof rooms. The only way we could hear each other was through our headsets. We'd be recorded on a separate track, so we could overdub any mistakes or anything we mightn't like.

Bobby brought us each a bottle of water and made us comfortable. I closed my door, and all sound disappeared, leaving me in a sound vacuum. It felt weird.

I put on the headset and heard Johnny talking. His disembodied voice came across as if he were right in front of me, unnervingly sharp and crisp.

I could see Hanna standing about ten feet away, but Mick was in a room outside my vision. Karen watched from Johnny's control room off to my left.

"Okay, run through your first song so I can get the levels balanced," Johnny said. "Just play like you normally would. I'll get everything where I want it, then we'll run through it again and have a listen. Take your time and let's have fun."

I felt like I had back in Yellowstone when I first played in front of people, as if I might pitch my breakfast. I heard Hanna count out, "One ... two ... three ... four ..." It was time to go to work.

After the two takes, we went into the control booth to listen. I felt giddy hearing ourselves for the first time. Karen spoke first. "Oh my God! You all sounded so great."

It did sound good. We listened several more times, then Johnny asked, "So, whatcha think?"

The three of us looked at each other. We all had huge grins on our faces.

"It sounds perfect to me," Hanna said. "What about you guys?"

Mick and I agreed. It did sound perfect.

"What do you think, Johnny?" I asked.

"Ya know, I've been doing this over twenty years, and nailing it like this on the first take? It's good. Really good. I like what I'm hearing. It tells me you've worked hard. Some people come in here and just waste their money. Let's keep going."

We got three more tracks down that day, three the next day, then four, then three and finished with our material early Friday afternoon. Sixteen tracks down rock solid. We had several redos: two tracks I had to do over; another I had to dub in two bars, and Hanna messed up on one. Other than that we were solid.

Frank sat in on six tracks with his banjo, and Gretchen, the violin player from our jam sessions, sat in on nine of the tracks. Andrew, the whistle player, joined for the three tunes that had a Celtic flair.

When we left on Friday, Johnny handed us three CDs, one for each of us to listen to. We had to be absolutely sure about quality and decide if we wanted to include all sixteen tracks before he sent everything off for our CD order.

Beyond ourselves with the sense of accomplishment we felt, we stopped at Roy's before we went home and regaled him with our success over beers and wine. He wanted to have a release party at the bar as soon as we were ready, and he wanted us to play that night. While tempting, our adrenalin from the week was draining off. We ordered pizza, more beers, and left for home, assuring Roy we'd play next Wednesday night.

Chapter 25: Spring

March moved into April, then into the first of May. Karen, Hanna, and I had started going to a Mindfulness Meditation group once or twice a week. Karen even managed to get Mick to join us. We all went to yoga class at least twice a week, and Karen glowed with health and happiness. She'd lost weight and looked more beautiful than I could ever remember.

The Stealth Movers gained more recognition and more gigs around the Bay Area. After the CD release party at Roy's, we'd gotten a good review in the local alternative newspaper. Karen worked on getting the band out on social media and essentially became our manager. We became the regular house band at Roy's and did gigs around the area: San Francisco, Oakland, Alameda, Berkley, and up as far as Santa Rosa and Petaluma— mainly in small venues like bars, eateries, and coffee shops. Some paid a little, others were for tips. But we got more and more exposure and refined our chops—musical ability. Our main money came from selling our CDs as well as singles on Apple and Amazon. We placed another CD order—this time for a thousand.

One night after a gig in a coffee shop in San Francisco, a woman came up as we were packing up. Mick asked her if she wanted a CD.

"Thanks, but I already have one. I'd like to talk for a minute, if you have time."

Hanna said, "Sure, what's on your mind?"

"I really like your sound. Have you thought about touring?"

"Touring? Like where? We've a lot going on around here right now."

"Yeah, I know, I've been following you for a while since I first heard you a month ago. You're good, good enough to be playing better venues, higher-paying venues. My name's Riley; I represent five other local bands, and I'd like to represent you as well. I have a good success rate in getting acts into the right venues where their music will be successful."

The three of us looked at each other, not knowing what to think.

"Think it over," Riley said. "Here's my card. Check out my website. As I said, you're good. I know I can get you some bigger venues, probably mostly warm-ups for headliners, but it will give you more exposure outside the Bay Area. Think it over and give me a call."

Hanna gave her one of the cards Karen had designed for us and promised to be in touch. We talked about it on the way home and decided that Karen would check her website and contact her for more details and references.

* * *

Karen and I had talked with our parents, mainly our mother, as usual, over the last three months. Our conversations revolved around Donny and his trouble with the law and his trial. Apparently Donny was cited for spousal abuse twice before, one aggravated assault. While he got off with hefty fines the first two times, this time he could be looking at up to a $10,000 fine and up to ten years in prison. Mom and Dad had gotten him out on bail, which he immediately revoked after he violated the restraining order Alice had gotten against him.

He apparently went to her parents' house, where she and Zoe were staying, and was belligerent, threatening Alice and her parents. He was arrested and put back in jail, where he'd been ever since, awaiting his trial set for mid-May. Mom and Dad were really worried and completely stressed out. With all the trouble with Donny, Mom had mellowed towards Karen and I, interestingly, causing us more concern than relief.

One evening when Hanna and I came in from the hot tub, I noticed I had a voicemail from Mom: "Russell, Dad's in the hospital. Please call me as soon as you get this."

Panicked, I immediately called her back. "Mom? I got your message. Hospital? What's wrong? Is he okay?"

"He had a little heart attack."

I couldn't say anything for a few breaths. "How bad? When?"

"Yesterday. He's in the Iowa City Hospital Heart Unit."

"How is he? How serious was it?"

"He had a dual bypass. There was a little complication, so he has to stay in the hospital for a few days. He'd like to see you and Karen. Could you come home?"

"Of course we'll come. I'll try to get us a flight tomorrow. I'll call you when I know. Are you okay?" I asked desperately.

"No, not really. There's Donny and now this. I'm at my wits' end. But the doctors here are very good. They say Roy'll have a complete recovery, but he's going to have to start watching his diet and start exercising. That'll be the hardest part for him."

"Mom, I'll call you as soon as I know something. Tell Dad hello and we'll be there as soon as we can."

"Thanks, Russell. I'll be so happy to see you two kids. This's all been real hard on us, you know, Donny and everything."

"I know, Mom. I know. I'm sorry. I'll call as soon as I know something. Okay?"

"That'll make Dad happy. Hear from you soon." She clicked off.

I called Karen, and she started to cry.

Hanna overheard and became upset. "When you go, I'm going with you."

"Not a good idea. You know our family dynamic."

"I don't care about that. I care about you. You and Karen both. I'm coming, no argument!"

Mick wanted to come too, but Karen wasn't ready to have him meet our parents quite yet. I was worried about bringing Hanna.

I managed to get us on a flight out the next day at nine in the morning with a three-hour layover in Denver. We touched down in Cedar Rapids a little after seven that night, picked up our rental car, and went to Iowa City to our motel. We were tired and visiting hours were over, so we stopped at a convenience store for a six-pack and ordered out for pizza at the motel.

I called Mom. She didn't answer, so I left her a message that we were in town and would be at the hospital first thing in the morning.

Chapter 26: Iowa City and Home

The three of us arrived at the hospital shortly after ten. Mom wasn't there, so we checked in at the nurses' station and were told we could go in to see him. We arrived at Dad's room and peeked in quietly. Propped up in bed, he saw us and broke into a huge grin.

"Karen, Russell, come in. Come in. Who's this?"

"Hi, Dad, this is my partner, Hanna."

"Is that like a girlfriend?"

"Sort of, somewhere between girlfriend and wife, I guess. How're you feeling?"

"I'm happy to meet you, Hanna. My, but you're a beauty. Karen, you look great. California must agree with you."

I was a little taken aback with his graciousness. He usually never said much, always being quiet and subdued.

He continued, "I'm feeling great. I had a little bypass was all. They've had me up and moving since the day after the surgery, but there was a little bleeding, so they kept me to keep an eye out that it'd be okay. All's under control now."

"When was your surgery?" Karen asked.

"Three days ago. I was pretty scared, but I feel better right now than I have the last few years. Guess there was blockage building up. Now I know why I wasn't feeling so good. Please, sit down. Here, Karen, sit here." He motioned her to sit on the foot of his bed. Hanna and I sat on the two chairs. "I'm happy you and Russell are 'partners.' I can see in his eyes how much you mean to him."

Is this the right room? This isn't my father. This is some apparition that looks like my father.

"Dad, are you okay? I've never heard you talk like this before. Are you sure you're okay?"

"Never better. This heart attack was a big wakeup call, son. I was afraid that was it, but here I am, and I'm tired of not speaking my mind. I need to tell you kids some things you don't know."

Karen and I looked at each other with wide eyes, both wondering what the hell was going on here.

"Thanks for coming," he continued. "I've been needing to talk to you two for some time, but, well, you both had your lives, and there never seemed to be a time. And then you were both gone to California. Anyway, first off, Donny, yeah, Donny … he's your half-brother. I'm not his father."

Karen and I said in unison, "What? Not our brother? Donny's not our brother?"

"No, he's not. I'm sorry you never knew, but we didn't think it would ever matter. But now …? Anyway, you don't know much about the early years, how I met your mother, and I'd like to tell you. Well, ah, back then, I was a shy single farmer, who never socialized or went out. I was getting older, and there weren't many eligible women my age around anymore. When I was thirty-one, your grandparents retired, moved up to Cedar Rapids, and left me in charge of the farm. Now I's out there by myself, trying to do everything around the house and farming 350 acres. The house was dirty. I barely got to town to get groceries, and I never learned much how to cook. I's living on mainly cold sandwiches and beans.

"I put an ad in the paper for a housekeeper and cook, room and board a possibility. Your mother applied for the job. She was pregnant, with Donny, as it turned out. She was the only one who applied, so I hired her.

"Well, one thing led to the other, and we ended up getting married. I didn't know any better. I thought this was the best I'd ever do. I guess it was one of those marriages of convenience. I didn't know much about women and marriage, but she took care of the house real good. We had our moments. We made you two beautiful babies. And, looking back, we done pretty good together all these years, could've done a lot worse.

"As you know, she's pretty opinionated and wants everything her way. I know she pushed you two awfully hard, maybe too hard sometimes, but I didn't know a damned thing about child-rearing, so I let her do what she thought was best. She always meant well, but sometimes, well … Now, Donny, he got away with everything, and look at him. He's in deep shit and is probably going to prison for a while. Well deserved, I might add.

"The good thing is, before we got hitched, I did then what you kids now call a prenuptial agreement of sorts. I made sure the farm was mine and would remain so to this day. Somehow, I was smart enough to do some legal wrangling back then."

I interrupted. "How many acres do you own now?"

"A little over 2,000. I rent another 1,500. I was smart back in the eighties. Prices were good and farmers were making money hand over fist. Some I knew were buying up more acres at too high a price, building big new houses, buying big new cars, new trucks, airplanes even. Banks were wanting to lend money as fast as they could. Times were good. Most of them farmers were leveraged way over their heads. I hung in there with my 350 acres and put money into the bank and some other investments. I figured that the bubble would burst, and it did. Commodity prices dropped like a rock, and all those friendly banks weren't so friendly anymore; they started foreclosing on delinquent loans without mercy.

"There were a bunch of farm sales every weekend. Land and equipment were selling for pennies on the dollar. I cashed in on my investments and bought more land then and some bigger machinery, and it paid off over time. Most of it'll be yours someday. I've set up Donny with 350 acres. He'll go bust and lose it in a year or so. Dumber than a post, that boy is. Won't listen; knows it all, and I just don't give a flyin' shit anymore."

Karen and I sat there, speechless.

Hanna spoke up. "I don't have a clue about all this, but I'm guessing the land you own is worth a lot. Why not retire? Sell out or rent it. What are land prices here?"

"To answer your last question first, anywhere from five to ten thousand dollars an acre right now depending on the land. Big shot investors from California, New York and other places are buying up Iowa farmland for tax purposes; tax evasion, mainly. More and more Iowa land is owned by absentee parties these days. Farm management companies are a growing business. A lot of farmers I know are mainly renters now, even me with my 1,500 acres.

"As for retirement—hell, I could live like a king, I suppose, but I don't know where I'd go or what I'd do. This's all I know. Right here."

"Come and visit us in California," Hanna said. "You'd love it out there. We'd love to have you come. At least come for a visit."

Karen and I looked at Hanna, our eyes still bugged out and mouths still open. It seemed as if Hanna and our father had some immediate karmic connection.

316

He threw her a big smile. "We just might. I knew I wouldn't be able to work this spring, so I made a call to a farm management company yesterday and was able to do some last-minute rental agreements, rented everything out, and they found some folks to take what I'd rented. So I have nothing to do now. All my land is taken care of."

"Dad, what …" Karen said. "Just like that. You're what? Renting?"

"I've been quiet too long and put up with too much. As I said, this heart thing was a wakeup call. Maybe it's time I made some changes." He chuckled. "Ya know, Rose and I have been wanting to do some traveling. We were looking at motorhomes last winter; darned things are about as expensive as a new combine. We're thinking we might go to Arizona for the winter like a lot of folks do. But now, this heart thing, things might have moved ahead for us. Maybe after the trial. California isn't that far from Arizona, and Arizona's too damned hot in the summer. Maybe California might be a good idea. Nothin' for me to do here for sure."

Just then, Mom walked in. "Earl, how are— Oh my God! Karen, Russell, you're here? Come here, let me see you. Oh, let me see; oh you both look so good, so healthy. Russell, your hair is too long; you need a haircut."

We got up, and she grabbed both of us in a big hug. She started to cry. We stood there for a long moment. I didn't know what to think. This was a different greeting than I expected. We broke apart, and I had a look at her. She looked as if she'd aged way beyond her fifty-five years. She'd always been trim, but she'd lost weight; her clothes hung loose on her; she had dark circles under her eyes, and her once-healthy, tanned face was pale and lined. Donny, and most likely Karen and I, had aged her. I felt sadness for her. Right then I vowed to do everything in my power to try to do better. What that would be, I didn't know, but I'd try.

Karen grabbed her and took her to one of the chairs—both now empty as Hanna stood next to Dad, holding his hand. Mom cried into Karen's shoulder. Dad and Hanna seemed like old-time friends. My head was about to explode.

Mom looked up and dabbed her eyes. "You must be Hanna. I'm surprised you wanted to come with all that's happening. You probably know all about Donny. It's pretty sure he'll spend time in prison. Just how long is the only question. I'm happy you came. though, so I could meet you." She turned to Karen and me. "Will you be staying at the farm? There's no one there, and it's lonely out there now. Earl's in here, Donny's gone, Alice and Zoe are gone. It's just me now." She started to cry again.

* * *

After what seemed like about a hundred years later with all that went on, we left Dad to rest after his lunch. The four of us gathered at the old farmhouse built by my grandparents, with the new addition of a master suite along with a remodeled kitchen—nothing fancy, no frills, simple and practical, and not much decoration, just some family pictures. We sat drinking coffee, and Mom served us up pie and ice cream after the ham sandwiches she'd made for us. There was an awkward silence.

Hanna finally broke it. "Rose, I'm really happy to finally be here and meet you and Earl. I can't imagine now hard all this is for you. I'm glad we're here to do whatever we can to help."

Mom gave her a long, intense look.

Okay, here we go. Now the shit will hit the fan.

But instead of a firestorm, Mom said, "Hanna, my dear, I'm happy you're here. Thank you. That's very kind. This has been

318

hard on me with Donny, and now Earl. It's all made me realize how selfish I've been with you two kids. I know I always favored Donny. He was my first, and I always thought he could do no wrong. Now he, and I, are paying for everything I did wrong. I know I ran you two off with my nagging you to be better, to do better, to follow the strict requirements I laid down. I'm sorry. I don't want to lose you two like I did Donny. I just worry about you both being so far away. Russell, when you were in Chicago, it wasn't that far away, but out in California … I got so upset when I talked to you, out there somewhere, not knowing. I was so worried about you." Her voice quivered.

Karen got up and went and held her. I sat looking down. A lump formed in my throat, and my eyes began to tear up. What I'd perceived as control was just her way of expressing worry.

Mom perked up then and said, "Okay, enough of that. Let's eat our dessert and have our coffee, and we can go back to the hospital. Do you kids think you might move back here?"

"I'm sorry, Mom," I replied, "but I don't think so, at least not for a while."

"I wish you would. What's so important out there?"

I told her about our music and our CD and that we were serious about what we were doing. I saw in her eyes that she wasn't too excited about what she heard.

"But, Russell, your college? Your career at the bank? What about all that? You're throwing it all away? Just like that?"

"I can always fall back on that, Mom. I know I can get good references from Americo if I ever need them. I could probably even go back there if I wanted. I'm all right and really happy with what I'm doing right now. Times have changed. We don't stay with one job or one career for life until retirement anymore. Trust me. I'm—I mean—we're fine." I looked at Hanna. "I have some CDs with me, and I'll give you one to listen to."

319

She didn't reply. The subject was dropped, but I could tell she was having a hard time accepting that. We made small talk while we ate. Hanna also asked her to come and visit in California as she had Dad. Mom acted as though going to California would be paramount to going to Mars or Pluto, or to some other solar system. We all tried to convince her otherwise and were making some inroads when it was time for us to go back to the hospital.

We all rode together, and I played some of the CD for Mom on the way in. As we got out of the car, she said, "That was you and Hanna? That's some real pretty music. Can I have some to give to my friends?"

That was way more than I'd expected.

We spent the afternoon making hospital small talk. On the way out, after Mother's incessant begging, we agreed to stay with her at the farm for the next five nights. Dad would be home in another day or so.

After we got back to the house, Mom had us sit, saying there was something she wanted to tell us.

She began with a quivering voice. "You don't know this, but I was twenty when I married your father. I was nineteen and two months pregnant with Donny when I started keeping house for him. We seemed good together, and we got married right before Donny was born. He did everything for that boy like he was his own. Still does. Earl was good to me, treated me like I was somebody, somebody special. He gave me a life I never experienced or expected. I'd walk through hell for that man.

"I came from a bad home. My father was a drunk and barely supported my mother and my two brothers and a sister. We never had money for anything—sometimes not even food. The son-of-a-bitch thought he could come in our room anytime he wanted and—" She stopped and dried her eyes.

"Mom, I—" I began.

She held up her hand, shook her head and continued. "Both my brothers turned out to be drunks, just like their father. One is dead now, killed in a car accident. He was drunk. Thankfully he didn't kill anyone else. I don't know where the other one is, haven't heard from him in probably twenty years. My sister, Mary, moved to Colorado as soon as she graduated high school. She's married and living on a ranch somewhere in the southwest part of the state. We send Christmas cards back and forth.

"Me, I had a wild streak, barely got out of high school. Hung out with a bad crowd. Of course, you already know I got pregnant. Donny's real father was a fun time but ran as fast as he could as soon as he found out I was expecting his kid. Never heard from him again. Think he went into the army or something. He just up and disappeared.

"My father could be really mean, especially when he'd been drinking—beat on Mom a lot. There weren't the support systems back then, but we survived, none the less. I guess that mean drunk gene must run in the family with Donny and all …" She stopped again and dried her eyes.

"I guess I wanted so much for you to be better, to make something of yourselves, wanted everything to be right for you, pushed you so hard, too hard maybe. I was so happy when you both graduated college. I'm so proud of both of you. You're doing things I have a hard time with, leaving good jobs, divorce and all. I suppose since my mom never left my sorry excuse of a father, I thought couples ought to stick together no matter what. Maybe I was wrong. I hated that you two got divorced. Hated it! But you both seem so happy now. I'll just have to get over it, I guess.

"But then Donny, he was a disappointment from the get-go. I blame myself for that. I know I favored him, always thinking if I cajoled him, he might be a nicer boy, nicer to you and others, but now … now he's going to jail. It's wrong for sure."

"I'm so sorry, Mom," Karen said. "We never knew … never knew about all you were dealing with."

"No, it's not your fault you didn't know. How would you? I'm the one who should be sorry, taking my childhood abuse, my frustrations, and my problems out on you kids. I didn't know what else to do. I just didn't know any better … I'm so, so sorry. Please don't hate me."

She choked back her sobs, put her head in her hands, and shook. Karen and Hanna went to either side to comfort her. I sat there, feeling numb. All the anger, the tirades, the never being good enough, now I was beginning to understand. This family had some serious secrets, now coming into the open. So much made sense to me now. I again felt a big lump build in my throat and had to dry my eyes. I looked around. We were all crying.

"We've never hated you, Mom, never," I said. I felt the pain of guilt stab my heart for all the times I thought I did hate her.

We heard a knock on the front door. Everyone became alert, dried eyes, and tried for some composure. Another knock came. I went and opened it and stared straight into Mick's smiling face.

"Hey, I found you. I stopped by the hospital, and you'd already left, but I managed to meet Earl and we chatted a few minutes. Nice guy, gave me the directions. Said you'd all be here. You guys left in such a rush, didn't want me to come, but after I thought about it, I decided to come anyway. And here I am." He stood with his arms spread wide in a gesture of triumph.

Karen screamed, "Oh my God, Mick." She ran and jumped into his arms.

This was all well and good except that Mick's real name was Miguel Espinoza. The only thing I could think of at that moment was Mom's reaction when I played with the two Latino boys at the swimming pool.

Karen, without hesitation, dragged him in. "Come on in and meet my mother. Mom, meet my boyfriend. Mick, this is my mother, Rose."

Mom looked and then took another wide-eyed look at the smiling Mick.

"Rose, I'm so pleased to meet the mother of the woman I love," he said. "You are so beautiful; I'll not be able to tell you and Karen apart." He took her limp hand, bowed, and kissed it.

I could tell she was in shock and had no idea how to respond.

"Oh my ... oh my. Mick?" Mom stuttered. "I'm happy you found us." A brief pause. "How long have you and Karen been dating?"

"Long enough to know I never could live without her. She's a treasure I've been fortunate to find, like a shining diamond come from the stars."

Mom didn't say anything for a long time. She stood there staring at this man, then finally managed a smile. "Mick, ah, please come in and sit down. Can I offer you something, water, beer, something stronger? Have you eaten? I think I'd like a high ball. How about everyone? Russell, will you get us drinks? See what everyone wants."

She managed better than I'd expected—so far anyway. Maybe the whiskey would help. We hadn't talked about sleeping arrangements, and I desperately wished we'd stayed in town. I knew Hanna and I sleeping together would be bad enough, but Karen and Mick? I sucked in a deep breath. "So, what can I get for everyone?"

We'd gotten some take-and-bake pizzas on the way home, so we all had pizza and beer. Mom had a whiskey sour. Then came dessert, and she had another whiskey sour and started to get a little tipsy. Mick doled out praise for Mom. Karen and I rolled our eyes, and Hanna smiled. Mom grinned, eating up everything he said. He was a charmer.

It grew late, and we were all drained from this day, ready to head to bed. This was a four-bedroom farmhouse, but I somehow knew only three would be used.

Mom said, "I'm going to bed. You kids figure out your own sleeping arrangements. There're clean towels. Have a good night." She came and gave us all a hug, even Mick. She turned towards her room, muttering something about not understanding and asking for strength, went in, and closed the door.

After she left, I broke the silence: "Karen, what has gotten into Mom and Dad? They're like different people."

"I think it had a lot to do with Donny, but now with Dad," she said. "Dad was always the good cop and Mom the bad. From what she said, her childhood was far from great, then being a mother and wife, being so young. God, I'm thirty-five and still didn't know how to parent two boys. Our lives are so different."

"I agree," Hanna said. "From what she unloaded to us tonight—didn't either of you ever know about all that?"

We both shook our heads.

"First I ever heard," Karen said. "She never shared much, neither did Dad. Family history was something no one ever talked about."

Mick spoke up. "To change the subject for a moment, remember that woman, Riley, who wanted us to tour? She called yesterday and can get us a four-week tour this summer: Arizona, New Mexico, Colorado, one gig in Utah, and ending in the

Reno Nevada area. There are several folk festivals and some indoor theater venues, like in Arizona, for sure. As she said, she'll do all the booking and arrangements. I told her we'd let her know next week. Are we ready to do this?"

We all looked at each other, all thinking the same thing—so this is it; on the road playing our music. I felt a flutter in my stomach. I knew my eyes had grown wide. I looked around. So had everyone else's. All four of us smiled and nodded in agreement. We were all in.

Karen and I led our weary guests up to the second-floor bedrooms. Karen and Mick elected to use her old one. Hanna and I went into my old room. I felt strange sleeping with a woman in my old bed. I'd never slept here with Dana; she never would stay at the farm, always wanting a hotel in Iowa City.

Chapter 27: The Finale

I heard Hanna's breathing deepen easily into sleep, while I lay awake with my mind racing, running through the events of the past year—so much, so much. I thought back to that day in Iowa when I came out of the coffee shop and saw the Westfalia campervan and made a spur of the moment decision to buy it. Why had I done that? It was so unlike me, so outrageous, but, for some reason, I had. And what a journey that van took me on. Maybe it's a magic van? I smiled inside. Maybe it is.

Was I different now, after the journey of this past year—a journey that still continued? Deep down, I thought I was different, but then again, not really. So many of my early beliefs had been shattered but not so easily left completely behind. Many still remained, but I saw my life differently and wasn't so hung up on all those do's and don'ts. Would I ever be free of my childhood programming? Probably not. I still had moments of conflicting thoughts and emotions, but counseling helped. Maybe someday I'd be free. It'd be a lot of work, but I'd had a taste of a new life and wasn't going back.

"Once you wake up, you can't go back."

What a road trip this has been.

I thought of Hanna, Mick, Karen, and music. Would I be a professional musician for the rest of my life? I had no idea. I let go of one career for this adventure. What's not to say I might have one or maybe more careers ahead of me? One thing for certain, I'd be with Hanna and her music as long as she'd have me.

I thought about my parents and all they'd shared that day. It was good to know something about their early life, especially Mom's. It helped me to understand both of them better and what I'd always thought was an abusive attitude towards Karen and me. They just wanted the best for us and did the best they knew how. I could see how hard it must've been for them and how difficult it was now with Donny facing prison time. For the first time I could recall, I knew I truly loved them.

I fell asleep with a smile on my face, looking forward to tomorrow's new opportunities and experiences and where this amazing journey would take me.

A Note from the Author

Did you enjoy my book?
If so, I would be very grateful if you could write a review and publish it at your point of purchase.

Your review, even a brief one, will help other readers to decide whether or not they will enjoy my work, so if you liked it, please let others know.

Do you want to be notified of new releases?
Sign up to AIA Publishing's email notification list and they'll let you know whenever they publish a new book, including one of mine. And they'll give you a free ebook—the award-winning magical realism novel *Worlds Within Worlds* by Tahlia Newland.

Visit www.aiapublishing.com and find the sign-up button on the right-hand side under the photo. Of course, your information will never be shared, and the publisher won't inundate you with emails, just let you know of new releases.

CPSIA information can be obtained
at www.ICGtesting.com
Printed in the USA
FFHW021317160319
51081143-56505FF